INDIGO VOSS

K. LEIGH

k. LEIGH

Editing by Maxine Meyer
Book Formatting by Alex Tackett and Kira Leigh Maintanis
Cover Art and Illustrations by Kira Leigh Maintanis

ISBN: 978-1-7368053-5-0 [paperback]
ISBN: 978-1-7368053-7-4 [ebook]

https://constelisvoss.com

K. *LEIGH*

To Trevor: I didn't know what unconditional love was until you came along. Thank you for seeing me for who I really am. Thank you for loving me. Thank you for being beautiful in the way that only truly kind people are. I will hold your hand until the end of time and beyond, for as long as I have one functional atom in my body, I'll be at your side.

To a special someone: I heard every word and felt everything. That's why this book is for both of us. Witness your demons so you can let them go. I love you more than you can feel. I hope you can feel it, someday.

To my cat: You're my hero, even though you'll never understand what that means.

Finally, this book is for all those who fell so hard they didn't know if they could get back up again. For the imperfect victims, the self-destroyers, the toxic-damned who took on everything raw and wrong without knowing it. I promise that you can escape and drop all you were forced to hold. It just takes time.

Breathe.

The following story contains depictions of mental illness, manipulation, abuse, exploitation, bigotry, violence, eating disorders and drug use. Triggering (accurate) depictions include: psychosis, panic attacks, dissociation, alcoholism, gender dysphoria, autistic trauma, suicidality and more.

There are also explicit consensual sex scenes depicted.

Moreover, it includes marginalized groups such as sex workers, LGBT+ characters and abuse survivors struggling in a different time, on slightly AU earth, across two countries. Please keep in mind that there is a difference between sex trafficking and sex work while you read.

Consider this your warning for a work of fiction that exists as a spiritual companion to books like Dostoevsky's Crime and Punishment and television shows like Sam Esmail's Mr. Robot.

Finally, I ask that you read with empathy, as this story hopes to reach and heal at least two real people, and hopefully very many readers. I aim to give you what you haven't been taught exists: mercy.

CONTENTS

PART THREE: PENDULUM

PART ONE: NURTURE

"People speak sometimes about the 'bestial' cruelty of man, but that is terribly unjust and offensive to beasts, no animal could ever be so cruel as a man, so artfully, so artistically cruel."

— Fyodor Dostoyevsky. "The Brothers Karamazov." 1880.

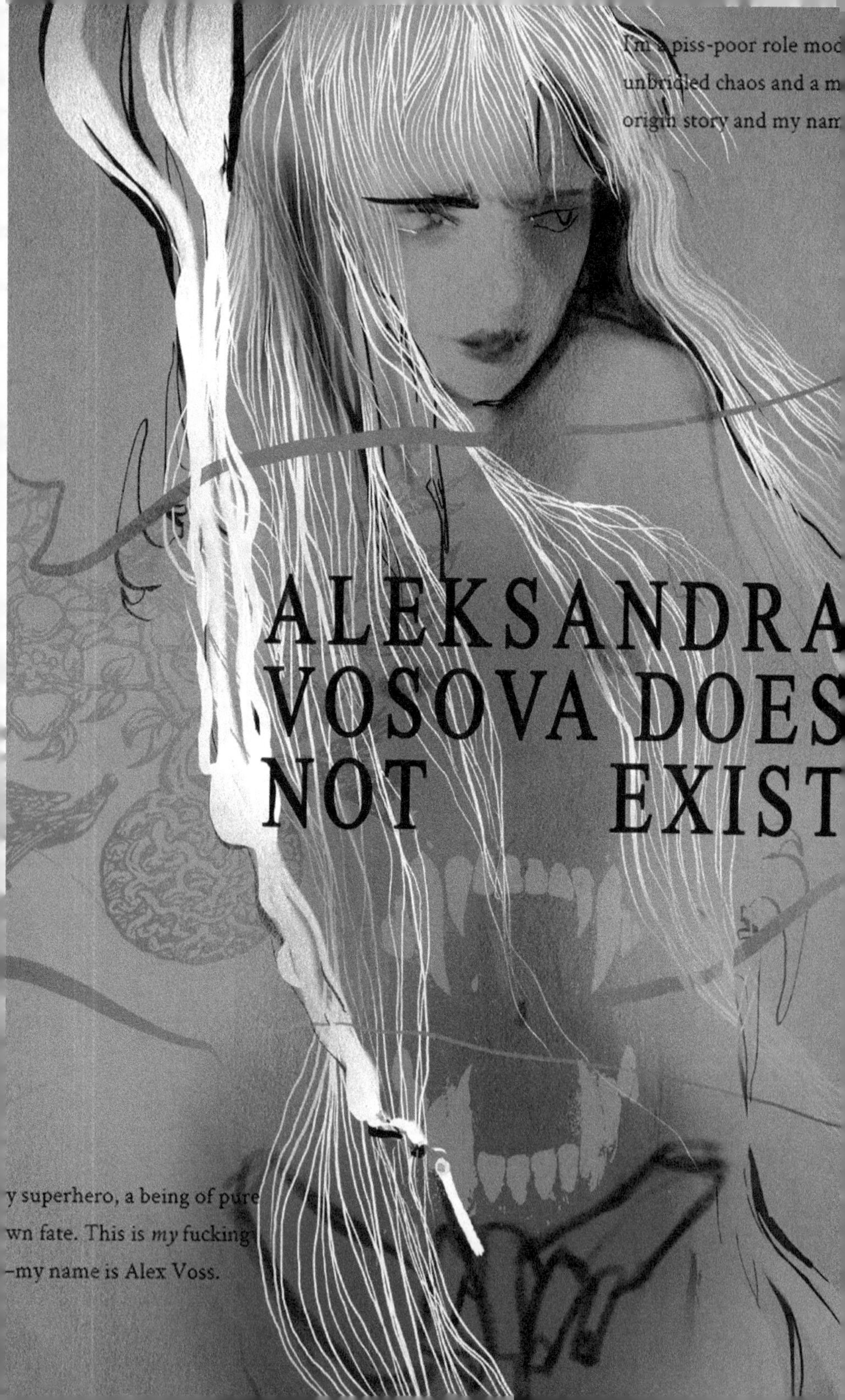
I'm a piss-poor role mod
unbridled chaos and a m
origin story and my nam

ALEKSANDRA
VOSOVA DOES
NOT   EXIST

y superhero, a being of pure
wn fate. This is *my* fucking
—my name is Alex Voss.

1 / THE END

I am an invisible man. I was born an invisible woman. I will die in invisible chaos and the most important person in my life will not know why I let it happen. As a gun digs into my temple—held in the sweaty palm of the man I like least—his cigar stink stings my war-blue eyes and oil-slick pigeon wings obscure my face, let me tell you an invisible story.

Let me tell you the invisible story of a life deemed so unimportant it was pillaged from my near-birth to my death, all the way into the future of breathing machines and dictators with stolen faces. Let me tell you the invisible story of a life I deemed so very unimportant that *I* let death stick his fingers in my guts and dig around until he found a toy to mangle: my invisible soul.

This is my superhero origin story. We start where all things end, with time.

2 / THE BEGINNING

Time is a tricky little minx. One assumes it charts on a straight path, plodding ever forward and leaving our bodies in its wake with each shivering decade. But that's only part of it. Time lives in the body, what it remembers and what it *hates*. My body was not made for the pageantry of womanhood. Neither was it made to be weaponized against its will, as no one's body ever *should* be. Suffice to say, the fucked up knife with an indigo handle doesn't take well to an entitled palm. And that is how you make a human weapon; *acute pressure over time until a bomb is born.*

The first time I weaponized was when I was small. Red-lipped and feral, I was starved for self-defense. The second time involves bible-beating; both metaphorical and literal. The third? Well, we'll get to that soon. To make it simple: walking wounds like me defy much to survive all.

Despite my painful life, at least I had time on my side and defiance to protect me. That is, until my mind unraveled like a loom and led me to embrace an outcome where a bullet brains me on New York streets.

However, at the beginning of it all, time certainly wasn't on my side. I hadn't yet sheared the locks, learned to fight like dancing, ruled my body by my *own* design and didn't understand what it means to be unkillable.

We are in the distant past in a land you know distantly from gangster movies and propagandized textbooks. I am slight, weak, stubborn and paper-thin with paper skin. The dark circles beneath my eyes paint me as a bloodless beast of burden. I am very pretty but awkward, as though my bones don't fit my meat. Nothing I wear is anything I own, and the very food I eat is someone else's property. As am I.

My room is filled with light. The sun blinds me. A cloud rescues me and hovers beyond the window; I wonder if someone owns that cloud. *They must.*

"Aleksandra Vosova." A woman with button-black eyes mutters my name like a curse. "You must watch that." She gestures at the small breaded sweet in my fist.

Saying nothing, I swallow what little saliva I have in my mouth, glare at the woman as my heart throttles like a motor, shove the whole confection in my cheek, and then she slaps me.

3 / STARVED

Tonight's thief is a silk-shirted beast stitched with geometric patterns. *Perfect geometry* and yet his hair is uneven. Devils always dress well but forget the scum layer that spies on them. *We all notice.*

His fist is in my long blond hair while I play dead. A mistake is made: I struggle when he shifts his weight. He stops to look down at my body, which they always do. His eyes gouge my navel, linger on my hips and stab my thighs. When he gorges himself on my face something in my chest snaps. *It's in the eyes, I think.*

It's the sort of glance a man gives when leaning too-far out of the passenger seat of a vehicle, braising the backsides of people who don't know he exists until they feel the hair on their necks stand up. It's the sort of glance a man gives a hunk of marbled steak he covets, drools for and whines at for no other reason than it's *there.* It's the sort of dog-hungry look I want to pluck from his skull and pop wetly in my *fucking* fists.

My teeth are in his throat. I tear with everything I have as he hollers out foamy pink screams. Scarlet drips over my face, leaks into my gold hair, infects my bird bones and dip-dyes my soul. Like a hunting dog crushing a pheasant, I latch on, ride out the flood of hot human paint and don't loose my jaws until he's good and fucking *dead.*

Sitting on the bed that isn't and will never be my own, in clothes that aren't and will never be my own, in a body that has never and will someday be my own, I'm catatonic. A violently stuffed vessel, I finally burst apart at the seams and exploded a grown man's esophagus.

Flickering back to life, my blue eyes trail across the room. The black-eyed woman is here haunting me, as she always does. She curses at me, as she always does. She raises her fist above her head to strike me, as she always does. I snatch her fist and ram my forehead into her nose, like I *never* do.

Possessed by defiance, I war against other body thieves who swarm in plague-waves to descend upon me—as if they'd need a small army to subdue something as frail as I am.

"Useless girl!" a single man roars, clamoring to pin down my jeering legs. My wings beat hard enough to bruise as the devils are surprised that I'm not made of glass. I spit blood in one's face, and for that I'm knocked out cold with just one thick punch.

When I wake, I notice I've been cleaned and dressed in a taupe slip with frayed edges. Bruises from my little war linger up my arms, now bound at the wrists. I can still taste the man's hot metal in my mouth.

The black-eyed woman peers at me as I rouse, blond locks muddying her shape. "Food," I command, flicking my head to loose my bangs and drill my eyes into the woman's skull, willing her buttons to pop.

She snorts and drops an empty dish on the floor with a clatter. I won't be fed until I behave. I will behave in order to survive. *Until I won't, in order to truly live.*

4 / BEATEN

It's a great deal of time after my first war and I still don't have mastery over anything useful. I'm taller now, but not by much. Mother nature keeps me small to make it easier to poke me full of holes like stabbing a fucking bug in a jar. *If I don't behave, I might even be crushed.*

After the first fight, I've behaved in order to survive. I may have even enjoyed behaving depending on how I've been treated. Today is one such day. An attractive man wraps his arms around my body and pulls me to sit on his lap. He smells like green things I don't have names for. Maybe he enjoys spending time in nature, which I remember doing in my watercolor-past where birds ink a canvas of sky.

"I was told ya were a biter," he says in a foreign language, chuckling into my back. "Butcha don't seem all tha' bad." He places not-unwanted kisses on my shoulder.

His words are untenable, but his warm mouth explains the rest. I don't hate their mellow, fernsome feeling. "This, I have never done," I admit, as he holds me closer. "Strange?" I ask, placing my hands on his arms to guide his flat palms against my chest. *I've never been held like this before.*

"What, bitin' people?" He chuckles into my hair and twists me around to face him. He's very handsome and not unkind. In fact, he's the only one who ever made sure I enjoyed myself. *I don't even know his name.*

"No." I shake my head, suffering a half-smile. "A feeling." My thoughts gurgle foolishly, which makes me turn away. He catches my fingers, drawing me back to the sun of his arms.

My eyes hitch as I scan this tender stranger. He's as tall as an oak with tanned skin, expressive brows and a broad smile. Later, I'll meet someone not unlike him and fall in love; I'll file him away as a secret. Much later than that, I will love a similar man and he will love me like a sibling. In the distant future, I will distort a spaceship to reincarnate the third man. I'll say it's because humanity needs his heroism, but that's a lie. *I need his heroism and so I imprint him wherever my ghost lives. Yes, even in the future. Maybe even in your world, too.*

The stranger smiles. "You mean...you've never?" He kisses my chest as I smile and don't understand him. Then, he places his hands on the small of my back where eyes will someday live. Eyes that will shame me and make me hate this closeness. *I don't hate it now.*

"N-no." I chuckle. In his arms alone, I'm a piece of abstract art to marvel at, not something to cut into chunks and swallow. *Why does he study a nobody like me? Why would anyone?*

"Didja enjoy it?" he asks expectantly. This must be new and unusual to him. Impressing me is also new; *nobody ever wags their tail for a bit of stale vatrushka.*

"Yes. Good. Unusual. Usually," I mumble, worrying my lips. "Treated difference—different-ly. Feels different." He studies me from below the mounds of flesh on my chest. Nonsense words form dark shapes in my mouth as I study him back.

"The parts...feel wrong," I explain, placing my palm to my breast. I hesitate, then curl my fingers off and away, as if unspooling a knot.

"Feels off sometimes, yeh?" he asks.

Draping my arms around his shoulders, I gaze into his eyes. "Yes. All off."

My body is a flesh-prison and I'm its poltergeist. No part of me fits; not the words I'm given to call myself, nor what I have that makes money I *never* get to fucking see. This feeling was there *before* I was ensnared, shoved into a wooden box and cut up for money. *I just didn't have the language for it. I still don't.*

"I am haunting this. I will tell you, maybe," I begin, briefly kissing this kind stranger's ear. "I had friend. We play by river, you know," I trail on, gesturing out the window, leaving my other hand to nestle near the nook of his neck. "Younger, we were like brothers—" My sentence is sliced with a grimace.

When he kisses my ear and places his hand on my back again, something unfurls in me. Maybe I'll try to talk to someone who seems like they want to listen. In later years, this openness will be beaten out of me as everything always fucking is. Much later than that, someone smart will help me find it for one single night, and after that it'll slip through my fingers when a handsome bastard breaks my heart hard enough to make me killable. That's the sad script of my life. *I never get to keep anything good for very long.*

"I didn't understand different—difference," I correct myself. "But with time, he sees difference in me. Treats me different-ly," I ramble as the man in my arms sits back on the bed to scan my face.

"I am ghost, I think," I say softly. "Haunting toy I do not own. Do not want." My fingers tap on his skin as my words traipse into native umber-syllables. *The kind stranger won't understand.*

"I am off." My words paddle back to English. "Nothing fits." I pause, slicking my lower lip with my tongue. "But with you I did not haunt."

My mouth goes dry as my hands drop to dangle limp at my sides. My words could mean anything; I'm talking about what it is I do, or maybe what it feels like, or maybe what it is to be a fucking object. Luckily, this archetype always wants to listen, but that doesn't mean they can always hear it. Even in my native language, so few people listen. Every language I've learned is for other people's fucking benefit and they translate nearly nothing. *It's no wonder I'm broken.*

Silence.

This stranger spots spies in my severe brows, sharp jaw and half-cut smile. He hunts my lapsed phrases, dips into the whitespace between each postured breath and reads the constellation of my awkward limbs.

Raising an arm, he threads his fingers in my hair and sifts through my long blond leash. "Y'know," he murmurs, "I think you'd look fetching witha bob." He pauses to look into my eyes. "We 'ave some o' yer lot." He wraps his arms around me to sweep me into the air, then sets me on my feet. "Noticed it when I walked in," he explains.

I don't know what 'it' is.

He presses his lips to my brow. "Kinda hard to miss, innit?" He speaks soft sounds into my paper skin.

"Explain more," I command, stepping back. I search for something unsaid, unknown, unseen, invisible and only conjured in the mangled cry of a bird who flies uselessly on wax wings they were never born to use.

"S'way ya move, mate." He kisses my cheek. "S'way ya speak. Kinda like one of me mates back home. Like he's stuffed with feathers n' all, but could bite yer 'ead off in a flash." He pulls back and snaps his fingers. "Like that."

The blue-eyed doll blinks wildly; I am Aleksandra's vicious confusion.

"T'be honest, you even look a bit like 'im," he reveals, looking away as if his own words would wound him.

I snort. "You choose me because I look like friend stuffed with feather?" When he laughs, I cock a half-grin then continue. "Ridiculous."

"Life's ridiculous, mate. And I think ya'd look ridiculously fetchin'..." He turns me around, then places his hand above my rear to steer me to the vanity. Clutching my hair, he pulls the long locks behind my head so only my bangs remain. "Jus' like this. Yeh?"

My eyes skim the smudged mirror as something like violets blooms within me. An anemic little bird squawks at the moon and this stranger heard its impossible language. *He's a fucking bird whisperer!*

I fumble for the drawer near my hip, rip out a pair of shiny silver scissors, slam the drawer shut and face him. "Show me," I command, holding up the scissors in my palm.

The man smirks and shakes his head. "Right now?" he snorts.

"Right now. Show me."

A not-thief is cutting my biggest selling point: long, fine, yellow-gold hair that curls when the damp clings inside my cage. Hair that men love to yank me around by. Hair I'm forced to wear by the button-eyed woman who slathers my dark locks in chemicals. Goldilocks, with her bowl of gruel in a dog's dish. Goldilocks, punished because 'she' dared to eat 'her' own fucking porridge. Goldilocks, devoured by scavengers who imagine themselves proud, noble men in any other fucking circumstance. *Beasts, all of them. Vultures, scavengers, thieves.* This man is nothing like them.

Slivers of gold scatter like bodies in war across sheets of blue. Blue, but not like heaven. This is the blue of space. It's dark, deep, purple and alien. I'm afforded this color because it's advantageous for displaying my corpse. It matches the marbles in my skull.

He sweeps my shoulders free, then guides me back to the mirror. "All set, mate," he says. His expression is open skies, verdant green fields and mornings where nothing hurts.

"What do ya think?" he murmurs heat across my ear.

I flick my fingers over the uneven ends. He's all but cleaved it off, leaving starts and stops like all my broken sentences. It's how a child might cut their own hair in all its messy charm.

"Aw mate, ya hate it somethin' fierce, yeh?"

I twist around in a flash and bite into his lower lip. Startled, he's thrown off balance and stumbles oafishly. I push him to the bed and straddle his lap. He's lying in a sea of blue surrounded by gold clippings. I'm backed by a pocked ceiling with my face framed in an awkward haircut.

"No," I comfort him, a devilish grin tugging at my mouth. "Perfect."

Soaking him into my skin is an act of gratitude and his warm arms are a response. He smells like heat-kissed landscapes, feels like real tenderness and he's given me something. Something I don't understand, something that feels like seeing myself for the first time, something like truly *fucking* living and he's *holding* me.

Knowing only one way to thank him, I kiss his shoulder and reach between us to grasp him in my fist. He makes a stunted sound as I spread fire between his thighs with a flick of my thumb.

"J-jus' like I said," he stammers as my hand quickens. "Can bite yer 'ead off in ahh—"

"Time up soon," I breathe into his skin. "Let me give." My words are lost in a delicious red mark I leave on his throat: *Let me give you something others take from me.*

Raising myself up, I spread myself over his lap. He drifts his knuckles over my hip and grasps my sides. Grinning awkwardly, I tilt back, wrap my fingers around his length and nestle his sex against mine. As I press down, he slides inside of me and I let gravity do the rest.

We settle, joined together, breathing and so very vulnerable. Romance isn't something I know, but he gives it to me by threading our hands, even as the clock ticks. With a quirked brow, I roll my hips just once. A sinful half-smile blooms as I make his eyes flutter and render him mute.

Most of them are speechless when I stop being a corpse, but he's not like most of them. He's not like most of them when I milk his cock with short, slight, bursts. He's not like most of them when he pulls me down to twine his fingers in my lacerated hair as I ride him. He's not like most of them when he slaps my ass. He's not different because he lets me fuck him into the bed while the springs whine. He's different because he wants to enjoy this feeling *with* me.

As I draw out our time together, we're soon covered in the remnants of my gold massacre. Sweat clings to our limbs as we chase the rush of pleasure, together. *I didn't know it could feel this soft.*

My cheeks flush as he places his hand to my chest to feel my trembling heartbeat. When he grasps me for a kiss, the pleasure in my gut flutters like a million wings, screws my eyes shut and pulls slight, soft moans from my mouth. He feeds on them, breaths shared as my brows twist and I ache beyond reason. *I didn't know it could be this warm.*

After enough heady kisses, he decouples and turns me as if in a dance. I chuckle as he splays his hand to the center of my chest, pulls me back to meet him and rests his mouth to my ear. Breathing against me, he slides the head of his slick cock just barely inside. Gentle, romantic, fluid, vulnerable, beautiful hot-white heat; the space between my legs burns. Kissing my ear, he waits for an answer I won't speak plainly. A murmur ricochets from my abdomen and drips from my lips. *There's your fucking answer, bird-whisperer.*

He wraps one arm around my waist and lightly grasps my throat as he pushes inside. With every centimeter I respond in half-gasps. My legs shake as he pulses inside of me, but not from pain. It's pleasure that parts my lips and floods hot blood to my face. *I didn't know.*

I'm not a poltergeist haunting my brittle body as he fills me to the hilt. I am not somewhere else frozen in time as he slaps against me and pulls from me throbbing vowels. I'm not separated from this skin. *It's mine. It belongs to me.*

"You are not," I gasp out. He makes speech difficult by repeatedly pounding my backside. "Wayward." I strike my hand to the headboard to level myself. "Virgin."

"Issat whatcha thought?" he asks, then swiftly snatches my hips to pin me to the bed, which makes me laugh into the sheets. I may have even snorted.

He kisses my shoulders, then raises himself to hook his legs under mine, pressing against me deliciously. A sunrise smile spreads across my face as he starts up again. The heat is impossible.

"Y-yes," I admit with a breathy laugh. "Staring at my painting." A ship would crack under the pressure between my thighs.

Concocting a devious thought, I blurt out, "Is because I look like feather-man?" My words make him press my head into the pillows playfully. "You imagine him?" I ask as his face burns into my back.

"What would he say?" The sound of our fucking echoes against the walls, but he says nothing. Nothing at all.

Tilting back, he listens to what my body says, and gives me leverage. I snake my hand between my thighs, twist my fingers inside myself and imagine my pleasure takes a different shape. A shape I never knew I could have. A shape that aches in an unseen, unreachable place that I can only fumble at.

"Tell me," I command, which makes his thrusts quicken. I don't care if he imagines I'm the friend he secretly wants to fuck and love and hold and kiss. I never get to have this. *I never get to fucking have anything like this.*

"'Put your back into it, Thomas," he stammers in an accent not unlike my own.

I cackle—I can't help it. "Put your back into it, Thomas," I mimic his foreign words and snicker myself stupid in between obscene sounds. Thomas must approve, because his crashing grows more erratic.

Pleasure pools in a place my hand can't reach as he holds me tight. My face burns, every brush against my erect flesh shoots lightning through my groin. I'm impossibly warm, my thighs drip and my fingers can't keep up with the spasms made by the hot-running blood this stranger boils within my very fucking veins. I still my hand to stave off small quakes. *I want this to last.*

Thomas groans until hoarse and slams his hips against me. Hot liquid coats my insides. He cloisters my body in his arms and jams himself into me at the base. My entire pelvis seizes with the blood-rushed feeling of my heartbeat. I flick my fingers, send a bolt of nuclear heat up my spine, clench down, tip the explosion into a scalding throb and screw my eyes shut as my body throws itself into a euphoria strong enough to boil an entire ocean to nothing but seabed. *Holy—*

"Блядь—" I groan as I ride out one of the best orgasms I'll ever have in my life. I remember this vividly. I imagine that this is what love must feel like. It's a pattern I'll cement so hard that the bowl of my mind (attached to my crotch) sieves into space because I'm *stupid.*

"Ah, mate," Thomas whispers, pulling out slowly for my comfort, "that was—" I wish he'd been able to finish his sentence. I wish to this very day we'd had even just one moment more together. Thomas falls into his clothes and is rushed out immediately. I don't even get to say goodbye as the door smacks his ass on the way out and I only just turn to see it.

He ran over time and a theft was starting far too soon. Too soon to get cleaned up, too soon for really anything at all. My gold hair is all over the bed, my shorn locks are ghastly, I am the worst creature in the world, and I've ruined absolutely fucking everything for daring to have any fucking fun at all. *No fun, never any fun. Never.*

At least that's what the button-eyed woman tells me with a glare cold enough to freeze anyone else's blood as she looms in the doorway.

Like a sated feline, I stretch on the bed and look up at her. She gawks down at me like I very much killed her entire family by setting her house on fire. All I can do is laugh in that joyous post-coitus cackle I'd come to learn in later years is usual of incredible sex.

Reaching across the end-table makes me wince with soreness. I fumble for the cigarettes and shiny silver lighter I'd stolen from an impotent devil and proceed to smoke in her face.

The woman glares. *She should take a fucking Polaroid.* She stalks forward, snags my hair in her fist, twists me around and yanks me from the cigarette I'm trying desperately to place at my lips. Even as she drags me about like a stubborn mule, I chase the damned thing.

"What have you done?!" she screeches.

I cackle ferociously, rip myself away and scamper back as she aims to strike me. Rolling around the gold-covered bed, I half-fall off of it, then half-land with a half-snort.

She screams at me in whatever words she can find as I croon into full hysterics. My laughter stops when she slaps the cigarette out of my hand and beats the side of my head with a book. A bible, left in my room for God knows what fucking reason, thwacks my skull.

On my knees, holding my head in one hand, I look up at this woman who I *suppose* I should consider my guardian. Truly, she is a devil, with small black eyes and an even blacker heart.

Usually, my expression would be vacant. Even after small wars, my resolve never lasts for very long. This time, my bright blue gaze is not vacant. I'm not catatonic in rage, nor am I split from my body and hovering. I am not a poltergeist in my skin. I'm not going to haunt myself any fucking longer for as long as I *fucking* live. This is a battle of wills I have never won—I reach for the discarded cigarette as we lock eyes—until now.

She raises the book to smite me. I launch up to drive the cigarette into her button-eye. The smell of burning flesh licks the air as she screams. Wrenching my hands in her brown hair, I jerk her head back and dig the smoldering paper into her wet socket with all my might.

Her skin immolates and I feel no sympathy for her sizzling screams. She will never again lay a hand on me for as long as I survive under her roof.

5 / TIME

Survivalism grinds time to a halt. Precarious and alone, those like me hide in the forests of our minds, for that's all we have. As I'm only ever surviving in this fucking prison, I freeze subjective time without knowing it. *Without knowing I can do far more.*

I am meat lying on a mattress on top of my blindingly blue sheets. A freshly killed corpse stops nothing because men like to imagine they've murdered me. Baring my fangs and dying is erotic for men who need death to feel something. I could pity them but the knife prefers to dabble in backbiting. *I will never not prefer it.*

I'm elsewhere. Plucked from one of few good memories, a river bleeds past my eyelids. Thomas is there, with bright eyes to match his smile. He doesn't love me, but I imagine he does under a blush-colored sky. I imagine I'm taller with broad shoulders and none of the careless weight on my chest. I imagine we're catching little fish in our hands as he's babbling like a brook about nothing and everything. I imagine the sun is setting and painting his skin in warm colors.

The man on top of me twists me over, which makes my eye twitch. The coral sun coats the entire sky in golden-orange ink. Reaching up to the heavens, my leg is jacked above my head. Even in all this hell, I draw a scene within my mind of a time where I will be *loved*. Maybe loved by a man like Thomas. Maybe loved by a woman. Maybe loved by anyone at all, really. I imagine *possibilities* of lush kisses beneath leaflets, sunrises in lemon-yellow, rushing water and a sea of a thousand beautiful birds above me. Birds that dot a clear blue sky where there's no violet-blue war, no theft and nothing hurts.

I'm twisted around again and my grasp on time falters. I drag my searing blue eyes over my robber's mug. My soul rejoins my body as a feral grin splits my face. "If you lift my fucking leg any higher I'm going to gut you like a fish and dump you in the *fucking* river."

The man lets my leg lax. Bringing it down comfortably, I resume concocting something better than all this. There has to be something better than all this. There has to be. *There just fucking has to be.*

I imagine maybe many people at the river. Maybe many people enjoy sweets, laugh, catch little fish and spend warm moments together. Maybe many people have a party. I've never been to a party. Maybe many people celebrate a special day—what's the most special day? *Is there a holiday to celebrate living?*

There's a quaint couple kissing, embraced by music; music that I must invent because I rarely get to listen to anything outside of what I hear through the walls; walls of wood that cage me as I paint a scene of eating fruit. The sweet-sour citrus drips down my chin. It's then that I realize what's being done to me. Too distracted to paint a prettier picture, my mind-body dissolves into the inky shadows of my skull. The clock stops, my corpse rots and nobody who *could* care or make a fucking difference gives a fuck.

I am an invisible woman, an invisible person, an invisible man. I'm a ghost, but not for long. I will spare you the details of further vanishings in this clump of frames. I just wanted to show you where the rage comes from—that matters, I think. Or maybe it doesn't matter. Maybe I've never fucking mattered. Maybe that's the depression using my mouth to speak.

The depression that invited Boris' bullet in to kill me dead, in cold blood, on colder asphalt with no one who could care anywhere in sight.

While I die in the present as a too-thin shadow against blood-splattered bricks, I know now that depression *always* lies. We must choose to live because it is a lying, agency-stealing thing. I wish I'd learned that lesson on Earth and not on a fucking absurdist spaceship in the future. And why the fuck would I get a chance to learn it then, *anyways? Who would ever care to help me learn what I never could?*

God isn't real, but there must be *some* cosmic dickhead who took sympathy on me in order to give me another chance at all this. Maybe in a way it gave *itself* a chance by letting me lord over a space that belonged only to me, in a body that could do *anything*. Why else would I be given that if not because something *else* fucking needed it? *I am given very little.*

I look at the space beyond and see a thing that hides between the letters. In an umber shadow, it glimmers in a sea of stars. I reach out my hand to touch the wet shadow. When I pull back, my palm is stained blue.

Do you cry for me? Or do you cry because you wish someone else would?

6 / PISTOLED

Today's thief looks rather important. To test just how important he is, I dig my hand into his pants pocket and steal his expensive cigarettes. As I pull one from the pack with my teeth, he marvels at me like one would a puddling butterfly. Important enough *not* to vibrate with machismo at my antics, here for a reason *other* than robbery and clever enough to know I'm unpredictable. Only the truly powerful have no reason to crush the discarded. Only the truly clever are smart enough to see the *something* beneath my skin. I steal his cigarettes without complaint, sup ephemeral blood and feel that *something* writhe.

Eventually, the *something* that I am must go *somewhere*. Those unlike me shut down, let it cake in the limbs like clay and atrophy. Those *not* unlike me become reactors primed on fucked-up actions they had no way of cleverly avoiding. Despite being *very* fucking clever, I will eventually react hard enough to ruin my life. That's the script and design that the clever thief sees. Stilled, he watches me move, translates my tells and grows more clever by the second.

The way I hold my head perfectly still as I flick my gaze to this expensively dressed stranger is a tell. The way I tilt my chin up as though he's beneath me is a tell. The way I burn his cigarettes and wield his lighter as he darts his eyes over my blood-sucking body is a tell.

I take a step forward as he eyes my slack right hand. My fingers curl around his shiny lighter. I *want to burn his fucking face off*. His cocked eyebrow tells me he knows.

"Do they know what you are?" he asks.

"Do you?" I reply, shifting my weight to my hip. I cross my arms as smoke from my nose rises to the ceiling in a thick gray ribbon.

The clever thief mulls his mouth with his hand, then stands and steps around me like a circling dog. He strikes out a fist at my naked ribs, time twists as I do, my foot slides back, I lock his arm in place, and his silver lighter clatters to the floor. *I didn't even move my head.*

"A natural, aren't you, little bird?" he asks. I let his fist go, then pluck the cigarette from between my teeth to flick ash.

"A natural at what?" I ask, eying the expensive-looking demon.

"Why do you think they keep you if you always cause so much trouble?" he asks, looking me over. *He eyes me like I'm a viper.* My smile is criminal.

"Not sure," I reply, inhaling smoke. "Maybe it's because I'm *very* fucking pretty."

He laughs, shakes his head and dares to walk toward me. Foolishly, he places his gloved hand to my clenched snake-jaw.

"That, and they're afraid," he says simply. He isn't afraid, it seems, but he *is* cautious. He continues with a smirk. "You'd do too much damage on your way out. Yet you bring in too much money." He pauses to swallow words he cleverly keeps from me. "It's a no-win situation, little bird."

"I'm not sure I like that nickname." I breathe smoke before recoiling from him. His hand hangs in the air for a moment before he places it at his side, then fumbles for something in his tailored jacket.

The glint of gummental begs me to stare at his palm. Magnetized, I'm drawn to it. He holds up the weapon, the cuff of his suit sliding as he moves. *Stars, snakes and other things I can't name. What are you?*

"Do you know why I'm here?" he asks.

I shake my head and continue glaring at the gun. He grabs my hand, curls my fist around the weapon and steps back. I hold the pistol loosely as if I'd have to warm it up to make it work. I study it like an artifact.

"Do you remember tearing out a man's throat?" I nod at his question absently, gorging myself on the details of his weapon. *I've seen many men with guns, I've heard copious gunfire and I've always wanted to be the one to litter the air with metal.* I linger on the weight of it, hoping it's loaded. I aim it at the clever client's head.

He smiles, then holds up his hands. I pull the trigger. Nothing happens. I gawk at the gun, then try again. *Nothing.* I drop my arm with a sneer as he bolts laughter from guts that deserve gunfire.

"We've been keeping an eye on you." He pauses to glance at the far corner of the room. "Boris wants to move you to a higher-end clientele who'd be interested in how much you can take." His words are sour. "Because he thinks you can handle it."

I cock an eyebrow. *He can fucking try.*

"I have a different idea," he says, prying the gun from my reluctant fist and placing it on the bed. He turns quickly and snatches me by the hair. The cigarette falls from my lips to the floor. I note it, then flick my eyes to the well-dressed devil's face.

"Tell me what you'd do if I tried to strangle you," he says.

My eyelid twitches before I speak. "I'd fall to the ground with you, brace the weight on my arms as I shove my knee in your groin and reach for the cigarette and lighter."

"Then what would you do?" he asks while my fingers play across the vanity at my back.

"Then I'd cozy up nice and sweet into your arms and offer you a fucking smoke." I wrench the drawer open, rip free the silver scissors and stab at him. He blocks and strikes me across the face, sending both me and the scissors clattering.

Pressed against the vanity, I make myself a static object. I watch him as he stoops, plucks the scissors from the wood and stands. He places them on the bed and gives me a rare smile; earnest and mild.

"Training starts today. I'm your new regular. Every day." He fumbles for his carton on the vanity at my side and continues. "This time. I've paid that awful woman in advance." He stoops, grabs his lighter and lights up a cigarette.

My eyes dart as he smokes. "Why are you doing this?" I hiss, slinking low to the floor to reach for my fallen comrade and shove it between my teeth.

When I stand, he flicks his lighter, bathes my face in orange and I inhale. *This clever thief is rarer than Thomas.* He's a boon in a sea of absolutely fucking *nothing* but the cities of my body robbed for profit that I'll never get to fucking see. *I need to know why.*

"I'm sorry." He flips the lighter closed, steps back, smokes for a moment and rolls his thoughts in his skull before he speaks again. "I'm sorry that I let them take you."

My eyes widen as I glare at a man I don't recognize. He isn't remarkable, nor is he arresting. He's average in every single way besides cleverness.

When he tosses me a boyish grin, something tugs at the back of my skull, settles itself in and twists its fucking fingers behind my eyes to show me moving pictures.

The river, the friend, the birds overhead, the yellow sunrise and pink sunset, downy clouds that brush the blue of the sky, the quivering fish in my palms, the way he treated me differently when I stopped looking like he did. Every single bittersweet note stings behind my eyelids. I can't escape them; they fill my mind with the only time I wasn't made into something I'm not. *Even then, I was mutating against my will.*

"I didn't know what was happening, little bird. You always loved watching them fly. I thought you'd remember me from that... I thought you'd remember," he confesses as his smile evaporates into the solemn ink of pain.

My lips part.

"I can't just *buy* you. It doesn't work like that." He gestures with his cigarette. "Buy your freedom. Buy you out of this cage. And certainly, I can't mistress a slave to set her free."

"Тыр..." I breathe out. My heart fills with putrid blood as it pummels my ribcage, my guts dissolve, bile floods my throat, I sag against the vanity and take a jittery inhale to choke the reel of memories from my eyes.

"But if you're very useful," he continues, solemn and sincere. "If you're very useful and very good at this, you can make a case. I brought the option to the table. Mind you, this has never happened." Tyr smokes and gives me a conflicted smile. "But Boris said he might entertain it. He finds you entertaining."

"Entertain *what?*" I bolt through my smokescreen as water leaks down my face without my consent.

"The girl we know, that no one knows but us, could possibly be the man—the prince—that everyone knows."

Instinctively, I jerk forward, a butchered marionette thwarted by time's trauma with every step. Every memory of the only point in my life when I wasn't used, abused, chewed up, broken, battered and beaten turns my steps to quicksand. I force myself to reach him in a sea of tar-fucked *nothing*.

"And you'll teach me to fight. To shoot the gun. To *kill*." I speak in absolutes against a backdrop of obsidian hell.

"Yes," he says as his eyes dart across my own.

"But, *why*? Why now?" My fists clench at my sides. "Why after all this time? Why now?!" His silence is deafened by my shaking, war-filled body. "And m-my parents?" My voice grows shrill. "Tyr—where are they? What *fucking* happened?!"

Curling my fingers in my hair, my heart jacks into my throat and I crumple to my knees. *It all deserves to fucking roast.* I want to burn this one alive and crawl back in time to meet my makers and rip their jaws open on the pavement with my heel on their fucking *skulls*.

I've reached the point where the *something* of trauma evolves into a nuclear-grade weapon. Usually, it doesn't atrophy like clay, for me atleast. It reacts in an explosion that, if directed, can pull off impossible feats. This time, that feat is feeling real pain. I twist like a snake, but Tyr's arms come out to catch my broken wings before I molt feathers for scales.

Folding into his body, I can do nothing but scream. He holds me as I wail at the loss of the child I was. I mourn, sob and dig my fingers into my once-friend's too-expensive jacket. Tyr can do nothing but haunt himself for what feels like hours as I break apart in his hands.

After a while of heavy silence spent sitting on my indigo platter, the tears finally subside. His arm is draped along my shoulders as he whispers why I was never rescued: *my parents loved me less than they loved surviving.* I can't be sure if this is the truth, but he seems earnest and his cleverness is comforting.

"Alright." I shudder, smearing my hands over my face. More tears threaten to fall but I hold them hostage.

"I want to make one thing painfully clear before we try to change my fate," I rattle, turning to face the man who was once a boy. "Don't ever treat me like a lost little girl or I'll *fucking* kill you."

These are my terms—this is not a becoming-thing or an escaping-thing. This is who and *what* I am and I'm fucking accepting it. I accept the offer to become the little bird, the would-be prince, the man everyone knows and something mostly unkillable. I accept my new destiny, a destiny where I'll someday free other little birds who never asked to be what they were made into. I will play at being a hero but only succeed at being a villain. I will find friends—better fucking friends than this one—and I'll use them to help me do *and* survive the impossible.

After all that, I will die because the king I used to play hero destroyed my heart. I will die because my trauma did, in fact, atrophy into my very fucking bones over countless decades. *It let the wrong devil dwell inside me.*

Afterwards, I will be found completely frozen in the river my body was dumped into, ice-capped in a blizzard. I will be found and experimented on—my Earth is not quite like your own—and even in death I will be fucking stolen from. Yet, this will allow me thousands of years in the future to do this all again as a machine of war.

And I *will* do it all again in every dimension I'm born within. I'm born within many, like a necessary virus. You've no doubt ignorantly passed my pestilent specter in the streets, underestimated what I am and walked the other way. This is the mistake of man: missing the manifestation of a promised *something,* he picks up the pieces of his empire from between *my* fucking teeth. That's the lesson never learned: *Me.*

I'm the promise of vengeance in a blood-stained smile, an indigo creature stuffed to the breaking point and forced to explode everything around me to survive. I'm a piss-poor role model, a necessary lesson, a survivor, a warrior, a being of pure unbridled chaos and a master of my own fate.

This is *my* fucking origin story and my name is Aleksandra Vosova—my name is Alex Voss.

7 / METAMORPHOSIS

It's been a year since Tyr began training me. He's driven by guilt, imagining I'm a princess he can save by teaching 'her' how to kill. Tyr, the knight who generously takes credit for freeing me from the button-eyed woman's abuses—as though me cauterizing her eye did nothing. Tyr, who pays handsomely so my thefts are infrequent, yet I'm still pilfered all the same. *Isn't that right, fuckhead?* Tyr, the chivalric knight who watches the drippings from the ceiling turn my floors to ice in colder months, sympathizes, yet never frees me from this wood-paneled *shithole*. I've never been a princess, but I did need saving and this *isn't* that.

My face is centimeters from the cold wooden floor as I prop myself up on my forearms over and over again. Sweat pours over my skin, my joints ache, my meat screams, yet I'm dauntless as Tyr speaks and I don't listen.

After enough repetitions, I stalk to the end table and pour cool water down my throat from a dingy cup. I place the cup back down and reach my hands above my head to stretch my sinewy muscles.

Tyr calls me by my old name to grab my attention. I'm not about to respond to that corpse's bullshit moniker—he gets a wall of thick silence.

Spindling my arm to the ceiling, I take a form not unlike dancing, which I'm very good at. Innate lust, imprinted rage, immediate distraction, Tyr's influence: all are weapons made to hypnotize. I will be a killer who masters tools most men wouldn't dare. *I'm not like most men, am I?*

The vanity gets a solid kick, which jostles the mirror as Tyr asks if I'm listening to him. No, *fuckhead*, I'm focusing on the way it feels when

I strike. I'm focusing on the rage of being given no choices but to recoil or lash out. *Choice is important, you know.*

As I raise my arm, grasp my elbow and stretch, I think about what's to come. If Boris turns the little bird into razorblades, will it cut everything in sight? *Will it cut even him? And just who is Boris, exactly?*

I smirk, swivel and bring my foot to crash against Tyr's side. He knows me enough by now to block. *This is a test.*

He lets my foot drop and I smile mutely as I bring it down. He's not looking at the trick of my mouth in its half-hitched truth: *he will die by my teeth.* The usefulness of his fucked up chivalry will run out. It always does.

"You probably shouldn't be teaching me any of this," I admit, sharpening my smile as I settle near the neglected glass of water. "Who's to say I won't dabble in backbiting?" I ask, taking a sip.

His response is a hesitant chuckle, which I mimic, then signal to him that he's safe in the language of sex. Over my shoulder sifts subterfuge; butterflied lashes, the slight hesitant quirk of a brow, the pretty lips morphing into a playful pout, the supine neck shown as I tilt my head. All of this was learned. *My brand of libido is never this precious.*

"I'm only kidding," I say as I wait for him to laugh it off. He doesn't, so I present my half-filled cup of water to him. "You think I'm serious?"

Tyr takes the cup from me and manages a cautious sip. "I'm not sure what to think, little bird," he says, licking his lip. "You almost took my head off the other day."

He passes the cup to me, which I take, stopping for a moment to scrutinize him. *It's in the eyes, I think.* Those fucking planets spinning stupidly in his skull, orbiting the girl I never was. He's waiting for me to warble, make a joke, laugh, coo, mewl, flirt, or twist like the prima ballerina. Instead, I dump the rest of the water down my throat.

"I want to get some work done," I say with a curious twinkle in my eye. "Do you know anyone who stabs people, rips useless shit out and sews them back together?"

Tyr mulls his hand over his mouth and looks to the left before he responds. "I may know someone. Is this something for princely endeavors?" He kneads his brow.

I scrunch my nose at his question. He's trying to be sweet but it feels like rubbing salt into wounds he can't see and will never fucking understand. After a moment of heavy silence, I place the cup back on its table, then turn to face him with a sugary smile on my face.

"Yes." I nibble my lower lip. "Princely endeavors." I'm a kitten asking for milk with my big, beautiful eyes.

"You will help me, won't you?" I mewl, slinking into Tyr's arms, who stares at me like I'm about to peel his skin off his body. "You owe me *that* fucking much."

"That I do," he says, opening his mouth to speak again. I steal his words with a kiss that isn't a kiss.

I pull away, smiling. My hands frame his face and I speak once more as the comely titted thing I was never meant to be. "Then take me there and spend your *motherfucking* money."

The operation—if one can call it that—is done far more off the beaten path than I'd ever have imagined. My hand is in his as we walk into what I can only describe as a brown-smelling, antiseptic-tinted, shit-sleeve of a building.

Tyr leads me as I step over sticky tiles. I pull up one of my heels and look down at the taffy-gunk on my shoe. Scraping it on the floor, I'm tugged over yet another ocean of tiles, all slightly warped—which is deliberate cross-story symbolism. *I'm a self-aware wraith of space-time.* Past-me isn't.

A woman scans me with her deep-set brown eyes. She's discussing something with Tyr—they're discussing me, which is apparent as she squints at my face. I don't know the language they're speaking in. She makes a comment, waving about my getup with thinly veiled disdain.

"It's camouflage," I offer with a shrug.

Tyr shushes me.

As the two speak, my eyes become thin slits. I'm not being let in on this little fucking conversation; a little fucking conversation about my little fucking *self*. I strike out my painted claws and steal the woman's clipboard. She fusses and swipes at me. I pivot away and laugh, pushing a few fake blond strands behind my ear as I glance over garbled notes.

"Little bird, you're causing a scene, let us fin—"

"Sorry, but can you speak in a language I can understand?" I ask, smiling dryly as I tip the clipboard to gesture.

He sighs and waves at me for the clipboard and notes.

I reluctantly hand the materials over to the woman, who snatches them dramatically. "*Fine* then, keep me in the dark," I spit, stomping outside to smoke. Tyr sighs deeply, yet lets me go all the same.

I lean on the side of the sticky, grotesque-smelling building to smoke and stare at the burning orange embers at the end of my cigarette.

After what feels like forever, I'm hauled in like a sack of meat. Then, I'm processed, which means stripping and vague cleaning. Then, I'm hefted onto a gurney. Then, I'm anesthetized with drugs. The drugs are rather *wonderful*. I marvel at shadows on the wall I hadn't ever considered the shape of before, until night takes me.

I awaken with wounds that need to be cleaned. I don't fucking trust whatever they give me to clean them and instead use liquor Tyr brings—I imagine—to dull the pain of merely dealing with me. I'm also given pills Tyr calls 'антибиотики' but as I don't know what that means either, I'm not sure about them.

Back in my indigo and wooden cage, I check on my new war scars, then ask Tyr a simple question. "You mentioned these." I point to the bottle on the end table. "What's антибиотики?" I smile vacantly, waiting for an answer as I hold a clean bandage in my fist.

Tyr buries his head in his hands. I repeat my question but he doesn't respond. My face falls. *Why is he so sad?* At the time, I think it's because I've removed the flesh he finds lovely. He's sad because he wishes for us to be like his fantasy: Tyr, the knight in shining damask armor. Tyr, storming the fucking keep to save the beautiful princess, whisk her away and lavish her in riches.

The truth is, he's sad because I'm asking a question I should know the answer to. *The label is written in my own fucking language.*

When you keep a bird in a cage for its entire life, starve it, beat it, and traumatize it, the results are unsurprising. You get a bird who doesn't know how to fly, a bird who perhaps cannot even understand common bird language, and a bird who doesn't know what worms it can eat, or even what worms are to begin with.

I frown and tend to my wounds. The bandage is unrolled. I clean the injury with a wince, pat myself dry with a towel, apply searing liquor, wrap my chest in soft white and reach across the end table for my water and pills. Wiping my hands inelegantly on my sheets, I place an oval pill in my palm, pop it into the back of my throat and take a gulp of water.

"It's a pill to help healing, right?" I hesitate. "But what does the *word* mean? What does it *do*?" *Expectant, nothing-thing knows nothing.*

Tyr looks up at me with a sad smile. He offers me a cigarette, yet no real answer. I take it and quirk a conflicted grin.

"Little bird?" he asks, lighting my cigarette.

Inhaling, I lean back to eye Tyr like a bemused cat. "Yes, родной брат?"

"Would you like to learn to read and write?"

8 / WONDERLAND

Symbols that were nonsense make more sense these days. I'm still not good at spelling, but I'm a quick study. I sit with a notebook in my lap, clutching a pencil awkwardly in my fist. I'm writing things down as the colors stain the window beyond my blissfully blond head.

Tyr is driving. He's taking me to a place he calls Wonderland; a reprieve from training, my usual work and my somewhat-prison. I'm taking notes about the world, what I see, things I want to remember and things that beg my curiosity. Curious like a cat, with nine lives, but no owner. *I'd rather that than a stomped avian shoved in a mold to make a fucking pie out of.*

It shouldn't surprise you that I was illiterate for a large portion of my life. It also shouldn't surprise you that I'm fucking brilliant despite this. One can be a kinetic genius and use their body masterfully: dancing, fighting, sports. One can be musically, scientifically, or mathematically gifted. One can even be good at cutting throats.

I'm good at exactly two things at this moment, a third I'm working on, and a fourth that's inhuman. The first two are fucking and fucking war. The third is my mortal boon: I am always underestimated. The fourth is a gift from the distant future that slipped between the panes of time via a hole in the glass. Or maybe it's always been there. *I can't be sure.*

I clutch my pencil and furrow my brow at these rude symbols. English will eventually make much more sense than this. My lip biting begins.

"It's this," Tyr says, reaching over to scribble in my notebook. He returns my pencil, then turns a corner. I scrawl the Cyrillic phrase several times before I figure it out. Proud of myself, I half-turn to show him my work but my face falls. *Glass shard, full-stop, nothing-man.*

Curling the notebook on my lap, I stare out the window, blurry-eyed. I'm still a mental infant. Tyr is not my fucking teacher, this is not homework and I'm smart enough to know what I've been deprived of. Pulling my notebook to my chest, I lean against the car door as my eyes water without my consent.

"Alex?" Tyr asks, flicking his gaze to my face.

I drag my palm to my mouth and cry softly. He makes a stunted sound as I blurt out stunted sobs. It would've been nice to go to school, make friends, learn and be praised for learning *normal* things.

We turn down a side street and drive a short distance while I try to scrape my tears away. We're at a bustling market. I will later know this is called a wet market—hardly a fucking Wonderland in the face of what New York eventually gives me, but this is my first time in a space like this. A space I could've never, ever dreamed up.

We park. I leave my notebook behind with its chewed-up pencil and exit the vehicle. I'm myself for the first time outside of closed doors. I walk through the crowd behind Tyr, who keeps an eye on me over his shoulder. We approach a stand with food I don't recognize. They're brightly colored and smell fucking awesome.

"What's this?" I reach for a fruit.

"This one is exotic," Tyr replies patiently.

I take it in my hands and turn it around. It's small, comes in a bushel and has a thin, brown pocked shell.

"Lychee." Tyr sounds out the awkward letters. "You want it?" he asks.

I nod, he buys me a bushel and it's placed in a crinkled brown bag. I pick through the fruits and crumple one in my fist. The skin peels away. I place the whole thing in my mouth.

"There's a seed, little bird," he warns me.

I half-chuckle as I find it by pulling apart the sweet flesh with my tongue. I spit the seed from my mouth and plop it into the bag. I've never tasted something like this. *I want more things I've never tasted.*

We mull around this colorful 'Wonderland' eating whatever we can find, until a shop off the beaten path steals me away with its bright blue door. I press my nose to the glass and marvel at garments hung like bodies on a line as my bag crinkles in my arms.

"Do you want to go in?" Tyr asks as softly as before.

Narrowing my eyes, I offer him a sideways glance. "Yes. But why are we here? Why are you showing me all this? Buying me all this shit?" I look back through the glass window and spy a shopkeeper. She's shuffling near a display. A pair of indigo heels hits the orange afternoon light. My eyes widen at the shock of blue-violet.

"Tomorrow," Tyr says hesitantly, placing his hand on my shoulder, "we present you." He licks his lower lip. "This experiment is a flight of fancy," he admits. I scan his face as he continues speaking. "We're trying the impossible. You amuse Boris. We need to see where amusing meets useful, outside of…" he trails off.

"Being invaded and robbed," I say, pressing my nose against the glass to gaze longingly at things I've *never* seen before.

"I really wish you wouldn't describe it like that," Tyr says with a deep sigh.

"Why?" I snort. "That's what it is." I scoff at Tyr and round to the shop door. I open it and stroll inside.

The woman manning the shop glances at us, then shoves herself as far into the back of the boutique as possible. Proud that I fit Tyr's design, I puff up my feathers. I don't want to scare her, but I'd rather be feared than appetized by shitheads.

I pick up a pink frock in my hands and look it over; attractive but not made with me in mind. I peruse more garments and flick my fingers over the price tags. They're all rather expensive.

"I think I'd have been fine with it if I'd picked it myself," I admit, pulling free a loud button-down patterned in buildings and kitschy colors. My sunny smile makes Tyr's mouth shrivel.

"Do you truly?" he asks, siphoning through clothes by my side. He's dressed like he costs thousands and thousands of lives while I'm dressed like a discount murderer in too-big clothes.

"Well, I don't have a problem with sex. I love it when I *actually* get to fucking have it," I reply with a dry smile. "Now…theft of agency?" I mutter, holding up the bizarre button-down. It has tourist patches plastered on it, but I don't recognize the words. I splay the shirt across my chest and continue. "That's what I hate."

"Little bird," Tyr says, grazing the shirt I'm partial to with mute disdain. "You will have to steal agency to make this work."

I glance around to make sure the shopkeeper isn't within earshot. "Not *that* way," I mutter with simmering cruelty. "Killing obstacles isn't the same." I snort.

Twirling to hunt for a mirror, I stalk to the first one that catches my eye. Placing the garment to my chest again, my reflection greets me with a half-smile. This is my style. *I have a style.* I didn't think I'd ever get a chance to try myself on like a better-fitting skin. *I didn't think I'd ever even get to go fucking shopping in the first place.*

"Isn't it?" he asks, scrutinizing me for a more ideal answer.

"You wouldn't fucking get it." I sigh, smoothing out the shirt's creases. "You were born in a body that lets you never have to think about it."

Tyr huffs as he sifts through ties he doesn't need.

"I didn't have that luxury. Do you ever imagine what it's like to be seen as meat in a market just by being born? Or fruit at a stand?" I pull my shirt over my head, then hang it on the edge of the mirror.

"Do you ever imagine what it's like for people to assume you're a pastel little butterfly—forced to accept that's *all* you fucking are—even if you're an *entirely* different species? That you don't get to define yourself, let alone own your name, just because?"

I meet his gaze with a feral smile. "If I'm an object, I want to define myself. You'll never have to, not the way I fucking do."

Tyr furrows his brows, rounds behind me and blocks me from view. Ah. *Does he worry about my 'fruitsome' limbs? No; it's the scars that spy.*

Wriggling into the kitschy button-down, I straighten it and preen. "Yes, that's more like it."

Tyr shakes his head, then mutters, "No, that's not going to sell this. We need to sell—"

"Violence?" I ask, twirling on my heel. My hands fold instinctually behind my back. *Kitten antics.* "Power doesn't look like wealth. That's a facade." I laugh then change tactics with a dead blue stare. "It's useless *fucking* posturing. It's nothing more than small men dressing big to appear bigger than they *fucking* are."

Lacerating with my tongue, the lashes last and yet Tyr lingers on my mouth and waits for another lick. *Hypnotized by a ghost, he's hopeless.*

"Better to disarm them with a smile and an awkward outfit. I think being underestimated is a skill."

"Do you?" Tyr asks, half-incredulously and fully distracted.

"For example." He stares at my mouth like he always does. "You estimate me the wrong fucking way. You're imagining my mouth wrapped around your dick. You're thinking of me like girl-meat."

Tyr protests uselessly with a shake of the head.

"I have been illiterate for a very long time but I'm *not* fucking stupid. You're only doing all this because you can't mistress me, all because you remember a love that never was. We were young. You remember a ghost, Tyr."

A pair of ruddy slacks catch my eye, and as we're in Wonderland, I deign to pluck them free. *They only just match the shirt.* I pull them to my body and eye them in the mirror.

"I don't think of you that way," he whispers.

My brows raise to my hairline. "You're not a very good liar," I chide. With a flick and zip, my pants are unbuttoned. They drop to the floor, I snatch them up, and finally hang them on the mirror's edge. The briefs Tyr loaned me vanish as I step into twice-worn skin. *It feels like home.*

"You think I'm a stupid little girl playing dress up," I say, buttoning the slacks. I look at myself in the mirror, ruffle my hair, smile, grab my old clothes and return to Tyr's side. "Isn't that right?"

He's speechless. My vicious smile looms. That is, until a shock of indigo tugs at me. Spotting the wrack of shoes, I lean, confiscating shocking blue heels and a pair of smart loafers. "I want these too."

"Women's heels?" *He asks a dangerous question.*

"And what makes them *women's* heels?" I snap. "'Normal' people are fucking *backwards*. You have rules for things that don't make any fucking sense."

I round to the front of the store and gesture with my chin. "Pay her." My command stings as I dump my new clothes on the counter. Tyr's mouth is drawn into a flat line, yet he pays the woman all the same.

We leave. I'm carrying bags of exotic foods and new garments I chose *myself*, happy as a pig in shit, and all Tyr can do is stare at me like my brain-matter is leaking from my ear.

"The world doesn't work the way you think it does, Alex," Tyr says as we walk. I hand him my bags (which he takes without complaint) so that I can swing my arms, half-skip and marvel at this *Wonderland*. The scents, the sights, the many people, the food, the lights, the bright sky—*it's a beautiful place.*

Later, I will live in a much more beautiful place. It's a city that embraces every culture you can imagine, a city host to thousands upon thousands of languages, a city that breathes in burning lights. Millions congregate and create friendships across borders, lifetimes, languages, and cultures. I will love it there and the name of the borough I love most will be called Queens. But now, I'm in a city I don't know the name of, in a country I never fucking understood—with a man who never understood me—who still stumbles on my name and the borders between words and worlds.

"How is it you know so many words and so many things but don't understand fucking *anything*?" I ask after a pregnant silence featuring me flitting through the cluttered landscape of sights, sounds and strangers.

"I'm not sure I follow." Tyr hesitates, then lurches to catch up. *I will always outpace men who plod on earth they imagine yields to their every step.*

"You've taught me to read and write, but you didn't teach me observation, the nature of words and how the fucking *world* works. If people make choices, they can unmake them. There is no God that dictates a shoe is only meant for women."

We approach Tyr's vehicle, he unlocks the car and drops my bags in the back. I slide into the passenger's seat as he takes the wheel, then we slam the doors in unison.

"They're mine. I am whatever I say. So, they're men's shoes."

Tyr grunts, turns the vehicle on and we drive. I'm back to writing again, but not of things I see. Concepts bleed from my fingers, but the only translator I've met is long gone.

"I'm not sure that's how it works, little bird," he says, cutting his sentence on his canines.

"Of course it is." I snort.

My pencil scribbles ruddy hieroglyphics as we chart broken roads. Next, I doodle a bird from a faded sign we've passed a few times, just so I remember it. *I'm not a very good artist.*

"How can you be so certain?" he questions me.

We lurch around a corner. "Because man thinks of himself as both beholden to God *and* the arbiter of reality. When something strays," I snicker, fiddling with my pencil, "he names a fake man in the sky as the fucking lord of all meaning. When he can't do *that*, he bastardizes logic in the name of his bullshit convictions—his personal beliefs about the nature of subjective reality."

Tyr licks his lips. "And how would you know all this?" he asks like chastising a child too young to know their ass from their elbow.

"I've learned everything I know about human nature from those given everything and grateful for absolutely fucking *none* of it. You're all so idiosyncratic. It's not hard to use nonsense to make sense of nonsense. You're useful for stealing vocabulary from too, because each of you imagines you're a fucking genius at *birth*," I explain, turning back to my letters and poor artwork.

This will be one of the only times in my shitty little life I share my naked thoughts with anyone I vaguely like. I'll learn later that I can't, because I'll think no one fucking cares enough to listen. The real answer is that they can, but I won't let them, because I'll convince myself I'm unworthy of listening *to*.

Tyr sighs, turns the wheel, we pummel down a rough side street and end up in a narrow alley.

"This isn't—" I hesitate as we park.

Tyr says nothing, exits the vehicle, approaches my side, rips open the door, snatches my arm, and sends my notebook clattering into the dirt.

"Hey!" I shout, struggling against him as he pries me from the vehicle like knifing a tin can. Two men stumble beyond us in the back of the alley as I claw at Tyr's arms.

"Look!" he shouts, gesturing at the puking masses of men too well-dressed to be civilians. "Look at them!" They're Tyr's type: stars, snakes, power, privilege. They're the type I will mimic, then overpower, as a much deadlier version. *That's the script.*

"Do you think they will *ever* understand how you think?! Do you think they'll ever look fondly on a man in heels, a queer painted bird without sense in his—" He forces me to face the strangers by vicing my head. "On a lost little girl playing at war with—"

His voice drums in my ears as he jerks me about, the sound fades as time yawns around me and I snatch his family jewels in my knuckle-white fist.

With a sneer, I pull his lever and he drops me. "What did I say about fucking treating me like something I'm *fucking* **not**?!"

On his knees with my claws near-puncturing him, he reaches into his pocket for a knife—a scare tactic. The puking messes in the alley skitter away like rats, he swipes at me, I break away and he raises his arm to beat his brick fist into my delicate skull.

I grin.

He freezes in time, eyes locked with my own. *I want him to hit me so that I can do what I've been planning to do for months.*

You may find me cruel for this. *Tyr's so lovely, isn't he?* He bought me things, gave me the power of literacy, taught me to fight, helped me step into my new snake skin and he even mourns my hardships! Oh, how fucking novel—the hero's journey—a piss-poor cliche like any *fucking* other! Tyr gave me the tools to not only escape my prison, but to survive, and eviscerate every obstacle in my path. I should be so *fucking* thankful that it only took him ages! I should be so fucking *grateful* he pays only just enough that I'm not *always* a broken heap and all I see in his *fucking* eyes is love for a girl who never *fucking* existed in the *first* place!

I laugh as tears roll down my cheeks. Perhaps it's because I find him lovely in a way; my only boon, my one saving grace, my one shot, my single chance. Perhaps it's because I know I'll still kill him. Perhaps it's because I know he's only here because he loves the girl I never was. Perhaps it's because this chivalry is far more fucked up than he'll ever know. Perhaps I'm crying because he wants me to live so *badly* that he'd teach me a brutal lesson about just how far I can fly before my wings melt.

"Thank you," I say through my tears, drying my eyes with the back of my hand.

Tyr lowers his fist, drops it at his side and gawks at me. "F-for what?" he whispers.

For caring. "For underestimating me."

9 / BIRDFLIGHT

I'm in Tyr's bed glaring at the ceiling. Yes, we ended up sleeping together. Don't fucking judge me or I *will* rip reality in half, drop through the fourth wall and puncture your eyelids with my thumbs.

I drag my blue gaze to his unconscious body. He held me like glass, yet nothing was tender, because he treated me like someone I'm not.

It's difficult to explain. I screw my eyes shut and shift beneath the patterned sheets. How can chopping things off and playing dress-up do much more than trick the eye?

I drift through dark fabric and saunter my way to the bathroom. At the sink, I twist the knob, scoop my hand into cold liquid and douse my face. How can you turn a woman into a man, and considering man's general nature, why would you ever *want* to?

Rising to review myself, damp symmetry greets me. Lacerated white-gold frames blue cold enough to burn and a feral smile spins a spell. I don't look like a woman, but I do look feminine in a way that confuses, which is deliberate. *Confusion is power.*

Confusion is dangerous for men because it's a formula that makes them weak. For many women, blurred gender is a calculated draw. I've thought about all of this, because I had to, and I had to in order to make sense of my own fucking nonsense.

That's why explaining it with any efficacy is difficult: If you've never needed to know what you're not, nothing short of *never* will make the mind-math make sense. Love, pleasure, desire, how we understand the world, how we understand ourselves and others—all of this lives in the head. That's what normal people don't fucking get and Tyr for all his cleverness is a *normal* man.

I'm not, and why *shouldn't* I project my mind onto my body and live the way I choose? "Who could ever stop me?" Whispering to my-self, I vainly twist my locks and preen at the scant tattoos I bribed Tyr for by mewling.

I towel off and return to my clothes to find Tyr sleeping peacefully. I believe he thinks he's done right by me and I would almost have to agree with him. If only he loved who I really was, which is an acquired taste, as I cut on the way down. *Unworthy.*

I pull on my briefs, plain slacks, loud kitschy button-down and my new smart loafers. Undershirt in hand, I nestle it beneath his pillow. He can keep it if he wants to remember us. *See, I'm not always a bastard, am I?*

Shutting the door quietly, I leave. Tyr can't give me what I need and what I need is someone to kiss my lips, not the mouth of a ghost. I need to know myself fully and Tyr can't give me that.

In the dead of night, while the sun sleeps in a blanket of navy-black, I make my way down side-alleys, look up at the stars and chart a path to a less seedy establishment than I'd been kept in. I've seen this place in passing; a bird sign, unassuming women, the tells of a certain kind of labor said in physical gestures.

I exchange knowing glances with a woman with almond-shaped eyes. She nods in my direction, I signal back to her with my body lan-guage, she raises her palm and I become her shadow.

Dipping my hand in my pocket, I pull out a cigarette and place it between my lips. Lighting it, my short steps keep me in time with the woman guiding me.

I notice how her shoulders scrunch when I get too close. "So you *do* get my type around here," I mutter. She half-turns, dark brown hair cascading over her shoulder as she inspects me.

She hesitates at what she sees. "Not as often anymore," she an-swers with an accent I can't place. "Not since Virginia, uh."

Blowing gray smoke into the air, I smile. "Virginia can crack me upside the head if she thinks I'm a threat." I pause, catching my mirror image in a tall glass window. "In fact, you can too."

She suffers a smile, then faces away again. I look from her to the dim lights of this hovel of a city, catch candlelight in windows and feel the sea of stars hover above me.

"Your words are funny," she says with a short laugh. "Like some-thing twice-laundered." She weaves us down a side-street, I smile, flick ash on the wet sidewalk and melt into her shadow.

"So are yours," I offer and quicken my steps to walk at her side. "Are the ones like me rough?" I ask bluntly.

She darts her eyes at me and quickens her steps. "Why?" she mum-bles. "Looking to get rough?"

I shake my head, dig my hand into my pocket and jostle a package of cigarettes in her direction. She hesitates, yet pulls one out all the same. I light it for her as we continue to stroll.

Licking my lips, I take a risk. "I used to become very still. They liked when I played dead. And, if I did it early enough, they exacted less"—I breathe and raise my hand—"pressure." My grin is a tilted tilde tainted by a five-letter word that makes up all I am.

"It's not as fucking fun for them when we don't put up a fight."

As I speak, the woman at my side examines me. She clips over the map of my face, estimates my short stature, drags her eyes to my chest, skirts across my limbs and scrutinizes how I hold my cigarette. *Compartmentalized pieces, perfect geometry, a flank of fabric, a decorative doe.*

"Plus, they couldn't kill me," I admit and hope she understands. "I made too much fucking money."

She surveys the pores of my face, looking for a hole in my story. All at once, I watch myself become a woman in real-time in the eyes of a stranger. *A yarn-haired doll with cotton skin and dead blue marbles for eyes.*

She chuckles warmly. "We have some like you," she says with a dry smile. "Sometimes it's the only thing they can do. There aren't a lot of options."

I nod as she speaks, then place my hand in my pocket as we pass through comfortable silence. She's not in a hurry anymore and neither am I, but to be plain, I never was.

"Did you have many options?" I ask, perhaps too bravely.

She shakes her head and parts her lips, but doesn't reply. I smoke with a solemn smile. She's not from here and I'm probably not either, all things considered. Being so far from a home you don't know how to go back to, or if it even exists in the first place, shrinks every option down to the head of a single fucking pin.

We arrive at the unassuming off-white door of a pale blue build-ing. The paint crumbles with age, propaganda posters peel up the sides and the wooden sign over the door is splattered in nonsensical Russian with an intricate bird design. *Little bird, little patterns, a million avians, and I never ask why until it's far too late.*

Someday, this bird will be my calling card for death. In the far fu-ture, it will be a code-word mumbled into my ear by a fuckhead with a stolen face who shuts my system down. I won't know what this means at first, but it's important.

"Nervous?" she asks, having already opened the door.

I pluck my bent cigarette from clenched teeth, drop it to the pave-ment and grind it beneath my loafer. "Yes," I admit.

She walks toward me and takes me by the hand. Her expressive eyes are sunny skies and open fields.

"Don't be," she says with a slight tug. "You're just where you need to be." Her voice sounds hollow and wet. *I don't ask myself why. I should've.*

10 / CONSTELIS

This building is a farce of a restaurant—something staged, but I guess that's the way of the world. *All the world's a stage. And all the men and women merely players; they have their exits and their entrances; and one man in his time plays many parts.* I've read much since Tyr taught me, though I often have to reread things many times to atomize them.

Drifting past the sea of too-perfect tables, I'm pulled through a beaded door that sifts around my shoulders like stars in a nebula.

"What's your name?" I ask the woman guiding me over the threshold of a place familiar and yet altogether alien.

"Natalya," she responds with a sardonic laugh.

"Well, *Natalya*, thank you for the conversation," I say with a starry smile. "My name is *Jacques*. I'm honored to make your acquaintance." I kiss her hand, making a show of gentlemanliness and she chuckles.

Tethered again, she orbits me to a table cloistered with more hovering beads. A delicate, mousey woman with brown hair looks up at me. Though she looks like she'd break in half if the solar winds hit her the wrong way, I know that looks deceive.

I present the most confident smile I can. "Virginia, I assume," I say. She smokes and leafs through colorful papers written in a foreign language.

Making vague eye contact, she taps the table in front of her. "Payment upfront. One hour limit. Don't get cute—no marks." Her voice is bright and thin. "Play by the rules and you'll be fine."

Natalya steps to Virginia's side, whispers in her ear and she takes a longer look at me. "Heck, really?" she says, a grin pulling apart her fragile features. "Hmm." Virginia sits forward and folds her hands on the table. "Tell me what you need, handsome."

"Two. I'm not picky, I just want to know what it's like," I say, softer than I expect and dig into my back pocket. I place a wad of papers on the table, slide the chunk forward with my fingers and lodge my hands back in my pockets.

"You've never been on this side of the curtain before, huh?" Virginia asks, scrunching up her nose. I shake my head.

"We'll set you up, милашка," Virginia says, gesturing at Natalya, then scoops my cash across the table.

Natalya reaches out her hand and I take it. She glides me toward a door that surprises me with its color, until it calms me with it. I know this color, I belong to it and it belongs to me; it seems something wants me certain of the path my star takes. *I didn't have the language for what this feeling meant back then. I wish I had, because it's deadly.*

I'm ushered in, Natalya closes the door behind her and the smell of heady incense curls around me like a drifting cosmos.

Graffiti is scrawled on the navy wall to my right, dripping in aerosols, but only half-written. I place my hand on the peeling letters and feel something bloom in me. It's a landmark phrase for my life. An English word of space, the sea of stars and patterns in nova-light. I'm *right where I need to be.*

I linger on it until a pair of strong arms comes from behind me and drape over my shoulders. My neck is kissed in burning heat from a stranger with honey-colored skin and hazel eyes. He snakes his hand up my body, underneath my loud shirt and grasps my neck. I tilt back and offer my open mouth. He feeds from it in slow, delicious circles.

A pale pair of hands with tattooed fingers finds me next. The woman in front of me has hair like fire and eyes so green they could threaten forests. She unbuttons my slacks and reaches her hand between my briefs and flesh. She steals my lips for a kiss and slides her fingers over the sensitive ache between my thighs.

There are no syllables here except the dreamy sounds the woman pulls from me with her slick hand in the shape of a claw, and the man with his consumption of my blood-flush lips. We're slow, deliberate and we communicate in skin. In pleasure—for them, a job—but for me, an experience vital enough to force a future where the word on the wall matters even in the dead rot of space.

Heaven weeps for what it will never know. My eyes cast to the hidden stars as I lay prostrate on sheets, scarred and inked chest heaving as the woman between my thighs kisses me, tongue inkling over hot flesh, feather-light, fierce, not at all and back again.

Pleasure is made of speech in things said and unsaid. That's what sex feels like, for those of you who've had only a mirage of it. It's language. It's a kiss to tented, blood-flush flesh, a rod grasped between lips to speak from base to tip, but it's also neither of those things. It should feel—even when it's awkward—like a vulnerability that people agree to experience. It should never feel scarred, unless one feels pleasure that way, and that takes a *lot* of fucking trust.

I trust these professional strangers to kiss me and not my ghost. I do not haunt myself like I had with Tyr. It feels like it did with Thomas and yet it's altogether different. I will know this feeling in the future in two distinct spots of color. The first will be something red-stained and so erotic that I can't speak but the breath of angels, yet it will kill me. *That* one's a bloodless fucking vampire.

The second will be the same, yet tender, like the man now feeding me oxygen. He is so unbelievably close and he waits for me every step of the way. She will do the same, but in pink—this time, it will be pink. True love is so bright it terrifies millions of people and so they run from the light into damage, foolishly, pathetically and foreverly. *I ran from love's warm color.*

I know this now as the explosion from Boris' present gun cracks the air, my life floods before my fucking eyes and we witness the memory of lust grow muddled like a blurry afterimage.

I'm so fucking sorry, Olivia. Someday, I'll remake your constellation as lovingly as I remember you. For I did, and do, and will *always* love you. I will worship you until trauma locks me in the cage of my body and flips my switch forever. *That's the shitty script that we're all forced to follow.*

The bullet careening at my head shifts on axis, the system reboots and we slide through the glass panes of space-time like a smeared bug leaking through a camera's pinhole.

11 / PROOF OF CONCEPT

A wraith in damask peels ribbons of smoke, hunches at his car and glares at me with the viciousness of a man who can't force his pet bird to stop shitting all over the carpet.

"Where were you last night?" Tyr bleats. I raise my brows, walk around him to the passenger's side of the vehicle, jerk open the door and flutter inside as he does. I glance in the back seat—my bags are nestled in the corner, but the shirt I left him isn't.

I shrug at him as he starts the engine with a vicious twist. We're driving toward the event we've prepared for—an event that really shouldn't exist.

I reach for my notebook and flick through it. From what I know of Boris—my fingers trail over my personal hieroglyphs—he enjoys being amused, quippy humor and 'usefulness.' I'm very good at being useful. I also know that he's entertaining this princedom out of pure, unadulterated boredom—at least that's my current intel. Moreover, I know that if I pull this off, I'll have to hide what I am, unless I gain allies. Which is the plan. I know how to pull it off because I'm a very clever little bird. I'm a clever little bird scrawling in my clever little notebook with symbols so nobody knows what I'm writing. *I'm a very clever, very fucking paranoid little bird.*

Tyr glances at my notes and huffs. "I asked, where were—"

"None of your mother*fucking* business." I turn back to my notes. Tyr slams on the brakes and I nearly smash my head on the dashboard.

"What the fuck is wrong with—" He strikes me across the face, which is something I didn't think he had in him. It also moves up our timeline *considerably.*

I lean back in my seat as we drive down a long, trash-littered road, only turning to look at him once my carnation-cheek starts throbbing.

"Ah, so you're just like I thought," I say in a precious voice.

He gristles a putrid sneer. "And what *exactly* does that mean, little bird?" he spits as he drives recklessly. I slink down into my seat; wilting Goldilocks lodged between a metal door and a looming, heartbroken beast.

"A big, strong man, who gets off on beating up women," I simplify. My body jostles as he curses and jags us up a thin alley, pummeling the tires over cracked asphalt.

He smirks at me, as though he's discovered the mystical secret of life itself. "But you're *not* a woman, though, are you?"

I raise both my brows, hand still to my cheek as I eye him like game to hunt. *A bird, a snake—which one am I? Can I be both?*

My sneer is criminal. "And what—exactly—*am* I?"

"Poison," he confesses before stepping on the gas. The car jeers and whips around a corner.

The jostling forces my hand to the dashboard. "Tyr, if you keep driving like this, we'll never make it there in one fucking piece." I grip the dashboard with both hands as we barrel down another thin alleyway as the car—and Tyr—grow more erratic.

"Why did you leave?" he asks, near-pained. We jerk over a pothole as he yanks his boiling head in my direction, as though staring at me could rip my words past my teeth.

I splay my palms flat, lock my arms in place and I hesitate on an answer. "I didn't like how you treated me," I admit, which is the truth.

"And how did I treat you, Aleskandra?! I bought you everything you asked for. I let you butcher yourself. I gave Boris a game to play—one you cannot win. I did all of this for *you*! For you, and yet you sneak out in the middle of the night and for *what*?!"

"You really think I butchered myself?" I sniffle, bow against the dash and bury my head in my arms.

"Aleksandra," he says with a sigh, finally slowing to an acceptable speed. "I-I'm sorry, please. Please don't cry." He touches my arm briefly, smooths my short hair, runs his fingers over my neck and pulls at me. I let him curl me to his side and bury myself against his chest. He wraps his arm around my shoulder.

"Tyr," I whimper. "How did you think this would play out?" I ask. *All the world's a stage. I play a part. I play many parts.*

"I'm—sorry?" Tyr's befuddled, while I have perfect clarity and a thin knife now lodged inside his guts. He feels the wetness first as red leaks into his too-expensive shirt. "Aleksandra, what have you—" The pain floods away his words. It always comes second during shock and I know this because I've felt it all.

I twist to look up at his face as his guts squelch around my blade. My fist is still on the knife's handle—fangs in his meat as I crush his organs like the feral dog that just won't stop tearing.

"Did you think we'd meet with Boris, his men would beat me to a pulp, then you could whisk me away and keep me all to your *fucking* self?" My voice serrates with each syllable. "Pay for me forever, but never buy my *fucking* freedom? Keep me locked in a cage?" I sizzle between clenched teeth, digging in the metal as his blood coats my hand.

We're almost there and if he fights me he'll lose. I will drag this entire blade up his fucking chest and gouge his brain out, crash the vehicle and miraculously emerge ready to take down a bunch of shitheads far outside my weight class because pain is *no* obstacle.

I lick my fangs. "Yes, that's *exactly* what you fucking wanted. Save the princess. But first, let 'her' get beat within an inch of 'her' life so you can sweep 'her' off 'her' broken *fucking* feet. You'd keep me working until the *day I died*, huh? Working, paying you with my body, you *fucking*—" I dig the blade in, he wrestles to snatch me by the hair and a demented smile splits my face.

"Eyes on the road *fucker*, or you'll murder your owner."

Tyr slams the brakes and halts us all of a few inches from a well-dressed man's shoe. The man gestures with his cigar at the human mutts surrounding him. They catch the scent of blood, then crowd the vehicle. *Boris apparently knows how to command an army.*

"You stupid bitch!" Tyr screams as I tear the blade from his gut, scrambling to rip me by my golden locks. I pummel him in the groin and swing my needled blade into his ear.

The blade pierces his eardrum and the friend who was never a friend gets a lobotomy. The only sounds that remain are his death screams and the squelch of brain matter mixing inside the bowl of his skull.

12 / AMUSING

Blood coats the windshield in a pane of red. I emerge from my side of the vehicle with Tyr's ink up to my arms, my kitschy shirt dip-dyed in his delicious death. *It's intoxicating.*

This should be a grievous offense, judging by the gaggle of Bratva that circle me, descend, rip the blade from my hand and jack me against the vehicle's hood.

Boris raises his hand, clears his throat and says, "Little bird, I presume?" His accent is very deep — something more old-world than even the button-eyed faux-guardian.

"Yes," I spit, twisting like a snake against the arms that keep me pinned in place.

Boris chuckles. I catch him stroking his chin from the corner of my feral eye. "Let him go," he says, repeating himself once more. The others finally free me.

I stand proud and tall, square my shoulders and clasp my hands in front of me. I stare directly ahead and wait for the bird keeper to tell me the rules of my new cage. *I won't know it yet, but everything he ever said was a lie. Boris always lies. Always.*

He hums to himself, puffs his cherry-smelling cigar and draws close to my side. "Care to tell me why one of my men is dead in the front seat of my car, staining its upholstery, *little bird*?" he asks, scrutinizing my face with thinly veiled amusement.

"He was in my way," I admit. I keep my head level, but lock eyes with Boris, whose expression shifts comically.

He smirks, blows smoke around me in a shroud of gray, sizes me up and fucking *pouts*. "Too short, too lean and doesn't respect chain of command," he muses behind his cigar, gesturing at the others. "Give me one good reason why I shouldn't have Nikolai put a bullet in you."

The man I assume is Nikolai presses a gun against the back of my skull. I don't flinch. Instead, I give Boris a vicious smile. I am the snake coiled at the base of the tree of life and he's the actual fucking devil. "If your enforcer can be taken out by someone like me, he wasn't very good at his fucking job, was he?"

Boris stares at me for a few moments then finally waves at Nikolai, who drops his weapon at his side. "What are you suggesting, little bird?" Boris asks with a deep laugh.

I tilt my head to the side and imitate his laughter before I speak the words he needs to hear. "I take his place. I'll be more useful and *entertaining* than he ever was."

Boris is not enchanted by me. He never will be and he'll always find a way to exploit me, regardless of how smart I am. For now, I'm safest as a powerful asset and someone who challenges him enough to be amusing. I will never truly learn how amusing I was until I become too broken to hold the truth.

I turn my gaze to the horizon, remain stoic and wait for his cherry-smelling laugh. It doesn't come.

With a wave of his hand, the others disperse dye-like to the building behind them and do whatever it is they do; drink, smoke, gamble, rot eternally. He saunters behind me and whispers in my ear. "And if my men find out just what you are?"

"I know how to gain loyalty," I whisper back.

He shakes his head at this, blowing smoke around us both. "Not the way you usually do, I imagine." He cracks a dry smile. "Tell me, pretty bird, how do we command respect?"

I pat my pockets for a cigarette, jam one between my lips and light it. Avoiding his gaze, I say, "Through fear."

Boris' laughter is infectious. I may end up hating him more than fate itself, but his laughter is a thing of beauty. Heady, warm, rich, and yet it borders on a giggle. It's a dangerous thing—a laugh so genuine it convinces you that Boris could *maybe* be an ally, even a friend. Boris will never be that, though he'll trick me later into believing it. *I'm a fool.*

I tip to peer inside the car. "But first, I'll dump the body, get that reupholstered," I offer, daring to look at Boris momentarily, "and I guess they'll have to haze me."

Boris steps away, traipses to the car and marvels at the mass of flesh that once made up his enforcer. "Yes, they will. But tell me, little bird." *If he had a fucking mustache he'd be twirling it.* "How is it you managed all of this?" he sweeps his arm across the viscera slathering his upholstery like frosting. *I made a mess.*

"Do you want the honest answer, or an answer to tell the others?" I ask, flicking ash to the ground. Boris doesn't reply and instead inspects my handiwork. I'm assuming he wants both. I hope I'm right, because every step of this initiation has to be geometrically perfect.

I'm blunt. "The honest answer is he had no intention of making this work. He loved my ghost. I used it against him. Men are weak to love; the illusion of control and beauty."

Boris nods at this and opens the driver's seat door to scrutinize Tyr's face. The brain matter leaking out his ear seems to amuse Boris, considering his musical laughter. At least Tyr didn't steer me wrong; I know how to be flashy, if that's what Boris wants. *And it is what he wants, for a reason I'm not ready to explain as the present bullet looms before me.*

I exhale a ribbon of gray smoke and swap to standing contrapposto. "As for the others." I sigh and nod in their direction. "Make something up about him dipping into your product to sell it out from under you and me being tasked with sussing it out. It's not a fucking stretch."

Boris chides me with a tsking noise, then walks to stand beside me, rolling his cigar between his fingers. "That'll position you far too favorably, little bird." He snorts and raises his palm. "Like my own personal pet."

Too-genuine laughter bolts from his chest. There's something behind that laugh that I can't see, crinkling in his eyes like black buttons, sideways looks in a wood prison and too-long pauses on my feral mouth.

I smile and half-hum my answer. "Aren't I?"

Boris' laughter catches the attention of his men. He laughs hard enough that he crumples to holding his knees, his cigar hanging between his fingers as he struggles to breathe.

I quirk a conflicted grin, inhale my cigarette and turn on my heel. He walks out in front of me, I trail in his shadow, then he starts babbling about something. I should be paying attention, but instead, I'm itemizing these shitheads to figure out which one of them is weak enough to control *or* confuse.

Setting my sights on Nikolai, I walk through the open doorway and slide into his booth. He scowls at me as he drinks what I assume is Turkish coffee; it has a certain scent I now know.

I smile, he scowls, I smoke, he drinks.

"Say, do you like gambling?" I ask, idling with my cigarette. I tip ash into the slight black ashtray on the table.

Nikolai narrows his dark eyes and turns up his nose at me. "Of course," he more or less spits.

I chuckle, tilt my head to the side, then blow my smoke away from him. "Well, if I said I could kill a man with a piece of fucking string, would you bet against me?"

Nikolai scoffs, pushes back in his seat, crosses his arms and sneers. "Absolutely. You're less than nothing," he says, sucking his teeth. "Small, scrawny, pretty boy got lucky with that one." He waves at the blood-soaked vehicle.

"Well, I *did* puncture Tyr's ear while he was driving, so I don't really know how you'd consider that *lucky*. He's got over a hundred fucking pounds on me," I muse behind my cigarette.

I flick ash into the tray as he raises a skeptical brow. "Prove it, then," Nikolai sneers. He's very pleasant looking; tanned skin, thick unruly brows, a thin nose, square jaw, coupled with closely shaved hair. He looks an awful lot like Thomas. *This worries me less than it should.*

My smile serates. "And if you win, what do *you* get?"

He thinks on my question, brows twisting up. "Your car," he says dumbly.

I snort and then break into sharp laughter. "It's Tyr's car—which is Boris' car—not mine, you fucking idiot." I'm cackling now, which has Nikolai's face pink as sunrise.

"Then…" He pauses, leaning forward, "you buy me a car."

I raise my hand, still snickering to myself, now using my cigarette as a shield because I find this too ridiculous. He's one of *those* men. Obsessed with motherfucking vehicles. *They're fucking cars. Who gives a shit?*

"Sure, a car," I sputter through my fit of laughter. "And if I win, I want you to dump Tyr's body and get the inside fixed up."

"Deal, крошечная собака. We'll take you out on a run," he whispers, looking around. "See how you do, and bring some yarn." I don't know if he really expects that I'll bring yarn, but that's not the type of string I had in mind. He must really want the car of his dreams. *What a strange, strange not-so-little man.*

Nikolai leans forward, neglecting his coffee and speaks low in the throat. "We've got collections. You know—our turf, our protection, our rules. They haven't paid up and we've gotta' exact." I nod as he talks, more or less gathering what he means.

He grimaces too dramatically. "They're a pain in the ass. Runners took out my car with a pipe bomb. They want to cut us out," he huffs, then sneers. "Expand and take our business. Can't let it happen."

I ash out my cigarette in the tray and lean forward. "And Boris doesn't know anything about this?" I whisper, locking eyes with my new broody, handsome, seemingly very thick-headed, car-obsessed 'coworker.'

Nikolai shakes his head. "Vasily was meant to handle it, but he's too busy with drugs and hookers," he admits. "Then, I was meant to handle it, but…" *His pause is fucking agonizing.* "My car."

I snort. "Fine, but I want one more thing." I grin viciously, swipe his coffee, drink it down in one gulp and place the mug on the table with a satisfying sigh. "If I prove I can kill with string, I want your loyalty. Eternal, undivided. Forever."

I smile as he scowls at the empty mug I've pushed in his direction. "Do we have a deal?"

"And you'll buy me a car? If you lose?"

"Yes. But I won't."

13 / CAT'S CRADLE

As we drive to deal with pests, I feel your unseen eyes thrumming the back of my skull as the car thrums over asphalt. 'If he can do all this, why didn't he just escape his cage?' Here's the thing about my type of murderer: I may be agile, methodical and have a high pain tolerance, but I'm more fragile than even I know. One good fucking clock to the head and I'm *out*. Back in the wood-floored cage, that's the way I was handled. *If the bitch bites, break your knuckles or ~~she'll~~ he'll never let up.*

To be more honest, when you're in a fish tank filled with shit for long enough, you get accustomed to shit-water and don't notice you're slowly drowning from it. *That's the sad reality of how hope dies young, or dies at all, for that fucking matter.*

Now halfway there, I sit in the backseat next to a man who smells like stale socks. I assume they're all mere grunts and imagine Nikolai is the smartest they have. For someone as powerful as Boris, I wonder how he manages to get anything done with these playing pieces. *Tyr must have been the mind and the muscle, and of course I just had to kill him.*

Sock-man smokes. I glance at him and take a calculated risk. "Give me one," I command, tinted with a half-smile. *I have to test how this group works.* They might respond to playful bravado, but I'm not certain, and 'not certain' could spell certain death.

Sock-man chuckles and hands me a lit cigarette. I take it, roll the window down slightly, inhale and blow smoke into the blurry street.

"Say," I begin, flicking my eyes to the smelly one, "what did Boris tell you about me?" I want to know how deep this runs—there's something behind Boris' curtain and it's much bigger than hearing that I ripped some dickhead's throat out during a fugue state.

Nikolai clears his throat. "Said you were born into it. Didn't say more," he blurts out while turning a corner. "You think it's a family thing?" He twists to look at me momentarily.

I raise my brows to my hairline. My family name labels me—for a long time, Russian naming conventions didn't have surnames. We had 'so and so, son of guy,' or 'so and so, daughter of woman.' *Vosova* is a woman's name.

I do the perhaps very brave/very foolish thing and mutter, "Vosovic." It's limp in my mouth.

Sock-man glances at me as he smokes, Nikolai repeats my last name as he drives and I flick ash out of the window, hoping I haven't already fucked everything up.

Nikolai twists in his seat. The man riding shotgun chastises him for not watching the road, but he ignores him. "That's Slovakian, right?" he mumbles, faces forward, jerks the wheel and we thud over a pothole.

Slovakian? I feel their eyes on me and turn into a statue; flat stone waiting for what I have to carve myself into to make it out of this bullshit alive.

The sock-man tilts his head to the side and scours my thin limbs. "I think Boris said Mohylévych?" he offers.

My eyes narrow into thin slits. Tyr explained as much as he knew, but considering where we're at in time, hierarchies are dispersed enough to blur bloodlines. *I could be anybody.*

"That can't be right," Nikolai says as he slows the car to a snail's pace, puts it in park and exits the vehicle.

I exit as the others do, still smoking, when Nikolai jags to block my path. He's working something over in his meaty head which makes me smile despite myself. He salutes me and says, "That would make you royalty."

My eyes widen. *Names mean something here and I can't even use mine. I don't even know what it is.* Later, in the city I'll move to, names will only mean as much as you can make them mean. There's brotherhood—and family ties matter—but making a name for yourself? *That's how you fucking win and lose in America.*

Here, I have a gaggle of men born as men gawking at me—including a handsome idiot who's concussed himself trying to figure me out—and Boris in the ephemeral background comically mulling his invisible mustache at the knowledge he's conveniently kept behind a curtain. *Fuck.*

I shrug, nurse my cigarette and blurt out, "Well, to be honest, I don't know much about my name." I pause, gesturing with my chin at the building where the pests are holed up. "But it'll mean something after all this is said and done."

Nikolai smirks, drops his hand and looks at me expectantly. "Have you brought yarn?" he asks. The others exchange various looks. I dig into my back pocket and produce a circle of sturdy metal twine.

Nikolai crosses his arms and huffs. "I thought you said string! That's cheating, you—"

"I didn't say what type of string—did I—you fucking Засранец?" I chuckle, thread the weapon around one wrist and idle with my cigarette. The others erupt in scripted laughter. I've figured them out, which means I'm safe. For now.

Finished with my cigarette, I flick it to the ground and ash it underfoot. "So...what's the plan?" I look at Nikolai, who shrugs sheepishly. "Really?" I scoff, surveying the others in all their comedic, ill-prepared glory. One of my 'brothers' has a plank, another has a gun, another has two guns, someone has a metal bat and none of them project confidence. Boris' small operation is just that—small. Small, unprepared and fetal, just like I am. I won't know until much later how much I helped create his empire by mere fucking observation. *I wish I'd known.*

Nikolai furrows his thick brows and sneers at me. "Well, you *did* say you'd take his place."

Mouthing the word 'ой,' I step forward. "So it falls to me then. Alright. I'm assuming they're all armed and pissed." I glance at Nikolai for confirmation; he nods. "Then we're going to play this smart, *not* hard."

"What do you mean?" sock-smell asks me.

I turn to him, smile, scrutinize his thick skull and ask him a simple question. "What's your name?"

The man gives me a half smile. "Yanov," he says, limply holding his firearm at his side like a sack of groceries.

"Who's Vasily?" I ask. A man with a crinkled, cheap suit raises his hand. "Alright, what I'm going to do is sneak in. The sign that I've cleared a path will be..." Rounding to the back of the vehicle, I pop the trunk and pull out one of the indigo heels I'd been stupidly keeping with me this entire fucking time. "I'll drop this thing," I say, raising the shoe. "Out *that* window," I continue, pointing with my other hand.

Nikolai steals the shoe from me and squints. "This for a girl?"

I chuckle at his question and snatch the shoe back. "Yes, actual—"

He cuts my lie off by blurting out, "She pretty?"

I screw my eyes shut and groan before I grab a rag from the backseat, wrap my fist in it, cleave left and break some poor family's window. Nikolai primes a half-question, so I point to a balcony. *It's the through-line to the second floor leading to the building we're meant to raid, moron.*

"Leave it to me, alright?" The others still don't seem convinced, but I guess Nikolai really wants his fucking car, because he nods vigorously. "And, if I die," I start up, raising my finger. "You don't get your fucking car."

Nikolai grumbles like a child.

Clearing the glass, I fumble with the lock and enter the home. Though it's very quiet, I slink my blade from my pocket and tread lightly. Surveying the home, I notice kitschy figurines dotting sills, musty books, scenic paintings, charming family photos adorning sage-colored wallpaper and children's drawings littering a rustic living room table. A comforting blanket is draped on a sofa that's seen better days. For a moment, I walk to it and wrap the thick knitting between my fingers. A bittersweet smile tugs the corner of my mouth. It's a shame they're in such a shitty province. *I might have liked growing up in a home like this.*

A noise from the stairwell startles me. I leave the blanket and strike out my blade into the shadows. I still my hand a mere millimeter from the face of a small girl. She stares up at me with her mouth slightly open, fidgets with the hem of her pastel yellow dress, yet doesn't scream.

I draw the blade to my side and kneel. She takes a step back as I follow her with my eyes. My expression softens.

I clear my throat. "Little one, can you let me go up your stairs to your balcony? There's—" I pause for a moment, holding up the indigo shoe. "There's a beautiful princess who needs her shoe back, but I need to use your balcony to get to her. Her father won't let me see her, because I'm not the prince she's meant to marry." I smile at the girl-child, who seems relaxed by my completely bullshit story.

She gnaws her lower lip then speaks in the smallest of voices. "A princess? Like Vasilisa?" My eyes dart over this young one's round, pudgy face. *I don't know this story yet.* There are so many that I don't know, so many that I should, so many that I never fucking will.

"Yes, *just* like Vasilisa," I lie.

She chews her lip again, nods and holds out her hand for me to take. She's too trusting. Nevertheless, I take her hand as she walks me up the steps behind her. We are as quiet as mice in a suspiciously quiet house. Drawing the girl behind my back, I glance around the narrow hallway. A door across from us is slightly ajar. I nudge it open with my foot and catch a flash of wet crimson on hardwood.

Turning, I kneel slightly and hand her the heel. "Can you hold this for me?" She nods, mouth forming a quivering pout as she takes my stupid shoe.

Placing my hand to her shoulder, I steer her toward a thin slate door without complaint. Pulling the door open, I'm met with folded fabrics, coats and assorted boxes. *Enough room for a little girl.* I usher her inside, she wriggles around, then stares at me with watercolor eyes. My wire-clad hand is locked in her small fist.

Kneeling, I whisper to her. "No matter what you hear, stay inside and keep close to the ground, alright?"

She looks at the floor, shuffles back into the closet, sidles between thickets of coats, draws the shoe between her legs and clasps her arms around it. Something rose-colored animates my corpse to ruffle her hair before I leave her hiding between coats.

I stand, shift the door closed, slink to the room with the bloody floors and suction to the wall beside it like a leech. Glancing behind me, I spot an unassuming red ball on the ground. I grab it, nudge the door with my foot and roll the ball through the crack. A man curses and another man mentions 'молодая девушка.' They must have done her the mercy of leaving her alive. Alive to see all of this and deal with it, alone. *Yeah, like that's a fucking mercy.*

A man yanks the door open, I loop the metal wire over my wrist, ensnare his throat, choke him out and wait for the second shoe to drop. Just as expected, another man steps through, trailing bloody boot-prints. Striking out my foot, he stumbles on it, raises his gun as he falls and I use the man braced at my chest as armor. Bullets split the air—no doubt she hears the gunfire.

I fling my bleeding shield at the man, skitter like a scarab and launch at him. He raises his gun again, but the body blocks him. I jab my thin blade into the second man's cheek. He curses out, flails his gun to fend me off, jerks to throw me, but it's too late. The meat between us makes him writhe as my inevitable skewer rises to pin him like a bug.

I stab into his jugular with a wet sound. He gurgles around the blood filling his esophagus, body twitching as I hold him in place. When I'm sure he's dead, I tuck my blade through my back belt-loop, take his gun and step through his blood to peer through the doorway.

I'm not going to have backup without a signal, but I don't give a fuck about that right now. I give a fuck about the child kneeling in a closet in shock, stuffed between coats, hugging my fucking shoe, listening to me *murder* people. No child deserves to go through this shit. *If she doesn't have any family to take her in*—my mind races. My new mission is to kill everyone in my path to make sure that doesn't *ever* fucking happen.

With blood-coated hands, I make for the back stairwell that leads to the balcony of this quaint home in the worst neighborhood I will possibly ever visit in my life. I've taken to instinct; it's not the color of red-meticulousness, it's teeth to the throat and the raw neon blue of war.

A man thuds down the stairs—I shoot him between the eyes. I don't wait for the sound to draw whoever he's with and plod up the steps, seeing without seeing, moving without thinking, leading with my gun as if preordained. *No one* is allowed to leave and no one fucking does.

I'm covered in blood with one bullet wound in my shoulder while I traipse over mounds of bodies that stain this little girl's floors. My 'brothers' have arrived; drawn by bullet-fire, but late like cowards always are. They follow me around the house and shoot questions that I bob and weave around. Nikolai yells, speaks with his hands and tries to pin me in place. I ignore his attempts to snag at my shoulder, until he pulls too hard and I glare.

Making my way to the bathroom, I flip the lightswitch on, shove my hand under the faucet, then dig my fingers into the wound. Twisting, I look at my back—clean through, which is good—and hesitate for one moment that freezes subjective time like slamming on the breaks. *Glass-flicker, guilty-eyed, blood-splattered nothing-soul.*

I note my clothes in the mirror, flick my gaze to the unseen closet, clench my jaw, screw my eyes shut and feel pain throb through my shoulder. My heart pounds out of my chest, the dirty mirror gets a viper's glare and I rip most of my clothes off.

The others burst through the door and bark at me as I say nothing, because I don't have to. The scars on my chest spill my secret in faded lines as I clean the bullet wound and sew myself up with whatever's in the cupboard. Cutting the thread on my teeth, I ditch the needle, scrub my hands in the sink vigorously, reach into my slacks, unearth my cigarettes and jam one between my teeth. The others gesticulate comically, I light my cigarette, shove the lighter into my stained pants, toss poppy-tinted towels to the floor, inhale, dart past my 'brothers' and dip into the master bedroom.

They follow me. I saunter, they gawk at my flesh and I ignore them. *My body is a fucking spy.* Stepping over the corpses of the girl's parents, I rip into the closet, snatch a rose-colored blouse, rest my cigarette on the end-table, pull the shirt on, button it and put my cigarette back in place. The others squawk as I step into a pair of crumpled gray slacks.

Nikolai hovers at my side as I round to the bathroom and slide my loafers on. He yaps, I lock eyes with him, then shove my blood-stained garments into his hands as he blinks wildly.

Plodding past the group, I kneel before the closet. My bleating 'brothers' magnet behind me and croon. That is, until I place my hand to the door with a heaviness that shoots them silent.

Steeling myself, I screw my eyes shut and knock. The little girl knocks back, I twist the handle, the door flings open and she emerges from bushels of coats. She rushes to my chest and I bury her face in the silk shirt of her mother. My indigo shoe—still clutched to her body—digs my ribs.

Collecting her, I make my way to the stairs. Hitching gingerly down the steps, the thick silence of men born as men twists like a noose that I worry about meeting—but not now. I lean close to the girl's ear, cigarette between my fingers and whisper only to her. "Do you have an aunt or maybe an uncle? Siblings?" She nods into pink silk and I continue. "Do you know where they live?" She nods again.

I leave out the front door with her clinging to my body. The others follow me. They haven't begun shouting again, and to be fucking frank, if they do I'll choke them out with my metal yarn.

They huff into the vehicle, all save Nikolai, who shoves my crap in the trunk, rounds the car, jerks Vasily out of the passenger's side and waits until I slide in. Only when I settle myself—and the girl—does Nikolai dare to sit at the helm and put his hands on the wheel. *He's more clever than I thought.*

As we drive, I ask the small one where to go, then tell Nikolai, who glances at me sporadically as the colors whip past the windows.

"So." Nikolai clears his throat. "Alex, Alexei, then—"

Ignoring Nikolai, I ask the little one her name. She mumbles out 'Sofia' in broken syllables as I smooth out her hair and she fiddles with my obnoxious shoe.

Nikolai sucks his teeth and tries again. "Alex Vosovic, then—"

I grunt and wrap my arm around the girl like a shroud. "Aleksandra Vosova." My corpse's name curdles in my mouth.

"Aleksandra *Mohylévych*," Yanov corrects me with a simple laugh. Covering the girl's ears, I crane my head to gawk at Yanov.

"You knew," I say flatly.

He snorts as he looks out the window briefly. "Boris let slip after too much drinking." He laughs. "You're royalty."

I pause, stuck in time as I scan Yanov's eyes. He smiles. It's a simple, good, real smile. "Boss of bosses," he adds with a twirl of his cigarette, "like your father, yes?"

Turning, I stare straight at the road that floods below our wheels.

Nikolai keeps looking at me, then the road, then the girl, then at me again. *A pinprick, a stain, a martyr, a slave.* "Yes. Like my father, who—"

Nikolai raises his hand to cut me off. "Don't care."

My eyes narrow. "What do you mean you '*don't care*?'" I snort.

"What you did in there?" Nikolai gestures back at the scene of a crime we'll have to call the cleaners for. "And if Boris knows…" Nikolai trails off as he turns a sharp corner.

My eyes bullet to his face as I slip my palms over Sofia's ears again.

"I'll kill anyone who gets in my fucking way. If you make this difficult, I swear to f—"

Vasily pipes up. "Yes, sir." Nikolai chimes in with the same sentiment, as does Yanov. Competence, compassion, strength and respect is how I won the loyalty of a small group of lost boys missing their north star.

Boris will, after far too much time, eventually fail because he lacked the one word I'd replaced with underestimation: Respect. A respect I earned every single fucking drop of. *A respect I forgot to have for myself when I walked into Boris' bullet in real-time.*

As I worry about a child stained in horror—and show you my mind-movies—the bullet hasn't clipped my skin just yet. I narrow my eyes as the car clatters over a pothole. *I don't think I'll let it.*

14 / FRUIT

When we dropped Sofia off with her relatives, Nikolai had to remind me to put her down. Locked in my arms as she was, he pried my fingers one by one. I didn't realize at the time where my reluctance came from, but now as I sit under a cloak of night at our base of operations and devour messy fruit, I understand all too clearly.

Nikolai stares at me as I eat. I guess he wants to ask me questions, but I assume he's afraid to even open his mouth. He looks away sheepishly, which amuses me, so I quirk a smile before I dig into my fruit again.

With a mouthful of fuzzy viscera, I mumble between bites, "Should I charge you for watching me eat?" He flicks his gaze to the far corner of the restaurant. My indelicacy forces his glance once more. He watches me lick the corner of my mouth. *I notice, but I don't hate it.*

Vasily and Yanov approach us, hesitate, then pull up chairs to sit on either side of Nikolai, cloistering him. He freezes in place. *Caught your hand in the cookie jar, hmm, you little shit?* It's Yanov who pipes up finally. "Sir." He clears his throat. "What you did—"

I roll my eyes and grind sweetness between my molars. Sucking the juices off my fingers, I toss the pit in a far trash bucket with a dull thud.

"I did what anyone else would do," I mutter and wipe my hands on my stolen gray slacks. Vasily shakes his head. I quirk a brow. "What?" I scoff at a man two times my size.

Vasily folds his hands on the table, leans forward, looks over his brothers, then locks eyes with me. "Not everyone else." His sentence drifts. "We would've left the girl," he admits.

I wrinkle my nose at this. "And?" I let my non-question hover as

I pull out a cigarette, light it and smoke. I pause for a moment, sneer, then jerk forward to drill my eyes into Vasily's thick skull. "Are you really all so *fucking* dense you don't know where she'd have ended up if she'd had *nobody*?"

The others grow quiet as I slump back in my seat, glare into the distance and tear my fingers through my hair. *These men should fucking know better.*

They should feel what I feel, and yet they don't, or perhaps their shitty little lives keep them stuck so deep in fucking dog-shit that they can't think about people so very small, so very weak and so very *fucking* helpless in a place and time that affords no agency for anyone at all and nobody who *could* care or could make a fucking difference gives even *one* single fuck.

Nikolai knits his thick brows together, which makes me stop trying to tear my hair out. I'm only ever distracted from rage when I have to protect someone or when struck by beauty. *I'll even let beauty gut me if it means I can flirt with it.*

I'll let beauty gut me many times over the course of my life. At least one very beautiful person treated me beautifully enough not to rip out my fruit-guts like I'm desecrating my food. *I've failed her, I know this.*

Boris' bullet pushes a millimeter into my skin as we watch my past self smoke in a stolen shirt and stare at a beautiful man who stares at him. I don't hate his stare—in fact, I find it flattering.

Offering the trio a real smile, I say, "I want to do something awesome and I need you three to back me up." I pause to lick my lips. "Will you fall in line behind me, or do I need to threaten you with a piece of string?"

Thick silence hangs like the stars overhead as I stream smoky ribbons and men born as men try to make sense of my nonsense.

Vasily leaves and returns with Turkish coffee, says nothing and pours me a cup. I drink the bittersweet brown brew, he sits back down and the trio speak without speaking. As they smile at me, I smile back.

I've found people willing to do what I want. What I want is to break something apart in my teeth—a target I can only vaguely sense—so that power never offers absolutes to little birds without families to protect them. *Just like me.*

These three are mine now. I sip my coffee. They won't be mine for long. I scan the horizon and smoke. If only I could've ended it all here, with them. *If only I fucking knew I could.*

15 / WATER

Why do powerful men always meet in bath houses, considering how homoerotic they are? This is where men go to meet and fuck. I don't think the others get that context, but what some of them *do* get is that I don't have the right equipment to be here in *this* context.

It's not that I shouldn't be allowed, but it's that I'm quite simply *not*, and if I'm discovered by anyone else, Boris will discard me, wash his hands of 'entertainment' and my hero's journey will be fucking lobotomized. It's a great risk, even if I think the others have enough respect for me that they'll defend me. At least I'm sure Nikolai will.

Nikolai hovers at my side when he doesn't need to—war has cut me enough to make me invisible and the scars have faded—yet he still shields me all the same. I nudge the inside of his arm with my fingertips and feel the smile on his face that I can't see.

Boris begins to talk with a man wearing eyebrows that threaten to connect to his hairline. I pull away from Nikolai instinctually and follow him to sit down in a too-warm, too-humid space, with too-evil men with *far* too much power.

A damp notebook in my lap offers obfuscation as I take notes and older men speak. The older men note it curiously, but Boris waves the idea away in cherry-smoke and too-genuine laughter. He says things like, "Little bird is strong," and, "Little bird has blueprints."

Nodding absently, I raise my gaze to the weathered, leathery face of a powerful man, nod again, then turn back to my notes. I have little respect for him, but I have to make the effort so he doesn't throw a fit about the politics of machismo.

Politics. I scribble symbology with my grubby pencil. Nikolai lingers on my completely fucking nuts flavor of note-taking. My grimace is slight. I hope he gets the hint, and he does, hiding a shy smile before looking off at damp, grimy tiles.

Throughout my life, I'll meet other quietly brilliant men like this and always fall for them. I will also meet someone very different, whose cleverness makes life impossibly simple. She will be the most beautiful part of my story, but I won't be strong enough to keep her.

Olivia, the bullet is here, you're so fucking far away and I'm crying enough to shame rain itself. I need you here, please. *I can't let it end like this.* The still-frames of my life fracture into a million points of light and burn around the edges. My past-pencil slips in my grasp like a record needle skipping and curiously falls out of reach. Nikolai picks it up. Taking it back, I don't linger, but I *want* to.

After our meeting concludes, Nikolai curtains me while I dress, then we walk from the bathhouse into dark streets filled with strangers. Boris glues his eyes to the side of my face, staring like I'm a bomb. My grin is criminal. Boris then begins his braggadocious schpiel, I take in what's relevant as his cigar-stink stings my eyes, then we drive back to our front and I think about the truth he hides and the home I don't have.

Up until now, Tyr's car has been my new metal cage. Considering I've collected cash with recent runs and earned a bit of respect, I should score a spot not baptized in the blood of a fake old friend. I've sent Yanov and Vasily on the hunt for just that purpose.

Rounding my usual table, I furrow my brow and sit. Yanov—eager to please a man—places clippings on the table like offerings at an altar. I suffer a mute smile as I flick through them. He's given me too-pretty homes where nothing grows, sweats, smells or breathes.

"Thank you," is all I say before I take to my nicotine habit. Nikolai joins me shortly, bringing much-needed Turkish coffee in a pair of mugs.

He smiles as we share a hot brew, only frowning when he eyes the ad-scraps and water-damaged Polaroids. He bravely nudges my leg with his shoe to ask me a question. I don't nudge him back. His frown hurts to look at, so I turn it into a smile by winking at him.

Our type doesn't do well here. Our type doesn't do well *anywhere,* not until much later, and even then we suffer and die for *nothing.* The world's bizarre hierarchy persists for 'pure' in-groups and 'pathological' out-groups. I will understand it more as time goes on, but it still won't make any fucking sense to me, because making sense of nonsense doesn't *always* work. *Some rules are just too stupidly, pathologically cruel.*

Nikolai pours more Turkish coffee into my off-white mug and grins; *fish in fists, gentle birds, a clear blue sky.* I rest my head on my palm and give him a smile before muttering, "Where do you think I should live? Seems those two keep giving me—"

"Castles," he cuts me off, then chugs his coffee. "Must be annoying, yeah?"

I nod, curling my fingers to my cheek. *He's very earnest, very gorgeous and very distracting.* If I wasn't distracted, I'd notice Boris metaphorically scribbling on everything around him to paint a picture of what I can't see just yet. Maybe that's why Boris pointed me in Nikolai's direction to begin with. Maybe he knew what would happen. But I never stopped to think about how he could possibly know. *I should've.*

After finishing up our coffee, Nikolai and I leave the scattered papers and our scattered brothers to get something *real* to eat. Street food—including kvas—which makes him laugh in my face and croon about "children's beer." It's a sweet drink that tastes lovely and new to me. *Almost everything is new to me.* The pelmeni we eat from crushed boxes with awkward forks, the kvas we drink in crinkled cups, the vulnerable flirting, walking these streets, hearing these sounds, seeing these sights, living a life—all of it is new. *I don't hate it, in fact...*

I shove a sloppy bit of pelmeni into my mouth as we walk. He watches me lick my lips, which makes me smile. Overhead, the sun dips low above the curtain of the horizon, coloring the sky in purples, pinks and blues. *This is romantic.* I'm sure no one else would think so. Not of us, not two men eating messy food, laughing loudly about nothing and everything, then chasing each other around in mock-fight foolishness. This is a date—a real date—the first I've ever been on in my entire *fucking* life.

Stopping short to mimic Boris and his arrogant antics, I wield a fork like a cigar and pretend I'm more important than I am. Nikolai bursts into blistering laughter as I huff, puff up my chest and act perpetually bemused. His laughter is breathtaking—I stop to stare at him and spot food on his face. I want to pry it from his cheek with my tongue. His quirked brow begs me to, but I can't. *Not here.*

Afterwards, he brings me to his home under the guise of letting me stay until I can find a place of my own. We haven't been very secretive about spending time together, but I'm certain I've at least earned Yanov and Vasily's silence. If you're at the top, nobody questions you. I'm not there yet, but someday I will be. Or rather, I'll be safely beneath someone who's at the top, but not nearly safe enough, considering how fucked up the world is. *America will be both better than this place—and far worse—because it pretends it's better than it is.*

Nikolai's lips are on the corner of my mouth. This is a slow thing, a butterflied lashes thing and a delicate thing that he won't let me turn violent. He kisses my temple next, then my cheek, then finally my neck. I'm worried he thinks of me in the way I'm not, but that thought is dashed when he wraps his arms around me and pushes his tongue between my lips. My eyes flutter closed. *He's not kissing a ghost. He's kissing **me.***

I dull the ache between my thighs by sipping his lips and lapping my body against his. Thomas may be the blueprint of the only type of man who never hurts me, Eric Hail may be the one I give to another to keep and Henry Thames in the future will be a solid copy—but *Nikolai Fucking Voronin.*

We kiss and do nothing else—which I'm not used to. We talk until the morning sun greets us through his window. We eat pelmeni in bed, drink kvas and I run my fingers over his mostly-shaved head. Kissing his eyelids, I pull away and I'm met with his thumb caressing my lips. *He's so gentle.*

I'll warm his bed until I'm thrown in a new cage by choice in order to protect him, because the only way to save his life is to let him slip through my fingers. *Why do I let the only type of man capable of loving me... leave me?*

16 / HUMAN COMMUNICATION DEVICE

Something inside my body crushes itself. Nikolai's sleeping face comes into view, then the bizarrely flickering wallpaper behind his head. Instantly, my insides explode and crack my lower back in half. *Fuck, damn, ass, shit—fuck!*

With wide eyes I plead with Nikolai's unconscious body. I don't know how to ask Nikolai for help, but if I don't, I'm— *How do I even fucking begin?!* My organs seize. *I'm a broken thing.* I could start there. *I'm probably dying*—another fact. The walls crawl, my guts twist, I hide a grimace in sheets and make stupid sounds attempting not to wake my lover. *Fuck!*

Sliding from the covers, I jerk to standing and feel my stomach drop through the floor. Half-falling to the discarded carcasses of careless bags left in recent months, I pluck through the entrails. Accouterments scatter on the floor as blood drips down my thighs and stains Nikolai's hardwood. Cursing, I twist to scan his face, but he's still in dreamland. *Fuck!*

Blind as a bat, my hands fumble until I snag something that crinkles. Clutching it, I struggle to stand and feel all the blood drain from my face. My head pounds, a fragment of a star blinds my left eye, *and* I'm anemic. *Fuck!* Twisting on my own limbs like an alien creature, my useless body contorts toward the bathroom. My hand crawls against the wall with every screw-eyed, shuttering, delirious step. *Fuck! Fucking shit!*

I didn't ask to be burdened with the 'miracle' of childbirth. The walls vibrate as the migraine pulls my gray-matter out in chunks. *As is obvious, I'd have fucking picked a very different fucking option.* Hellscape patterns blind me as nausea thrusts my stomach into my throat. *Fuck!*

Staggering into the bathroom, I rip off my shirt, toss it to the floor and turn on the tub's faucet. Once the tub is filled, I slide into bone-biting frost with a gasp. Slapping the fiddly package on the ledge of the counter, I finally drift into the cold depths. *Fuck!*

Submerged, I wrap my arms around my knees, open my eyes, glare at the damp ceiling and pray for death. Death, not hearing my despair, leaves me to tint the water pink. *Fucker!* I scream below the surface for millions upon millions upon millions of years. *As if that'll fucking do anything!* After wasting oxygen for a factual millennia, I let my waterlogged corpse bob to the surface with a flat scowl on my too-pale face.

Snarling, I snatch a bar of sandalwood scented soap from the rim of the tub and cleave my thighs with it. My nails dig angry red lines as I scrape, shiver, wince and whisper-cuss. *Fuck!* The suds on my hands are stained, the water is stained, Nikolai's floors are stained, my relationship is *stained*. I fucking broke it by being what I am!

Dear voyeurs of my tragic life, you may be wondering why I'm forcing you to witness me scream as my inner organ skins itself. Well, it's because *I* was forced to live it. It must suck to experience something you didn't consent to—in a story that doesn't call for it—in a life that never fucking called for it, huh? *Fucking blow me.*

My purification leads to a zigzag-crackle that knocks the vision from one eye. The soap slips. I drift into my pink sea with a feeble whimper, a useless, dying extraterrestrial melting in a vat of my own juices.

Glancing to the door, I beg my voice to travel out my throat and into the air, then reach his ears—magically. *Maybe if I just float in here all night that'll be fine.* Maybe I can sleep my way through the agony ricocheting my skull like a thousand fucking bullets. Maybe I can *drown* myself if I try hard enough. Slipping below a pink sea, a martian coated in its own blood writhes in the dark, submerges itself in a frigid lake and *weeps* in pain.

A noise startles me as I flop instinctively. Nikolai rubs his bleary eyes and pulls at his boxers. I struggle to snort in amusement despite the migraine. He screeches.

"Sorry, sorry—fuck." I thrash and reach out to him, yet he spots my sea and shirks back. "Ah…" I mumble. *I'm a terrifying, broken child's toy.*

Nikolai's thick brows raise to his hairline. "Are you having a stroke?!" He stumbles toward me and tries to gather me from the tub. I slap wetly at his arms and wriggle like a caught fish.

He pauses, arms out and then takes to a slow kneel. "What can I do?" he asks. I manage an approximation of the words 'pain' and 'kill,' or perhaps 'kill me,' but I can't think. The patterns bleed across my eyelids as I'm left to snivel, partially blind and fully malfunctional.

Nikolai fumbles, my gauze contraption drops off the edge of the counter, he rips open the medicine cabinet and scours the shelves. Jamming a pill bottle into my hand, he tears from the bathroom and I'm left to bleed and curse God all alone.

After a moment, he returns with a cup of water, then flicks the light switch. I shrink from the bulb like a vampyric extraterrestrial—I might have even *hissed*. He slaps the light off, kneels again and holds up the cup like an offering.

With a violent twist, I scatter the pills in my palm and pocket two in my cheek. Snatching the cup, I slug the water and drugs down my throat. Scattered pale ovals are left as casualties of war in my grotesque sea. *I hope they'll take me with them as they dissolve in little smears.*

Nikolai takes the cup from me as I sink into the water. He searches my face in all its agony, mute at my distress and I can say nothing. I can't even speak normal words about normal things, but now? *Fuck!* Nikolai gawks at me like I'm dying. *Maybe I fucking am, fucker! Maybe I fucking am!*

Nikolai places the cup on the counter and returns to kneeling. Tears dribble down my pathetic face. This isn't morphine, it's not a fucking opiate, it's going to take forever and this is fucking horrible and I'm in a lake of my own blood while the man I'm falling in—the guy I'm fucking—stares at me in horror and wonders if I'm broken. *I am broken, that's the fucking point!*

"Alex," he starts up, reaching his hand across the lake of me. "Tell me what's wrong, Прекрасный человек." His voice is like a purr. What feels like a lifetime ago, I'd imagine he was stupid. My mistake. No, he's *far* smarter than I am, because he's trying to calm me down. *Moreover, it's working!*

"I don't want you to fucking see me like this," I blurt out, thick tears rolling down my cheeks. "I'm having a migraine. I—" My words fail again. *This isn't who I am. This isn't who I want to be. I never fucking asked for this. I don't want to be like this. Fuck this fucking shit!*

Nikolai furrows his brows then sits back on his rear, crunching my alien apparatus under his leg. He picks it up, raises a brow, then places it in his lap. "Why not?" he asks me, stupidly.

Stupidly, I don't have an answer and decide to stupidly shut off all human communication devices entirely. As an alien, I don't speak. I stare straight ahead, let my inhuman corpse bleed and stop responding altogether—dysphoric, catatonic, agonized.

At some point, the pain relievers kick in, and at another point, I realize Nikolai has pulled the tub's stopper. He stands me up, helps me from the tub and I mechanically complete the process I shouldn't have to and hate with every fiber of my *fucking* being.

When I'm finished, I crush the menacing device's shell in my fist, stand and jerk forward to make a break for it. *I'm never fucking coming back here ever again.* I've had plenty of lovers by my choice since escaping that shit hole, which is why I know how this fucking goes. *Never.*

I *never* want to deal with *them* dealing with *this*—but now that 'them' is only one fucking person and I'll lose him for this. *I just know*—Nikolai's fist clasps my wrist, locks me in place, the wrapper crinkles in my palm and I bow my head like a beaten mongrel waiting for the words I know he'll say. The words that I think he'll say, that I project into his skull—magically.

"Come." His voice is baby's breath. "Come," he repeats and my mistake of a corpse is pulled. The crinkled paper drops from my fist as my face burns into his perfect chest. It will take me years to unlearn this self-hatred, but at least Nikolai got me started. *It's astounding what love can do. Sometimes, it's enough to change a person forever. Sometimes, it even defies fate itself.*

Nikolai helps me over the edge of the tub, then turns on the rusty shower. Cold water hits us both as we shiver in unison. He looks into my eyes, trails his dark gaze to my neck, charts the faded map of my chest, lingers on my tattoos, flutters my hips, then below that and ends staring at my legs with a sunny smile.

"It'll turn up soon, give it a minute."

I nod, my arms wrapped around my chest as my eyes narrow. My glare should frighten him off, but his smile doesn't fade. A grimace does nothing, so I up the ante and *scowl.* I'm giving him the opportunity to discard me and he isn't *fucking* budging. *Obstinate prick.*

"Why are you so scared?" he asks and I can say nothing as the water pelts my feral body.

"You can tear up anyone. You can kill anybody," he murmurs, pressing me against the tiled wall. He kisses the shell of my ear as my eyes close. "You're war on two legs." He chuckles, threading his fingers through my serrated locks. "What are you so afraid of, 'blondie?'"

He speaks this strange nickname in English. It will be a label the people who love me will use. It's a pattern I cement for eternity; I decide this as Nikolai breathes hot against my ear then feeds on my throat.

"Myself," I mumble into the sky, the sea of stars, space-time, the air and it's all so very fucking horrific being an alien in your own motherfucking body, but he kisses me and I forget.

He slides his hand between my legs and makes me forget how much I hate myself. The water is warm. His smile is warm. I forget how to speak human language again. He turns me into the stuff of paintings on ceilings all with one curled hand. Even at a time like this, Nikolai doesn't treat me like something I'm not. He doesn't find me disgusting. He doesn't think I'm an alien. *I love this man.*

The water warms up, he warms the one part of me I let feel anything good, and I hold on for dear life. As beautiful as this moment is, I will have to let him go to save him. I will *truly* let him go—no recreating him elsewhere, no forcing fate to let me keep him for myself.

As you stare at my mind-movies as my shitty life flashes before my eyes, you might be wondering *why*. If you're from the future that sucks far worse than any past could, the question possibly remains. As you watch Nikolai kiss me and turn me into the stuff religions are born from—perhaps the question thrums as his hand does.

Nikolai's an error in my machine. With his variable, no heroism takes place. Keeping him would've meant my death in Russia. Keeping him would've meant no New York escapades. Keeping him would've meant the end of an entire species in the future. *This may all be a lie, as people are good at running away from love when pain's all they've ever known.*

Once, I loved a man named Nikolai Voronin. On this night, he'll draw the pain from my body and carry me to the bed I will want to live in. We'll drink kvas, eat leftover pelmeni, he'll rub my aching back and make me feel powerful before we drift off to sleep with our foreheads pressed together. Soon, the man I now *know* I love will be absolved of all sins and I will lose my humanity to protect him. We will never speak again for as long as we both shall live, but we will love each other madly.

I will never let anyone have this, I promise myself.

It's a promise the script says I'll keep.

17 / PERFORMANCE

We've spent a week together; warm nights, soft speech, wet stars and more closeness than I've ever dreamed of. However, the pink glow of morning turns into a red warning when we emerge for breakfast. A sack is placed over my head the moment I step outside, but I don't resist. Despite making plans with Vasily, Yanov and Nikolai to do 'something awesome,' I have apprised them of nearly nothing for a very good reason.

As I'm bound and jostled, I listen for Nikolai's breathing. *He's still with me.* We're dragged about like heavy sacks, then thrown into a familiar-smelling vehicle.

Men talk around us in hushed voices, the car door slams and I'm reminded of when I knew all of this was so much *more* than just me amusing some overinflated, arrogant asshole with a cigar fetish.

The last name of Mohylévych would make me royalty. After Sofia, I followed that thread off-camera like a bloodhound. And every time I followed it, there would be a car, a color and a smell — in that exact order. I know what you're thinking: *He's mad.* Yes, very much so. *But I'm also never wrong.*

Assuming paranoia just like you, I ignored my fight or flight response and kept my bird-brain thoughts at bay. This obviously couldn't last. After passing the same sort of vehicle enough times — especially when you're out gathering intel on *yourself* — the coincidences become a pattern. Moreover, men in red shirts were in every single car like demonic little beacons. I even swapped to dresses a few of those times to see if they'd let up. They didn't, which meant someone spilled their guts about me to someone powerful enough to have me **followed**.

Tyr told me that my parents had been poor and sold me off, but what if he'd been wrong? Was I the illegitimate spawn of a very powerful man? If I was, would that make me a threat? Well, I wouldn't have been as a woman or a slave, but I'm neither of those anymore. *Curious.*

Hunting for intel in this memory of memories, I emerge from the little-bird brothel in comely camouflage, only to be met with a car, a color and a smell. The car—the same make and model as Tyr's. The color of the man's shirt was red—a stranger. Finally, Boris' cherry smoke stung my nostrils. This telltale pattern trailed me for *fucking* months.

I didn't tell Nikolai because his ignorance means he gets to live. I didn't tell *you* because detailing every single time I'm followed isn't narratively interesting. By now, you shouldn't be surprised that my life is a morbid fucking fascination for too-evil, too-powerful, too-impotent men. *There's a reason for that. One I'm not ready to show you just yet, even as the present-day bullet hovers and Boris grins in putrid triumph.*

Memories flicker across the inside of my burlap prison, Nikolai and I are spirited to a location in silence, the car we're in jerks about and I nearly pop my arm from its socket trying to find my lover with my fingers. I brush against his skin, he makes a soft sound and I know he'll let me protect him—my way. *At least, I hope.*

After flinging the pair of us into a rust-smelling room, our hoods are ripped free, we're lodged onto metal chairs, bound by rope and face to face with Vasily and Yanov. Bludgeoned, bloody and unconscious.

Boris whisks his cigar in the air (inconvenienced by my meager rebellion) and directs his men to bash my skull in. This doesn't go as planned. After far more violence than most men can handle, all his grunts manage to pull out of me is blood-stained laughter. The man slapping me around can do nothing but shrug. *Pathetic.*

Boris mulls his hand over his mouth then gestures with his chin to an intimidating-looking man. *There's only one choice now and that's to prey on my emotions.* A gun is raised, I give Boris no ground, Yanov and Vasily get bullet lobotomies and I just keep laughing as their gray matter leaks down the teal wall adjacent.

Nikolai is next on the chopping block. I make no normal declarations of bargaining, because I'm *not* normal. "Boris," I mumble through a busted lip, "how about we make a deal?"

Boris raises his palm. "What deal *exactly*, little bird?"

"I'll renounce." I pause, "Whatever it is you're worried about." I lick the iron from my lips, tilt my head to the side and lock eyes with the man I like the least. "And you let *him* go. He doesn't know anything. And he's stupid."

Boris settles his cigar between his lips and seethes sweet-smelling smoke. He glares at me for a moment before lifting my chin so he can stare into my dead blue eyes. "That's not good enough, little bird." He wags his finger, then drops my head.

My cheeks burn hot as blood dribbles abstract art onto the concrete from my tight lips. *I need to find his trigger. He needs to boil.*

Changing tactics, I glance at Boris in the language of sex. "Then what is it you want most?" I ask in a velvet heat. "What do you want me to do? What role do you want me to play? I can be *whatever* you want." I laugh again. He cuts off my crescendo with a slap, casting red ink in a long stroke. Nikolai winces—I notice.

"I want you to stop twisting everything in your path, you fucking whore!" Boris roars. *Oh, I've made him fucking mad now. Good. Boil and fester like the fucking tumor you are.*

I laugh, which makes him vice my jaw in his sweaty palm. *He's steaming like a nuclear fucking kettle.*

"They weren't meant to *accept* you, Alex!" he screams, temple-veins sizzling. "They were meant to discover what you are and *hate* you for it!" *His tea kettle whistles.* "You've been a thorn in my side for months! And this one!" He points his cigar at Nikolai and bellow-screeches, "*Adores* you?!"

I laugh again. Boris prepares to hit me with a fist this time, but stops short when my jaw unhinges. "It's not *my* fucking fault your men fucking *hate* you. You're pompous." I lick my fangs. "And as lazy as a fucking sloth." Boris steams in place while I bullet every blistering word from my mouth with the skill of an expert marksman.

"The *only* reason shit ever goes your way is because Tyr cleaned up your messes." A bound devil thrashes. "And now, me. *I* clean up your messes now, Boris. *I'm* the brains of your operation. *I'm* the muscle you'll never have—right between your *fucking* legs. You impotent, garbage-smelling, walnut-dicked, *petulant*, filthy, abscessed little maggot! I survived *hell*! And what have you done, you *prick*?! Nothing but crawl along the ground like a parasite in your good fucking suits, stuffing yourself with cigars to rid the stench of shit, and for what?! To play make-believe. To convince *everyone else* you're more than you are. But I know the truth: you're **weak.** "

Boris' face is red, he's sweating, his cigar has been all but forgotten in his grasp and I've fucking **won**. I brought the Cheshire-fuck to mute fury. He can be angered, which means he can be exploited. *Sadly, I'll forget this much later, because he's far smarter than I've ever given him credit for.*

"Kill him," Boris directs one of his cronies in Nikolai's direction. A gun is raised as his handsome/terrified head.

"Wait," I say softly, feebly, prey-like, beckoning. *Take pity on the frail, battered, crazy 'woman' masquerading as a plucky prince, fighting against all odds to survive in a cruel, cruel world.* "Wait. *Fuck.*"

I'm crying—I can cry on command. I can become *nothing* on command and that's *exactly* what I'm doing. "Stop." Men like Boris like to see the hope drain from your eyes before you give in. *Then* they get to flatter their ego by giving you things that *aren't* gifts. *That is how they're most entertained.*

"You win."

Boris rolls his cigar between his fingers, takes a deep breath, puffs out his cheeks, blows smoke, grimaces down at me and then twists his face in mock-sweetness.

"I'm just scared," I stammer, sobbing hot, wet, heavy tears. "Please just let him go. I'm sorry. I'll do whatever you want. I mean it. Please."

"*Whatever* I want, little bird?" he asks, taking my chin in his hand yet again to scrutinize my tears like a demon fueled by misery. "And no complaints?"

"No complaints. Just let him go and forget he exists. Please. He knows nothing. *I'm* the problem. He knows nothing." *I hope you like this performance Boris, because I'm acting my motherfucking heart out.*

"Well," he begins with a Cheshire grin. "You wanted to play at being a little prince, hmm?" He chuckles. "Do you know what happens to little princes who commit crimes?"

I shake my head when a thought creeps in: *he can't kill me. If he could, I'd already be dead. Why can't he kill me?* My eyes flick to his demented smile.

Boris continues, "They do time for their crimes. Well, sometimes they do time for the crimes of others, too. Let's kill a few birds with just one stone, clip your wings and Nikolai can go free. What do you say, little bird?"

I lock eyes with Boris. "How do I know you'll keep your promise?"

Boris' laughter—that disarmingly genuine kettle-rattle that I can't help but admire, which makes me fucking hate him more—ricochets. "You don't, little bird. But I do always keep my promises. And so, I promise."

Nikolai's bravery finally outmatches his wits. "Alex, you can't—" Boris chides Nikolai into silence with his cigar, then dares to sneer in his direction.

"Boris," I trill, which pulls his eyes to rest on my feral grin. "If you harm a single hair on his head you will be dead within a year."

The man I like the least turns to look at me with a clever twinkle in his eye. "I know, little bird."

"I've never found it hard to hack most people. If you listen to them, watch them, their vulnerabilities are like a neon sign screwed into their heads."

— Sam Esmail. "Mr. Robot." 2015.

KNOWLEDGE
STRATEGY

18 / INKED SYMBOLOGY

They have a saying in the States that all cops are bastards, but I'm sure at least a handful of them took the job to do *some* fucking good. Here, the police *know* what they are. They're the worst criminals housing other criminals—many of which were jailed for the crime of existing—as all hands of power are the same and all of it comes from violence.

Our government will ferry poison to foreign journalists who investigate 'off limits' news items. Boldly, they'll use the nerve agent Novichok, which is only accessible to the KGB. They want others to know just how powerful they are and how few scruples they have. Here, power makes the biggest statement. The entire country works like this. *It will never fucking not work like this.*

I will work like this in the future, as I do now, but not with my face buried in the sheets against my will. It's with my fist buried into someone's guts, with my hand surrounding a stubby pencil, blood coating my skin as their muscles twitch. That someone is a guard, because *that* someone was in charge of my inspection and I was certainly *not* thrown into fucking women's prison. They thought they only needed one inspector for the scrawny blond with a cunt. *They were misinformed.*

Guards pour in like an infestation as I'm jacked against the wall, nude and still massacred from Boris' bullshit interrogation.

Once I'm pinned, the tallest guard pauses, looks me over, and raises his brows to his hairline. "There must have been a mistake, who's this one again?" He gestures as another guard gathers the blood-splattered clipboard off the floor and hands it to him. The tall guard flips through pages, brows twisting. Another guard enters the room and makes a bee-line for the tall one, whispering in his ear. His dark eyes hitch my way.

"Well, if that's how it is, it can't be helped. Throw him in—four days. No meals."

I don't need to linger here with you, but if you want to see where the ink lives, I'll show you my symbology. I'm not ashamed of it at the hour of my death. *Whether you'll understand any of it, who can say?*

We're passing through to my cell—I don't deserve to be in here, the fucking guard does. Pissed off and stuck in a box of concrete, I'm occupying my mind by imagining a beautiful sea of stars, a beautiful river and beautiful people spending beautiful moments together. I am hollow and bloodless, but the inner paintings of my mind are ravishing. I'm playing music stolen from the reel of time in my ears without knowing it. An early gift to cope with starvation. *Can you hear it?*

We pass through the wall and now we're in the cafeteria. The food they serve is hardly more than sticky gray paste, but eating means living and I'm greedily ingesting anything I can shove down my throat even if I have no fucking appetite.

In order to prove I'm not to be fucked with, I've taken to making a meal out of a much bigger man's neck using my fork. It snaps off before it manages to do much damage, so I puncture his neck with my teeth. *They always forget about the teeth, huh?*

Blood spurts into the air in a pane of red. We pass through that pane together, ghosts in the machine of my brutal memories.

We're in the medical wing; a shoddy operation with a green-garbed nurse and a doctor who looks like he wants to be anywhere but here. The nurse treats me gently, we speak nothing-words and she dares to touch my shoulder in softness. I get the gauze from her. Without it, I'd be stuck ripping up my pillow case to shove shreds in my body. *They never talk about that part in stories like this. I wonder why.*

We flip through the sands of time as the sun reincarnates every morning, a strobe through the small rectangle barely registerable as a window. In the resounding weeks, I present the nurse with small gifts to pay her for her kindness. I've scribbled ruddy drawings of birds for her. She seems to like them and I like her enough to let my baby blues linger.

She's the type of beautiful many men miss because they're looking for malleability, not wine. I like the way her eyes crinkle when she smiles. I like her strong nose and jaw. I like the way she always seems embarrassed when I kiss her, even when the rushing feeling melts her voice. As though she could ever deny her pleasure with my hand between her thighs.

We pass from this scene and into one where I'm forcibly held down by inmates and given a boar tattoo. It marks me as a woman who sleeps with women. I'm obviously furious about this, but I let them gore my skin with piss and shit ink because—to be fucking frank—I have no other choice. There are far too many to fight and humiliation is the goal. *I can deal with humiliation. I might even like it on rare occasions where I get a choice in the matter.*

Through this gaggle of limbs and my war-scream jaw, we move to walking the yard, bartering with cigarettes for tools, and me being surrounded by a trio of much larger men who've challenged me recently. As much of an ego-death as it is to have someone less than half their size take them down several *thousand* pegs, they know what I am enough to know they're safer with me than against me.

We smoke and talk of 'something awesome.' I trust none of them, because I'm paranoid. Paranoid and *certain* they're in contact with Boris. We zoom in on my raised brow. *I can't figure out which one the cherry-cancer demon owns, but I know he owns one of them. Can you?*

This leaves us sliding into the communal bathing area. The steam is a wall we hit as we parse the frames. We hover over my prostrate form as a fist cracks into my bird-skull with a deafening thwack. I dared to shower without my entourage and so what we expect to take place is trying to birth itself like a piss-poor fictional trope.

A hand is around my neck as I lay limp and perform the corpse-bride. I'm an unconscious man, covered in blood, grappling for strength. The man on top of me positions himself, calls me whateve sludge he can slop together in his trash-skull and gorges his eyes on my flesh. *I'm a woman to him.*

My eyes shoot open, I bite into his lips and tear. He dribbles blood at me, I twist, pull back and skitter using the wet floor to propel me away from his sweeping fist. Wiping my mouth, I spit red ink on the floor and grin with bloody teeth.

He rushes me, I jag in close to slam my fist into his throat, but he snatches my arm and cracks me against the tiled wall like a rag-doll. Winded, I crawl like a bottom-feeder, close to the ground, low on my heels. My hand curls around a mere pebble as I glare at my enemy.

He glares down at me, shouts obscenities, bleeds and froths. I cackle as he launches at me, tears at my shaved head, gets his thick fist around my throat and drags me to standing.

As he crushes my windpipe, I strike with my pebble—he assumes it's a shiv and jerks back—that gives me leverage. Jerking my hips, I flick into a half-fall, surge forward and swing my leg at his ankles. When he drops onto the flooded tiles, I drop my elbow into his face. I keep dropping my elbow until my arm is stained scarlet and his skull cracks. I don't stop even as the guards rush in. I don't stop even when I'm jacked into the air and wheeled around like an overclocked marionette made of razor wire.

The baths ran red that day. No other inmate would try that fucked up shit with me for as long as I survived in this prison. *They got the hint.*

We pass from this violence into a tender moment with the nurse. She gives me a sweet after I gave her something sweeter. She eyes me curiously, shoulders scrunching as she hesitates on the question taking up space between us. "What are you, exactly?"

Smiling, I nibble on the vatrushka she's made for me. Swiping crumbs from my face, I say, "Alex. Alexei," and nothing more.

She shakes her head and pushes a few dark strands behind her ear. Growing brave, she sidles closer on the cot we rest upon. "No, no. I mean—" she whispers, pausing. "You're different." She lingers on my too-feral, too-pretty face.

"Obviously," I reply, then take her hand and plop a bit of sweet bread into her palm. I smile and continue eating. She brings the food to her lips, darts her green to my blue and devours her food with an awkward grin.

I like the way she eats; it's when she forgets to be timid. She's a baker and certainly loves what she makes. If only she could be anywhere but here, making delicious things, instead of tending to violent sociopaths like me and my on-again, off-again empathy. With her, I can flick the switch a little, which is why I'm so endeared to people like her. They need the love I've convinced myself I can't feel, not the wrath that bursts all bulbs when time's trauma weaponizes me.

I break off another piece of bread and perch it against her smile. She grins around the foodstuff I push past her lips and gently kisses my fingers. I take a moment to run my thumb over her beautiful mouth.

"Why are you in this place?"

She pulls away, draws her hand to her chest at first, then places one hand—then both—on her lap.

"That bad, huh?"

She nods. What we're witnessing now are the wheels of a plan turning my empathy off as we slide through rooms like a dollhouse rigged on metal rollers. It's a never-ending cascade of violence in cells, the yard, the cafeteria, the communal bathing area, in the halls and beyond. *I like this nurse, but I haven't brought up her name for a reason.*

We're back in my cell with one of my new grunts detailing eyes on my lower hips. This tattoo marks me as a homosexual—the cock is meant to form a man's face—as juvenile as that is. I don't have one, and when paired with the boar tattoo, I'm a bit of a contradiction, aren't I? *I never fucking fit.*

Someday, I will replace these eyes with burning red flowers—borrowed from a friend I should've made an effort with—meant to symbolize the drug between my thighs that I'll use to get what I want. The eyes will be placed on my back as a genre, marking me for life. I thought it was clever to glare at people while they fucked me. *It won't be.*

Boris' present bullet presses into my skin as my life flashes before my eyes and I regale you with just one more reason why I'm such a terrible creature. Yet, the bullet is not just moving forward. It's pushing left a fraction of a millimeter at a time. *Were you listening?*

We peel through the scenes like layers of paint stripped with thinner. The thick swatches of color scramble backward, scraping up and away from the gridwork metal and plaster walls. The space is blue as we sift through a scene of mass chaos. An insurrection I caused is passed on by as indigo smoke bathes us both.

The space is yellow as I share a passionate moment with the nurse. A fistful of vatrushka is crushed in her palm as I bob between her thighs. She hides her face with her arm as her hips jerk. *I mean this kiss.* I didn't have to give her pleasure to pull this off. *I wanted to.*

The space is red as I wield the nurse forward, not very much later, with a scalpel to her neck as the entourage I've gathered finally joins me. "How are the pigs enjoying the show?" I ask the shortest one, a man with thin brows and a broad mouth.

"Just like ya said, sir. All stuck in the pen," he replies. I nod and step forward as the nurse's heels scrape the floor.

I thread my fingers through her hair to jerk her head back. "Are you going to be a very good girl and let us out of here, or are we going to have a problem?" My dreadful question is monotone because I don't mean it. It's an act. *I hate it.*

She's crying and I don't want her to cry, but I tried appealing to her emotions earlier and that didn't fucking work. I hoped that if I'd developed a personal connection, she'd take pity on me and bend the rules. *I would've bent the rules for her.* I would've broken *any* fucking rule, just to make sure someone who didn't deserve this shit got a chance at **living**. *This is my resolve: justice for the broken innocents. It begins to die here.*

But she isn't like me, I'm not like her and these men aren't like me, either. They're here because they want to escape, that's it. They have no loyalty, not like Nikolai and not like Vasily and Yanov, for that matter. The latter paid for their loyalty with their lives, yet I don't feel it now because I can't. *There is punishment for every crime, though it can sometimes take a bit of time.*

Her shoes scuttle as tears roll down her cheeks. "I don't want to hurt you. You know that, right?" I ask in her ear, my lip quivering.

She jerks her head like a terrified mare—my heart breaks. The space hue-shifts to mint-green because coloring horrible moments with beautiful things is something I have to do. *It's survival.*

I plod forward as she cries. A guard rounds the corner and the man with the broad mouth stabs him through the neck with a shiv. He falls to the floor like a stone. The nurse's shoes dig around the tiles to avoid the gush. She mops the floor crimson with flailing hooves.

We meet a checkpoint with a glassed-in guard who makes a move for his gun. I press the scalpel into the nurse's neck who's praying to her God now, which makes me hesitate. *I can't hesitate. Not now, not here, not ever.*

"Beautiful." I clear my throat. "I am *telling* you that I didn't want it to be this way. I *want* you to be happy, baking your sweets, living your life, enjoying moments with people not like me."

The nurse shakes and jerks her head away to sob hot, wet, heavy, horribly ugly tears.

"That's why you've shelved yourself here and why you even like me to begin with, hmm?"

Her crying grows into a shrill bleat. The guard at the window is still on alert, but not for very much longer. I look over the nurse's jaw-line to her beautiful mouth, which contorts in pain.

"She's out there. I *know* she is. Someone who doesn't endanger you. Someone who isn't a worthless criminal," I whisper in the most gentle words I have. "Loving women isn't a crime, Anastasya. You don't need to be here because your God told you to suffer." She stiffens like a petrified lamb in my grasp as I mention her name for the first time.

"Let's make this easy, please—" The guard at the window lurches for his gun, which forces me to press the scalpel. Anastasya bleeds, crying softly, but no longer struggles. I lock eyes with the guard, then gesture at the three men I've conscripted, who are all standing by uselessly.

"Do I need to fucking hold your hand for everything?!" I roar at the trio. "Open the *fucking* door or she's dead!" I hiss at the guard, then snap my head toward one of my playing pieces. "You—take his *fucking* gun!" Idiot number one jolts to attention and busts through the guard's booth to confiscate his weapon.

I thread my arm underneath Anastasya's head to lock her against my body, then thrust out my open hand at the fool with the gun. "Give it to me." The grunt stares at the gun for a moment, looks at my hand, the nurse, the guard, then his fellow idiots. "Give me the gun, идиот! Before you shoot your fucking d—" Idiot number one drops dead when a guard peels around the corner and shoots him in the back of the head. Blood sprays Anastasya's skin. Her wails beat my ears and cascade against the walls like a cacophony of horrors.

For a perfectly frozen mint-green moment, I look down at the petrified woman in my grasp. I see—more clearly than I ever have before—just how much of a monster I've become. "I'm sorry," I breathe into her hair. "I'm *so* fucking sorry." I mean it. *I'll always mean it until I can't mean it anymore.*

As more guards gather, idiot number three reaches for the gun. He's shot. The gun clatters just out of reach. The guard behind the window bolts to snatch the gun. Idiot number two lunges for it, grapples with the guard and the gun skitters close enough to leap for. As more guards approach, they raise their weapons and I do the unthinkable. I fling Anastasya into the fray, who stumbles between the second moron and the guard. Moron number two steals her in his chest and mimics my hostage theatrics. I peel toward the gun, snatch it as I roll and shoot the closest guard between the eyes. He drops, idiot number two twists around with Anastasya in his grip, yet she bravely manages to wrestle herself free.

No!

Anastasya takes a look back at the guards, bright green eyes growing wide against a sea of uniforms. She'll be stampeded because I had to beat my fucking wings hard enough to summon a human ocean. I foolishly try to defy fate itself and snatch her wrist. I try to play the hero even though I'm not one. Even though I'm the reason she's in this fucking mess to begin with. Even though I'm the villain of this fucking story—*I try.*

She hesitates just long enough for the guards to raise their weapons at me and I have to do the twice-unthinkable in order to make it out alive. I use Anastasya as a meat shield. She's shot, as is the last of my expendable pieces and now I'm out of leverage. What results is an agonizing shoot-out and series of stand-offs that has me leaving a sea of broken bodies in my wake. *I destroy everything I touch.*

The mint-green fades as I burst outside with Anastasya in my arms. A car is waiting for me; a man smokes beside it, seemingly in no hurry as I throttle toward him. Perhaps Boris finally realized keeping me in here is wasting my potential, even if I am a potentially very dangerous weapon to have in his arsenal. Maybe it's something more than all that. I don't know. All I know is that I'm being given a shot. *I have to fucking take it.*

I'm carrying her as I run—we'll make it. *It'll be alright.* She'll find someone to love her, find a life worth living and spend her days treating a beautiful woman who treats her right. The space is white. *The space is blue. The space is yellow. The space is white. Lights blind, the indigo door sears shut.* **Stop.**

I jag toward the vehicle. The driver eyes the woman in my arms. "Who's the broad?" he asks.

"It's Anastasya."

The man locks eyes with me and I see it: pity, which I hate. Pity at this shell-shocked youth holding the body of a woman he didn't want to hurt. A butchered-nothing with new ink, new scars, thin as a piece of bone—a skeletal devil with a shaved head and a rotten nothing-soul.

"It's Anastasya," I repeat. The man nods, helps me heft her into the vehicle, jams me into the backseat with her and we're off.

I hold her as though cradling a child and smooth out her beautiful brown hair with a trembling hand. "Now you'll get to open a bakery. Won't that be nice?"

The driver says nothing, but he does keep looking back at me. I don't know why he's gawking, or why he hasn't acknowledged Anastasya. I don't—my chest is warm. I pull away and stare at my red-stained palm.

Fuck.

19 / MIRROR'S TOUCH

He went into that place months ago. It's all I can think about as I do my morning routine. The same thing I've done every day since he dropped off the map. Get a pack of cigarettes and some alcohol in a brown bag, take the long way back to my place, pass by thousands of strangers, walk up my steps, listen for his voice, and hear nothing. Nothing at all.

I know I'm being watched, but they'll probably let off in a few years when they're certain I'm not going to start nothing. I eat old bread and stare at the spot on my bed he used to take up. The alcohol comes next. I don't care what it is. I just need a drink.

I thought I could handle this job. I thought I'd be good at being the muscle, cause I don't have the brains for anything else. Going to have to find something else, maybe get my lungs carved out by radiation, or bust my arms in a machine. I thought I could handle this job, though. Really did.

The bag crinkles in my arms as I fumble for the cigarettes. I pull one out and stick it between my teeth. I pat around my green jacket for a lighter. "Where'd I put you?" I ask, swerving my head, and a ghost greets me. He flicks on a lighter for me.

My brown eyes meet piercing blue. He's such a strange guy; wears blond like it's feathers, but not for a bird. Like some kind of demon made pretty and human, but a nice one. I smoke with a ghost—a memory—as he loops his arm around my shoulder. Presses our heads together as he speaks to me like I'm the only man in the world that ever mattered.

I know I'm not right in the head. I knew that a long time ago. Buried how I felt and tried my hand at being a big, bad, tough guy with a gun. I thought I could handle this job, I really did. Until this one showed up, looking too pretty.

The ghost looks at me like he's trying to figure me out. He scrunches his nose as he smiles, something wicked at first, then funny. I reach for the bottle of alcohol, let it burn past my lips and down my throat. I need to drink until he stops looking so damn pretty.

I wonder if he's still out there. I wonder if he thinks of me. I glance at the mirror at the end of my room, drink, smoke and wonder if I mattered.

I was in that shithole for fucking months and all I can think about is if Nikolai made it out and if Boris kept his fucking promise. After my shock with Anastasya, the muteness was palpable for about a week. Boris was generous and let me acclimate to living in a space not always caked in violence. Surely, my life has always been violent, but not like that. *Not like that.*

The only thing that kept me going was knowing that someone else would survive because I suffered and damned so many others. Was Anastasya's life worth my own? Was any of what I went through worth knowing Nikolai would be alright in the end? *Yes, it was.* And I'm not fucking sorry for saying it, because it will catch up with me later—it always does.

Nikolai. He's all I can think about as I do my new morning routine. The same thing I've done every day since breaking out with a body in my arms. Visit the local corner store and grab some Vatrushka—reminding myself of just what evil I've wrought—cigarettes and some kvas. I don't like getting drunk right now, it's an easy invitation to a haunting.

I take the long way back to a place Boris has secured for me far off the beaten path. I pass by thousands of strangers, walk up my steps, listen for his voice and hear fucking nothing. Nothing at all.

I know I'm being watched and I know they won't fucking let up, ever—but I don't know *why*. I eat sweet bread and stare at my empty bed. The kvas comes next—I'm drowning myself in flavors just to feel anything else. *There fucking has to be something better than this. There has to be.*

I thought I could handle this job. I thought I'd be good at killing and fucking and fucking killing, because I didn't know anything else, not really. *But now I do and it fucking kills me that he isn't here.*

The sweet bread leaves crumbs. I swipe my palms together and drag my too-thin hand over my mouth. I reach for the small end-table of this claustrophobic rectangular shithole, snag my cigarettes, pull one out and stick it between my teeth.

I pat around my tourist's blouse for a lighter. "Where'd I put you?" I ask when a ghost greets me. He flicks on a lighter only I can see.

My violent blue gaze meets a brown, lovely, patient one. He's such a bizarrely normal, gorgeous man; he wears his brows like a beacon, so it's always easy to tell what he's thinking. *I can't believe I thought he was stupid.*

I smoke with my secret and I loop my too-thin arm around his shoulder to press our heads together. Shifting my cigarette to rest between my fingers, I talk to him like he's the only man in the world that ever mattered. Because he was, and he will be, my guarded secret—my hidden, important thing. *That's the script.*

I know I'm fucking crazy. I knew that a long time ago, even before being thrown around, stolen from, pillaged, ripped apart and made into a machine of war. I buried my heart so that I could survive, tried my hand at being a murderer and it drove me madder than I even know. I thought I could handle this job, truly. Until this brilliant/simple man showed up.

Scanning the ghost's face, I try to figure out what makes Nikolai so special—outside of love—as though there needs to be any other reason. I scrunch my nose and smile, devilishly at first, then he grows bashful. In my mind's eye, he's looking at me bittersweetly. My face falls, I twist away, sup my cigarette and coat the air in tar. I need to smudge the ghost with tobacco, or he won't ever let up.

I wonder if he thinks of me. Glancing at the small oval mirror at the end of my room, I smoke and hope he knows how much he matters.

I hope he knows he matters—so much, in fact—that I set him free of everything I ever was and will ever be. Tears fall down my gaunt cheeks. They're happening against my will, as everything else always seems to do, which is why I try to bend the world to my aims, though it never sticks.

This one time, can't I just fucking keep him?

20 / PERHAPS

Nikolai's ghost haunts me less in recent months, but I still feel him in my bones. I'm always waiting for his fingertips to graze my shoulder, knowing it'll never happen. What haunts me most of all now is a beast, one I can't ever seem to escape. *Why does he fucking keep me?*

Boris glances at me with his token heady bemusement. He offers me a cigar, I take it and sit back in my chair. Flicking my lighter, I roll cherry-smoke around in my mouth, then smear it into the air from too-tight lips.

"So...you want me to do what again?" I ask bloodlessly, trailing my eyes down to the loud carpet below.

I look at my shoes with muted indifference. They're modest heels in red—not powerful enough for war. Up from my heels come two long, pale flesh-colored stockings, and above all that is a slinky red dress that sparkles. *I hate this color when it's not between my fucking teeth.* My eyes are lined in kohl. My long blond wig hides the hair that's still struggling against its shaving. The tattoos have been obfuscated in makeup. I'm less thin now, but I *am* back to where I fucking started.

I'm back to being someone I'm not, reconfigured in order to make money—or so I'm told. *I tried to plan for a little bit, but without any allies—impossible.*

Boris smiles, bolts his disarming laughter and says, "We're going on a trip, little bird." He sweeps out his arm, eying the details of his own hidden devices in perfect theatrics. *If I crack his dome like a fucking fruit, will I get to see behind the red curtain?*

I grimace and tilt my head to the side, staring off into the distance for a time before I mutter, "A little trip that's going to make you very rich and powerful, yes?"

Boris cackles and slaps his thighs. Wincing, I lull my head against the loud pattern of the loud chair. "Why do I need to go with you again? Why don't you just fucking kill me?" I half-ask, half-joke but I'm very serious.

Sinking into the puffy chair, I beg it to devour me. I command it to suck me into the blue-black nebula of space. It doesn't comply with my fucking demands. *Nothing ever does.*

Boris gives me a cherubic smile. "You're the meal-ticket, little bird. Or was it a blueprint?" he says as I arch a brow.

I have no idea what he's fucking talking about. Moreover, I'm high, so I don't *really* fucking care. Yes, I went the drug-route to deal with the trauma of merely fucking existing, but if you're going to judge me for embodying a stereotype, I'm going to ram my fucking fist through the fourth wall and rip your organs out in chunks. *I'm fragile and absolutely alone.* What else can I even fucking do, what job could I *ever* get and do you think anyone would *ever* help me exit the bird cage? No. *I have nothing and nobody.*

The bargaining starts. At least I get to pick who I fuck and keep some of my goddamn money. At least I have drugs now—scant time spent *not* feeling like I'm drowning in a fish tank full of shit. At least I know Boris will make good on his promise to leave Nikolai alone, as long as I'm his. What else is there, but this? *That's the sad reality of how hope dies young, remember?*

But maybe—I click the lighter open and closed as the room swims and I inhale Boris' cherry poison. *There has to be something better than all this. There has to be. There just fucking has to be.*

I cast my eyes to Boris' stupid face. He's snorting a line. He offers me some with a hazy smile. *I don't know why he bothers sharing.* I let him pour the powder on my pinky, plug one of my nostrils and inhale. Rubbing at my nose, I deflate in my plastic chair and glare at the ornithological wallpaper by my head. I stare, maybe even into time itself. I stare with blown-out pupils into what could possibly happen as patterns flutter over walls.

"What do you say, little bird?" Boris asks, leaning forward. I've done a good job at letting myself be subjugated lately. He thinks he owns me, I think he doesn't. *I'm good at convincing myself of my own fucking lies.*

"We take a trip, we move on up, and maybe—" He lets his sentence dangle, carrot-like. He's being generous, which jerks off his ego beyond all reason.

A devilish smile tugs at my red-painted lips. I bargain. "Maybe you'll let me be something more if I prove myself, hmm? Prove I can bring more value as muscle, prove I can be...trusted?"

Boris's warm laugh shoots me. "Ah, ah, ah," he chides, wagging his finger. "I will never trust you, ever, you *fowl* little nightmare."

I offer him a stunted chuckle and reply, "Neither will I you, you putrified piece of sentient fucking shit." I laugh, he laughs, we laugh. We're both laughing. We laugh for centuries until it dies in a smear of cherry smoke and drug-fueled time-lapses.

Men walk around us in a flurry of noise, light and shadow as the wallpaper crawls and my body grows translucent. Boris talks to the others, I'm given more drugs for no known reason, I take all of them and lean back. The chair swallows my torso as stencils of birds peel off the wall and skewer my flesh. My body is a hand grenade, but the drugs make me forget about detonating. *If only I knew I could've ended it here. I could've ended it years ago, and all it would've taken was one single murder.*

After much drug-addled nonsense, Boris flags my attention by rudely snapping his fingers an inch from my ear.

I lull my heavy head to look at the face of the man I like least. "If I prove myself again...will you at least let me fucking try?" I bargain because I'm only ever surviving *and* bargaining for survival.

Boris' face glows with the only actual genuine sympathetic expression I've ever seen him wear. I blink a few times, unsure if I'm hallucinating.

He shakes his head. "Aleksandra—"

Flooded with emotions, I grasp his hand when he says my corpse's name. He doesn't rip himself away. We actually connect as humans capable of empathy, for all of one sliver of a fraction of a millisecond of a moment. *He has it in him.* It's small, but it's fucking there—barely holding on for dear life! *God, please help me.*

"Alex," he says softly, like speaking to a wounded deer, "if you become what you're meant to be, I'm out of the job. And so is, well, anyone who crosses you." *Am I hearing this right?*

Boris clasps our hands together and scans my face with light in his eyes. It's not pity, or amusement, nor faux generosity. I am the thing he destroys on principle, for profit, for reasons I don't understand and he knows it's fucked up. He's *aware.* I'm looking at Boris the man—not the villain—and he's looking at me like I'm an *actual* person.

"I'm not going to lie and say I didn't want to do this to you. I'm not going to tell you," he says, holding up my palm to unfurl my fingers like a flower, "that I don't enjoy watching that arrogant smirk fall from your face, but I'm not stupid. You belong with your fists up, little bird. Not pinned to a blue plate by the wings by people like me."

"No one does," I blurt out, a false lash sticking to my lower lid as I wrestle with learning Boris has a heart. "I'm a fucking *prisoner,* Boris,"

I add, voice warbling. "This—this isn't the life I *wanted* to live. I never asked to be this—you've stolen my *life*. You know this, right?"

My eyes are glassy as I agonize over his round, disarmingly sympathetic face. *Who is this dual-natured beast? Are they* all *like this? Is it just that power's too fucking strong? Is it that the path of least resistance to achieving it is always fucking justif—*

"I'm just a businessman, Alex." He sighs, shaking his head. "You're only good for a certain kind of business if you can be controlled, and you can't be, so here we are—in the second business you're also very good at, that makes more money than you can possibly even imagine."

"Why not just let me go?" I stammer out, scraping away from the loud chair and his loud sympathy. I topple toward the table and traipse my way against a tapestry hanging on the wall. He's not making chase, but he does stand and he *does* help me up. *Why does he fucking bother?!*

I stagger back again, point at him and snarl. "Why the *fuck* does it have to be *me*?! Can't you find someone else to torment?!" My rage makes me trip backward on the heels I should be an expert in. *Thin-limbed nothing-thing, a ballerina in chains, an empty jug, a meal-ticket.*

When I fall, I don't get up because I fucking can't. I'm too broken, battered, lonely, traumatized, alone, fragile, weak, drugged, pillaged, piled-on, reconfigured and coerced to make a stand any longer. *I'm a nobody who has absolutely fucking nobody.*

Boris kneels before me and lifts my chin to meet his eyes. Tears trail down my cheeks as he looks at me like I'm **real**. Not a piece of meat, not an object, not a toy to wind up and be amused by as it falls off a ledge repeatedly. *God, please help me.*

"Alex. For what you are—here, it's too dangerous," he remarks dryly.

My eyes go wide. "You're trying to *save* me?!" I screech and reel forward, bloodless and impotent. My fists twist in his shirt as I feebly terrorize this cherry-demon. "By forcing me to be what I'm not, just like *he* did?! I killed him for that, you fucking—" Dragging at his collar, I thud weak punches. Boris refuses to fight back. "Why won't you just fucking *kill* me?!" I sob, struggling against this monster of a man.

"You know that I can't," he says hollowly, admitting what I already know.

"Then *why* won't you let me go?!" I howl, he snatches me by the arms and I writhe but can't throw him off in this state. *I can do fucking nothing.*

He locks me in place as I let out one single sniffle. "It's just business. Nothing personal," Boris says mechanically. We lock eyes—I'm angry again. Anger gets shit done. *Anger lets me live!*

"Because I make too much money." I stifle an acidic, lilting laugh.

"*Nobody* is worth this much effort." I know I'm not being kept around for money. It can't *just* be that. **It can't**. You can't fucking steal someone's life and torture them just because it pays the *fucking* bills. *What am I not seeing?!*

"Boris, you sorry excuse for a man—" I snap, using all the energy I have to latch onto his shirt. "*Tell me*. Just. Fucking. Tell. Me. *Please*."

He looks over my face. For just a moment, he's sunny skies and nothing hurts. "Mohylévych makes you royalty, little bird. What would a king think of a discarded princess who thought herself a prince?"

My expression cracks in half. We're tilted off axis as the room spins around us like a camera tipping. *I was right!* Scanning his eyes for deceit, I loose my hands from his shirt, sit back on the floor and splay my legs like a knob-kneed fawn. As much as I pride myself on being observant, it's a skill that doesn't come naturally. I'm not like *them*, not like **you**.

I don't live in your world of social rules, status and boxes—yet I'm always forced to. *Forced to play parts and roles that never fucking fit.*

"You're inconvenient, little bird," he begins, measuring his words. "Your mother's politics complicate matters, you know." Time stands still as Boris tells me *only* what I can handle. "You were taken, then found, then taken again. Then, I was meant to observe. Then, to turn you into a lesson." His pause is a vacuous space where sympathy managed to grow. "To cut you down and bury you," Boris admits, then stands away from me.

"You weren't meant to survive, little bird. And you certainly weren't meant to grow wings. Least of all not ones made of gold." There's something he's not saying. *What is it, you piece of shit?!*

He reaches out his hand to me. I hesitate, but finally take it. He pulls me to stand on my red-clicking hooves.

"But now we must leave. For both our sakes. I'll…" He pauses for far too long. "If you can show your worth again, in a space with different rules—then yes. Perhaps. Perhaps, if you prove yourself," he trails on.

"Is that a promise?" I ask him.

"Perhaps," Boris parrots, then pulls away to do whatever it is he does—maybe he finally grapples with his fucking conscience for once. I have no fucking idea, nor do I give a flying fuck.

Boris gave me a 'perhaps' and I need to believe that's a promise.

21 / CARRY-ON BAGGAGE

Whatever Boris didn't promise me wasn't going to come to pass without great fucking effort on my part. Proving myself is no longer about power, or cleverness. It's about playing pieces and performances. For that reason, allies are non-negotiable.

The first one will come in the form of a baggage mix-up. They're heavy artillery none would think is powerful, but they're a deft weapon of intel in the right hands. In fact, most would imagine she's a bubblegum-nothing. Yet it was in Blake Anne Percival that I saw potential on two fronts: a real friend and a real asset. I will use her, love her despite using her, and she will hate me. I am a compassionate monster, but I cannot win a war without toy soldiers. *Nobody can.*

We descend from the plane. I'm dressed impeccably and carting the one carry-on bag I have behind me on hitching wheels. I'm meant to be trailing Boris and his goons, but instead I'm meandering by a kiosk. I spy a pair of black circular sunglasses on display and place them on my face. Gazing at a mirror on the top of the swiveling merchandise rack, I smile. As I'm enjoying something for the first time in months—how I look in these fabulous shades—I'm too distracted to notice the blond woman beside me, smacking her gum and eying a pair of heart-shaped lenses.

I take the shades from my face, approach the vendor, one of Boris' many muscle-heads joins me and then clasps his hand on my arm. The vendor casts a glance; a universal eyebrow raise. I contemplate making a scene to be rescued from Boris' clutches, but that rescue comes with a price. For starters, I know our passports are fake, I have no form of ID and no family I know of on this continent. Moreover, if they send me back, it'll be worse—Boris fled for a reason. *This is precisely how they get people like me into predicaments like this.*

I shirk Boris' goon from my arm and gesture at the glasses. He digs into his pocket and produces American money. *This is a small victory.* Placing the glasses on my face, I twist to look for my carry-on. Instead, I spot a curiously similar one, albeit with a different pattern.

"This...isn't mine?" I say to the muscle who curses and sweeps around in a circle. Perplexed, I swivel to look for the gum-chewing girl. Boris' goon has started up his own brand of pink-faced tea-ket-tling. *Insufferable.*

"I don't know why you're so fucking pissed, it's just my clothes and some random shit I like," I say with a sigh. He tosses me a blood-freez-ing glare.

"Let me guess," I say, raising my palm, "there was something else in my carry-on you don't want lost?" I rake my fingers through my long wig.

"Boris is a fucking moron." Turning to the blockhead, I speak in a voice fit for patronizing children. "Go back to him. He knows I'm not going to run off—I don't have anywhere to go, and I know where we're going next. I'll get it back. All of you are too fucking conspicuous. Tell him."

"Good. Alright, Aleksandra. But don't try—" My pitying expres-sion stops his sentence short. *I don't understand how any of them get through the day, considering powering their egos must cost all their fucking braincells.* I sigh and fix my glasses as he breaks off to join the hoard of devils.

Wrapping my delicate fingers around the handle of the wheeling tote, I hitch forward in pursuit—a perfect debutante. A perfectly incon-venienced debutante. A perfectly inconvenienced murderer playing at being a prostitute playing at being a perfectly inconvenienced debu-tante. *Hah! At least I haven't lost my fucking sense of humor.*

I scuttle forward and glance at signs I can't quite read. It doesn't take very long for me to find the gum-smacking blonde, but she's un-usually spry. She idles at an exit, I groan and bolt forward as quickly— and delicately—as possible.

Somehow she's gone again. I twirl about on a busy sidewalk I've never been on, in a city I've never known, in a country *very* foreign to me. I can't spot her in this crowd. Clicking forward, I break into a run when I finally catch sight of her bobbing blonde head—at least I *hope* it's her bobbing blonde head.

The street looms, but the people stop, which fixes me in place. There's a beeping sound, a woman speaks in English and everyone starts up again. I cross, buffered by bodies, hunting for the blonde.

Sure enough, I see her walking over a cobbled path beyond an iron fence.

It's then that I'm hit with the scent of something *divine*. I push through the crowd, still stalking after the woman, but I have to find the source of this aroma—*Wonderland haunts me.*

There's a man with kind eyes manning a street stall. He's selling pinched little pockets he fries in a pan. He flips them in oil, then beams at me with pride. Hurriedly, I investigated the woman's bag. Digging around, I find green and off-white papers, pry them from their small pouch and hold up the wad.

"You want dumplings? How many?" the man asks. I garble out muddy English. He chuckles and notices that I'm standing on tiptoes to look behind him. He swivels his head, then when he faces me again, I flap a single bill in his face.

The man waves his hand. "Fifty? No, no, too much. I can only give you four," he says with a toothy smile. He holds up four of his fingers. I nod, stuff the bill in his hand, snatch the box he holds up, grab the woman's tote and I'm off.

I'm off, a piece of food stuffed in my mouth, trailing some American woman who probably has a tote full of drugs so strong they'd send even *me* on my ass. How Boris got it past customs is *beyond* me. How he even fucking got us here to *begin with* is beyond me. *Boris is far too clever for his own fucking good.*

As I rush through the park, I see oval leaves that rise beyond a glistening river, marvel at them and gorge myself on divine fried snacks. People of so many shapes, sizes, colors and sorts part the green grass, laugh, eat and talk. This is a melting-pot city—*I've never seen anything like it.*

I polish off one of the dumplings and take chase again, bursting from the park. Spotting her, dumpling container under my arm, tote wheels scraping, I jerk forward and throttle across asphalt.

She stops abruptly and I stupidly get spooked. I can't explain why, but I hide behind a metal partition. Beyond it, she idles with a payphone. We had those in the bigger cities, but mostly in residential districts, not bright blue beacons on sidewalks. I lean against the cool metal as I listen to her coins clink and hear her speak.

She mentions something familiar—landmarks—which is good. After this, I have to meet Boris. If I don't, it'll end poorly for me. *America offers me nothing but a fucking tumor to turn to.*

The blonde woman is ecstatic, but I can't hear her English warble over the sound of traffic. When she's finished with her call, she turns to leave and I lunge for my bag. She tugs it forward, huffs, then looks over her shoulder. We lock eyes. She glances at the bag by my side and the one she *assumes* is hers, that she still hasn't fucking let go of.

"Hello," I say, the word awkward in my mouth, "*that* is mine." I point. Her eyes widen as she looks between the totes again.

She laughs. "Oh my god! I'm, like, *so* sorry or whatever!" she blurts out, scanning me as everyone always does. I'm dressed immaculately; the perfect facade of some jetsetter's Russian trophy wife. *Boris cast me yet again in a role I hate. A role I'm apparently perfect for.*

I scan her all the same: poker-straight, shoulder-length blonde hair, large eyes, a long face, bright magenta lips, and to top that off, wearing a pink mini-dress with matching heels. *She's very stylish and far too cute.*

She pulls her hair behind her ear before muttering, "You were that woman at the, uh, what is it? Like, the kiosk, you know?" She gestures wildly, pointing to my glasses. *Her mannerisms are beautifully American.*

"Yes." I hesitate, as whatever English I learned in my youth has atrophied. "Supposedly." I furrow my brows.

She notices me struggling with my words, giggles and says, "You're, like, not from around here, huh? Not uh-mare-ih-can?" She lags her letters for my sake, which is fairly offensive, to be blunt.

I shake my head, chuckling. "No," I reply with a pained smile. "Supposedly," I say again—*Jesus Christ, Alex!* I sigh, which she turns into a moment to snatch my hand and shake it frantically.

"I'm Blake. Blake Anne Percival," she says as she rips my arm from its socket, "and like, this is crazy—" *She has a lovely, bubbly voice.* "But, like. I just. I just got a job!" she shrieks, breaking all glass windows across the northern hemisphere. "Do you, like, wanna go for a drink?!"

I laugh. *She's so infectiously excitable.* "Percival—" I roll her name around on my tongue. "Ah, Per-cee. A drink?" I pause for a moment, collecting my thoughts. "For job. Yes? Sure."

"Alex," I say, prying my hand away and placing it to my chest. "Cannot stay long." I offer a deep frown. "But maybe one drink. One for you, yes."

She shrieks, jumps into the air and then *hugs* me. I pat her back with one hand—I guess this job is *very* important to her. Important enough to celebrate with a well-dressed strange 'woman' she just met.

We swap bags and walk. *She's awfully trusting for a twee American girl.* To test this, I gift her a dumpling by saying nothing and holding it out for her to nibble from my fingers. She takes a bite and smiles like she's just won the lottery. *Maybe she has.*

I gaze at her as she prattles with the speed of a fucking jet. It's her body language that fills in most of the blanks—her face is very expressive, moreso when we make it to a local bar and she has a few diabetic-looking drinks in her.

I haven't ordered anything. I don't know that I can and I don't know what to ask for. *I've never been to a proper bar before.* "Like, do you want one, or whatever?" she asks, noting my weak expression. I nod, she waves at the bartender, he notes us and stares at me for a moment too long. *I'm guessing she's a regular.* I don't know how to ask her about that, either.

She smiles from behind her straw, wiggling her brows. "It's, like, a *super* popular girly drink. You'll totally love it," she says, before sipping her concoction.

When mine comes I nod thankfully and take an impolite gulp. My eyes go wide. "Americans...drink this?" I marvel at the drink I'd likely bathe in, if that were even possible.

She laughs at my expression, which must be hilarious considering how much she's snorting. "Yeah! Like, it's a Cosmo!"

I'm not sure if I'm supposed to knock these back or not, so I take slight sips. "Cosmo," I repeat. I'm sure in the bigger cities we had this, but it wasn't like I had a chance to *live* in the place I came from. It wasn't like any of that was living to begin with. *Maybe this is where living starts.* It's also where dying starts, but past-me doesn't know it just yet. *I wish I could tell him.*

I stay for far too many drinks and glean more about Percy's life while she reteaches me a few English phrases. She hugs me before we part ways. Percy is Cosmo-sweet; infectious laughter, prone to flights of fancy, gossipy and affectionate. I like this 'Blake Anne Percival' but I forget to ask her for a way to contact her.

Now walking alone in the dark, unafraid yet intoxicated, toting something illegal and dressed like a temporarily embarrassed heiress, I gaze at the stars above. They're so bright in a city made of stars itself. *I wonder if they twinkle just for me.*

A few men holler at me. I stop in place, sneer and fumble in my flashy coat pocket. I find a crumpled paper—assume it's important—and stash it again. Digging in my other pocket, I pry free a convertible plastic knife. *I wasn't patted down. Boris' cleverness can be beneficial after all, huh?*

I gesture lazily at the orchestra of men who seem intent on making me notice them. *They should've never fucking dared.* They spot the knife. Flicking the blade open, I do a few drunk tricks and sneer. *I can kill them tanked and they need to know it so they'll leave me the fuck alone.* I want to enjoy this beautiful city without the eyes of men making me into girl-meat.

"Отвяжись!" I break into a staggering cackle as the men scatter. *They're weak vultures all of them, anyways.* I return the knife to my pocket, smoke as I walk and manage to make my way via hazy, illegible landmarks.

On my way there, I spot the street-food vendor from earlier with his stand of heavenly foodstuffs. He's pulling up to a ruddy inlet below an apartment. A dingy storefront with a claustrophobic kitchen, an area for prep-work, cart-space and a gated-up window takes shape.

"H-hello!" I wave, perhaps stupidly. He does a double-take, stops unlocking the gate of the shop, raises a slow hand, then waves.

"Hello!" he yells across the street.

I say it back once more and laugh, drunk and very happy. I'm also teary-eyed and I don't know why. *Is it normal to cry because you're so happy?*

Smiling, I jag across the street to meet this food genius.

"Ah, you are drunk," he says. I nod excitedly, snatch the little box of dumplings that sit snugly on top of my carry-on and rattle the container.

"Delicious," I manage, though blurry.

He cracks a grin, then points at his shop. "Tomorrow, here. You gave me too much," he explains, waving at me.

I twist my brows and look from his face to the shop, my container of food, back behind myself and finally meet his kind brown eyes again.

He huffs, exasperated with me already. "Tomorrow. Here!" He points. "For you. Dumplings." He curses at me in a language I haven't heard before.

I chuckle. "OK," I say, giving him a thumbs up. *That's the universal symbol of agreement, right?*

"Yuen," he says, pointing at himself as he scans my face, looking for any sign of sentient life. *Sorry, Yuen, nobody's fucking home. I'm sloshed.*

"Alex," I say and mimic his pointing. He curses at me again and waves me off as if I'm an irritant. I find this hilarious, but stagger off at his behest.

"Tomorrow!" he says. "Too much! Tomorrow!" he yells at me as I drift away with my tote and delicious dumplings.

Where I end up is an unassuming, plastic-looking apartment complex on a narrow side-street. With a raised brow, I approach the door, slap the button of the intercom and plaster my mouth against the receiver. A voice blares in my native language, asking what I want.

"*Boris.*" His name dribbles from my drunk mouth. "I saved your poor, powdery baby." I snort, laughing myself stupid.

The man on the other end curses, the receiver goes dead, men meet me outside, I'm ushered through the door, the tote is plucked from me and I'm giddy as can be even with these fuckfaces passing me back and forth. I light up a cigarette—which is difficult, considering I'm drunk as hell—and let the shitty shepherds guide me.

Boris arrives and holds out his hand for me. "Little bird," he says softly.

I narrow my eyes but take it nonetheless. "Boris." I scoff, leaning on his arm as I stagger with him down a hallway. For a moment, I foolishly forget that I hate him.

"Do you mind telling me what took you so long? I was worried," he dramaticizes.

I laugh but stop short as my face falls. *There could've existed a timeline where we weren't mortal enemies.* There could've been a world where Boris didn't fucking *suck.* Where I didn't have to be repeatedly brutalized for some nonsense reason that I don't *fucking* understand.

"I was on a date," I say, no longer giddy and light. Instead, a tear slides down my cheek. Boris wipes it with his thumb and wraps his arm around my shoulder.

I let him in when I should've sealed the blue door with a fucking blowtorch. *I'm a fool.*

22 / ACTUAL WONDERLAND

Shopping. I've retooled my English in recent weeks, enough so to purchase pretty things. Call me a vain little fuck if you want, but I *like* shopping. New York is where you shop. I have money, and as I've only now been free enough to shop alone and only for *myself*, that's what I'm fucking doing.

I vainly look at myself in a store's tall window. Long boots, tall heels, black and leather, short shorts, a pink floral box blouse, and a loud fur coat. Happy as a fucking clam, I convince myself I don't care about what I had to do to get any of this. *I get to choose who I fuck, I get to make money, I get to wear what I want when I'm not working, Boris is nicer to me now, I eat good food,* this is all bargaining. What I do is *not* what others do, who I work for is *not* your standard criminal and I *am* an easily manipulated idiot.

As I glide over the streets of New York carting colorful bags, eating food I've never even heard of, drinking sweet drinks and smoking, I *know* I'm living the life I always wanted. I'm Vasilisa, except I have no prince, my shoes are not glass and I'm certainly not a fucking princess.

"Actual Wonderland," I breathe out as I twirl around on a sidewalk. Gorgeous light, gorgeous smells, gorgeous people, conversations, scents, and dreams—dreams can happen here. *So can nightmares.*

I slide into a hole in the wall with a pastel pink sign. The store is manned by a woman with a metallic-looking tattoo over one arm. She has bright eyes, long blonde hair and is mostly wearing nothing. She smiles at me like we're both very normal. *Perhaps we are.*

"This." I stumble on my words, swiveling to place my bags on the floor. My eyes go wide as the shelves expand around me. I stalk forward and wrap my fist around a glow-in-the-dark cock. Snorting, I turn it around and glance mutely at the bottom. Pressing a red button, it vibrates in my fist. I cackle.

The woman at the counter walks beside me and speaks to me in English, but her accent is strange, which makes me stare dumbly. "Not American. Can speak slower? Not too slow."

She smiles like the sun. Everyone here is so nice, even though they're abrasive, like Yuen—I remember the food genius and grimace. Making a mental note to wander his way later, I turn my attention back to the inked woman. Now, I want to shop. *I want to shop for what I was rudely not born with.*

"We have all sorts of sizes, like this—" She snatches something from the shelf and accidentally drops it. "Aw, bull crap!" I snort at her phrasing. She rises to her feet and wiggles the plastic cock in the air like I had.

Tilting my chin up, I gaze at this rather tall woman and say, "Swearing?"

The woman looks at me bashfully, then shrugs. "I don't cuss. It's not ladylike." She giggles. I laugh as well, and soon we're both in hysterics, though it dies after a while.

She takes my hand and places the object in my fist. I squint at it. "Too much. Modest…" We talk like this for a while with me stumbling on English while she's far too patient. She gifts me new words for old desires, phrases I forgot and I get to leave owning what I never thought I could.

Before I go, I pluck a business card from the front of the store and stare at it curiously. "Penny's…What is this?" Raising both brows, I slide the card in my back pocket and stomp up the street carting far too many bags.

This is a walking city, yet it's very big. I don't quite know how to use the trains just yet, but I decide to make a go of it. Clobbering down into the subway below, I'm met with a wind-tunnel, a cacophony of echoes and the smell of people. Passing by a bushel of bodies, I dig into my pocket for quarters and approach a silver machine. Plopping my coins into a slit, the machine whirs and spits cold tokens into my fist. *What an odd way to go about it.*

I finagle my bags and walk to the turnstyle. The tokens make a pleasant sound as I drop them into a slot and I'm let through. A train whirls past me, fluttering my cropped hair. Suddenly feeling someone's eyes on me, I drag my nuclear glare to land on a small child. She's holding her mother's hand and peeking behind her hip to look at my shiny boots. I give her a sun-warm smile. She shyly tucks herself behind her mother's side.

Another train whips past, a pigeon scatters above us and I scour for the neon orange letters I need in order to get to Yuen's shop—my new landmark.

My train approaches, the doors open and I step through, carting my mounds of materialism. The little girl and her mother trail behind me, then we're abruptly packed-in like sardines. The small one's face is lodged against one of my bags. I put them down to give her respite as the train jerks sharply. She falls into me. I catch her, drifting her to her mother with my other hand tethered to the slick metal handle above my head.

"Thanks, sorry," the woman says softly. She pulls her daughter into her arms and looks down at her pudgy, round face. *Stillness, hope, love. I've never*—my arm blocks their moment as something sour curdles my mouth. The train rattles, they embrace and I wonder about the life I never had. With a conflicted smile, I collect my things when the orange letters signal my stop and leave.

The walk isn't long. Soon, I'm in front of the dumpling shop. Yuen waves from behind the counter. I sidle up to it and look around; there aren't many people here, they're mostly passing by. I glare at them as I set my bags down. *How could they not fucking eat the most delicious food in existence! It's so motherfucking*—

"Disrespectful." Yuen snorts. "I'm the greatest!" he chortle-bellows. Nobody else can hear him but me and yet he's *roaring*.

Chuckling, I tap my fingers on the glass. "Yuen. Sorry. I forget." Yuen scrutinizes my face, glares daggers into my clothes, turns up his nose and then finally his eyes sparkle.

His laugh is not unlike the cherry demon's, but earnest in a way his will never be. "The drunk!" he shouts, wagging his finger at me. "Alex, yes? You paid too much!"

I beam with pride that he remembers me, I can understand what he's saying and he isn't just calling me a tipsy broad. However, "Yes!" is all I say.

"You seem happy," he says. I gnaw my lower lip, then scan his face. We have a connection and I'm not sure how it happened—all I did was devour his dumplings, yet I feel like he knows me already. He smiles, but turns his back to me all the same.

With raised brows, I pull away and light up a cigarette. *Did I offend him?* He disconnected so fast that I'm *convinced* I've done something wrong. I sulk as I smoke, flick ash to the street and tend to my bags like bushels of dying plants. Leafing through colorful fabrics and garish patterns, I soothe myself with products. As though that'll ever stop me from feeling dismal. Looping forever into a tar and something far worse, I don't know my patterns just yet. *They're deadly, even this one.*

Yuen slams the glass with his hand. "Hey!"

He startles me, I stand and walk to the silver counter, resting my elbows there. He opens the window, pushes through a large box with a daisy sticker on it and grins. The scent coming is divine, but—I frown. Yuen darts his eyes from me to the street and then he flits away again.

Taking the box in my arms, I wield it to the ground, then lean through the window to search for Yuen. Not a moment later, he pops through the small door to my right, jerks down the heavy gate with a crash, locks up, then turns to look at me with his hands firmly planted on his hips.

"Where are you staying, strange little man?"

I snort at this. *He's so fucking brisk!*

"Uh…" The words in my mind are shredded English. "Not far, but too far."

He plucks the cigarette from between my fingers. My eyes go wide. *The fucking audacity!* I explode in a fit of laughter. He's just this short, strange little man himself, smoking *my* cigarette and acting like he owns the fucking city! *And maybe, just maybe, he does.*

"I have a proposition. That one." He points at the stairs to my left. "Empty. Can't rent it. College kids don't like me." He pauses, friendly eyes growing dark. "I don't like them either," he whispers, like it's a state-secret.

"What do you mean by this?" I ask, marveling at the glint in his eyes. Maybe he wants me around because I'll pay fifty fucking dollars for four dumplings. Maybe I don't care if that's his game, because I'm *certainly* having the fucking time of my life.

Chuckling, I ask, "Is for rent? You are landlord?"

Yuen nods triumphantly, smoking *my* cigarette with his eyes sparkling.

If living above his dumpling shop means I get to eat all of his fragrant little meat pockets whenever I want, "I accept."

After a gentleman's agreement (ending on me huffing dumplings and Yuen complaining about 'stupid college kids' for an hour) his leathery hand places cold keys in my slim one. *I have a real home to call my own now.*

I thank him, the door closes and I'm in my own private oasis. The floors are dark hardwood that my heels make pleasant sounds on. I place the keys on the sill of a large window and twirl like a ballerina. *Large rooms, open space, sun-kissed silence.*

A brand new mattress in the corner of the master bedroom catches my eye. Traipsing through the doorway, I slide then fall onto the sticky plastic. There's a yellow note on top. Stretching, I take it between my fingers, turn it around and scrutinize the chicken scratches. It's in broken English.

"Miss you. Come h-home." I sound out the words. "S-soon…" I trail off, confused about the contents, but not confused about who this was meant for. Judging by all the dust in the apartment, Yuen's kid isn't coming home anytime soon. My heart hurts for him, but a smile tugs my mouth regardless. I can't replace Yuen's kid, but I promise I'll be the best son I can. *It's a promise I can't keep.*

Flopping around the slick plastic, my loud coat shifts and a piece of paper slips free. Picking it up, my smile blossoms. I swivel around to hunt for a phone.

A mint-colored box sits on a pale wall. I click toward it, jab at the buttons, place the receiver to my ear and listen.

"Helloooo?" Percy's American girl charm makes my face heat up.

"Percy." I roll her name around like a sweet. "I have gifts." I have more to say but she cuts me off by squealing. "Would you like…to come to my place?" The telephone cord is making my knuckles white.

"Yes! Like, totally, oh my god!" I tell her where I live. The scene turns to watercolor from the mist in my eyes.

The light that filters into the flat is yellow. Bright yellow, until it hits the wood, the walls and finally turns orange. Drifting to the floor, the sun paints golden wheat-shapes, umber furls and countless exotic patterns in beautiful shapes.

In the future, Percy will be named Polly. *I rename many symbols so it hurts less when I break them.* She'll run through fields of wheat with a man who will love her immensely. A man I will fall in love with for a short period of time (during this era) before meeting a person who will change my life forever. A person I'll steal from Percy on purpose. *I'm a monster.*

In this future, I'll recreate all my beautiful friends as my code breaks down on a planet-sized ship, puke out a shitty story about our lives all over its innards and try to stop my fucked up man-mind-machine from destroying all of humanity. *Our lives are always so tragic.*

Curiously, I'm not alone, but I can't see the ghosts staring at me. Colorful doppelgangers watch my past self revel. We're a triptych of specters. All eyes turn to this one clueless walking contradiction as he marvels at the short-lived Wonderland of his not-really-wonderful life. We're a triage; morally-gray errors who haunt a damaged species in hopes of saving it. Yet all we do is make it worse. *We only ever make everything worse.*

You may be wondering—as past me hangs up the phone and wades through a sea of paper bags—what all this means. When I stretch myself on the plastic bed, you may question why these ghosts are here, watching me bask in the light. It's sorrow for a future that past-me is unaware of; time ripping apart and taking me with it. *I die.*

Time is a tricky little minx. One assumes it charts on a straight path, plodding ever forward and leaving our bodies in its wake with each shivering decade, but that's only part of it. Time lives in the body, what it remembers and what it *hates*. This, I have learned. He hasn't learned and isn't meant to. *That's the script.*

In the present, Boris' bullet clips my temple in slow motion. To answer your dizzying questions: *I'm trying to keep an impossible promise.*

Hop in, losers, we're fucking with space-time. But first, we need to manipulate many people, lose our minds and melt our wings off, one wax-feather at a time.

23 / BLAKE ASSET PERCIVAL

Percival arrives after her shift at work. The anemic space is filled for her comfort; I bought a sofa, coffee table, colorful ashtray, record player and a stack of records I didn't bother examining. The fridge is stocked with Yuen's dumplings and too-sweet alcohol. *A farce of adult living. It's all I know.*

Percy makes a beeline for the sofa and faceplants into it, her legs flinging up as she groans and babbles about her boring, sad, annoying day. *I don't know why people dump their loud feelings on others without warning.* Picking up words in clumps, the particulars scatter as her feelings expand across the room and possibly half the country.

Sweeping over the coffee table, I spread my legs, rest my elbow on my knee and place my head in my hand. Percy pours her heart into my useless bucket and doesn't know that *I* don't know how to hold it. As she screeches and rolls about, I reach beside myself, pluck a cigarette from the table, light it with a Bic and catch a word that makes me lean forward.

"Police. *Politsiya,*" I repeat, scanning her green-latexed back. *She has a perfect sense of style — I'll have to ask her if I can borrow this.*

Percy turns to look at me so she can reply, but instead of speaking, her bright magenta mouth hangs open. I'm hopeful that my face and accent hit home that my night as a drunken debutante was just a masquerade. *I hope.*

Her eyes are as big as saucers. "Uh, you look, like, totally different, or whatever. Where— Are you like, *sure* you're not her brother?" she asks, I snort, yet she shrinks into the sofa all the same. *Fuck.*

"No. There's only one me," I mutter, raise my palm for impact, bring the cigarette to my lips and take a drag. Blowing smoke, I wave my hand so she's not accosted by it.

Percival scans the room. *A strange woman becomes her friend, a strange man takes her place and she's been led to a strange apartment with strange furniture.*

"You are safe. I was...camo, ahh." *My English is still fucking terrible.*

"Camouflaged?" Percy stammers as she borderline vibrates while gawking at my tattoos. *She's an anxious little thing, isn't she?*

I don't have the words to explain what I am and explaining too much is dangerous for her. Moreover, explaining might yield a label that feels alienating to me. *It's dangerous to announce yourself and doing it repeatedly is **fucking** exhausting.*

Turning away, my leg bouncing begins. Knee vibrating my elbow up to my palm, I knead Russian thoughts into English inside my stupid fucking skull.

Percy dramatically mouths the word 'OK,' then tilts to catch my downcast expression.

"So, you're like a cross-dresser, right?" Percy struggles, because she doesn't have a word for what I am. Not many people do.

I shake my head. *I'm just a guy with a cunt.* Many people hate that word, as though the rough diminishes the delicate. *There's nothing delicate about bleeding for seven days and not fucking dying.* I flick dry ash into my thin tray as Percy's questions wear my patience to its bare bones.

"Then you're like, you know...gay?" she tries again, which accelerates my leg bouncing. Percy rolls her eyes to the ceiling. "So, you're, like, a guy, or whatever?" *She got it.*

I nod, raising my brows at 'whatever,' which she notices. "I didn't mean to deceive." Smoke spirals from my nose. "You like women, yes?" I ask, yet she's too distracted by her own confusion to reply. "I do too. But, would like more to be friends. Is this good?" *I feel like I'm making a fucking business deal with a terrified animal.*

"That's, like, totally cool. Yeah, I mean," she mumbles as her cheeks turn rosy. "I've already got someone I like, or whatever." She pulls her hair behind her ears.

I cock my head to the side. "Is cute?" I ask.

Percy nods slowly, begins to giggle, then that giggle turns into a fit of magenta laughter. That laughter falls away soon enough. She resumes telling me about her day again, barely asks anything about me and prattles about someone named Olive. Again, she mentions the word 'police,' which makes my leg bouncing die.

"You work at police station?" My question slithers. "Secretary, yes?"

She nods, then stampedes all conversation until I'm mute. We move on from her day and she points at my shoes, yet again talking too quickly for me to pick much up.

"Oh!" I exclaim, stand and round by my buffet of bags to pull out a box patterned in a brand's logo. Cigarette hanging from my lips, I stalk to Percy's side and present her with her gift that's not a gift.

"For you. A gift for friend, yes?"

Percy's gawks, slides the box from my hands and runs her fingers over it. With mute amusement, I watch as she unboxes a pair of very-tall, very expensive bubblegum pink stiletto heels. *They cost a small fortune. I cost a small fortune.* Boris made sure of that, which is another reason it's hard to hate him now, though I should. *I should always fucking hate him.*

Percy holds up the shoe, then looks up at me, conflicted. "You can't, like, be serious? We like, barely know each other—oh my god," she blurts out, eying the price tag. She immediately stands and kicks off her flats.

To set the spell, I kneel before her, place the Cinderella shoes on her feet and look up at the bottle-blonde barbie who will be a powerful weapon in a war I've deluded myself into thinking I can win. Then, she will help me become a king, which is something I've also deluded myself into thinking won't kill me.

"Do you like?" I ask too sweetly. *She's not listening to me.*

Percy tests out her new shackles by clicking about the apartment. *She's a very useful friend. I'm never letting her go.*

24 / SAGE AND SEARING TRUTHS

I'm working tonight, which means a masquerade. I have to be realer than real and it's wearing me down. The emotional labor of packaging yourself in ten thousand different ways would run anyone fucking
ragged, even if they'd chosen this job, though nobody *chooses* to work
for Boris. *No one chooses to work for a fucking tumor.*

The man who flags me down has such a thick accent that I can't
understand what the fuck he's saying. He has unruly brows and kind
brown eyes. I can't see his mouth, but his eyes tell me he's smiling.

He cranks down the window. "Sorry, mate, lemme start over."

My face falls when he smiles. *He's Thomas in a city of lights. Nikolai
in sage green. Handsome, simple and dangerous.*

"You are new to this. Conspicuous," I mutter as I lean against the
car. A pale bird flies overhead. I stare at it for far too long.

The man lets out a sheepish chuckle. "Got piss-poor luck w'the
ladies," he admits. "Feelin' lonely is all. I dunno, jus' need someone,"
he half-asks.

Turning my attention back to the man, we negotiate as he grows
less secure with each passing moment. *This man needs a lesson, not a
fucking hooker.* Exasperated, an idea strikes me. Jerking the car door
open, I crawl in the back seat and direct him to Percy's bar. *He stupidly
complies, but it's not like I gave him any other choice.*

I force him to park, clop from his vehicle and grin.

"Ah, mate?" he stutters as I snag his hand and drag him through
the doorway, which he stumbles through.

The bartender waves at me, I narrow my eyes, wave back and yank
my patron into a booth with me. "You do not want this." I scoff, before

nodding at the bartender. Assuming everyone loves Cosmos, I raise two fingers. *Who fucking wouldn't?*

My patron furrows his thick brows. "I'm pretty sure I do, mate," he argues.

I wave my hand in his face, sit back and cross my arms. "You do not want this, and you do not want *that* anyways." I grimace as English breaks apart in my mouth. *I'm brilliant in Russian, but in English? I'm a fucking idiot!*

With a sigh, I drop the mask and speak with the bravado of a murderer caked in hard-won prison stars. "Pleasure is nice. But feeling lonely," I borderline hiss. "You are awkward." I pause, scanning this stranger's handsome face. "Loneliness is not cured in sex. This is lie told to men. Loneliness is cured with companion." I slap the table. The man jumps in his seat. "I will teach. Find women, find friends, find love. It's easy, no?" *If it was so easy, I wouldn't have let Nikolai go.*

The man in front of me is a marble-mouthed mess. The Cosmos arrive, I smile, push one of the drinks toward my new 'friend' and take a sip of my own. *Delicious.*

"What is name?" I ask gruffly. The man folds his hands in his lap. Nudging the drink with my finger, I slide it across the table as he grimaces.

"E-Eric Hail, mate. Name's Eric." He takes the drink and sips it, instantly souring like he'd swallowed an entire lemon, rind and all.

"You are stupid." I scoff, taking a gulp of my sinfully sweet liquor.

He gawks at me. "Wha' makes ya say that, eh?"

"Drink, we talk. I will teach you." I run my hands through my long blond mane and snicker. "Easy."

"Yeh, yeh, awright. Easy." He skitters out a disbelieving chuckle, tosses back his Cosmo and eyes me hesitantly.

"Alex," I offer before he asks.

I'm meddling in this man's life for one reason and one reason only: Nikolai would've pulled this exact same shit when left to his own fucking devices, just like Thomas had. Their pattern is obvious to me: they can only speak with their faces and they're *hopeless* romantics with no backbone. That changes today. I *will* be the hero. *As always, it's a promise I can't keep.*

Eric knocks his drink over, cursing. I smile at this man who looks like the only man who's ever truly loved me.

"Eric." His name is velvet in my mouth. "We will talk, but after. You will try to ask another—" I half-ask. Eric isn't sitting in front of me. I wheel my head around—he's at the bar. He returns with a tall glass of beer. My grimace is ghastly.

"Sorry mate, that shit's nasty is what." He huffs at the Cosmo in my grasp and I huff right back at him.

"I ask: if after we talk, will you try again with another?" Licking my lips, I continue, "One like me, yes?"

Eric looks up at the ceiling for a millennia, as if studying some ancient painting carved there. "Yeh," he mumbles into his beer.

I deflate, sink back into the booth and hunt for his gaze. "I will show you why not. Then, I will show you how flirting is. Deal?"

Eric shakes his head, swigs more of his beer and waves in my direction. "Mate, this is fairy-godmum shite is what. You're mad, yeh?"

My smile's vicious. "Yes to both. But let me do this. For you. I do not want to see another like you in this," I admit, leaning forward to swipe my Cosmo and dump it down my gullet.

Eric's brows knit together, forming a single caterpillar. "Another like me? Whaddaya mean?"

I shake my head, wave to the bartender, raise two fingers, gesture between us and wait for another round of booze. The bartender points at the tap and I stick up my thumb. *Eric can have his disgusting yellow piss-water if it makes him happy.*

Raising my brow, I pause to sift through English and pluck free the closest words I can find. "Man like you, came to me. Has feelings for friend, but never told. I thank him for much, but he went in wrong way with me. You must go to love, not to mimic." I hold my hand out and wiggle my fingers in the air. "Mimic of love can help, but is not same."

Eric opens his mouth to speak but I barrel over him. "Second." I inhale deeply and rock back from the table. My Cosmos arrive, as does a pitcher of beer. I treat the first like a shot.

"Second, I loved." I click my nails against my glass. "A lost boy — your kind. Your kind does poor without tenderness. I regret leaving." Downing my second Cosmo in record time, I lock eyes with Eric. "Loneliness maybe is death for lost boys."

Eric wags his brows as he works over my words in the empty caverns of his skull. "Y'know what, mate?" he starts up, pouring his mug full of beer. "I think yer onta somethin'. Yeh. How izzit ya know so much?" he says, polishing off half the yellow piss-water in one go.

"Observing people-patterns. They are easy to see." I pause. "Mostly." I frown at all the things I can't see and know exist right outside the camera's lens. *A learned skill. I'm not like you.*

After we're properly liquored, I guide Eric somewhere he's not meant to be and somewhere *I'm* not supposed to be right now, either. Considering I've been allowed to come and go at my leisure and we entertain clients here often enough, I don't think much of it as we park.

I pull Eric behind me through rooms inside of rooms, down stairs, around, under and through. I aim to have him talk to one of my co-workers. *He needs to see behind the curtain to find his way out of it.* It will end poorly for *him* if he never learns to try with people he can't pay for. *I don't note this irony, when I should've. I pay for all my friendships. I'm never not transactional.*

We step into a bizarre room. A room I've never been in with just one solitary carpet, two narrow exits, one closet door and blank white walls.

"I have lost us, sorry." The voices of men prick my ears. I snatch Eric by the wrist and drag him with me inside the closet. Cracking the door open, I look through the crevice with just one blue eye. After the voices fade, I hear a distant bleating noise, then silence. Finally, there's no sound save Eric's pummeling heartbeat and the birdflight of my own.

When I'm satisfied we're alone, I trickle out into the room and jerk my head back to look at Eric. "Stay here," I say, digging into my flashy coat pocket for my plastic knife.

"W-wait mate, ya canni jus' leave me—"

My hand latches to his mouth. "Quiet. I will return. Promise," I say, peeling my fingers from his face.

"Scouts honor?" he asks, raising his pinky. He repeats himself, mouth pulled tight. I hold up my pinky finger. He links them together.

He's waiting for something else. "Scouts...honor," I mumble, push him into the closet and shut the door.

Stepping out into the room, my heels muffle on the loud carpet. Dizzied by the avian pattern, I slink low and hug the wall. The sound returns, fogged by distance. Disembodied men speak. I follow the wall and search for the warbling sound accompanied by thick accents. My stomach bottoms out as the noise becomes a damp blue sob.

When I duck through a doorway, I'm left standing in a windowless box of white. *The lack of color is so cold it burns.* Lips parted, eyes wide, I scan the stark floor: remnants of ash, scuff marks, a single pastel-rose dollop treated with assumed bleach. Silence, a bleat, a man speaks and I see nobody.

Nobody at all.

My baby blues trail to the far wall; it's draped in a blood-red curtain. Magnetized, I chart a milk-ocean, place my hand to the soft velvet as the sound continues, swallow hard and rip the crimson tapestry through the dead air as unseen men laugh and make familiar disgusting sounds.

The curtain slides on automated rollers to reveal a floor-length glass window with an indigo door on the left side. Speechless, I peer within to find an expansive room. My eyes narrow at the blinding lights above, reflected by umbrellas. They cast against a hulking gray tetrapod. Squinting, it becomes a studio video camera. Beyond that is a behemoth television set with a jittering screen. The curdled cries come from its expensive speakers.

My eyes wander, landing on a blown-out gray lattice. Beneath it rests a canvas with a ruddy stain in the middle. I draw closer to the glass, my eyes adjust to the light, the bars sharpen and the gore of a body no longer there announces itself like a coffee stain on a napkin.

The speakers explode with thin screams, all the air sucks from my lungs at once and an ancient word strikes me stupid: *Observe.*

Flicking my gaze to the television screen, I rake down to the thick stacks of gray tapes underneath. Daring to fix my gaze on that demented, scan-lined rectangular portal to hell for just one brutal moment, my heart stops completely.

My eyes are single dots in two seas of bloodshot white.

"I'm the blueprint."

Skittering, I fumble toward the indigo door and find it locked. Wheeling back to the window, I rip my coat off, wrap my hand and stop just short of shattering it with my fist. *Would it even shatter?*

My eyelid twitches as I press my nose to the glass. The light grows dimmer the closer I get. "It's a two-way," I whisper in my native tongue. Gawking, I hold my coat dumbly. *The screams ebb and flow in time with the laughter of men born as men.* My arm falls and the loud faux fur slides down to my wrist. *Observe.*

The television screen glitches, the tape reels back and my mouth hangs open as Aleksandra Vosova dyes herself with the red ink of a man. A man she killed in self-defense. Self-defense observed from the corner of my wooden prison that Tyr could *never* keep his eyes off of. *Observe.*

Forehead pressed to the pane, I mull through millions of scenarios as my hot breath fogs the glass. *If I manage to break in, Boris will know that I know.* This is so much bigger than I ever fucking imagined. This is so much fucking bigger. *This is so much.*

A foreign avian screams. I screw my eyes shut. If I escape *all* of that—carting evidence to Percy's place of employ—I'm an illegal. *A prostitute, murderer and mistake. Nobody will miss me if I'm gone.* My strong brows knit together, the greatest hits of butchered bodies blast over static-soaked speakers and I die the deaths I hear through them.

I will be questioned, prosecuted for my 'crimes' and lost to the system. If Boris owns *that*, they might even ship me back. Then, no one who could ever care about anyone like me *ever* will. If I don't break in and fix this now—my fur coat drops to the floor—I'll have to live with knowing what's going on behind the curtain. *Observe.*

My cheek to the window, I slide against the pane like a gecko until I'm a seated, sulking heap. On the floor, I draw my knees to my chin and clasp my arms around them. A broken thing not lucky enough to make it out alive begs for God, begs for help, begs for her life, begs for her mother. Every brittle breath butchers the air until the behemoth television dribbles out gurgling sounds. I bury my head. She's silent. *I lived this.*

"I'm the blueprint," I scuttle out as something in the back of my skull drips hot liquid down my cheeks. *This is evil.*

I curl my coat into my arms like collecting a dead pet, stand and feel my eyes water *with* my consent. Against a blown-out space of white, my pale features dissolve, and for the first time, there's no war in my blood. *No flash of resolve. No action. Nothing.* I take just one step from the glass. I flee.

Pulling my coat over my shoulders, I jag across the white room and stumble around a phantom of my curled up body. Tripping, I stare bloodlessly back at my sobbing once-self. The corpse-bride's cut into slivers of pie by immaterial knives. Her crumbs bleed on the floor, staining everything with sweet, sugary blood.

Staggering back, I trail sticky syrup on the floor with my heels, trip, whirl around and bolt on weak legs. When my hand fumbles for the wall to steady myself, I feel slickness. I peel my fingers back. A red smear dribbles from my handprint.

Dyed in blood, heart in my throat, bile in my mouth, temples throbbing, I back up toward the door. Crimson creeps from my mark and crawls the floor like a leech. *I don't scream. I don't breathe. I don't fight. I don't freeze. I don't speak.* I flee.

Bursting from the room, I make my way to the closet, turn and find no river of red on my heels. Wrenching the door open, Eric streams free, speaks his marble-mouthed nonsense and I don't listen.

Eric stares at me as I begin to pace.

I have to figure out who owns this fucking city. It's not Boris, I know that much. I have to smoke them out, pin them and figure out how to wrap them in my fucking fist so I can pop Boris in my fingers like the bloated, maggot-infested tumor he truly is. Boris and *every* fucking person who would ever call this shit *entertainment.* **That fuck.** That fucking piece of filth in a fucking man-suit. I'm—*help, police, stop, murder.*

If these are your thoughts, you've been force fed the American dream, not the American reality. You watch your precious little television programs and imagine you'd be saved from this by law and order. Never.

Eric speaks but I don't hear his words—I hear the sounds of death. *God, please help me. Please, don't kill me. Please.*

After a thick pause, I hold out my hand for Eric to take. He stares at it for a second, scans my face, then his expression goes dark like someone stole the sun from the sky. He pulls my coat up to cover my chest, takes my hand and we walk as though we've just returned from war, *because we have.*

Eric gleans how I'm feeling; his eyebrows say as much. *Something terrible happened.* I know he knows as we find ourselves outside in the cool night air and he grasps my hand tenderly. We pass his car, which he looks back at momentarily, but leaves behind all the same. I drag him with me on a heavy plod where we say nothing and I feel *every-thing.* Past the dumpling shop, he trails me like a kite. Up my steps, he follows me like a comforting green shadow. Closing the door, I pull Eric into my bed, which he doesn't resist. *We don't fuck.*

I don't sleep that night, but Eric does. He drifts off blissfully against a blue sea of sheets, his arms around a stranger who holds him back. This is what he needed, that I couldn't explain to him. The tears rolling down my face tell me that this is what I needed, too.

As I cry silently, I think of myself as a very, very brave little bird. *Tomorrow, there will be scant time for tears, as war is here.* I am built for war, and for them, I will wage and win a war. For those like me, I will defy the conventions of every piece of media I'm written in to break our cages. I will be the hero (flawed, imperfect, maligned) no one asked for, but desperately needed.

I'll be the hero who never came to save me.

Frozen in time, I stare darkly at the invisible shadow outside of space whose heart aches. Hating himself for not being there for some-one when they needed him, I imagine that I must do what he cannot. *I promise I'll make it right. I'm a fucking superhero, aren't I?*

INTERLUDE: REMAIN NAMELESS

"I was born in a big grey cloud screaming out a love song. All the broken chords and unnamed cries. What a place to come from. I wish to remain nameless and live without shame. 'Cause what's in a name, boy? I still remain the same."

— Florence + The Machine. "Remain Nameless." *Ceremonials.* 2011

25 / GODLESS/FAITHED

Sitting in the pew of a Church, I stare dumbly at the ornate gold ceiling. I don't know why I'm here—not really—aside from catching the building from the corner of my eye as I stalked sleepless up my sidewalk, smoked and thought my way through surviving a swap of genre and the downfall of an empire I don't fucking know enough about to destroy.

Faith has never been something near or dear to my heart. Growing up where I did, there were many living Godlessly while praising a sky-man who's either cruel, apathetic, or imaginary. As with anything else, I didn't fit the mold of believing in something that never believed in me. Worse yet, if it *did* believe in me, it had a very fucked up way of showing it.

Yet here I am, sitting in this gilded church, gawking at a beautiful ceiling, horrifying statues, paintings that make me uneasy and pews that stretch on for miles. I need something bigger than myself to believe in right now. *I won't find it here.*

Masquerading as the girl I'm not, I twist strands between my fingers and scrutinize the gold, glory and ghost I'm meant to beg for some sign, some path, some way out. I'm alone, aside from one man in an outfit that looks like it's choking the life from him. He looks at me sympathetically. I shrink in my pew.

A beautiful woman in a hairnet enters the church and makes a beeline for the confessional. She picks her damaged nails while she shuffles on squeaking sneakers. *She looks mostly fucking miserable.*

"At least she knows where she's going." I sigh to myself as I loose my hair once more, stand, click to the door and look back at the miserable/beautiful woman. Her hand to the confessional door, she turns to lock eyes with me. Deja vu, but I don't ask why it strikes. *I should've.*

Back outside, the sky above me is blinding blue-violet. I dig around in my fur coat and lodge the kiosk sunglasses on my face. I'm walking to think, yet nothing comes to me. *I can't pull this off without an army. I can't pull this off without protection. I can't pull this off.*

Eric will not be a protection for my body or my life. I know this when I return to my flat and he's still there, sifting through my records with his caterpillar brows wiggling.

"Hello." I break the silence, close the door and startle the man I forcibly injected into my life. Eric knocks over a stack of records, I hide a smile behind my painted claws and stoop to help him.

Our hands touch briefly, which makes my mouth pull tight. *He doesn't—and won't—want me.* It's a mistake to love someone just because they're familiar. An unfair ask of a kind stranger, even if I want it.

"Mate, cha' listen to this one yet?" he asks with a warm chuckle, lifting up a record.

"No. No time. Work. Do you like?" I ask with a half-smile.

He takes the circle from its sleeve and holds it up like it's made of pressed gold. "Yeh, yeh mate. It's brilliant."

I gesture to my new mint-colored record player sitting neglected near a lonely outlet. "Go for it, Erica." I pen a pet-name; he doesn't correct me. Eric sets the record, places the needle on it, plugs the machine in and twists the knob.

Then he dances while I sit dumbly on the floor. *He's awkward and charming.* He even tries to get me to dance with him by pretending to reel me in. The weight of all I haven't done keeps me pinned in place like a bug.

Eric shows me he can't dance worth shit, which bolts laughter from my chest to break my pitiful spell. I take the hand he offers and we dance.

We're too close, he's too warm, too kind and he smells like green wonderful things I now have names for. I know this isn't how my story is meant to go. "Eric, stop. This—this is not what you want."

He furrows his brows as I pull away. "C'mon now, mate, why not try?" I groan audibly at his question and try to peel him off of my body. He won't let me, collects me in his arms and imagines that I'm the pretty red packaging he can see.

Prying him from me, I pluck the wig from my head which makes his expression flatten. Still dancing like a goofball, his movements falter when I unpin the wig cap, toss it and remove the inserts in my bra. When I drop the cutlets on the floor, he stares at me. It's not an uncomfortable stare, but it's a fucking stare, regardless.

"Uh…" he mumbles. I walk away from him, a sigh escaping my lips. *I hate having to come out over and over again.*

I spindle into the kitchen and come back carting a box of dumplings under one arm, a sweet bottled girly drink in my fist, a six-pack of beer and my cigarettes set on top of them. Placing it all on my coffee table, I light up my cigarette and sit like I'm accustomed to. He sees me for the first time, which makes me wince.

I look away, smoke, he says nothing, the guitars pick up on the record and he plops down beside me. Eric snatches a can of beer, pops the tab and slurps it down. Flitting his eyes to the side of my face, he snatches a dumpling from the box.

Gnashing his food, he speaks between bites. "That's whatcha meant, at tha' bar, yeh?" he asks, raising an unruly brow.

I nod slowly and glance at him from the corner of my eye as I tip ash into my colorful tray. *Deja vu again, but this time a natural one.*

All is quiet. That is, until Eric digs his keys from his pocket, frees another can of beer, punctures the center of it with a key, holds it in front of my mouth, stares at me and I stare right fucking back at him.

Eric is well versed in the art of war; distraction and confusion are methods of it and he's smashed my defenses by perching a bleeding can of disgusting piss-water at my lips.

He force-feeds me alcohol. *This is what men do with men they're friends with, I imagine—at least in America.* He croons when I finish off the deplorable brew and wipe my mouth.

"You're…very strange man," I say with a chuckle, then take to drinking my fruity bottled concoction to wash the yellow taste from my mouth.

He chuckles, then abruptly jags to the record player to crank up the music. *So let's sink another drink. And it'll give me time to think.* I quirk a half-smile as Eric continues his awkward dancing as if nothing's changed.

"So are you, mate. So are you," he says in sunny-skies and verdant fields, yet everything hurts.

Eric won't protect my body, but he'll protect my heart by being the *strangest* normal man I've ever met. He dances and treats me like any other guy he'd hang out with, even in a dress, even in heels. I don't have to tell him who or what I am. *He accepted me and all it took was beer.*

I've made a new friend, one who will be the glue that holds the rest of my army together with his perfect simplicity. Perfect simplicity that will also ruin us much later, but we'll mend as we always do, until death by Boris' bullet. *At least that's the script.*

I have faith in something now. *I have faith in the kindness of men born as men who are friends and only that.*

26 / THE PATH

It appears I've become complacent. I work, Boris assumes he has me in his clutches, I stuff myself full of good food and into claustro-phobic dresses, and that's that. Truthfully, if I'm hasty, my plans will fail. This isn't like the movies where the perfect hero manages to un-dermine the kingpin without ever being discovered, damaged or de-railed. *Without knowledge, I lose.*

For this purpose, I've taken to letting Percy gossip about whatever she wants, but mostly about work. I glean what I can about the local police district, the movements of my enemies, give her gifts to keep her tethered and catalog what she tells me in thick symbols.

I've combined her babbling with my notebook scrawlings and turned the back wall of my bedroom into a planning space. It's an in-sane topology of post-it notes, Polaroids and ridiculous symbols that Percy and Eric are both curious about—*initially.*

Eric drops the conversation after I tell him I won't explain. He doesn't comment on it for the remainder of our friendship. A solid chap.

Percival, however, is far trickier. In this memory, I'm currently leaning with my head in my hand as she barrages me with eight hun-dred questions while speaking seventy-five miles a minute.

"Percy, sorry. Today is not so good," I admit. *She's fucking agoniz-ing.* "And I don't know how to explain."

Percival crosses her arms. "Like, OK. But, like, I need to know if you've gone off the deep end, or whatever," she huffs, then points to my wall. "Cause this is *totally* some kind of psycho shit, Al."

She drops her arms at her sides. "I'm, like, worried. That's all. Are you in trouble? Just tell me if you need help or whatever, I can total-ly—" Her words drift as my patience dies.

"Yes," I admit. "Trouble."

She's pulling this out of me like a pink motherfucking industrial drill. "But not in way you think. Please," I beg. "Leave this alone. Just leave it."

Percival, unconvinced, puts her hands on her hips. *I have to switch tactics.*

"If you want me to explain," I murmur, raking my hair, "you may-be teach me more English, yes?"

Percy whines and stomps her foot. *What a petulant spoiled brat.* "You *totally* know enough by now, you just like, don't want to tell me," she sputters.

"C'mon! I've, like, told you tons of secret stuff!" *This is an appeal to emotions.* "Like, what's with all the bird drawings? Are you like, men-tal?!" *She's wearing me down.* "And, like, you have tons of weird Pola-roids of, like, random stuff up there!" *Not just wearing me down. This is torture via verbal water-boarding.*

"Are you, like, a serial killer or whatever?!"

*I'm going to be if you don't shut the **fuck** up.*

"Percy," I try again, sagging against the wall. "I do not know how to explain and have other things to think on." Even if I told her, she wouldn't understand, not that she'd let me get that fucking far. We never talk about me, even when she asks. *Percy plods paragraphs for fun.*

Percy groans at me, irritated, her fists balled up. "Like what?! God, you're, like, **so** irritating!" *Did the bleach rot your motherfucking brains?! I'm irritated! You don't get to be irritated, you fucking banshee!*

"I have to pay bill—requires maths I do not know. Have to call someone in follow-up. English hard. Please, tackle immediate thing now. I need you." Generally good at acting, I can't even put in the effort this time around.

"You are only one who can help. I am lost without you, Percy. Please help? You are smartest woman in world," I state.

Percy perks up and skitters toward me, placing a hand on my shoulder. "All you had to, like, do was ask, Al."

This was a catastrophic mistake.

We're staring at math equations in a big blue binder on my fucking coffee table. All I asked was for her help with simple math—that I do need help with—and English, which I *also* need help with. Percy's flaw is making everything more complicated and painful than it needs to be. *It's terminal.*

"I-I don't understand this. Any of it," I admit, leg bouncing as she throws me into algebraic bullet-fire.

She giggles to herself, sits closer to me and tries to explain again. "See, it's like when you substitute, like, a letter for a number, and guess around it. There's, like, totally an easy formula. Here." She scribbles out some actual fucking witch language as my eyes glaze over.

"You are too smart," I say, leaning forward to hold my head in my hands. At least I'm honest in the face of feeling fully fucking incompetent. *It's not a great feeling, let me just say.*

"I'm sorry. I am stupid." I attempt an appeal to emotions so she'll stop torturing me with new problems. *It probably won't fucking work.*

She shakes her bottle-blonde head. "Silly," she says, pinching my cheek like a babushka might. "Some people are just, like, better at some things, or whatever. And like, worse at other stuff."

I give her a half-smile and push some of her golden hair behind her ear. Even if she's maddening, I can't hate her. *She will hate me eventually, even though I love her.*

She giggles as I kiss her forehead. "I think that maybe, I love you." I'm not saying this for any other reason than I've just realized it. *It's confusing and maybe more than a bit concerning, considering she's irritating as fuck.*

"You're, like, totally not my type." She cackles, pushing away to scoop up a sweet bottled drink from the table. "Besides," she says, twisting the cap, "I've *totally* got a girlfriend."

I snag one of the bottled drinks myself. "Oh?" I half-ask, tipping alcohol down my throat.

She mimics my drinking, cutting it with musical laughter. "She's, like, totally a tiny nightmare, or whatever."

"When will I meet this 'tiny nightmare?'" I ask with a sunny smile on my face.

Percy's face lights up. "Like...how about tonight?"

"Sure, I would like this," I say into her hair as I nuzzle her affectionately. "I will try not to be too aggressive."

Percy cackles. "What do you mean by 'aggressive,' or whatever?"

I shrug my shoulders. "If she is no good, then she is no good." I punctuate my sentence by raising my palm. "Only the best for you, yes?"

She shoves me and we laugh.

We spend the day dancing not unlike I did with Eric as birds perch by my window and coo. It's a bit too romantic and co-dependent, but even drunk, I keep it platonic. *Despite how irritating she is, I want her. I kill the part of me that wants her, because it's rotten.*

Any kind person is liable to attract me and that's a problem, because kindness can *lie*. This is a lesson I have a hard time learning, but a man will soon force me to learn it forever. A man who I will use to solve this horrible mess, kill many bird keepers with just one stone and divest myself of a genre I *never* fucking asked for. He'll also be what kills me.

We dress up for the night—I wear Percy's green latex dress and she wears my lavish red prescription. I don't bother with the wig, but I do opt for some of her glitter. I'm not trying to be anyone but myself tonight (a blurry androgynous line) and maybe borrow a bit of her kitschy sweetness.

She takes my hand and we're off on foot. The lights around us sparkle as we pass, though I know now I can't be distracted by them. Fraught with opportunities for failure, my plan can't afford complacency. *Sadly, my resolve won't last. I wish it had.*

When we return to her usual haunt, the bartender lingers on my face. Paranoid, I opt-out of alcohol for the night. We wait for the 'tiny nightmare' she wants to show off, I sip a diet soda and we talk about nothing and everything. Which means *she's* talking and *I'm* listening.

Despite how annoying she is, I love basking in Percy's glow. She has this quirkiness that fills my empty spaces beautifully. Sadly, in future times, she will very much hate me. For as big a brain as she has—and an even bigger heart—she overthinks, which I will use because I don't know how to do anything else.

A too-genuine, tea-kettling laugh snaps my head around. I duck down in the booth instinctually.

"H-hey, like...what's—what's up?" Percy asks, a fry in her mouth. "Al, what are you, like, hiding from?"

I scuttle underneath the table like a feral squirrel in green plastic. Percy repeats herself, "Alex?" while poking at me with her foot.

Pushing her foot away, I rake my eyes over the busy bar. Heart pummeling my ribs, my ears chart that laughter like a beacon and land on the fucking devil himself. He's surrounded by lackeys. *Why the fuck is **he** here?!*

A man with dirty-blond hair wearing a russet suit walks toward Boris. He's handsome, well-dressed, has a devastating smile and he's tall as fuck.

Percy prods at me with her pink stiletto. "Alex?" She stupidly ducks her head underneath the table. Worst of all, she snatches my hair in her hand to wrestle me from my hiding spot.

"Stop." She kicks at the back of my fucking head! I push her leg away and shuffle forward to gawk at the men across the room.

The tall man turns as he speaks. Every move he makes forces the men around to move like the sea. Even *Boris* has his head slightly bowed.

"I've found him," I breathe out. Percy wriggles her foot again, distracting me. Naturally, I slide her shoe off to keep her heel from braining me.

She squeals, fidgets, then drops beneath the table. "Give me back my shoe, *oh my god,*" she shrieks, prying at my fingers.

Without looking, I drop the shoe, reach back, yank her by the hair, clasp my hand to her mouth and force her to watch the men I'm watching. Her eyes widen in my grasp, which grows tight as I hold my breath and stare at my future plans.

Uncomfortable, she slides back toward the booth, taking her shoe with her. I lean to keep my hand plastered to her lips. She mumbles beneath my fingers. Fingers that dig into her jaw to shut her trap.

A vicious smile tugs my mouth. *I've found him.* Percy's eyes fill with tears. As you and I watch my life flash before my eyes, let me put a pin in it. *This was when Percival figured me out.*

"The king," I marvel as the tall man commands his entourage with gestures. I glance back at Percy's face twice, then peel my magenta-stained palm from her mouth.

"I, like…" Percy pauses, rubbing her jaw. "Don't really get it, or whatever." She giggles nervously. "But, like, I'm like, not gonna pry." She drags her wrist over her lips to swipe her smudged lipstick. "But you'll, like, tell me, right?" She searches for my eyes.

"Yes, Percy. I will tell you. I promise," I lie. I lie and wait for the men to leave, which they do, as we sit in pregnant silence below a table and Percy sees me for what I truly am.

When I'm sure they're gone, I let out a sigh. "So, where is mystery girlfriend?" I ask.

Like clockwork, a pink sneaker brushes my elbow. Startled, I shove my hand into my coat pocket but freeze as Percy's glare serrates my skull.

I flick my eyes to her face, linger on her pink-stained mouth, offer her a grin and slide my fingers from my pocket.

"That's Olive." Percy smiles mutely, notes my coat, then wipes her mouth with her curled fist.

"Hey!" a plucky voice trickles from above our heads.

We claw out from underneath the table in unison to peer up at a very short, very buxom woman in a daisy-print t-shirt. She has a mess of bright pink curls on the top of her head. Almost like she dip-dyed it all in highlighters.

"Whatcha doin' down there, huh?" she asks with a nasally laugh as we wriggle into our seats. We don't respond.

Olive latches herself to Percival and showers her face in kisses.

"Liv, oh my god," Percy squeals. "S-stop. We're in public."

"This is Alex!" Percy gestures at me. "A-Alex, this is Olive!" Percy smiles at her girlfriend who is glaring a hole into her bottle-blonde skull.

I reach out my hand to shake Olive's. She snatches my digits in her fist and nearly breaks them. *Holy fucking shit.* Olive slides into the booth next to Percy, grinning like a fiend at my possibly-broken hand.

"Nice ta meetcha finally," Olive says with a toothsome smile. "Heard a lot aboutcha. How yer wicked crazy, but wicked cool."

I mutely mouth my pain at Olive's mangling then shoot Percival a look. She shoots me one back. Olive shoots me a grin, then shoots Percy a glare. We're shooting each other in heavy silence while none of us can decide if we're fucking angry with each other or not.

"Yes, wicked crazy, wicked cool." I break the silence, giving them both a thumbs up with my not-really-broken thumb. The three of us break into wondrous laughter but I don't notice that Percy's laugh is so dull. *I've broken her trust.*

I *should've* noticed, but I'm trying to look anywhere but the pair of love-birds because they're blindingly beautiful, especially Olive. It's hard not to notice her. *I'm not trying to be one of those men who describes women who breast boobily and tit downwards, if you understand me.*

Olive. Liv. Livvie. You won't be a weapon in my army, but I will be a weapon in your life. You will judge me for nothing and I will love you like dying—and I will die—despite loving you.

Boris' present bullet tries to right its course into my skull. This memory makes me want to let it. *I'm so fucking sorry, Liv.*

As the three of us laugh, share food and talk, I notice how lovingly you gaze into Percy's eyes as her cheeks turn pink. You want to kiss her and she wants to let you. She does love you, you know. *She's just scared.*

Watching you both in this moment and knowing your breakup will be my fault, I know that I can't die. Not just because I love you, but because I have to make it right by Percy, too.

I have to apologize to her. I have to tell both of you that my heroism is just vengeance with a good reason slapped on top to make me suck less. I have to tell you both how much I love you. I have to let Percy know that she was fucking right to hate me. Olive, I'm worried that you already know and love me anyways, when you shouldn't, because nobody should.

I can't die like this.

27 / FELINES & FELONIES

Despite seeing the path, Boris keeps grinding me down. Moreover, it's *working*. Work is steady to the point of plentiful. Plentiful to the point of invasive. Invasive like all thefts are. Thefts like a murder of crows picking the celluloid entrails from my carcass. The tape of my trauma spools from my guts for all eternity. That is, until it lets Boris **kill me**. *Fuck!*

All I've managed to do is map out a problem I only know the half of as my fish tank fills with shit. Maybe Boris is poisoning me to death. Maybe that's the only way to *actually* kill me. *Maybe that's the fucking point!*

With wild eyes, I sit in my room at the crack of dawn and work over the gristle of a plan only *I* understand. A feral thing, I chew my cheek, naked and completely alone. Placing my hand to the wall, I scour looseleafs like a madman. The orchestra of my inner universe plays out in snapshots of living color that melt before my eyes.

It's hell in here.

Plucking free a Polaroid of a pack of chewing gum, Percy's symbol takes shape before my eyes. I've boiled her down to just one image to use her gossip for illegal bullshit. *It hurts less in pictures.* My cigarette dangles as I pin her back in place.

I hate myself.

I idle with another Polaroid and pluck it from the wall. It's a green caterpillar. I won't do much with this except love him from afar and lean on him for whatever kindness he gives me. I will think I'm helping him, but really, I'm just sucking up his empathy like a fucking vampire.

I don't know how to ask for help.

Rising to my knees, I lean for a daisy-stickered, blank snapshot. *I can't put her anywhere near this.* Tossing Olive's symbol atop of a stack of dust-covered records, I wince.

Can anyone even help me, anyways? Can my friends? Can they do any of this fucking shit? Think about it, even? No.

Boris' Polaroid is next. He's a cigar of course; heady cherry-smoke cancer. I reach for a pen and scribble underneath it a nonsense-drawing that only makes sense to me. I skewer his forehead with a pin when I put him back on the wall.

Closing my eyes for a moment, I wilt back to the floor. With one palm on the cold wood, I drag my other hand through my matted hair and try to still my rapid thoughts. *They're all so fucking deafening*—my phone rings, which makes my eyes flick open.

I stand, leave my dim room, swipe my hand across the coffee table that's now littered with alcohol bottles and snag a full one in my fist. On my way to the screaming phone, I snatch my cigarettes and lighter and slug down a quarter of the bottle. Picking up the receiver, the voice on the other end makes my heart seize. *It's too early for him to call.* What the fuck does he want *now*?

"Yeah?" I mumble, sitting on the floor as I knead my eye with my fist. "No, I'm busy tonight—" I light up another cigarette as he speaks. *Wasn't I just smoking a moment ago?*

Payne's gray spirals from my nose and flits near an open window as I listen to a tumor speak.

My expression twists. "I can't—" Boris steals my choices by reminding me I have no other option. *He's right. I don't.* "Alright." I reach up and slide the receiver into its holster with a click.

I'm worthless except when I'm very useful.

Staring off into nothing, I imagine my life in moving picture. Beyond the box, beyond the glass, beyond the curtain comes Boris' laughter. He's ground me to dust. Worst of all, I've let him.

Cold air buffers my cheek, reminding me that I can feel. I crush the cigarette in my fingers, burning myself and drop it to the floor with the rest of the trash littering my flat.

I will never be anything more than a victim, and if I escape that, I—

Standing, I stumble to the open window as the light beyond it ebbs orange. The sun drowns below the horizon, I slam the window down after far too much effort, place a hand to the glass and sag against it.

A small mewl catches my ears. Twirling, I spot a dirty white creature in the corner of the room, pressing its nose into a pile of empty pizza boxes from Rosalin's—a little Italian place I'm a fan of.

For a moment, I forget my madness, my fish tank, Boris' repeated stomping on my already-brutalized psyche and my fucking faux-heroism.

I need real heroism now for just one dirty feline with a sunken face who crawled through my window looking for a meal. *Looking for safety and maybe even love. Me too.*

The cat shrinks when I move toward it, each step met with its ears pulled back. Stooping, I reach out my hand and make a tsking sound. It quivers.

"You too, huh?" With my finger, I flick open one of the pizza boxes and let it snack on remnants of cheese. It eats greedily, eying me with each bite.

Struggling to stand, I trail to the kitchen, pass by yet more garbage and thousands of cups filled with mold. *A home reflects its owner.*

Flinging the fridge open, I remove a carton of milk and a can of tuna. Intoxicated, I struggle to pry open the can's lid. Grimacing, I stomp to the living room, fumble around on the coffee table for my knife, return to the can and puncture angry holes in the brittle metal as the juice stains my fingers. I dump the tuna into a blue plastic bowl. The milk is next. I steady myself on the counter as I pour it into a saucer as my head swims.

With both bowls in my hands, I glide to the starving creature and place the food in front of it. Back down to my knees, I hug them and watch the cat sniff my meager offering. After a few moments, it takes to the tuna, devours it and licks its chops. *I imagine that it's happy.*

As it laps up the milk, I hold my hand out for it to smell. "I've never had a pet before," I mumble. It licks at my fingers, hunting for yet more tuna on my skin. *I've bought its trust with food.* I place my other hand on its head ever so gently. The feline purrs for me.

It curls into a ball, stretches out, then reaches up its paws to the ceiling. I think it loves me for just one act of kindness. Maybe it does. *Maybe it's just like me.*

After doting on the furry thing for far too long, I manage to take a shower and carve away all the hair on my body with a scrap of metal without drunkenly falling and breaking my stupid neck.

Emerging from the steam, I wrap my fists around the bottle from earlier, down the rest of the booze and look around for the cat. It's made my sofa its bed, sleeping soundly between my discarded bags. Its tail covers its nose as it breathes soft, slow and *finally* safe.

Bleary-eyed, I watch it doze. "I will call you Diana. Seems fitting." The rest of my words die in my throat as I prepare to die over and over again for a genre I never chose. *I didn't want this fucking life.*

I stalk away, cake my inked flesh with foundation, and stare down at the naked eyes on my hips. They glare up at me. Missing a piece and still fucking branded for it. *I didn't want any of this.*

With a grimace, I find the most flattering, clean dress I can and slide it over my thin frame. It's a death shroud made of blood. The shoes come next; I stumble when I put them on. I don't bother with undergarments. They're just going to be peeled off my body, and the faster I get this shit over with the better. *No one chooses to work for Boris. No one. He steals people.*

Diana purrs as I pet her. "Goodbye, little one," I whisper. She trills and twists her tail into a question mark for me.

I hope I don't fucking ruin this one's short little life, too.

28 / MOSTLY MISERABLE

The path doesn't matter if my metaphorical legs have been cut clean off by a cherry-scented tumor in an expensive suit. None of my friends notice me wasting away, dropping pounds a week. *None of them ever will, save Olive.*

I am small, weak, stubborn, paper-thin and eternally exhausted. I am very pretty but awkward, as though my bones don't fit my flesh. Nothing I wear is anything I own, because a dog never owns his collar.

What other job could you get, little bird? You don't have an ID. You don't even have a name. On paper, you don't exist. You don't exist. I don't fucking exist.

Even the very food I eat is someone else's property, as am I. Does Boris own the very clouds in the night sky above my head, too? *He must.*

The air is cold on my skin although the coat around my shoulders buffers it. Oil-slick birds flitter by my head, and in my drugged stupor, I imagine they're one living, bleeding, breathing beast. They roar behind my eyelids and blur the street as I walk to the cage I'm actually in. The cage I never left. *The cage I'll die trying to escape from.*

Distance doesn't mean I'm not behind bars. Distance doesn't mean my mind isn't stuck in that wooden box. Distance doesn't mean you're not reading my tragedy like a voyeur. You're just as complicit as you watch my death and the death-march of my life. I fucking hate you and I *deserve* to hate anyone I wish.

Slapping the buzzer of the unassuming apartment complex, the static prickles my ears and I'm in. Head swimming, I enter various rooms and lay about in various appetizing poses as I'm stripped, cut into slices and eaten raw. My eyes go blank as I stare at the ceiling and freeze subjective time. Willingly, I daydream, but all the film reels are stained. Birds scream in human sounds. A man strangles a doll in the river. The earth bleeds.

I wonder if Boris records this shit. I wouldn't be fucking surprised. I'm the blueprint. The starter meal-ticket. The basis for this New York operation. All rivers of rot run through me and yet he won't let my waterlogged corpse just drift down the fucking river. Why? *Why can't I choose what I do with my own fucking life?*

After, I leave on weak limbs, high on something I don't recall taking. Smudging my wrist over my mouth, a permanent red stain lingers on the back of my hand. *This color ruins fucking everything.*

This must be my rock-bottom; a path I'm too depressed to follow, a home filled with rot, a body reconfigured, a life broken and a mouth silenced with a lipstick ball-gag while I can do *nothing* for those like me who die and make money by dying as my soul withers, rots and dies all the *fucking* same.

Anger fills my corpse as I plod wet, gray streets. Anger gets shit done by reminding me I need fuel to function. I have no appetite, but decide to force it. *I always force it these days.*

Instead of going home, I make my way to Rosalin's via the subway. The scents, colors and lights around me vibrate the walls of the metal tin can that barrels through space. I exit the train, trudge up the steps and dodge a migraine with my hand to my temple.

Rosalin's opens with the sun. I hustle inside, purchase a single slice of white pizza with garlic, thyme and rosemary, sit quietly in a booth and eat.

The woman from the church is in the back of the restaurant, arguing with who I assume is the manager. Deja vu takes over. A thousand toppling thoughts skewer my gray-matter. *It's so fucking loud.* I bite into my messy pizza and scrutinize the interaction as my pulse races.

She glances at me—the only customer in the restaurant looking like a feral cat huffing pizza. She's around my height, painfully gorgeous, and looks mostly fucking miserable, just like I do. She's like me. *She can be me, if she has anger.*

I'm angry enough to gnash my pizza to shreds. I'm angry enough to form a desperate plan to reach the path I need to at any cost. I'm angry enough to move my limbs mechanically to sit. I'm angry enough to find anything I can to pull myself above the shit-water of my fish tank, claw my way beyond the lights and wriggle past the gray bars. *Even if that 'anything' is a mostly-miserable, beautiful stranger.*

She goes on her break, and like any demented stalker, I round the back and watch her cry and smoke. She's pacing back and forth to think just like I do. *We're the same. This must be fate. This must be. It fucking has to be.*

After a while, she confiscates some alcohol from the kitchen, sits on a metal drum and drinks herself stupid, like I would. Empathy begs me to stop her from drowning herself with booze. Vengeance begs me to use whatever I find to dominate my enemies. *Vengeance wins.*

I turn off my empathy, wipe my hands on my dress and traipse beyond the brick wall. The disheveled drunk stumbles. "Ahh, fuck," I mutter, ending on a curated laugh.

The woman flicks her eyes to me, looking horrified for one brief moment. Her expression softens to graceful overwhelm. She stands on wobbly limbs, and reaches out to me. I have to be weaker than she is so I can lure her, figure out what she can handle and if she fits into the insane patterns on my wall. *It's all patterns, right?*

"Um." She hesitates, holding me at her side. "A-are you OK?" she asks with a slight accent. I nod then play my part; mining my trauma to queue waterworks is easy for me. *I'm a brilliant actor.*

As she dips her head down and hoists me to sit with her on another barrel, I scan her face. She's gorgeous, even with her hair stuffed underneath a net, her fingers pruned and her soul as broken as mine. She can be my mimic in earthy browns, full lips and comely optics. She can't see it now, if she ever could.

She could get anything she wanted, if she was very clever.

"Y-yes," I gurgle. "Sorry. I'm too drunk. Long night."

She nods and leans against me, idling with a cigarette.

Quirking a feline brow, she offers me one, I take it, she lights them, we sit in not-quite comfortable misery and I siphon smoke like I plan on siphoning her soul from her fucking body.

"Me too. Fucking pendejos run me ragged," she hisses from a beautiful grimace. She can do this. *It's easy if you have rage.*

I lean against her shoulder. "Don't they always?" I offer, breathing smoke into the air. She can't see what I am and thinks I'm just a lost little girl like she is. I know this when she holds my hand, desperate enough to seek comfort in a complete fucking stranger. *Desperate enough.*

"What's your name?" I ask, sweet as pie. *Come to me and be more than you think you are. If you must kiss me for it, I'll let you. If you must hate me for it, I'll let you. If I have to fucking die for it, I will.* **I need you.**

She smiles dryly. "Moira. You?"

My empathy flies free, maybe forever. It's drifting like the errant papers swirling in the alley near us. It circles the drain as I perform what I need in order to survive and **win**. My life has been nothing but a series of fucking *performances* based on survival. I react and react and react, the lightswitch turns off and I'm pressed into a mold. My wings break off with pressure and I drop like a stone to hell. *A monster.*

"Alex," I reply. "Moira Angela Darling, hmm?" I say, a dreamy twinkle in my eye. "Saw movie, very good. Are you like her, maybe? Savior of lost ones like me?" I force my eyes to water again. *The Lost Boys and Girls need their Moira Angela Darling.* Because Boris will always see me coming from thousands of miles away, this doesn't work without her. I'm the one who's easy to read, yet so many 'usual' people can't. *Boris is not usual.*

Moira hesitates, but wraps her arm around my shoulder all the same. She's far too kind, of course she suffers. *Only truly kind people do.*

"I saw that one too," she says. "Darling, hmm? I like it." She's dangerously beautiful with cat-like eyes, perfect eyebrows and a mouth made to whisper with a forked tongue.

For a while, she talks about everything, I listen, give her nothing and lie for days. Her words blurt and twist like drunk butterflies, unpinnable and easily distracted. *Good.* Moira sighs; she's taking too long with her break and we both know it.

Before I leave, I press a seed into her head from my pretty mouth. "You know," I begin, shaking out my blond mane with my fingers. "A girl like you could get whatever she wants. If she was very clever."

Moira chuckles, pulls pieces of her hair back into her hairnet and looks away. "You really think so?" she asks, shaking her head. "I don't know about all that. Tried forever at anything else," she admits. "Acting, singing. Modeling, even."

"I model," I muse with a dry smile.

"You do?" Lingering on my shape, she finds my too-pretty face beyond a mess of blond hair. "Hmm. Yeah, I could see it."

She's disarmed because I'm camouflaged as girl-meat. I'm not a girl. I'm not even a man, either. *I'm just a devil.* A devil that doesn't want to hurt her. *I don't want to. I just* want to teach her one skill that requires nothing but getting some asshole drunk and strong-arming him. That could work. It could work. *It has to work. It's fate.*

Leaving, I gift her a wave a princess might make—elbow down, arm straight, palm out. Moira mimics me and chuckles. *She's good at mimicry.*

I visit Rosalin's every week for years in different skins. I will try to have very many conversations with Moira, all of which she'll forget. I'll even lure Boris with me one of those times to test my theory about men and their weakness to beauty. She'll forget how I had to wield him away, proving my concept. *She always fucking forgets.*

Moira will take forever to conscript into my war, but she will be the missing piece, the snake, the partner in crime who solves this mess by merit of mimicking me so well she might as well *be* my fucking twin. She's desperate enough to try *anything* if it sets her free.

We're the same. But if I'm honest, she's better at it than I'll ever be.

29 / COMPARTMENTALIZE

My home is an avalanche of trash. Records, kitschy figurines and nonsense lamps act as lighthouses in a sea of filth. The lie Boris forces me to live bleeds out in the junk in my destroyed apartment—the junk I keep fucking accumulating. *I've become a hoarder.*

I am fully depressed in a fishbowl full of shit, but able to survive because I compartmentalize all of it. *The mind is powerful, the mind is weak, the bird is broken, the path is nowhere in sight.*

Quality time with Percy is spent at her place and only occasionally at the bar she likes. Because Boris haunts it and the bartender makes me fucking paranoid, I force us to leave early and often. Percy badgers me about this and badgers me about why I won't let her visit my flat. I offer that I'm having it redecorated. She buys that after much materialistic bribery, which she *also* badgers me about. Sometimes we even spend time with Olive, mostly at a cafe she likes, who I have trouble looking at because I very much want to look at her. I play at normalcy with these two bright, lovely people who haven't yet noticed I'm not worth spending time with.

An expert compartmentalizer, we're at the cafe today. Olive orders something from the barista while Percy and I sit and talk. By talk, I mean Percy barrels over any word I might say while glaring at a parking lot just beyond the window. I remember when she was ecstatic about work. *I don't know what that feels like. I've never worked a job I didn't hate. Save murder.*

Percy prattles foolishly about her precinct, gestures at the lot and I sip a small black coffee. She's bubbly and excitable again, which means I need to act the part. I laugh at all her jokes, flatter her and give her a little gold bracelet. If she notices my bribery, she isn't calling me on it. In fact, every gift makes her eyes sparkle. I wish I knew how to talk to her without bribery. *Or any of them, for that matter.*

When Percy goes to the bathroom, Olive returns and sits across from me. As she's distracting, I struggle to keep myself from dragging my eyes across the table. She snorts her piglet snort and drinks down a metric fuckton of hot chocolate.

"You're going to get sugar—a sugar high and crash later," I say with an earnest smile. My English has greatly improved but my rottenness hasn't. I'm still a bloodless vampire in their midst, stealing Olive's perpetual pluckiness. She lets me and I don't know why. *It's wasted effort.*

"Haha!" She giggles to herself. "Prolly." She snorts. "I dunno. I don't really care, ya know?"

My mouth tugs into a half-smile as she jams a cream-filled donut into her face. My half-smile tugs in the opposite direction—a dismal grimace—when Olive leans over said table to hold a donut to my mouth.

"Ya wanna bite?" she asks.

Helpless, I'm forced to lock my eyes on Olive's stuffed cheeks to avoid what's directly hovering in my line of sight. *Stop, for fuck's sake.* Olive waves food at me as my face burns. She grins, then jiggles on purpose. *She's fucking evil.*

"Liv," I say with a sigh, then stupidly take a napkin and bap it flat against her mouth. She looks like she got in a fucking fight with a bag of flour and I'm *not* staring. Olive grins, jams a donut at my mouth, *I don't stare*, she shoots a laugh directly in my ear canal, the donut flops to the table, then she bounce-dashes away like a *demented* goblin.

"Haha!" she screeches.

"You're such a fucking—what is word?" I hiss, pausing to gnash the donut. "Dork!" I shout and chase after her. We meet Percy at the bathroom as she stretches her arms over her head.

Percy stops short when she sees my face. "You have, like, a ton of powdered sugar all over you!" She cackles, then snags Olive by the arm to giggle with her. "Did you, like, assault him with a donut?" Percy asks the buxom dork she is very much in love with.

Olive nods and reaches for Percy's hand. Olive's paw sits idle. I notice.

Scrunching my shoulders, I look away like they might blind me. *They're too cute.* Finally, I steal to the table and sip my coffee. They trail behind me and talk to each other. I can't hear what they're saying but I imagine it's lovely, romantic and bright. *Everything I'm not.*

I check my new pager for something I haven't apprised them of.

"He's here."

The girls exchange curious glances across from me. Olive looks around then leans close to my ear. "Who's here?" she whispers.

"Oi, mate, s'far out is what. Butcha said tha coffee's mad, yeh?!" Eric shouts then barrels into my chair. He wraps his arms around my shoulders from behind. My eyes flick to his pleasant face. *I love him.* I want—*I'm absolutely fucking broken beyond belief.*

"Oh!" Percy trills and wags her finger between us.

"Eric, Percival—Percy. Olive, Eric. Eric, Olive. He is surrogate—my surrogate boyfriend." I chuckle, Eric snags me in a headlock and grinds his knuckle into my skull.

"Poncey lil shit, c'mere!" He struggles to keep hold of me as we tussle playfully, chair scraping as he lifts me about.

"Stop!" I cackle, feigning war because I *never* want him to stop, actually.

Percy leans forward, folding her hands."Surrogate, like...what now?"

Olive giggles and gestures at Percy, filling in the blanks. "Doncha know anything?" She snorts. "Besties!"

"No, no, they're like, totally, totally doing it," Percy says, rolling her eyes.

"It's alright, and no." I pause. "Though we have spooned. So, a *surrogate* boyfriend."

Eric doesn't correct me, instead, he wrestles me from the chair, hooks his arm underneath my chin and playfully chokes me.

"Agh, fuck, stop!" I groan, kicking into the air.

He drops his arm, locks me in a bear hug and nearly breaks my spine. Percy and Olive screech with laughter while Eric squeezes me. *This is too much.*

"Oi, mate, why ya tensin' up? Don't be such a bloody porcupine." When he finally lets me go, I slide into my seat, pull him to sit beside me and finally punch his shoulder.

"Now all my favorite people are here. This is a good day."

We enjoy a moment together as friends away from my madness; eating sweets, entertaining wild, joyous conversations and existing as normal people doing normal things. Normal ends the minute a cherry devil hammers my pager with numbers. Numbers that tell me where to go, what to do, how to live and who I get to be. *I would fucking kill to be normal.*

Souring, I offer an excuse to my friends who want my worthless self to stay. All of us embrace before we go our separate ways. When it's Eric's turn, I flood into his arms as he holds me.

He studies my face, then his expression goes dark. "Call me if ya need a ride, yeh?" he whispers, lingering painfully.

I screw my eyes shut as I resist burying my face in his shirt. I can't ruin what we have. *It means fucking everything to me.*

As Eric pulls away, I don't want to let go. I don't want to let go of *any* of them. I want all of them for myself even though I'm fucking worthless.

What's wrong with me?

30 / SNAP

I'm properly pillaged, poisonously pretty, perfectly pissed-off and making my way back to my biohazard of a flat in the dead of night. High as a kite, I float through a sparkling cityscape and imagine I have even just *one* tool that lets me unearth the path I need to walk away from this bullshit for good. A twinkling shadow catches my eye; *a sloppy drunk who knows a guy who knows a guy.* The street-sign before me melts into a yellow smudge; *an ailing grandma whose granddaughter knows a daughter of a daughter.* I know the red king—but he doesn't know me—and because of this, all roads lead right back to hell. *I'm fucking drowning.*

Sifting over dead asphalt, I spot a blue payphone; a lighthouse on a littered sidewalk. *Percy's lighthouse.* Percival and her pretty magenta mouth. Percival and her infectious, excitable laughter. Percival, the one I lie to most of all. Percival, a girl I'm in love with. *Why am I in love with all of them?*

Glaring at the payphone for too long, I finally part the sea of shadow-pedestrians that shimmer between me and my color. Every step creates more shapes, as though they're born from the ink of my guts. *Maybe they fucking are.*

When I finally push past the shadow-people, I bump into a long-haired woman with a large duffle bag on her shoulder. I don't apologize. She moves around me like I'm a virus in human skin, her white braids swaying like willow branches. *Maybe I am. Maybe she can smell it on me.*

Reaching my hand into my coat pocket, I unearth the scraps of paper my meat is worth and dig for coins. The payphone drips blue ink on the sidewalk, I plop quarters into the fiddly slot, dial a number and place the receiver to my ear. The demon answers after the fifth ring.

"Boris." My lower lip quivers. "I don't want to fucking do this anymore," I admit, despite all my planning. I admit, despite all my nothing-efforts. This is the plea of my twisted soul. Maybe it's manipulation without trying. Maybe I'm so *fucking* desperate to escape my fishtank that I'm banking on the scrap of empathy he let me chew on God knows how long ago.

A deep chuckle flits through the receiver.

"You told me." I suck my teeth. "You told me that if I proved I could be more, that you would give me *more*. You told me that if I tried my hardest to show just what I was fucking capable of, that you'd *get me out*."

Boris wafts excuses through the receiver. I also know he didn't promise me shit, but *I don't fucking care*. He knows that *no one* deserves to be a prisoner and he *knows* he can stop any time he wants. But he won't. *Why?!*

"It's just business. Nothing personal." The demon's rolling accent batters my ears like the wings of birds.

I slam the phone on the receiver with a deafening clatter.

Hand to my head, the world quakes around me. *I'm so fucking tired.* Digging around in my pockets for cigarettes, I jam one of them in my mouth, flick my Bic, inhale cancer and stalk to the subway. I won't call Eric to pick me up, though I should. *He can't see me like this again. Never again.*

Everything grows deafening as I walk: the cars, the people, the laughter, the smells, the birds, the screams, my thoughts, my heartbeat.

I take the subway to my next destination. Boris keeps moving me offsite and into the arms of more dangerous monsters. I don't bother asking why. I assume he's driving me into the dirt because he wants to break me like a horse. He wants me too weak to vanish into my mind. He wants me too weak to do anything at all but suffer. *If that's the case, he's already fucking succeeded.*

It's time for another dysphoric theft. I flick my cigarette onto the sidewalk, ash it with my heel and shuffle up the steps to a tall apartment complex. Men nod at me, men guide me, I follow them and when they look at my face, I smile. When they look away, my smile dissolves and I'm back to being a blank fillable jug. *Please, God help me.*

Glaring at the ceiling above me, I focus on a crack. It spirals out to make a river in a seam, reaching for a far window I can't see. I peer over the shoulder in my way, trying to get a view of just how far the faultline travels. It's far more interesting than what I'm putting up with at the moment, to be honest.

"I don't know why he has me with Sicilians; we're fighting over zip codes anyways—maybe this is why." My leg is jerked over my head. "He's sent me to a shithole, with grunts, like peace offering. When the way to solve this *fucking* problem is kill you fucking cunts and be *done* with it."

The man handling my meat makes an awkward expression, speaks in a language I don't know—though I know several fluently at this point—grunts and falls on top of me.

"I wouldn't even care if I had a fucking say about it. You know? He keeps strangling options. Do you even fucking understand a single word I say?"

The man rolls off of my body and reaches for a pack of cigarettes, leaving me yet again staring at the broken ceiling.

Another man enters the room. "I've heard you were the best on Boris' list. Entertaining, he said, but you look like a dead fish," the new man scoffs in English.

Tall, square-jawed, an obvious gun at his side, he mulls for a lighter in his pocket. He gestures at the man on the edge of the bed, who tosses him a package of cigarettes. New-man pulls one out, lights it, walks closer to my corpse and scrutinizes me.

I avert my gaze. "Give me a cigarette," I command. My mask is streaming down my face in kohl eyeliner. *I'm crying against my will.*

"Oh, she's making demands?"

"*He*," I correct him, my feral eyes locked on his face. My bird heart flutters in its cage of ribs. *I want to crush this man between my teeth.* Do I even fucking know how to do that anymore? *God, please help me. Somebody.*

"*She's* making demands. Didn't think Boris would give me a mouthy slu—" Sightless, I lunge for his gun and blow his brains out all over the wall. The body drops like a heavy stone. The man on the bed is next, now but a mere red stain across a dripping TV screen.

Seeing without seeing, moving without thinking, I tear through the penthouse with a gun. I find more guns easily. I find more people to kill easily. *I kill them easily.* My possessed body kills a maid because she's staring at me like *I'm* the blood-stained monster—not the men who she saw shove me into a room. *I'm* the villain. *Fine, then I **will** be.*

I kill a mechanic who's fixing an air conditioner all because he's in my fucking way. I kill everyone I can find between my path to leaving the building, even people who *don't* deserve it. I feel this, but I'm not inside my body and I can't stop myself. *I just can't fucking stop.*

Luckily for the humans of New York's streets, my war-mode ends the minute I wander into a familiar back-alley, startle a gaggle of loud pigeons and find a heavy gun in my hand.

My eyes widen. I look down at my hands; they're covered in blood. I look down at my dress; scarlet splattered in scarlet.

I destroyed an entire wing of a rival group without injury, without being seen by anyone who could say anything, anything at all. I'd have never made it this far if I'd left anyone alive. *I cleaned house. How?*

My hands shake. "I'm...so fucked."

Back at my apartment finally, I pass by Yuen like a floating apparition. My bloody fists are jammed into my fucking pockets. I fade out of view as he cups his hands to shout at me. *He* wants to feed me like I'm a stray cat. *I* want to pour solvent all over my body, burn my skin off with a lighter, run into the ocean and drown myself.

I push myself against my door, adrenaline thrumming my bird-heart to smithereens, then traipse around the feline playing beneath my heels.

"Hello, beautiful." I fetter my fingers over Diana's ears and scratch underneath her chin as my skin crawls.

The bathroom calls to me to scrape the bug-like sensation off. I strip and turn the water on. Jerking the nozzle to frigid, I step in and try to freeze my skin off. It doesn't work. *Why the fuck won't reality just give me what I fucking want?! Why can't I just—*

Pouring lavender-scented soap on a loofah, I scrub my skin raw. The foundation comes off like peeling the scum layer off a rotten bowl of soup. I finish up, wrap a towel around my vessel and stumble to my phone.

I have to call Boris. If I wait on this, it'll be worse, but the room spins. The distance between my damp body and the landline expands. I jut my hand out to the wall to steady myself as my body gives out. *This isn't a migraine.*

Diana threads herself around my legs as I sag under the weight of something I can't see, but feel caked into my very *fucking* bones. My heart is beating far too hard for my lungs to catch up. Something ancient and clay-like clogs my airway. I can feel my blood pressure drop as my entire body shakes like a fucking leaf.

"*Fuck,*" I curse as panic grips me. *Not now, I can't have one of these now, please—God, please. Help me.* My thoughts railroad each other in a hailstorm. With a hand against my chest, I suffer to skitter Diana from between my ankles and sink to the hardwood. *I'm dying. I'm going to fucking die.*

"One, two, three, hold—" I suck in sweet air but it's barely a gasp. "Four, five, six, seven," I sputter as I lay like a suffocating prey animal choking on its own bitter fluids. *A dying fish flops uselessly. Disgusting.*

Anger is terror's twin. As I've had enough anger for a few thousand lifetimes, I was bound to develop the other response at some point. *I just wish it could've come at any other motherfucking time.*

Diana nuzzles into my side, nibbling my hair. I struggle to reach for her and manage to scoop her into my arms. She lets me clutch her as my heart crawls up my esophagus. *She's so very warm.*

The vibration of her purrs settles the birdwing beat of my frantic heart. The heat of this little creature that relies on me for *survival* calms my thoughts. I breathe shallowly. She purrs. I breathe deeper. *She loves me.* I breathe.

"Y-you're a little life saver, you know that?"

She mewls in response. I suffer a teary-eyed chuckle, lay with her while I breathe and accept the unconditional love she gives me for only this handful of minutes. *That alone is the hardest pill for me to swallow and I can never keep it down. I'm not worth it.*

Steadier now, I shift her from my chest to the floor and drag myself up from my knees. With slow, deliberate movements, I stand and stumble to the phone again.

I call the devil. *He already knows.* I stare off into the sea of stars and beg the invisible man for help, but I see no specters, feel no ghosts and I'm pitifully, pathetically, mortally fucking alone.

I can't tell if Boris is going to send a fleet to murder me in my own home. I can't tell if he's upset. I can't predict what's going to happen and I'm terrified again. *What happened to the fucking path?!*

A clattering chirp-screech startles me. I place my hand to my chest, flicking my eyes to rest on the source. It's just Diana eating dry cat food from her bowl, nothing more.

Boris asks me a question, offering me absolutely no fucking answers at all. "Y-yeah, I can do that. I'll be right there." I hang up the phone as my heart seizes in my chest.

My inner camera peels the paint off the walls as I'm left standing in the void of black water. Ink laps against my ankles and skirts around my knees to climb up my body and devour me. We're watching panic take its course because the God of War has forsaken me and Boris has rendered me a prey-like, psychotically depressed nothing. I reach through the metaphorical bars above my head, ask for no help from anyone at all and drown in my own rotten sludge.

In the present, I press pause.

The mind movies we're watching as Boris' bullet flies at my head stop. I push the bullet away from my temple with a finger. I take just one step and turn to look behind me, directly at you. *Yes, you—the viewer.*

I want to ask you a question: would you help me if you could, or would you loathe me for how I think, what I am and what I've done? Think carefully, because depending on your answer, you're a deadlier animal than I could ever possibly be.

The mind movies reel back with a bolt of fragmented frames. In the past, I flag down a taxi and make it to Percy's bar in a fugue state. *Why he wants to meet there is beyond me.* That is, until I enter through its doors, lock eyes with the bartender and all becomes clear.

Boris owns this too, just like he owns the clouds, my food, my money, my things, my life and every single fucking telegraphed road I've walked until now. *Of course he does.*

31 / CRACKLE

"Little bird," Boris acknowledges me when I slide into the booth. I'm wearing my usual 'annoying punk tourist' getup. I bounce my leg as he scans my bloodless face with a bemused smirk.

This place is no longer full of Percy's magenta light or Olive's plucky pinkness. *I get it now, so I hate it here.* I didn't want to look outside of what I can control, which is fucking *nothing* but the shitty back wall of my shitty apartment stuffed with my shitty fucking things. Why else would the Bratva meet here if they didn't *fucking* own it? Why couldn't I see it? *Why am I always missing the obvious?*

"What have you done?" the man I like least asks, his furry brows tilting. *I can't read him and that terrifies me.*

"I've killed them. All of them. I'm so fucking sorry, I just—" Boris raises his hand. My voice drops off like a perfectly trained bitch. *Who am I? This isn't me. What happened to me? Where did I go?*

Boris leans forward, brown eyes gleaming. He's looking at the devil of a man I truly am and not the abused jug he keeps forcing me to be.

"Can you do it again, but with purpose?" he asks.

"I'm—" My leg bouncing accelerates. Pitch-black panic has swallowed my blue war by smearing me in red and cutting me to shreds. *How do I flick the lightswitch off? Can I even do it anymore?*

"Can you do it again, little bird?" Boris sits back in his chair. His expression is a familiar one. "This is more your style, yes? This is how you're useful. Perhaps this—little bird—is how you sing."

The 'perhaps' has come into play finally and all it took was me coloring so far outside the lines I risked his fucking enterprise. I'm harrowed by the lesson I keep not learning: *I am made for so much more than all this.*

I press my head against the table as he takes to his cigar habit and wafts cherry cancer into the air. As he smokes, I force myself to remember my repeated pillaging. I tape the image of the bloodied cage behind my eyelids and begin to boil. I relive prison's gore and feel my fists ball up on my lap. As his cigar stink stings my eyes, I tap the vein that lets me get shit done. I tap the vein that lets me live. I tap the vein that lets me fucking *survive*. Blood fills my cracked vessel with the only thing I ever truly fucking owned and earned myself: rage.

The stench is annoying. The ash pisses me off. He pisses me the *fuck* off. I'm going to fucking kill him and enjoy digging around in his guts as he screams and screams and begs for his fucking God. *My lightswitch flips.*

"Yes," I mutter, taking a deep, shaky inhale.

I lift my head to glare at him. "Yes. This is how I sing."

32 / POP

I'm amusing and useful again. A great act of violence afforded this, because a great act of violence *always* does. What I won't understand is that this was all designed. What I won't understand is that this is just *another* distraction. What I won't understand is that this, too, makes Boris money. It isn't about me, it's about **labor**. *Boris is too fucking clever.*

With anger as my tool yet again, I've convinced myself I can *finally* get back to my great work. Which isn't cleaning my house, nurturing my relationships or salving my life. I lie to myself constantly and nobody bothers telling me the truth. *Worst of all, I'd refuse to listen, even if they tried.*

Perched on the floor, I raise my hand and shuffle a series of sticky notes. Sticky notes with shorthand on them. Sticky notes affixed to Polaroids. Polaroids of people I know, my little army, people I don't, and one of a particular man I've wanted to stab for years. A poorly drawn bird takes up the white-space below this man's face; a symbol that says more than words ever could.

My moniker of murder is finally in play: a little bird. A symbol born from Tyr's love of a figment, based on his memories of my fascination with them in youth. This pattern reappeared again on the faded sign of the brothel where I borrowed a word I'll use in the distant future. A distant future I'll control and ruin by being what I am.

Just like I control the back wall of my room, I bargain. Just like I'll control an entire organization now that I have more playing pieces, I've identified the path and I have rage again. That's the plan.

I need control. I fucking need it.

When a mass murder of convenience happens, an unassuming

card is left behind. This is the work of the Bratva, and therefore of Boris. It's a show of strength, but not mine, because I'm just a tool. *This is not freedom but it feels like it is, because the card has my bird on it.*

I take Boris' Polaroid and hold it between my fingers, blond wig announcing itself by fluttering over bare shoulders. I stand, saunter to the far wall and reach for a thumbtack on the table. Boris is skewered in the forehead. I smile.

Another Polaroid is plucked from the floor, this time of a woman with messy curls stuffed beneath a hairnet, who looks mostly miserable in the blurry shot. I glance at her pleasant features with a blank expression. I skewer the white part of her Polaroid with a thumbtack.

I snatch a pack of cigarettes off the table, pull one out, flick my Bic, and blow smoke over a plan forged in pain, a plan steeped in rage, and a plan solidified in the pain of others used to justify its birth. *I should've just gone to the police. I should've.* I didn't for a handful of real reasons and one glaring truth: *I'll be made into a villain no matter what I do.*

Contrapposto in heels, I survey what will be my nothing-masterpiece as birds chirp out my window. This is Operation: Something Awesome.

"Hello, Moira Narvaez. Moira Angela *Darling,*" I say from behind a veil of smoke, "I have an opportunity for you."

33 / VIOLET VIOLENT

My resolve didn't last.

Suffice to say, the fucked up knife with a blue handle doesn't take well to an entitled palm. In fact, it takes well to one thing and one thing only: painting roses red and steeping in their blood. I've been convinced I can never be anything more because I *like* the way this feels and Boris knows it. *I'm his blade.*

My expression is sinful as I straddle some man's lap. Some man Boris wanted dead for a reason I didn't ask about. Some man whose wrists are bound to bedposts. Some man made of meat. Men murder, and as I'm a man, I *must* murder. I have no method right now besides the vengeance I can't exact on my bird-keeper. And why can't I? *Pay attention.*

I lick the side of the man's face, then edge the gun in my grasp further down his boxers. "Don't be shy," I say, breath hot.

This is ownership, agency, control, power—isn't it? Or, is it just a robbery in reverse, like looking in a dark mirror, seeing your own hideous reflection and *reveling* in it? I click off the safety of the gun and bite the man's ear. *I like how this feels.*

"L-let me go, please!" he begs me. I don't. I nudge the gun far too lasciviously because I fucking can, and as far as I'm concerned, he *deserves it* for falling prey to what he sees. Which is what he *wants* to see, because I designed myself to his specifications for tonight's 'date.' My thoughts railroad each other and war for supremacy. I don't notice. *I should've.*

Reaching between us, I pull the gun free and inspect it. "Aren't you having a good time, handsome?"

He jerks at his restraints, sneering at his beautiful indigo death. I'm in a blue jumper with a thick belt—something name-brand, expensive and stylish. My tattoos peek through the foundation of my shoulders, flooding broken symbols all the way up the back of my neck, to my wild, chopped locks. My smile is criminal as I graze my lower lip with my teeth.

I see you observing me just as he observes me all the same. Observation costs something, you know. *Do you know what it costs now?*

Adjusting my position, I lean back and press my hand into damp sheets. Blood leaks where I stabbed him in the thigh earlier. My palm wraps around a house-augur lodged in his leg. I pull it free millimeter by millimeter. His flesh squelches around my needle as he screams.

Settling on his lap again, I glance at my blade, then at my gun. "Which do you prefer, handsome?" The man reels and writhes, pinned between my thighs like a moth.

He stammers, "W-what?" His heart pummels in his chest cavity, vibrating my legs. *Heat, gored-meat, delicious*—give it to me. *I fucking need it.*

My eyes blaze in neons against the low light. The black hole void of my blown-out pupils paint a far clearer picture of me than anything I could ever wear. *This is how the little bird truly sings.*

The gun is raised in my shaking grasp. "I'm giving you a *fucking* choice, *insect*." I smirk. "The gun is fast. Little mercy for you, hmm? I'm in a charitable mood." I heft up the blade next, licking my lips. "But the blade will be way fucking better—for me, at least."

The man below me naturally screams. I naturally smile, place the blade in my lap and naturally snatch his cheeks between my fist.

"Tsk, tsk, tsk," I chastise him. "Nobody can hear you." I chuckle in a sing-song cadence. "Nobody is coming to *fucking* save you. So I ask again, which do you prefer? I'm giving you a choice. That's a rare thing in this world, you know," I ramble, punctuating my sentence by forcibly jerking his head. "I've had very few *fucking* choices. No fun, never any fun, never." The man doesn't answer me.

My nails cut half-moon shapes into his flesh as I press his skull into the pillows below. "Tell me," I simper-plead, intoxicated by my power over his very fucking life. He *still* doesn't answer me.

"Be a considerate lover, or go quick?" I insist. "You're boring. Why are you so *boring*?! I *like* when you're vocal. Why won't you tell me what you want? Please…" I breathe, break into a vicious cackle, fling the gun across the room, snatch my thin blade and raise it above my head.

My chest heaves as I hold this position and imagine his guts all over the bedsheets. Outside of doting on my friends, this is the *only* time I'm happy. If I'm honest, this is better than sex, better than any drug and truthfully makes me happier than friendship *ever* did. *I fucking need it.*

I push the blade into the flesh, penetrate the meat and press past the muscle, slow. It has to be slow. Dead-eyed, I stare down as the man scream-cries and gurgles. *He's trying so hard to fly but he can't fucking move his wings!* My laughter is rich. The skin pushes away from the wound and a long line of red draws down his chest. *Slow. It has to be slow.*

This is what I was born to do: fuck and kill and tear and mutilate disgusting shitheads who see me as something to exploit. I'm only *ever* exploited. *And why and why and why?* I wasn't born to be tortured! My thoughts ricochet around my skull like bullets and bleed every drop of empathy from the back of my head. *And yet, and yet, and yet, and yet that's what fate continually deals me and why and why and fucking why?!*

As he dies choking on the blood he pukes up his esophagus, I smile. I rip the blade free and watch as his wound pours scarlet paint down past his navel. Shimmying down his body, I dig in his guts with my blade like playing in a sandbox.

A knock on the door draws my intoxicated head back. I turn to look behind me and find Boris standing in the doorway framed by light. In an instant, I forget I hate him, that I promised to make it right and even who I am. *Boris is good at making me forget.* He's been observing me for *years.*

Boris is all smiles as he tosses me a pack of cards. I catch them with bloodied hands, open the package and place my moniker on the man's forehead. Sliding off of his body, I take some of his blood with me and look down at my splattered indigo clothes. *Gorgeous.*

I pocket the pack of cards. Next comes the gun. I snatch it, flick the safety on and slide it into my jumper pocket. It's heavy against my thigh. I place the knife in the other pocket like I'm collecting pretty stones by a river.

Boris offers me a cigarette, which I take without hesitation. *He's turned me into his own personal weapon.* He lights my cigarette, sups his cigar and we leave with his arm wrapped around his toy's shoulder.

The sun's bright white light blinds me as it breaks through the car window. Blinking wildly, I look down at my body, touch the dried blood on my clothes, stare at the knife in my fist and twist it awkwardly in the air.

Cigarette dangling from my lips, eyes wide, I flick my gaze to the back of Boris' head. He's sitting in the passenger's seat, smoking. The driver casts a glance at me. I force a grin that drops when he turns away.

What the fuck have you done to me?!

34 / PERCEPTIVE PERCIVAL

Unable to answer that question, I convince myself I'm happier than I've been in a long time, which is a lie. It's a lie to save a life, but only temporarily. For this reason, I've let my friends in a little more. However, I still haven't cleaned my apartment, though Percival doesn't seem to care.

Percy and I are lying on the floor, cushioned by a comforter, many blankets and pillows. She's talking on the phone with Olive, the long spiral cord of my landline pulled taut across the entire room.

My furry orphan is nestled at my side as I idle with a too-sweet glass of pink wine. I have my black circle shades on with the illusion of clothes on my body. *I'm a Goetian God in my obscene majesty.*

Percy is my perfect accessory in a peach-pink vinyl dress paired with white go-go boots that I bought her. In fact, everything she's wearing I own, because I've bought her friendship. She's a very useful friend considering how much she vomits about her fucking day-job, which serves aims I say are my own, but they're not. Boris owns me and I pretend he doesn't. *I'm an expert compartmentalizer, remember?*

Percy scowls at me. I hold the glass in the air as she only half-listens as Olive talks about her day. Percy giggles vacantly. *Can she hear my thoughts?*

I take a sip of my wine to clear my throat. "Did she make a joke?" I ask. Percy's nod is stunted. I missed when I lost her trust. *Well, she should've never trusted me anyways. I wouldn't fucking trust me.* I slug the rest of my wine and place the glass next to my side on the hardwood.

Nestling into the downy pillow below my head, I ruffle Diana's fur with my fingers. She's grown healthy and strong. *I'm proud of her.*

She purrs as I pet her and take inventory of what I have to do to make this work.

Percival is mine by choice; she could leave any time, take my gifts and flee, but she won't and I *need* her gossip. Then, the path needs pinning. *Who would know him?* After that, my mimic comes into play — Percy cuts my thoughts in two by knocking her heel-shackle against my foot.

"Liv wants to, like, know if we want to go to a party, or whatever. I guess she, like, *totally* already asked your boyfriend already." Percy makes her joke.

She's been teasing me about Eric more and more lately, which stings, because it's obvious I'm attracted to him. I'm attracted to *all* of them, but why? What can't I see? *What am I not hearing?*

"I'm, like, just kidding!" Percy protests, but she isn't very convincing. "Oh, Liv says there's going to be, like, live music. Totally rad, yeah?"

I nod slowly and reach out to twist a few strands of Percy's hair between my too-thin fingers.

She tilts her head at me, bird-like. "Are you, like, OK?" she asks, hand over the receiver. I open my mouth to say something real, but Percy plucks the sunglasses from my face before I can even utter a single word.

"Listen, I like, totally know something's on your mind. You don't have to tell me, but like, please don't pretend you're OK, or whatever."

Her eyes plead with me as if to say, 'tell me something real for once.' She's perfectly adoring in peach-pink, as still as can be, begging me to open up to her and I can say fucking *nothing. As if she'd ever let me.* She'll just invent new problems that won't ever fucking — something crashes against my window, startling me but not her.

Hesitating, I lick my lower lip. "I just don't want to lose you," I admit without context. *Try, Alex. Please try.*

Percy squints at me, puts the receiver back to her ear and tells Olivia she'll have to call her back. She scoots toward me and lays flat across my chest, making my problems with platonic intimacy even more problematic. She doesn't fucking understand me at all. I wish she could, but she has to speak my language. *She can't.*

I wrap my arms around Percy and hold tight, rousing Diana, who stretches and patters away to nibble her food. The sound of her eating is more deafening than whatever's *still* banging against the fucking window.

"I just don't want to fucking lose you. I'm not the good guy, Percy," I whisper into her sunny hair. "Not of this story, or any story, for that matter." I tell her the truth as whatever empathy I have tries to flick itself back on for her. *You're my first real, true friend. I love you.*

She nods into my chest. "I know," she says in a voice that melts brown around the edges. My heart skips a beat.

35 / ALONE, NEVER

Grasping at normalcy is all I can do to keep my head afloat, and so the party Olive invited us to surfaces like a raft in my sea of tar, murder, filth and bird-shit.

It's in an old warehouse with hundreds of people all laughing, drinking, dancing and basking in the colorful lights. A beautiful woman on the stage sings into a microphone. She has long braided hair in a shock of white. The metal wire that hooks from her nose to her ear jostles as she sings.

I'm spellbound as she fills the room with falsettos and baritones I can feel in my very skin. We lock eyes for a moment; I recognize her, but I can't remember how we met. She smiles at me, as if she feels the same, as if she can see into the bowl where my brain sits. *Is it fate?*

Olive and Percival dance under the thrum of orange lights. Olive is in flared pants with long chains on them, equipped with her token daisy shirt. Percy's peach-pink in vinyl. Eric is in sage and jeans. He wags his brows at the girls as they dance. He abruptly butts in as a joke. The trio laugh. Their beauty is painful for me because I want them all. *I ruin everything I want.*

Eric strolls off to hit on a pretty woman who immediately rejects him. He slides next to a pretty man who also rejects him. *He's hopeless,* I snicker to myself.

I watch my friends as I drink alcohol from a red cup. I'm wearing nothing of note, saying nothing of note, doing nothing of note, and siphoning their essence to catch just one eyeful of their bright lives.

I watch them with a smile, but I'm not here with them.

Even when Percy dances her way toward me and screeches as the woman on stage bewitches us with her voice, I'm not here. I'm somewhere else, but I'm not thinking of my plans, either. I'm not *anywhere*. I'm haunting them and myself. *I have no idea why anymore.*

Giving Percy a weak smile, she tugs me along so I can dance with Eric. He gyrates oafishly toward me, then places his hands on my hips. I rest my head on his chest, yet I feel him sulk as we sway.

"What's wrong, Erica? Strike out again?" I ask into sage fabric. I should end on a laugh to razz him, but I don't. He nods, because he's lonely. *We are lonely creatures, aren't we?*

"Hey, fuck, don't sulk about it. Here, here, let me show you." I grasp his hand and pull him across the dancefloor.

My explanations most likely go in one ear and out the other, but he's trying. His caterpillar brows tell me as much. As I explain that you have to make people comfortable and not just accost them with badgersome flirtations, the camera tilts.

The perspective zooms out as I'm left to watch myself. My life unravels in a million LEDs as I stop subjective time and float outside of my body. I'm not connecting with Eric right now, I'm solving his problem and hoping he'll grasp it by himself. We're not spending time together. I'm handling this like business, when all he wanted was to dance with anyone at all, really. No, that's not true. *He wanted to dance with me because he loves me.*

Traveling back to the present, I'm standing on damp streets as Boris raises his gun. The white-gold explosion at the barrel flickers. My hands come up behind my head. *I'm trying to turn back the clock. Time fights me every step of the way. I fight myself harder.*

I float, defy death and think until the thoughts spill to the ceiling: I don't know why I can't connect, why I use my friends, why I fall in love with all of them and why I can turn off my empathy like killing a lamp. *Is it trauma? I don't feel traumatized, I feel empty.*

I'm hollow inside, of course I'm always alone—Olive snatches my hand and rips me back into my body. Crashing into her, my cup spills on her shirt. She laughs until she's snorting, then tears at my hand again to drag me through the crowd. I have no time to think as she jerks me behind her, no time to plan as she rips my arm from its socket, no time to act as she forces me to run with her for no reason.

She yanks me after her with the gravitas of a fucking pylon driver as we whip around strangers. Wheat fields clip into view as birds fly overhead. *Does she see it too? Does she know?*

"What the *fuck* are you?!" I spit as she flings me to a makeshift bar.

Olive slaps her palm on the plastic table. "Hey buddy, ya got anything wicked sweet and hella strong?" she asks the makeshift bartender.

"Sure thing," the bartender says. "Cream soda with Malibu rum alright?"

Olive nods and digs around in her pocket. As she searches for cash, her tongue sticks out of her mouth. She slaps money on the table. "Gimme two of 'em, and make 'em big, okey dokey?" she says, turns to look at me, then wiggles her thin brows.

As we wait for our drinks, she crosses her arms and stares through me. It's not Percival's magenta obstinance or Eric's eyebrow assessment. *Olive's trying to cobble together what makes me tick.* I laugh sheepishly, running my fingers through my hair.

When the drinks are ready, she snags them in her fists and thrusts one into my hand. I take it. As we drink together, she hitches her hazel eyes over everything I am and everything I'm not. *I'm nobody.*

Olive snatches my wrist with her free hand and twists my arm as it dangles limply in the air. She scans my tattoos as though she could ever translate what no one else dares to.

"Ya got a lotta stories, huh?" she asks.

I pull my arm back. *I don't like this. I don't like this at all.*

Her bright pink curls jostle as she cocks her head. "So why doncha ever talk about 'em?"

I don't know what to do with this fucking question, Liv.

"Are ya worried we won't get it, or somethin'?" she asks, staring up at me like she can see right through me.

When I take a step back, she takes a step forward. "Hmm?" she demands.

Olive's more fucking persistent than Percy and thousands of times more deadly.

"Nobody," I stammer out starstruck, tongue-tied, marble-eyed nothing-syllables. "Nobody would get it. It's—"

Olive nods at my stunted mind-vomit as if she understands, which is *impossible*. I lick my lips, hesitating, but she gives me no ground. Every passing moment features my stomach curdling. Every passing moment is punctuated by her wrinkling nose, until she bounces at me on purpose and grins. *Fine, you fucking tit-demon.*

"I've learned so many *fucking* languages for other people's motherfucking benefit. I can't speak and no one translates, because they're too *fucking* stupid." My truth is a neon bullet I shoot between her eyes while I screw mine shut, prepared to be wounded for the sin of honesty.

After a moment, I peel my lids open and find Olive still very much alive. Orange lights flood over us, people dance nearby, she contemplates while sipping, I stand dumbly and the beautiful woman sings on stage.

"I get it, ya know," she admits, flicking her eyes over my face. "I'm tha same. Nobody listens ta me 'bout nothin'."

I take just one step forward. "What do you mean?" I ask.

She shrugs again. "They all think I'm some kinda kid, ya know? That I'm stupid, or somethin'."

"You're definitely not a fucking kid, Liv." My brows raise as my hand instinctively follows suit. "And you're also pacing yourself, right?" I say, jiggling my nearly empty cup in her direction.

"Yah!" she chirps cheerfully.

"We're all getting fucked-up tonight, and you—" I say, cutting my sentence on a sip, "will have to babysit. Yes?"

She nods and slides her drink across the plastic table near her hip. The music picks up as she digests my face again. "But even Percy does it, ya know? Treats me like I'm stupid or somethin'." She braces her chest, which is a feat. "Thinks I dunno what she's sayin', but I just dunno how to tell her, ya know?"

"You just don't know how to tell her?" I repeat distantly, remorsefully, foreverly as I think on all my fucked-up life choices. Searching my past, peering at my present and boiling under the nothing-star of my nothing-future. *I can only fucking*—Olive tugs my hand.

"Hey, ya did it again." She snorts, clenching my fingers.

"What do you mean by this, Liv?" *A half-smile, a syllable, silence, a noose.*

"You disappeared or somethin'. Doncha know you do it?" Her hazel eyes narrow as I wince. "I do it too. 'Cept I laugh or make a joke, ya know. Pretend I'm here and stuff, cause I'm stuck up here." She points to her pink-colored head.

"Tell me somethin' real," she blurts out. I take a step back, yet she chases me all the same.

Wheeling my head around, I spot an exit and jerk away to leave her and her horrifying questions behind. She nabs me by the belt loop and whips me around with no effort at all.

"C'mon, don't be sucha wimp," she says, shoving me. She even steps on my foot to keep me in place, as if that'd work. *It does, which makes my face flush.*

Scanning Olive's face, I try to find something that makes a lick of sense from all the rotten nonsense I'm made up of. *Might as well placate her with*— "Doncha think 'bout lyin' either, ya big baby."

"*Fine.*" I take a deep, shaky inhale. "I know Percy won't do anything for me, unless I'm groveling or giving her jewelry." Olive gestures with her chin for me to continue. "Even if she *tries* to fucking help, she wants to 'feel my fucking feelings' with me." I spit, yet Olive doesn't seem to mind. "And that won't *fucking* work." My upper lip curls into a sneer. "She can't *fucking* handle them, because she can't even handle her *own* mother*fucking* problems without making more—out of thin air." Snarling, my words drip into native colors. "Like she is bored, so must invent new problem. She doesn't really give a fuck. If she *did*, she'd meet me where I am. I can't explain in *her* way. And it's fucking...selfish."

"It's wicked annoyin', huh?" Olive sputters out. *I can't believe what I'm hearing right now.* If Thomas was a bird whisperer, Olive's a fucking snake charmer.

Ruffling her pink hair with her fingers, she continues. "And Eric acts like he can't do nothin' fer himself, like thinkin' anything, right? Hadda fix his sink the other day. He knows how ta do it!" Her fists are balled up like she wants to fight a man twice her size. A man far away from us. A man dancing oafishly, alone. A man who deserves none of her venom.

Dumbfounded, I ask, "Why don't we tell them? Why can't—why can't we fucking talk?"

Olive lets out a deep sigh, sagging her shoulders. "Dunno. Cause we love 'em," she grumbles. "I don't think we think tha same as them."

I drown myself in liquor at this unacceptable non-answer. *Ah, to be the type who mutes themselves for the comfort of all others. Is that us? Are we really so fucking broken?*

Olive bobs her head to think. "Can I just tell ya when I think stuff?" she asks, burning me with her smile.

When she smiles, I want to fucking smile—and venom doesn't smile for anything less than devilry. But I smile, because she's her, and I'm me.

"Yeah. If I can speak my way, which—"

"Do the picture thingy," she cuts me off. I mouth the words 'picture thingy' and scowl at her.

She snarls. "Yah! Yer pictures, ya know? Stuff on yer wall, yer arms and crap like that."

I raise a brow. "You aren't gonna fucking understand it, Liv," I say honestly. *You'd need a motherfucking encyclopedia on symbology just to—* She snarls at me again. *Incredible.*

"Yeah I will! Stop bein' such a dang dickhead! I'm smarter than ya think," she huffs, hands on her hips. "Smarter than you, anyways." Olive looks at me like she wants to fling me down a flight of stairs. *Maybe she should.*

My expression softens. "*Fine.* I'll trust you to figure me out and I'll let you do whatever you want, say whatever, whenever you wish. I'll do whatever the fuck you want, too. Sound 'rad' to you, you little fucking demon?"

Her smile is an actual supernova. "Yeah! Sounds wicked."

"Wicked," I mock her.

"Yeah. Wicked," she says with a hiss.

"Wicked," I snicker, warmer this time.

"Shut up, ya big, stupid idiot!" she blusters.

"You first, you pint-sized, pixie-stick snuffing tyrant-ass gremlin." I'm far more feral, yet all she can do is grin.

"Hey, buddy. You can eat my whole ass, ya know?" She snorts.

My brows raise. "Holy *shit*, Liv."

This is the moment I fell in love with her. Not infatuation, not lust, not my stupid 'every single one of my friends is attractive' nonsense, nor my 'kindness must be love' bullshit—true love. I buried it for years because she belonged to Percy.

In retrospect, I was (as I've said before) the *only* reason Percy and Olive broke up, because that was the moment she fell in love with me, too. However, as we both don't know how to talk, we took years to admit it.

Funny how that shit works, huh?

"The true measure of a man is not his intelligence or how high he rises in this freak establishment. No, the true measure of a man is this: how quickly can he respond to the needs of others and how much of himself he can give."

— Philip K. Dick. "Our Friends From Frolix 8." 1970.

36 / LAUREN'S POPPIES

The mirth of our earlier party is choked out like I choke out marks at Boris' request. Born for war yet gifted empathy, of course whatever bulbs of normalcy I discover rot in my hands. I can hold onto nothing, least of all my dying psyche and quickly unraveling life.

I sit in the lap of a man I made into a mess, black out and I'm left to stare at the body and my quivering crimson hands. After the usual bird-card, clean-up, journey home and cold shower, I make my way to the park in the sweltering heat to contemplate how much I suck. As the sun boils me in my loud black garments—the mirages of clothes, really—I rest my head in my hand. It's roughly noon.

Sitting on a bench, I gaze at happy families, radiant butterflies that lick across the violent sky and flickering tree-shadows dappled with light. *Maybe that's why Olive magnetizes me.* Her light makes my shade into 'something awesome.' What she finds beneath the roots of it all, well, she'll probably despise just like I fucking do.

I imagine her digging around in my guts with a shovel, ripping out a snake that's swallowed a wax-covered crow and dropping it in disgust with a wet plop.

A cardinal whips past. I notice a woman now sitting beside me on the bench. She cracks open a can of Josta and looks out at the currents of grass that sweep in a gale. I'm momentarily distracted by her enough to inspect her long face, dark skin and shock of white braids. Distracted by beauty, always. *I'm helpless.*

I clear my throat. "You know, that's probably going to fucking kill you," I mumble, sucking on my teeth. She casts a glance to the side of my face, mimics my body language and furrows her brows like mine.

She clears her throat. "You know, that's not your *damned* business, is it?" she huffs, then sits straight up to pour the caffeinated drink down her gullet.

I raise both my brows as she chugs the heart-attack in a can. "Bad day?"

She bumps her fist into her chest, lets out a burp, wipes her mouth and mutters, "Yes," before she hunches forward to knead her temple.

I examine her more closely. *She could fit into my design, I think, but on second thought*— "You were at the party." I gesture from ear to nose. "With the war jewelry and killer pipes."

Her topaz glare annihilates me on the spot. "Excuse me—'war jewelry?'" She makes a stunted sound, shakes her can, tips her head back and downs the rest of her noxious drink.

"I—sorry. I don't know the word in English. Not American," I admit. She cocks a brow at me and peels her laser gaze from my face to settle on the scenery. Even the gauzy clouds are immolated by her severe expression.

Scanning her face, I hesitate. *Beautiful, dressed impeccably, very tall and extremely fucking pissed.* "Do," I mumble, "do you want to talk a—"

"You look strong enough," she says, scours the area and launches her empty drink into a distant trash can with a loud thunk. I wince.

"I—yeah, pretty fucking strong. Short, but..." I sigh, shrug my shoulders and lean forward in unison with her. We lock eyes; I examine her like one would a puzzle, she examines me like one would a maggot.

"Carry something for me," she commands. I'm not used to people belting out orders anymore, but I oblige her, for no other reason than I don't want to go home right now. I don't want to pick apart my chaos. I don't want to make the move I know I have to make for it all to work out.

Truly winning is terrifying.

When she stands and struts forward, I trail in her tall shadow and let it keep the sun from my eyes. As we cut through blades of grass beyond bushels of damp leaves, her deafening silence mutes me. We chart a silent course through oval-shapes in Kelly green and deep turquoise, trickle over a stone bridge that blankets a river and end up on the far end of the park.

She points to a tall cardboard box in front of a car. A car that has a busted fender and massacred window.

"Fuck, what happened?" I blurt out, rounding the vehicle. "Some dickhead ram up your ass?" She nods at my question, her arms crossed. "Shouldn't you call somebody?" I ask, turning to look at her face, but her eyes are glued to the ground. She's trying to force a handful of pebbles to explode by sheer willpower alone. *I know the feeling.*

"Alright," I say, raising my hands. "Alright, yeah, fuck. I will carry box—the box." I wipe my palms on my pants, make my way to the brown heap and stand with my back to it.

"Hoist it up so—" I begin, but the woman's already behind me. I drop down, she hefts the box against my back and we work together to angle it across my shoulder blades.

"I am fucking pack mule now, *lovely.*" I snort, stumbling forward, the weight of it driving me into the pavement. She stalks ahead of me, but I'm far too slow to keep up. Staggering as fast as I can while the box digs into my bony fucking body, sweat pours down the side of my face. Soon I'm drenched, the vinyl of my pants making its way up my actual ass crack.

Stopping to catch my breath, I jerk my head up to search for her. She's standing directly in front of me with a scowl on her face. "H-how much further—"

"You wanted to help? So help," she cuts me off. I make a disgruntled sound and heft forward, outpacing her out of stubbornness, or perhaps she's slowed down for me.

She chuckles behind her hand as she watches me sweat, hiss, grumble and drag about like fucking Atlas if he was a short goth in vinyl.

"You *could* help," I grunt as the box gouges my shoulders.

She chides me, moving to walk backward as she looks down her nose at my sweating face. Her long white braids sway like willow branches.

"I am having too much fun watching you try your best to help a stranger," she says, ending her sentence on a baritone chuckle. I crack a half-grin and follow after her as her smile blooms like a poppy.

We continue on like this for decades, with me stopping every ten minutes to wipe the sweat from my brow and her stopping to watch me with amusement dancing in her eyes.

As she flits up short steps that lead to a simple home lodged between two tall apartment complexes, she chuckles. "My name's Lauren. Lauren Roberts. I did not expect you'd help me, you know..." she trails off as I drift the box down and kneel.

I place it against the building, put my hands to my knees and try to catch my breath. "The fuck is in that thing? A fucking *boulder?!*" I hiss as my legs finally give out and I plant my ass a few feet in front of her steps.

After a few haggard breaths, I look up and find her missing. "Lauren?" I ask. Not receiving a reply, I do the only sensible thing, which is splay myself out on the too-small driveway, close my eyes, let the sun boil me and listen to the birds chirp cheerfully from the single tree on her lawn.

A few moments later, Lauren blocks the sun. I crack one eye open. She's holding two glasses filled with pale purple liquid. "Here," she says, kneels and offers me a glass. "You have earned it."

For a moment, I grimace at her, but relent and take the drink. I tip it to my lips and drink something pastel, floral, light and lovely.

"It's lavender lemonade," she says and takes a mouthful herself.

We sit on the small plot of pavement, roast under the sun, sip our lemonade and don't speak. It's a comfortable, albeit vulnerable, silence.

Lauren plays with a blade of grass, her jaw clenched like she wants to strike like a scorpion, yet doesn't have anyone to sting. I'm bloodless and stewing under the raw sun; I can only offer her a fatigued smile. I'm far more tired than I should be. *Why am I so tired?*

Slowly, then all together quickly, she gathers our cups in one hand and takes me by the shoulder. "Come," she says softly. *"Come,"* Nikolai's voice crackles in my ears. I force a smile as she guides me up her steps.

"What's your name?" Lauren asks as she closes the door behind me. My shoulders scrunch. "I asked, what is your name?" she asks more forcefully this time as she places the cups on a driftwood end table.

"Alexei," I stammer out. "Alex," I correct myself, blues eyes darting across memories of Nikolai that won't let up. I smile weakly as they blind me.

With a raised brow, Lauren moves to stand before me and flicks her finger beneath my chin. She tilts my head up so I'm looking into her eyes, then steps aside. I'm treated to the garden hanging from her walls. Dark ivy winds itself around natural columns, lush orchids dot every crevice, a thousand different sorts of fauna speckle her home and a pair of poppies announces itself in a shock of red near her far window.

I wander toward the plants, hand outstretched. With my lips slightly parted, I point at a white, folded little bushel. "Lily of the valley," she says as she swells with pride. I point at a shock of indigo. "Vanda Orchid." She chuckles. "Or if you're versed in horticulture, simply *V.*"

I hike my thumb toward her door. "And the box?" I ask, my eyes darting across the breathing painting Lauren's turned her home into. The plants swell around us, as if growing in real-time. *Pay attention.*

"A mid-sized, very old petrified tree," she offers with a bemused smirk.

My lips part, about to ask her why she'd want something that wasn't even fucking alive, when the poppy flowers bewitch me. I drift next to them, brushing the petals with my fingers.

"You have whole—a whole fucking rainforest in here." My voice sounds distant in my ears. *She surrounds herself with beauty and I surround myself with mold and madness. We couldn't be more different.*

Lauren stands beside me and crosses her arms. "Well, a home reflects its owner," she says simply as my heart skips a beat. "Alex, would you like to see the rest of them?"

"There's more?!"

On this day, a beautiful songbird saved me from myself by showing me that beauty still lives in the world and that you have to choose it. I couldn't choose it before, but now I'm trying to fight Boris' bullet for just that reason.

I want to choose beauty, Lauren. I really fucking do. I *want* to go back to your place, drink your lemonade and serenade you with my piss-poor guitar skills while you fill the space with real music.

As per the script, Lauren will eventually sing at our parties and I won't understand that I have to invite her to spend time with us, because she's the type who needs to be plucked from the earth.

More honestly, I won't invite her into our garden-party by choice. Everyone I rip from the ground I'll use in some way to either panacea a wound, or as a stepping-stone. *I didn't want to ruin her or her flowers—that's my reasoning.*

The paranoid, realer reason is that I think she sees me for what I really am, which is rotten and worthless. *A home reflects its owner.*

As I drag my feet back over asphalt, framed by a brick wall, lit by the blast of a gun—I'm making you a promise Lauren. If I can defy my fucking fate, I'll take you by the hand, bring you through the blinding lights of your stage, off your pedestal, out of your garden and show you the beautiful parts of my life. *Olive would like that.* I think you two would make great fri— The frames scuttle, the space turns white and my mind-movies wilt.

I'm in a space where nothing can live, nothing can grow, nothing breathes and nothing hurts. My eyes dart over a terminal of sorts. I flick my fingers over cyan, yellow and magenta symbols that twist in the air like mobiles.

I have to go back. I have to—

37 / RED

Time passes, deaths of convenience cascade together, little bird cards scatter across bodies and my antics antagonize news outlets. I spend many nights washing blood from my hands, many mornings listening to a cacophony of pigeons outside my window and spend many afternoons placating my friends. Especially Percy, who cleverly pries. I field her from my life by smothering her in gold gifts. *She takes them and never asks me why, not even once.*

Every day is exactly the same, but today won't be like the others. Today is when the tapestry weaves itself together. Today is when what *must* stop begins to end.

Today, I will learn that sympathy can get done what threats can't. Tonight, I force myself on an indigo platter to spite my least favorite man. Tomorrow, I will become a bishop by courting a real king. After spending enough time on my back to secure the path, the matron of lost boys comes into play and I *will* put the tumor in checkmate with a fistful of toys. *That's the script.*

Operation: Something Awesome is a success. That is, until the chewing-gum piece destroys the daisy, the true king breaks my heart, we live our messy lives and I die because I consent to it. *I'm the villain, I don't get to live.*

If none of that makes sense, don't feel too bad. The play of my mind is for the marvelously mad, not the unimaginative. Only people who've truly struggled will understand. *I'm trying to teach the lost, not comfort the found.*

I wake to the sound of morning-doves cooing, wash myself up and paint the roses of my lips red. The long, selling-point locks in all their faux gold glory come next, then concealer to mask my skin-stories and finally I step into red fabric.

Diana mewls and rubs her face against my hand as I step into tall red shoes. I draw her into my arms, hold her to my chest, and kiss her furry face. She purrs, I breathe, she purrs and I leave to smash fate's family jewels to dust.

What I knew to be Percy's bar is something that those like and unlike me own, but the nature of the one who owns it is *exactly* what I need to find out to make this work.

In burning crimson, I enter and am noticed by the bartender. I raise a hand and wave, princess-like, then walk through a sea of day-drinking people to take my place on a stool.

The bartender is a short, average-looking man with dark hair. He knows that I come in assorted packages, but who he's allied to, I can't exactly say.

"Your usual today?" he asks.

"No, today let's make it count. Moskovskaya, please." I smile as the bartender locks eyes with me. I reach into my loud coat to plop a cool hundred on the counter.

"Are we going to have a problem?" I tap the bill.

He eyes it like a hovering fly as he swirls a rag inside of a dirty glass. Glancing at the other patrons, he says, "We don't have any—"

Another hundred is placed on the bill before us. I click my perfect red nails next to it. He freezes in space. I produce another hundred dollar bill, press my fingers to the trio and steer them across the counter.

He pockets the money, motions with his hand, makes my typical Cosmo and I take it graciously. Poised on a drift of wood in the middle of an ocean of patrons, I drink, he swims about, I look out at the crowd, he paddles somewhere, I finish my drink, he swaps his shift with someone I don't recognize and flashes me four fingers as the waves crash.

I order one more drink, watch the clock and when the time is up, I'm on my feet and parting the human-sea to the ladies room.

A curious sign greets me—out of order—I knock on the door and hear four knocks in return. After four of my own, I'm pulled inside by the very nervous bartender.

"Hello," I say. "You *do* realize that I'm one of them, yes?"

"No. No, you're not," he hiss, checks the door, locks it and drags me into the back of the restroom. With muted amusement, I watch as this man sweats, fusses, pulls at his collar and does everything he can think of not to look me in the eyes.

My mouth tugs into a half-grin. "I am—"

"No, *sir*. You're not. Boris has..." he cuts me off again, then annoyingly trails off. With raised brows I wait for the bartender to finish his sentence. He doesn't and so I produce another hundred, grab his wrist and slap it into his palm.

"Fuck, Jesus Christ—" *He's a nervous little pissant, isn't he?*

"If you don't want to tell me fuck-all, why are you taking my money?" The bartender slumps forward, sighs and takes to leaning against the nearest stall.

"You know why I'm here—" I begin, yet he cuts me off again.

"Listen." He raises his hands. "Alright. Yes. Fuck," he stammers, pulling at his hair. "I'm just supposed to keep an eye on you. Is that what you want? You want to know what he's doing?"

I wrench his mouth shut in record time. "I already *know* what he's *fucking* doing. I don't mother*fucking* care that he watches me like a fucking bug in a dish. I want one thing and one thing *only*, and you're going to answer me honestly, or I'm going to take the knife in my pocket and play around in your fucking guts. Understand?"

My teeth are on edge, my heart pummels my birdcage-ribs and everything is electric from the tips of my toes up to the back of my neck. I enjoy inciting fear in men who've wronged me, even in the smallest of ways. It's a drug. But I won't get what I want if I tear apart my food, not today, not with him, not here.

He nods beneath my claws. Satisfied, I peel my hand from his face and cross my arms. "Who runs this city? What's his name, when does he come here, who does he go home with—tell me everything."

I've rendered the bartender mute. Feeble, he raises up his hands, so I do the only sensible thing and fumble around in my coat pocket for my knife.

Exasperated, I threaten him. "I'm not fucking around. I've gone through too much fucked up shit to get here and you *will* answer my fucking questions, you limp-dicked little пизда—" The rest of my tirade is taken up by provincial Russian, off-brand Spanish and hackneyed English.

He gawks at the knife. *Are we going to fucking do this all day?!*

"W-why?" he asks. I wave my blade. He scrunches against the stall. *I should just kill him out of spite.* "Because I'm interested," I offer.

The bartender squints. "Come again?" he asks.

"I'm interested!" I roar. The knife clearly isn't motivation enough, so I do the only unreasonable thing I know how to: I reach my hand between his thighs while sliding my blade below his chin.

"I'm interested. Is this going through? Are you fucking picking up" —*I could crush him to death at any moment*—"what I'm putting down? God, why the *fuck* are Boris' men so *fucking* stupid?!"

"Interested?" He gulps as I remove my hand from his family jewels. "Right, that. Uh."

I pull the blade away. His hands are still raised. I snort. *I've given this man money, threatened him with death and vaguely molested him for just a handful of simple questions. Do I have to do an interpretative fucking dance?!*

"Well," he starts up, lowering his hands. "Markov Sevastian—new money, old family. You know how it is: dad dies too soon and the golden son steps in." He looks at me sheepishly. "Comes in every Thursday night, right around eleven." He pauses to lick his lips. "Unless you're here." *Silence.*

"He goes home with, uh, I don't know. They're—why do you need—" he stutters. I press my knee into the bartender's groin, drive him into the stall door and seethe.

"I'm going to let you in on a little secret," I say, my mouth pinned to the shell of his ear. "You know all those fucking mental crime scenes that the news just can't fucking shut up about, with the playing cards?" He swallows hard. "With the little birds on them?" I pick at his collar with my blade. "Who do you *think* the little bird is? Why do you *think* Boris wants your eyes on *me*, you fucking moron? Why do *you* think he keeps *me* from his *fucking* owner? Hmm? I'll give you one guess."

"Oh holy shit, please don't kill m—" I cut him off with a tsking sound.

"Then answer me! I gave you my money, you stupid little man! I need to know what type of women he fucking goes home with. I'm not trying to kill him, I'm trying to see." I look up into the bartender's eyes, searching for a marker of sentient life. "How I can get close to him. You know what Boris does, right?"

"Yes," he says solemnly.

I back off, lock eyes with the little pissant and try a fucking appeal to emotions. *Is that enough, fucknozzle?!* "What would you call it?" I ask.

"Evil," he says. "Evil." *No shit! Of course it's fucking evil!*

"I want it to *stop*. The only way to do that is to get someone strong on my side." I take a step forward, he takes one back. Chasing him into the stall, I snatch his jaw and shove him against the porcelain pony.

"Someone more powerful than Boris." *He's loyal enough not to bend immediately to money, violence, or sexual antagonism.* That means he has skin in this game. *Disgusting.*

I take a risk. *Please let basic fucking human decency work.* "Please," I plead, softening my expression and my grasp on his skull. "Tell me *everything* you know about Markov. And please—don't tell Boris."

I've used every trick in the toolkit besides getting on my knees for this guy. *This is fucking exhausting.* I've been planning war for far too long, and every day I don't make a move is one more day Boris gets to press plucked birds into my rotten mold and sell their deaths like fucking Blockbuster video!

"Well, you should've led with that, but...yeah. Yeah, OK. I'll tell you what I know, and—"

I cut him off. "If you tell a soul we had this conversation, I will fucking kill you."

What I learn from the bartender is several things: the first being that every single person's inciting action is different. Some people actually do respond to sympathy, but sadly I've met very fucking few of those. The second being that Markov picks women seemingly at random and shows very little interest in retaining them, which I think is a boon. *It isn't.*

The third being that Boris has apprised Markov of his bird-brained project, but has kept me under wraps. According to everyone else (save my drink-slinging monitor and the cigar-demon) I don't actually exist. *I'm the unnamed blade.*

Boris has worked very hard to keep me a secret. I wonder just how hard and what the power behind that secret really is. That wondering leads to tonight, where I place the variable of myself directly in the thick of Boris' games, surrounded by an armada of men I don't trust and hope beyond all hopes I've learned enough about the king to trick him.

My fucking life depends on it.

38 / INDIGO PLATTER

The wet moon beyond my window greets me as I pull an indigo shirt over my head. Tonight is the night. Tonight I'll win by placing my leash in someone's hands like a noose around their throat. *That's the plan, at least.*

I have to be underestimated; I feed Diana, her dry food clinking in the metal dish. *Then, I have to be good at fucking war;* she nibbles her food and flicks her tail. *Then, I probably have to be good at fucking;* I plod to my room, snatch a Polaroid I've marked with a red floral sticker and stab it into the drywall with a thumbtack.

"But then what happens?" I ask, my hand against my chest. The decades between my human-self and future-machine curdle. *Which part am I meant to play? Who am I, anyways?*

After a pregnant pause, I pluck Moira's blurry Polaroid from the wall and stab her between the flower and cigar. "Diana." I tsk at the feline rolling around on the floor. "Remind me to conscript Vasilisa, hmm?"

She trills and curls into a ball. I stoop, pet her and smile as the decades shiver around me, stars hover dimly beyond my window and I feel faux kismet kiss my cheek.

As the me of the past pulls on the rest of his clothes, bolts through the door, ducks below startled red birds, stumbles down the steps, hails a yellow taxi and hustles to the bar he once thought of as a normal space for normal people, the me of now is exerting pressure. It's a gift from the future. A gift I won't waste to keep a promise that every version of me wants to keep. *Yes, even him.*

We're witnessing one fractured life from three distinct perspectives. My past perspective: a man-made villain playing a hero because vengeance is control. My current perspective: I fight death itself as my life bleeds before my eyes. Your perspective: you've set up camp in my head and appetize my shitty backstory.

There is one *other* perspective here, one you might not know.

The space is yellow. The space is gold. The space is indigo. The space is pink. The space is white. The space.

The still-frames flutter backward in time. We're left with a blistering blue-violet me in a Bratva-owned bar at a closed event, let in by *the bartende*r. I'm certainly not meant to be here right now. Boris had tasked me with more marvelous murdering, which bloodlust always forces me to follow. This time, I've decided to bite the hand that feeds me.

Standing against the backdrop of countless murderers, drug smugglers, human traffickers (and one pain in the ass bartender), I'm nothing but a disheveled welp.

Markov—taller than most men and who dwarfs me by comparison—stands in a muted red suit idling with alcohol, while Boris idles at his side like the tumor he is.

"Who's this?" asks a looming man with a thick mustache. Ignoring him, I wave at Boris, who jerks his head in my direction. The color drains from his face. Markov turns to follow his glance, but he's soon obscured by a fellow in a loud suit.

"If I chirp at you, do you think you'll fucking figure it out?" I mutter to the mustached man, swipe a bottle off the table, steal someone's glass and act untouchable.

The mustached man curses, what I stole is swept from my hands, I'm snatched by the limbs and patted down for weapons. I've brought nothing with me save my winning smile and the one skill I need now more than ever before.

Boris stomps toward me, raises his hand and streams smoke in my face. "Let him go. He's one of us." The other men do a double-take before they drop me.

"Little bird." Boris drifts to my side. "Why are you here? Didn't I give you a job to do?" he asks me with a curious twinkle in his eye.

I offer him a feral half-smile, reach for the alcohol again, pour myself a shot and knock it back. It burns down my throat. "Well, you hung out the meat for me to eat and left me unattended," I hum. "I decided on a bigger kill."

Boris puffs up his feathers. I raise a feline brow, pour another shot and offer it to him. He takes it and knocks it back as Markov—the man, the myth, the legend, the path—strolls our way. Boris takes my arm to sweep me out of orbit and far away from the *one* person who can give me the protection I need to take him out.

"Why are you leading me away from your owner?" I snort. "Worried I'll sink my claws into him?"

"I'm not, little bird," Boris lies, then drags me to a buffet of alcohol. He gestures at a lone Cosmo with a piece of paper under the glass. Plucking the paper free, he grins at it, then waves it in front of my face. *'Hands off' in shitty Cyrillic.*

"Ah, so the bartender told you," I mutter, rolling my eyes.

Boris crumples the paper in his fist as a bemused smile blooms on his pleasant face. "Well, little bird, it's hard to believe someone like you can do what you say you can. It's not *his* fault, really," he offers and places the glass in my hand.

Boris wants a fucking reaction. He wants to gloat and the opportunity to be *gracious*. Instead, I sip my drink and give him absolutely fucking nothing. His face puckers. *Boiling your kettle, am I?*

"Boris," I start up, taking inventory of the men in the room, "wouldn't it be funny if being underestimated was a very good skill? Oh, that's right." I pause, wielding away from him.

I beeline toward Markov, who's preparing to sit down at a table to eat a savory looking stew.

"Little bird," Boris says as his steps quicken after me, casting ash from his cigar with each jag. "Alex—"

"You weren't there when I explained that to Tyr, huh?" Ducking away, I swoop past a tall man who chuckles at me, slaps my shoulders and shoves a vodka bottle into my arms. Abandoning the Cosmo with a clatter, I twist the cap, toss it and pour liquor down my throat without breaking eye contact with Boris.

"Alex—" Boris almost makes it to me, but he's hardly limber. I slide in and out of a poker game, leaving him huffing and angling around human obstacles as I chug more vodka.

"Wouldn't it be funny if I never *needed* to wait my fucking turn for any of this?" I ask over my shoulder, carting the alcohol in my arms. Pausing, I pass it off to a buxom piece of eye-candy who takes it with a giggle. "I love your dress, get it at Saks?" I don't wait for her response.

I've led Boris around in circles. He stops for a moment, places a hand on his hip and raises his voice. "Alex, if you do this—"

"Wouldn't it be funny if you ground me into the dirt because you needed me to think I couldn't ever win without playing the game *your* way?"

Spotting a plate of sweetbread, I snatch a handful, swivel to catch Markov's glance, and shovel food into my mouth. He's watching our game of cat and mouse with a bemused smirk perched above his silver spoon.

"Wouldn't it be funny—" Boris staggers to catch up, I dip through a wall of men and emerge to wipe crumbs off my mouth while he shoots his arm between bodies to swipe at me. "Wouldn't it—" Boris bursts behind me, snags my arm and twirls me in place.

I grin as he squeezes me like I'd pop. "Wouldn't it be funny if the barbed-wire bitch you built an entire fucking empire on just slithered out of the cage, punched through the glass and broke your fucking camera?"

The tea-kettle isn't rattling. It's empty. "*Aleksandra,*" Boris warns me, but freezes when Markov clears his throat.

"Boris, who's this?" Markov asks in awkward Russian, as twice-laundered as my own.

"Like I told you, sir." Boris frees me and straightens his shirt. "Born into the group, but you know how it is." He chuckles and blows smoke rings. "There are just so many grunts." *He needs to be appear gracious and he can't fucking kill me. I can win.*

"Well, if he knows you enough to drag you in circles, then he's important enough to meet, isn't he?" Markov asks, sipping a glass of rosé. Boris says nothing as Markov's arresting gaze locks him in place.

When Markov turns his attention to me, I look away to contemplate my angle. His glance pulls me back without any effort. *Fuck. However I play this, I can't get caught in that stare. It'll fucking kill me.* It's actually his mouth that'll do me in.

I approach the table, Markov gestures, sips his wine and I sit. Boris surveys us with thinly-veiled disdain, then floats somewhere within earshot, but not close enough for me to use him as leverage. *Asshole.*

I pick up a fork in front of me and wag it against my palm as Markov pours me a glass of pink wine. *I'm nervous.* This man has real power and it's *exactly* what I need to peel Boris off my fucking shoe forever.

"I'm happy to finally meet you face to face—sorry, fuck. That's stupid, wait. Let me start again." And start again, I do. Many different times, in fact, and in several borrowed languages.

Markov (who is infinitely more patient than I imagined) watches me with Boris' heady amusement and none of his vitriol. I fidget and babble, he quirks a grin and asks me questions, we drink too much wine, end up moving to beer and I tell him far too much.

He's dangerously easy to talk to. It helps that he's criminally beautiful, if a bit lonely, surrounded by older, seedier men of the even older, seedier world. He's a different breed; almost as ill-prepared as I am, it seems.

"And you're the one who took them all down? All of them?" Markov asks, followed by a gulp of beer.

"I am," I reply with a modest smirk, taking a sip of my piss-water.

Markov rubs his hand over his mouth in disbelief and scans my face as I fidget with a fork.

"Do you doubt me?" I ask, now fueled on liquid courage. I turn around to look for the man I like least. "Boris," I croon, wagging the fork to my palm.

Markov watches me with a bemused grin. When Boris floats to the table, we both sour momentarily and exchange a glance. *We both hate him.* This is why Boris ground me to dust and had me fucking monitored—we're allies against him and he *knows* it.

"Little bird calls and I answer. I do like to hear you sing," Boris says with a hesitant laugh. He reaches for my idle mug of beer, which I let him take. He rests his other hand on the table as he inhales it. I lean back in my seat, flick a glance to Boris' hand and tap the fork on the table's edge like a metronome.

I lock eyes with Markov. "Care to regale Mark here with my fables?" I say to Boris as a feral half-smile splits my pretty face.

"Mark..." Markov is baffled *and* fascinated. *Good.* My arrogance came on like a hand-grenade and Boris just so happened to pull the fucking pin.

"Aha, of course—" In an instant, I jam my fork into the meat of Boris' hand, breaking the beer-thief's words in half. *I've wanted to stab him for fucking years.* Now, with a supportive audience, I *can. Fucker!*

Markov, rendered mute in all this, should be angry. He should be furious with me for stabbing someone far above my paygrade. However, he isn't furious—he's laughing. Boris pours out broken swears in every single color and Markov just *laughs.*

"If you remember what I'm capable of, you'll remember not to fucking call me 'little bird' ever again," I snarl, much to Markov's amusement.

"Is it a nickname?" Markov asks, ignoring Boris altogether—who's attempting to remove the fork but only succeeding at screaming.

"No," I muse, claiming my mug of beer to sip. "It's a genre. Or, you know what? Never mind, I don't think you'd get it."

Boris unlodges the fork from his hand, spurting blood across the tablecloth. As he curses and bleeds, he attracts a garrison of men to hum, fret and fuss over him. I suffer absolutely *no* consequences, for I now have the ear of a king gifted his father's empire. A king who has *no love* for men like Boris. A king who will protect me as I surgically remove the tumor from both our lives, one leeching tendril at a time.

Markov Sevastian—you are, to this day, my most painful regret.

I regret Anastasya's needless death, feeding Yanov and Vasily to Boris' wolves and leaving Nikolai behind. I regret so many things that you haven't seen come to pass yet. It's a script I have to live, but want more than fucking *anything* to break.

But falling in love with Markov, someone with a silver spoon for a fucking *brain* and patently incapable of real love? This regret wounds me across oceans of lifetimes. It's the damage, the errored code, the broken feathered-nothing. Every little data failure comes from you, Markov.

I should've never let you consume me in record time like you polished off that bottle of beautiful rose-colored wine.

39 / MOVE

It's been roughly two years since leashing myself to Markov as a guard dog, yet he hasn't figured out that I'm steering him with every step, every flick of the brow and roll of the tongue to lap a language he fumbles at and I intoxicate with. At least, that's what I tell myself as I scrutinize his stack of soggy chips and cheese.

The men around us flutter at the speed of light in our local front, we sip sweet drinks, smoke in gray, cluck about war against a cancerous dickhead and I catch myself avoiding his dangerous smile.

Markov inhales a drink *I'd* even find too sweet to stomach and grins at me behind his glass. "You've got a plan then, hmm?" he mutters between sips. "I've seen you set your pins." *Liquor makes him stupid, talkative and far too charming.*

I half-smile, eye the shadowy figures that move past us and peel piddling flecks off my damp napkin. "Yes, but we're going to have to be very fucking careful, or the cherry'll pop."

He nods at me with a heady smirk, only vaguely paying attention as he waves at the bartender to deliver more alcohol.

"Mark, why do you always get fucking tanked—" He cuts me off with a burning chuckle, leaving me with a head full of static, sitting perfectly still save my paper-plying.

Alcohol bottles glint and pass like lights, the men around us converge and change lanes and I crash my gaze to the wall to avoid Markov's traffic-stopping smirk.

I dare to look at his face. He moistens his lower lip. Sadly, I haven't figured out that I'm falling in love with him. Worst of all, he already knows.

Markov savors a mouthful of cheap nachos before speaking. "You've taken care of my current obstacle then, little bird?"

Genre bristling up my spine, I quirk an acidic smile, pry a soggy chip free and muffle my words via chewing. "We're back to business then?" I wipe my mouth with the back of my hand. "Yeah. Yes."

Markov's handsome face dons a grin fit for devils. He points at my cheek. "You have a bit of cheese." He reaches to rid me of the offending yellow sludge. I lean back before he has a chance, siphon Sprite through my straw and dart my eyes around at the men in our midst.

"You're awfully nervous." He places his elbows on the table and folds his hands to peer down at me behind them. If he could see my innards he'd find them twisted in knots. *Fuck. Stop staring at me like that, you prick.*

"We can't— You can't act like this, here," I admit, hesitating. "Elsewhere, maybe. Not here."

He looks at me like art, meat, conquest and every other word I've known men to look at me like. "I'm like this with everyone." He chuckles, not quite getting what I'm saying.

I pry free another chunk of cheese-covered chips, finagle the mound into my mouth and aggressively gnash. "That's," I begin, pausing to chew, "a fucking problem." I lick my finger, which he lingers on.

He raises his brows and inspects my face like a nearly-extinct insect he wants to stab, frame and place on his mantle. The look fades to something tender; green leaves, small fish, sunrise. It changes again and I'm a distant nothing-thing. *I can't read him and that means I'm in big fucking trouble.*

This is a fucking mistake. I want to bolt. *I need to get the fuck out of here.* But I'm stuck on the way Markov's mouth makes me feel. I want his head between my thighs. *I'm hopeless and something else that I'm not aware of until it's far too late to save my very soul.*

"If we're 'very fucking careful.'" He smirks, raises his palm for effect, then digs into his chips.

I reach for my tattered napkin and wipe cheese from my mouth. "Are you careful with *many* people?"

Looking momentarily hurt, Markov lapses into a hazy smirk, wraps his fist around the neck of a vodka bottle and takes a swig. "Would it hurt you if I was?" He chuckles, then downs most of the liquor as a flock of birds bolt past the window behind him. My heart leaps into my throat.

"Yes," I admit, sit back in my seat, cross my arms and stare off into the emptied bar. *How is it we've been here for fucking hours, when we've only just sat down?* "I don't fuck around, Mark—"

"I understand, but we must keep up appearances, right?" he interrupts me, takes another gluttonous swig, licks his lips and my fate is sealed. *He wants to destroy me and I want to let him.*

After hours of verbal foreplay, we're in a seedy hotel far off the beaten path, naked, with his hand inside of me. He curls his fingers, says nothing about what I don't have, I arch off the bed, make obscene sounds and I should know it's all over for me.

I should know I'm done for as he pulls away, climbs on top of me and pushes my thighs apart. I should know he's nothing but poison as he jacks my legs up, buries himself in my guts and churns an ache so potent it would nuke a star if it could. My atoms burst with every touch. There's no shelter from it because he won't even let me fucking *breathe.*

He twists his tongue past my lips and holds me in place as I gasp into the mouth of certain death. I've been pinned like a bug and all I can do is wallow in it. *Stop. Please, God, don't fall into this.*

If I could erase this fucking point in time, I would. I've tried, but all I'm left with is repeatedly watching them fuck like sex is oxygen. They breathe together and it's a farce. Every pulse between my thighs is primed on nothing but lies. Past-me is turned with his face in the sheets and he smiles about it because he's *fucking* stupid.

"Блядь," I moan as Markov fucks me hard enough to leave me a quaking, groaning, shaking mess on sweat-soaked sheets. *I'm no longer in control.* He leashed me and made me into nothing. What's worse is I want him to do it forever and ever and ever and ever until the day I turn to *fucking* dust.

He kisses my shoulder like he means it. He trails his hands to the small of my back—I've moved the eyes here to stare at men like a cosmic joke—but he avoids them. He snatches my hips, slams against me and curses out as he fills me with what I think love is.

I knew love once. I turn as he removes himself and I kiss him in the way I would've kissed Nikolai. *I knew it once.* It's a slow, meandering, butterflied, giving-thing. *I knew it once.* I'm giving him romance yet his hands don't wrap around my tattoo-lined shoulders like I *need* him to.

Meaning this kiss, I open my eyes to look at him, but he's already broken away. *Why won't he hold me? What are we?*

Markov pushes me back against the bed. I stupidly laugh. I bargain playfulness while he aims to distract me with his mouth. He scoops my ass in his hands, angles my hips and breaths hot against my slick thighs. I'm a painting spilling his ink as he dives his tongue inside of me. If I could've seen his expression, I'd have known there was no art here.

There was no romance. There was only an addiction. Being loved is what I needed. Markov will never give me this. *He doesn't know how.*

When I reach the end, higher than heaven, more sinful than any devil and shaking like a leaf, he pulls back. He leaves no kisses on my newly-inked hips, marked by Lauren's poppies. Markov wipes his mouth with his hand and with eyes deader than anything I've ever seen in my life, takes to fumbling for a drink of water.

At this moment, I'm just something curious and new: a man with a cunt who can kill with a piece of string. I'm the weapon hidden from him for years: a shiny blue blade who's fascinating, amusing, entertaining, very useful and *too* willing. Lust is not love. Lust isn't even my friend. It's something else. *Can you hear it?*

Curled up in the sheets, I see him clearly for one bullet of a moment as the bloodless fucking vampire he is. He's hunting for a cigarette. My mouth opens but no words stream free as I stare at the patterned wallpaper near his blurry head.

Maybe he's not that much of a romantic. I bargain with myself that this isn't just lust. *Maybe that's just how he gets after sex.* I lie because I want Markov to be Nikolai's second coming, but no man will ever measure up. Men born as men seldom live up to their potential, especially ones born with privilege thick enough to blind them like a silver spoon in the fucking eye.

I smile weakly, reach for my cigarettes, light one up, jam it between my teeth and observe Actual Satan. "This is…dangerous," I offer, letting smoke wither from my mouth to the ceiling.

It spirals like a swirling nebula, flits through an open window, I flick my gaze to it, catch a pigeon battering the glass and frown. Pulling the sheets onto my lap, I give Markov a hesitant smile. His glance is dead-eyed nothing.

I reach across the vast expanse between us to give him an unlit cigarette.

"Yes, but I'm sure we can handle it." Markov regurgitates a limp line and takes the offering.

"Can you?" I ask, looking him over like he's a potentially feral beast as smoke orbits my face.

Markov smirks, sits forward, runs his fingers over my spine, skips over the eyes on my back and grasps my side to reel me closer. Facing him, I glare through his head at the shifting wallpaper with my cigarette dangling from my lips.

"Don't make me regret giving you things." I breathe out a warning of smoke in his pretty face. *It's a threat.*

"It's just a cigarette." Markov takes it literally. I search for any sign that he understands as he looks around for a lighter he doesn't have to hunt for.

He's giving me nothing. "God, you're fucking ignorant," I offer, leaning to tap ash into a pink yarrow ashtray near the window sill. "And you're avoiding it."

"Avoiding what?" Markov asks, rummaging through an end-table with a potted plant on it. He jerks open the drawer, toppling the plant, which makes him curse.

"The genre…There's a reason I'm here, and I do what I do, so I'm asking you not to make me regret giving you—" Markov plucks the cigarette from between my lips, steals my words with a kiss and dissolves me on the spot.

I am nothing but a prey animal and I can't even see it.

40 / VASILISA IN SNEAKERS

There's just one last playing piece I need to claw my way to vengeance. Dangerously obsessive, I've spent years trying to ensnare my Moira mimic and yet she'd escaped me at every turn. A curious rabbit, I'd half given up trying to cut her into Vasilisa's shape, that is until Markov and I took to our front to discuss business and she'd found herself foraging where she shouldn't.

A bird flicks through the air beside us as we walk, which makes me bump into Markov's back. I'm dwarfed by his shadow as he smiles at me, the door opens and I notice a familiar model/actress sipping her beer. With an insidious smirk, I thank my cosmic meddler and fall in line behind the handsome man who holds my leash.

Watch me smile and imagine I rule the world. Watch me be none the wiser about all I've lost. Watch me die by bullet in real-time because I'm an arrogant fuckhead who can't help but be led around by my crotch.

The disheveled would-be debutante turns, big brown eyes narrowing to slits. Grinning, I arch a brow. *Of course she'll remember me.* All she does is inhale her beer. *Maybe not.*

Boris makes a too-loud joke in Russian about Moira that I can't translate, but do *not* find fucking funny. Markov slaps my shoulder, startling me. I smile weakly, then gesture with my chin at Moira Angela Darling.

Markov flicks his gaze to Boris' stupid face, then leans closer to me and points at her vaguely. "Vasilisa, hmm?" he asks with a charming smile. We make a play of visually appetizing a woman I assume neither of us want. *My mistake.*

"We could give her a necklace," I offer, raising both my brows. "Or a noose, or a shoe." This makes Markov chuckle, but not in the way I expect.

"What?" I ask.

He shrugs his shoulders, looks off to the side and then says a phrase I should've known was true. "I'd give her a necklace."

"Careful, you sound just like our favorite tumor," I chide him, catching his vacant expression. "Not for me. I'm too fucking busy with baubles, bullets and bullshit," I mutter.

Markov's hand is still on my shoulder. "Why not?" he asks. We exchange glances. *Is he fucking kidding me right now? He needs to take this shit seriously.* Markov may have money, muscle and status, but Boris is the old guard and he's not about to give up his stranglehold willingly. He still has power and he *still* has this place, which is far more important than even I know. I flick my gaze to Boris' face. He winks at me.

Markov breaks my concentration by leaning far too close to me. "Don't tell me you've flown the coop entirely, little bird," he half-asks. "Or are you in your nesting phase? I thought that was only for—"

My expression flattens, but that isn't what stopped his sentence short. My gun is drawn and pointed at his crotch. I nudge his junk with the barrel. He sighs as if all this is just some terribly boring inconvenience.

"Careful, little bird. Wouldn't want to mortally wound your meal ticket," he warns, adding a wink to put me at ease.

I pull my gun away, sit forward to tuck it into the back of my pants, he moves his arm away and I'm left scowling like a chastised child. *Is that how he thinks I see him?* It isn't. *Wasn't that the plan?* It was.

Markov knocks back a shot, entertains one of our accessories' jokes and then, while several idiots laugh hysterically, leans to whisper in my ear something sinful that makes me forget I'm angry with him. Smiling, I look toward the door and ignore the leash he metaphorically places around my neck.

Moira, who's been glaring at us the entire time, inhales her beer and tries to stifle a thunderous burp. She fails. Markov and his minions grow quiet as I snicker to myself.

"Um...sorry..." she says, obviously not sorry at all. Buffering a yawn with her hand, she stretches, then swivels on her barstool. She's preparing to leave. *I can't let her.*

I bolt out of my seat, Markov looks at me, rests his hands in his lap and finally seems to be fucking paying attention. He meets Moira's gaze, who gawks at us. He narrows his eyes. *What, is he fucking jealous? Too drunk to pick up my plans?* Probably. *Asshole.*

When I stand and fix my shirt, Markov resumes talking to his in-bred arsenal of idiots. One of them slams their fist on the table, the other men cheer, I roll my eyes and make my way to the would-be debutante.

I slide onto the stool next to Moira. *I hope she remembers me, camouflage and all.* I've gone to Rosalin's as a man playing at being a woman, as a man, as a drunk, as a panhandler, as a faux-drunk 'model,' and yet—judging by her body language—she doesn't remember me. *Fucking how?!*

I rest my elbow on the bar, place my heavy head in my hand and flash her a cheeky smile. "You know, you're awfully clever to be working as a dishwasher. Or was it a waitress? Or was it a singer? A model, actress?"

"E-excuse me? Um…" Moira shirks away as I roll my eyes like Percival might. *She's impossible.*

"You've got a hairnet stuffed in your purse. I tried to flag you down earlier. Plus, we've already—"

She cuts me off. "Ah, um…yeah. Yeah, well clever don't mean shit…"

"Sure it does," I reply with a Cheshire smile and order the same beer she's having. I'm trying to reestablish familiarity, but she's not making it easy. *She never fucking does.* Once my beer arrives after far too many minutes of a disgruntled Moira glaring at me, I play my fingers over the glass rim.

I quirk a smile, take a sip of the piss water and speak. "See, a girl like you could get whatever she wanted. If she was clever. You really don't rememb—"

"You…really think so?" Moira cuts me off again, as though she only knows how to wait her turn to speak.

"I know so. You think I got to where I am with just brute strength alone? Fuck no." I take another sip. "There are a lot of ways to get ahead. Some more obvious than others."

Her eyes hitch over my face as she dissects me. *I can't believe she doesn't even—* I catch sight of her gripping her purse and put the pieces together. *She thinks I'm hitting on her. Fucking lovely.*

I mean business, not pleasure, you dizzy idiot. Sadly, my current business is murder and it comes across despite my best efforts. "I mean, you already know what we do. It's obvious. You're pretty bright, which is why you were going to get the hell out of dodge before I sat next to you. And why your hand is desperately clutching your bag more tightly than I'd handle someone's throat," I say, ending on a quaint chuckle.

"You're…an arrogant little dog, aren't you?" She spits with a sneer. I laugh nervously, but she ignores it, intent on finding me insidious.

"Yes, yes I am. But you already knew that, didn't you?" *I'm not here to fuck with you, Moira. Work with me here.* Instead, she shuffles off the stool to make a break for it. *Fucking shit!*

"Wait, you seriously don't—" Moira jabs her hand into her bag, pulls out her pepper-spray, presses her finger down and maces me directly in the eyes.

"You stupid idiot… I'm trying to—" My companions erupt into hysterical laughter as I dig at my raw, burning eyeballs.

Curses dribble from my lips as my eyes water. "Give you a fucking opportunity that we've already—" I snatch the hem of my shirt and viciously scrub my face with the fabric. "Fuck! It burns!" I fall to my knees; a consummate agent of war felled by none other than Moira Angela Darling and her fucking two inch spray-can of watery battery-acid.

Markov's laughter booms over the others, I screw my eyes shut and try to calm myself down, but his baritone digs into old wounds that haven't healed.

"Эh, брат…hairnet woman with bad taste in beer took you down. With bottle of girl spray," pipes up one of our 'brothers' in English.

"Aha! Girl spray. Like perfume!" snorts a buffoon with slicked hair. "Who is big strong man now, eh?" He teases me as I wrestle with momentary blindness.

I'm going to fucking kill all of you. "It's mace you fucking inbred piece of—fuck," I struggle, batting at some invisible pepper-demon that fucking jizzed in my goddamn eyes. I thought being kicked in the ribs was bad, but I taste this shit in my mouth, its traveled up my nose and my sinuses are fucking *screaming* at me.

Through my bleary gaze, I catch Moira smirking. She kneels in front of me and tries to take my hand. I slap her claws away and grind my palm into my searing sockets.

"You…really weren't trying to start something, were you?" she asks, prying at my fingers.

"No, I'm not that kind of guy. And we've already had this—not every guy is trying to get into your pants or sell you on the black fucking market, you know…" I grimace, ripping away from her.

"Let me see," she paws at my face.

"No," I say, jerking away, but she's dauntless. She sidles closer and digs her nails between my fingers.

"Let me see," she repeats, more insistent this time, peeling back my digits one by one.

"Fine." I let her inspect the damage. Through my blurry vision, I see her face contort in pity. *I hate when people pity me. I fucking hate it.*

Moira cackles. "You poor, poor boy." Her laughter is velvet-rich, her hands are warm and pretty soon I join her laughter despite the fact that she mortally wounded me. Every few laughs, Moira snorts and I can't help but wish in hindsight that I'd never made this play. I should've just let her live her fucking life instead of dragging her into mine. *Nothing grows here.*

As I grind my knuckles into my eyes, Markov walks toward us. Moira stops laughing when she notices, but I don't.

"Alex, you'll be fine, but flush out your eyes." Markov pauses for a moment. "As for you..." Moira skitters away from him, a smear of colors.

"Calm down. I'm not going to hurt you—don't mace me. Please." I can't see anything, so I can only assume she's raised her weapon at him. "Please, miss," Markov continues. And that's when the sting became a cataclysm that smashes up my sinuses like a full frontal lobotomy.

"What the fuck do I do!?" I half-sob, digging at my eyes again.

"Wash your eyes out, like I said. Go to the sink," Markov repeats.

My heart leaps into my throat—*there's no fucking way I'm leaving her alone with them.* "Fuck no, Boris is going to try to take her away in his child-abductor minivan..."

"She'll be fine. She'll be fine," Markov reassures me, and for a fraction of a moment I doubt him, if only because his earlier joke tugs at me. *I should've trusted my instincts. It wasn't a joke.*

Grunting, I stand using Markov's shoulder for leverage. Skittering away, I half-walk, half stumble toward the bar. The bartender doesn't miss a beat and points toward the bathroom. I wave him away, vaguely feeling along the wall to hobble to the door, kick it open and tumble inside.

I fumble for the faucet, find the knob, swivel it, dunk my hands into the cool water and splash my face. It does nothing to stop the stinging, but with every subsequent wash, the headache subsides. Pretty soon, I can spot the hazy afterimage of my face.

"I look like I fell out of a fucking ugly tree and hit every goddamn branch." I scoff, scoop water into my hand, then rinse my eyes.

"*Fuck.*" Sneering, I wash as much of the caustic shit out of my eyes as possible and stumble around for paper towels. Squinting, red-eyed, I slap my hand against a taupe metal holster on the wall. It's hollow. "Fuck!"

Jerking open a stall door, it slaps back on its hinges and tries to shut itself. Irritated, I rip it open, dive for the toilet paper and wrench out ribbons of paper-guts. Dabbing my eyes, I take to squatting on the closed toilet seat.

"What's your name?" *I hear Markov.* My ears prick up. I lean to listen more closely, still pressing the toilet paper to my burning face.

"Moira."

"I'm Mark." The way he says his name stops me dead in my tracks. I stand, drop the roll of paper to the floor, don't bother cleaning up anything and stalk to the front of the bathroom.

With rage burning my insides worse than this mace bullshit, I snatch the door handle, but then stop short. Screwing my eyes shut, I slide my forehead against the wood.

I pride myself on being observant, but my greatest weakness is society. I have no idea how their world works until it's too late. I pull the handle but don't open it fully. *My second greatest weakness is confusing sex with love.* I step through the doorway and compose myself. *My third greatest weakness is getting lost in Markov's smile.* I pull on my mask and saunter toward the both of them. *I have so many fucking weaknesses.*

"Russian?"

"Yes. You?"

"Hey, Markov...I think I got it all out," I interrupt them on purpose, rubbing my eyes while I speak. "The acoustics in this place are fucking awful. I could literally hear Boris scratching his balls from the stall—" My words are ignored. *That fucking prick.*

"Puerto Rican," Moira says, turning to look at me briefly before she gestures with her chin "Him?"

"Annoying, but very useful," Markov replies, barely looking at me. I grow quiet, my expression flickers, dies and I'm muzzled. *Useful is all I am, huh?*

"Them?" Moira gestures at our 'brothers.'

"Idiots." Markov smokes and scrutinizes the young woman I'd turn into a princess if she'd let me. *I bet he offered her a cigarette.* He always offers them to beautiful women. He only ever takes mine from me. My eyes burn from more than just Moira's mace.

She has absolutely no idea that he's looking at her like a conquest. I glare down at Markov. He has no idea that I'm looking at him like he's a maggot.

"Al, you look like you got high and fell down a flight of stairs..." Markov says, a bemused grin tugging at his perfect mouth.

"Thanks, Mark—" I spit, but he cuts me off.

"And like you got hit by a truck," Markov continues as I narrow my stinging eyes.

"Thanks, Mark—"

"And like you fell out of an ugly tree and smacked every branch on the way dow—"

"Alright! Markov. Shut the fuck up already!" I warn him. *I don't have time for his bullshit right now.*

I round Moira's side and kneel on the balls of my feet. *I'm going to fucking try this again and if it doesn't work now, it never fucking will.*

"I'm surprised you don't even remember me," I mumble, blinking wildly. "We've already—"

"I'm not becoming one of those 'red light' girls, rollin' on their backs for money," she cuts me off. My heart sinks in my chest. *Is that what she thinks I'm trying to do?*

Momentarily stunned, my brows knit together, my lips part and Markov charts the atlas of my face for a literal century as I hold the conversation hostage with my awkward silence.

The one thing that I wasn't counting on when it came to stepping into who I really am was how women would treat me differently. How they'd view me as a certain kind of threat, when I wasn't and will not ever fucking be that. *I'm not Boris.* That job has to be fucking picked, and with who I run with, it never *can* be. Not with us, not with them, not with him. We don't have a Virginia here. *I would never.*

"I'm not asking that of you." I hold up my hands in protest. "I never would. We're just going outside. You can mace me if I'm lying."

I meet Markov's gaze with just one eye, the other pulled too taut and watering again.

"Just what are you planning, little bird?" Markov asks, heady and enthralled. *Oh, so I guess he really wasn't fucking listening. Dickhead.*

"Something awesome. God, how many times have I asked you to stop calling me th—" *And how many times do I have to tell you shit until you fucking listen?!*

"Should…we wait up for you?" Markov takes a drag from his cigarette, blows smoke and licks his lower lip. *I'm supposed to be angry at him, but I can't be.* He leashed me with his tongue and all he had to do was blow smoke. *I hate him.*

"Naw. Later," I blurt out.

"How late?" Markov asks.

"Not too late," I reply, grimacing, but not from physical pain.

Markov smiles, and just like that, he turns his back to us, walks away and sits down on a stool with the trio of fools. Soon, they stammer away again, gesture wildly, Markov laughs and the table is slammed with someone's fist.

I don't belong in their world.

I don't understand how they're so comfortable sitting next to each other, knowing just who and what they are. Knowing just what Boris is and how much pain he's caused. My expression falls. *I don't belong in any world.* The ceiling cracks above me like that murderous night so many years ago. I pretend I don't notice it, but I do.

Standing, I reach out my hand for Vasilisa in sneakers and wait for her to make her move. She hesitates, but takes to me all the same. I help her up, then flick my baby blues back to look at Markov, but he's facing away. *When he's not looking at me, it feels like he forgets I exist.* Maybe I don't exist, unless my life's recorded. *Maybe I don't exist at all.*

Moira glances between the two of us as I lead her toward the door.

"What?" I ask over my shoulder.

"You two are doing a horrible job," Moira says, shuffling after me. I hold the door for her, now ruminating horrifically. *If it's obvious to her, that means I'm in danger. We're in danger.* This is so much worse than Percy's reluctance with Olive. It comes with a side of organized fucking crime and the rules of men born as men. *It means death.*

For a glitch of a moment, Moira spots a potted plant near the sidewalk and reaches for a rose that's not meant to exist. The moment fades into piddling data failures, the flower fades and she's left walking behind me as I shove my hand in my pockets. *Past-me ignores the moment, imagining he's merely tired. He's been tired for months and never asks why. Care to take a guess?*

The me that's still fighting Boris' bullet (and fate itself) wishes I could warn him, because past-me has no fucking idea what horrors await him. *All I can do is try to stop my own murder. Sounds impossible, doesn't it?*

Dragging quicksand limbs from Boris' fated gun, I rewind in a smear and I'm right back where I started. A dry smile splits my face. *You can't really defy fate, can you?* I always die, staring down this fucking barrel, because the problem *isn't* lack of trying on my part. The problem is that I'm helpless, yet no one ever tries to rescue me. *I wish they would.*

"What do you mean by that?" I ask her after far too long. I dig into my pockets for my cigarettes, pull one free, finagle my lighter and I'm about to light up when she speaks again.

"It's written all over your stupid faces. Those dumb shits will figure it out at some point," Moira says, spots my cancer sticks and waves at me. "Give me a cigarette."

"You didn't let Markov give you one," I say with a sour smile. "He always offers when he smokes." *But only if you're a beautiful woman.*

"He's intimidating," she replies, fidgeting with her bag's strap.

"And I'm not?" I ask, cigarette dangling between my lips.

"No. You're short, carajito. A pissed-off little dog," Moira says, fairly harmlessly. I raise my brows, crack a grin and light the cigarette. I inhale a few times, pluck it from my mouth, then pass it to her.

She takes the cigarette from me, glares at it for a few moments, then puts it between her lips. "Aren't you worried?" she asks while foolishly inhaling. She sputters, coughs, then wheezes in that order. *Pure tobacco, not those shitty American menthols.*

I raise my brows and shake my head. "Definitely. Uncharted territory," I say, tipping my head. "See, clever. Like I said—"

"That's not what I meant," she says. She gestures the next sentence as she speaks. "You know."

"What?" Squinting, I can't quite grasp what she means.

"The news. What they're saying. You know," Moira explains as best she can, made worse by all the coughing.

"Ah. Ah, right. *That* news." My words hang heavy in the air as I break away on instinct.

I don't need to shove you into every single frame of my personal life, but suffice it to say, I get tested. By sheer dumb luck, I've avoided what so many people like me can't and won't be able to, by design. *We don't matter and we did it to ourselves.* It's all over the news and that's what *they* say. As always, America acts like it's better than the rest of the world, while 'normal' Americans treat the different like a disease.

'Normal' people can be so fucking cruel.

I bristle, cross the street without waiting for the light to change, briefly look up at the hum of the city against the blanket of stars, and cup my cigarette. I relight it, orange and yellow dancing across my face. *I want to burn her eye out with this fucking thing for just that one fucked-up question, but I don't. She's ignorant, not evil.*

"Um…hey! Wait!" Moira yells, shuffling after me on destroyed sneakers. She flicks her mostly neglected cigarette to the street, and for a moment I hear the sound of breaking glass. *I must be tired.*

The glitch scuttles, time rewinds and the sound never comes to pass. *Pull back on the input, it's too much. We can't crack the path here.*

"What about that opportunity?" Moira pleads with me as she rounds my side. I don't know how to explain her disrespect and I don't think she'd get it, anyways. I've spent years trying to form a connection with her. *Years.*

"I don't know what's wrong with the world right now. People, I guess," I say with a hiss, ignoring her question in favor of plodding ahead.

"What—" she starts up.

I cut her off again. "I've been nothing but kind to you, you maced me, you're prying at shit you shouldn't, and we've already—" Rage curdles in my mouth. Rage that's not necessarily her fault. Rage that belongs directed at a man who keeps chaining me by the throat with his mouth. Rage that belongs directed at a man who made a business off of *my* blueprint. Rage at so many things that are much more deadly than she'll ever be.

I halt when we hit the sidewalk, the smoke around my head filtering the light above. I turn to face Moira, resting my back against the post, arms crossed, eyes narrowed.

"It could happen! Hey! I don't know where you've been. I'm just—" Her words trail off into the air like the smoke peeling from my mouth.

"All I'm trying to do is help you," I mutter.

"And I have no idea what you're trying to help me with!" she shoots back at me. *Oh, so you want to play war, bitch? Fine. Bring it.*

"And where, exactly, do you think I've been?" I wave my cigarette in the air as I speak, punctuating my sentence.

"You're projecting! I didn't mean it like that!" Moira throws up her hands in defense and every idea I ever had to take her under my broken wing dissolves at once.

"Maybe I am, but..." I start up, shifting to lean my head against the pole behind me. I raise my chin, flick cigarette ash to the street and prime my smile on razor-wire and *death.*

"Seguro que no eres un tremenda sata?" Moira gawks at the familiar words in my unfamiliar mouth. Illiterate for most of my life, but like I said, brilliant. A *brilliant,* pissed off, paranoid, beaten little dog who barks violently because nobody will pick his broken, trampled body off the fucking bloodstained streets.

"Fuck you, pendejo!" Moira shouts, raising her hand to slap me. *I want her to hit me, so all I do is smile.*

"No. How do you like insinuating fucking questions? Makes you feel like shit, huh?" I hiss, looking down my chin at the only person capable of my worst flavor of war, yet I almost gave up on her. All for an ignorant question. *An ignorant question that kills people like me every single day.*

"Enough of this. You're not worth the fucking effort." Turning to leave, I almost end it. *It could've ended here and it probably should've.*

"I was going to give you a way to get that bar. The bar we were just in. Like some fucking..." I spit my cigarette onto the sidewalk as I stalk away. "Fairy godmother bullshit, but you're just not clever enough."

"No. Hey..." Moira pleads, stumbling after me.

"I don't want to see you here again. And I don't want to get us in trouble," I say over my shoulder, looking around for a taxi.

"You'd get in trouble? With your boss?" Moira asks stupidly.

I twist my head—then turn my entire body—to look at her. Long brown hair, big beautiful eyes, beautiful skin, misery, loneliness, fatigue, flight, fear and desperation. *I need someone like her and she needs anyone but me.*

"He *is* my boss." I grimace. "So keep your big mouth shut, or I will shut it for you. And you just lost a longtime fucking customer."

"E-excuse me?" Moira stammers out.

I pull my flat palm across my face. "I wanted you to be the one to run the bar." My exasperated hair-pulling begins. "I go to Rosalin's every Tuesday and Thursday. I have for the past two years. Best pizza I've had in my entire life. I don't expect you to remember everybody, but we've had this fucking conversation before, Moira." I sigh, holding up my hand.

Moira crawls her memories, stares through me, at me, around me, over me and then at the inside of her skull. She blinks wildly when she finds what she's looking for, then jams her eyes shut. "Damn it..."

An opportunity, strictly business. Bad tourist shirt. An obnoxious blond guy. *This* obnoxious guy. All guys are obnoxious—I'm watching her expression and filling in the blanks. *It's a learned skill.*

"You're smart, but you're just going through the motions. You also seem mostly fucking miserable." I sigh.

"You've...been spying on me?!"

"It's my job to be very, very, very observant. Plus, Boris took a liking to you—which you don't remember—and I had to pull him away, which you also don't remember." The years tick on, shit happens and we forget. She forgets more than most. *I forget and convince myself I don't.*

"I don't date gangsters," Moira protests. My shoulders sag under the weight of pulling Vasilisa from her fucking carriage.

"You sure about that?" Silence. "Don't come back here," I say, yet again trying to cut her free from my trap.

"Alright."

"I don't want to see you here ever again."

But I did find her in my trap every night for the next month, standing at that corner with a bag over her shoulder, the strap clutched in her hands, watching as I entered the bar with Markov and the trio of idiots.

Sometimes it rained and she still stood there watching, waiting and hoping for something more. Sometimes I'd bring a girl on my arm to keep up appearances, as Markov said. Sometimes I'd bring no one. Sometimes I'd look at her, sometimes I didn't.

It's mid-day, months later. The light's low; however, it's too early for baubles, bullets and bullshit. We'd shown up early for coffee, just the two of us—not a date. *We don't get to have those.* I've only had one date in my entire fucking life.

Hovering at Markov's side as we plod through the snow, I chart his cheek and smile, yet he's not looking at me. He's noticing the dark-haired would-be debutante, princess, caught-rabbit and so many other symbols I've hoisted on her. Standing in the snow, she watches us. Soaked and cold in a thin coat, I notice her shiver.

Sucking my teeth, I break away from Markov and stalk to Moira. "Hey," I mutter. I look at anything other than her face, which happens to be a flock of geese above our heads.

"Hi," she replies to me, likesome avoiding my eyes.

"Why..." Moira chatters, blue-lipped. "Why did you want me to have the bar?" *That's a very dangerous question.* I flick my eyes back to Markov, who nods at me from across the street. I hold my breath for a moment, twist my brows, nod back, then look into Moira's eyes.

"Boris has it now. I don't like him. Neither does Mark, but we can't do much about it. He's dumb. And a man," I offer, rocking back on my heels as snow dusts my mustard-colored beanie.

"Yeah?" Moira stares through me, trying to coax the words free.

I lock eyes with Markov, who raises a palm. I nod again, chew on the words and continue. "He took an interest in you. You're beautiful and very clever. At least, I had hoped."

Moira scans my face for the flecks of a frozen plot. This is when I knew I'd made the right decision—she's the missing piece. A gust of wind whips through her dark hair and frames her widening eyes. She sees the forest and the trees through the snow and my cold blue stare.

Moira steels herself. "What do I need to do?"

"Dress the part. Use what you have. Get him to sign it over," I reply, wincing as the cold wind bites my cheeks.

"You act like it's the easiest thing in the world. Do I have to, you know?" Moira asks, gesturing with her hands as she had months ago.

I weigh my answer with a wry smile. "No, he's a lightweight. Just get him drunk and make a show of it." I pause. "I'd do it if he swung that way. I also can't use that trick on any of them. They know how I operate, and it'd end badly," I admit, playing my hand a bit too much, but Markov isn't within earshot. *He already knows, anyways.*

"He can't protect you?" Moira gestures at Markov.

My brows twist as I look off to the far left. A cardinal hops on the pavement and cocks its head to stare at me. Turning my attention back to Moira, I wince. "You...don't know a lot about where we come from, do you?" I ask softly, then look back at the bird, but it's gone.

"No..." she admits, freeing bits of snow from her dark curls.

I inhale sharply. "In many parts of the world, if you're like me, you're either in a certain job, you keep it under wraps, or escape. Sometimes all three at different times," I say in my token accent. "Shit like this doesn't fly. We'd be too obvious if he played favorites any more than he already is. My leash is already very, very long."

"Oh…" Moira says, glancing at my face. I've gutted myself in a cup full of snowy scant syllables and she has no fucking idea. *I hate this.*

"So, are you going to try?" I ask.

"I…don't even know you. Why are you doing this?" Moira asks, teeth chattering.

"Why have you been standing in this same spot for weeks?" I sigh, shift my weight and stare at a piece of flapping paper on top of a trash can.

How the fuck do you explain a life like mine to literally anybody at all? Let alone my goals, where I've come from, and why I need Boris to fucking suffer in the most convoluted way imaginable? *There's no simple, easy answer.*

"I'm desperate. I need him crippled in any way I can."

The nearby trees jostle with bodies. I drag my eyes to them, spotting nothing but a murder of crows. I'm immediately, irrevocably, foreverly unsettled as my heart jitters faster than Percy rambles.

"But why?" Moira persists, cold air sweeping her skin.

"The minivan joke after you maced me…wasn't just a joke." *It sweeps mine all the same.* "I've come a long, long fucking way. I can't pull the con again and I need…" *My silence is deafening because the concept is deafening.* That's the script. That's the plot. That's the thing unsaid in the future of futures. That's the core of black-watered trauma that will lead me to look a gun dead in the face and decide to let it blow me away.

The pregnant pause yields only when my voice cracks. "I need it to *stop.*" My yellow beanie has found its way in my hands. I piddle its edge uselessly like the damp napkins of old. *A nervous habit.*

"So…you're going to use me to get it done," Moira says flatly.

"Yes. Yes. I am. And I'm not giving you another option."

Moira scans my face. A cacophony of birdsong drags my bloodshot eyes to rest on the trees again. *The crows are all gone.* My hat-fidgeting stops as my heart does. *Something's terribly wrong with me.*

"You know too much. I'm using it as leverage," I admit, meeting her eyes again. A sharp smile quirks my too-slim face as she sees me for what I *really* am: *vengeance and nothing more.*

"So that's how it is." She sneers as my heart starts beating again.

"That's how it is," I parrot her, dead-eyed while everything hurts. *Why?*

"You're ruthless," she snarls over birdsong. The crows have returned. *They're loud as fuck. Doesn't she hear them?*

Markov finally deigns to cross the street and join us. He scuttles avians in his wake, as well as an aggressive taxi driver, who he shuts down with a mere glance. *About fucking time.*

"You don't know the half of it," I add, my teeth chattering. I pull the beanie over Moira's head with a smirk.

"Ah! Hey..." she protests with a slight smile on her face. *They're screaming now. Can she really not fucking hear them?*

"You're cold. I don't need it. But I do need to meet with you later."

Markov looks between us, a very ugly scarf framing his very handsome face as I witness the gears turning in his very blockheaded skull.

"Your boyfriend is, uh, blackmailing me." Moira chuckles, pulling the hat snugly over her damp brown curls.

"He's not my..." Markov dares to fucking breathe such a thing. I watch his lip quirk, scrutinize every micro-expression, but can't tell if we're playing the game of appearances or not. *If we aren't, he's fucking dead.*

I look away, zip up my jacket and fumble around in my coat. "To-morrow, here," I say to Moira through the fabric, tucking a piece of paper into her pocket.

I turn to leave, look back just once, and I'm off with Markov trailing behind me, plodding oafishly after vibrant, fragile war. A war he seems to like whipping into a frenzy with his tongue, but will ignore at any other fucking time. *Bodies on a line. My body on a line, but he's face down in my trench, sucking up all my fucking blood. There are consequences, idiot.* I shiver.

My frozen exterior is the perfect symbol for what I'm now doing, which is icing Markov out. We round to the small coffee shop, walk by cooing pigeons, he holds the door for me and I let other caffeine-fiends pass inside before I enter.

He asks me a question, which I ignore. We order coffee. I pay for myself, though he offers. We're not staying, even though he wants to. While our drinks are prepared, I acknowledge Markov for a moment. "I'm stepping out for a cigarette."

"Alright. I'll grab the coffee and meet you outside."

My hand in my pocket, fumbling for my cigarettes, I head up the sidewalk and just keep walking. I don't stop until I'm back at my flat. Yuen greets me, birds twitter by his trash cans, I order dumplings, pay too much for them, snag a few boxes under my arm and stalk up my steps.

The warmth of my home bathes my face, I close the door behind me, set the boxes on the coffee table and make a tsking noise to summon Diana. She knocks over a pizza box from Rosalin's, stretching toward me. Scooping her into my arms, I smile. It's a distant thing, like I've lost something in the crow-filled trees. *Have I?*

I nuzzle my frozen face into her fur, feeling her purr against my ribs. This fuzzy orphan gives me unconditional love, which is what I need. Not control, not war, not a path to fake heroism. Yet, it's also the one thing I'll always run from. When you're truly happy, you have something to lose, don't you? It's terrifying to win after a life spent losing. How terrifying can it be and what's terror for a man like me? Listen carefully.

Can you hear it?

41 / TEETH ON EDGE

Markov loves expensive vehicles, rare drinks, expensive clothes and rare objects. Anything that holds his attention for longer than a handful of moments is liable to set his teeth on edge, especially if it routinely surprises him.

I'm a rare object that he drinks with in his expensive vehicle to celebrate perfect victory before he drinks me down to the last drop. A rare bird, the rarest of birds—a bauble, a trinket, a jewel. *Marble-eyed, yarn-haired nothing*, yet he kisses me like I'm worth something. *Am I, truly?*

"That's one down." I shove my words into his mouth with my tongue. He tilts my chin as he kisses me, trails his hands to my obnoxious tourist t-shirt, slides his flat palm down my stomach, unzips my fly, wrestles my pants past my thighs and cups my sex. This isn't love but I want it to be. *I would give anything for it to be.* A crackling sound distracts me.

I fight through it to speak. "Did you like when I blew his brains all over the fucking w—" He steals my words by slipping his fingers inside me. As he feeds on my mouth, I grind myself into his palm.

"Ah," My moan sounds strange in my ears. It's too dark, thin and hollow in the middle. *Something's wrong.*

He chuckles against my lips, turns me into heat, blinding nuclear summers, fluorescent rose-wine and nothing *should* hurt. But it does. *Something hurts, but what, exactly?*

"It always sets my teeth on edge, little bird," he mutters against my neck. Something flits against my ear when my label leaves his lips. I pull back slightly, but Markov takes that moment to tug me forward and tangle his tongue past my teeth. My brows twist as he coaxes foreign gasps from my guts, my heart flutters and I try to hold onto how this feels. *This is love, isn't it? Please, let this be love.*

The orange glow of a streetlamp bathes me and muddies my blood-stained cheek in an umber smear. With lust-shut eyes, I feel it move leech-like as my skin crawls. Instantly, I stare at the shadow as it morphs in plain sight, but Markov *won't* slow down. I mumble into his mouth, he obscures the shadow, it writhes, my eyes close and his hand feels like the pure energy of two God-like souls melding in perfect spiritual synchronicity as angels weep and I— *Stop.*

He licks a long line up my jaw, tasting the war on me—a useful war, a useful tool. Birdsong splits my skull as he devours my mouth; a useful mutt who thinks no human thoughts, feels no real pain, kills only for pleasure, has no real conscience, a snake, a symbol, a little bird, a manipulator, indigo-war, violet violence, little fish in fists, a victim, a victim, a tape, a victim, a worthless nothing-nobody with a nothing-soul who deserves no love and will *never be a hero.*

Markov churns my guts, I jerk away to break his spell, the shadow beyond the window twists and I stare at it, horrified.

"Never be a hero," says nothing. Nothing at all.

I place my hands on his shoulders. "Markov." My hands frame his face. "Markov, stop." He keeps kissing me, I keep lapsing into divine heat, but there's a *sound* in my ear, the shadows keep moving, my thoughts are too loud and something is *fucking wrong.*

Markov grins into my throat. "You're so wet," is all he says, which makes me freeze in place. *Immediately, I feel the cold hand of death carving at my insides.* He rips his shirt over his head, then drags me into the back seat, biting at my lips as the windows shake.

"I love watching you work," he chirps in my ear. My eyes shoot open, two blue dots in twin white lakes, blood-shot and frenetic.

Markov peels the slacks off of my body. I freeze like a prey animal. My heart beats out of my chest, my thoughts paint my eyelids and I have the distinct feeling—in this warm vehicle, safe from the murder I just committed, safe from Boris, safe—that I'm in mortal *fucking* danger.

"Markov," I whimper, lying prostrate in his back seat as he hovers over my corpse. *I've started hacking away at Boris' supply lines, I've conscripted Vasilisa in sneakers, but something's wrong, he's not stopping to let me catch my breath and my brain feels like it's spilling all over the fucking seats.* I twist my head and feel the wetness of mortality slick my cheek. *Help me.*

Markov grips my thigh and raises it like a wing. I snatch his wrist in my fist, grit my teeth and hiss. "I said. Stop."

He looks down at me with pity, which I hate. His expression shifts, he becomes unreadable, then his features blur like acetone on paint. Markov sits back, hand to the smear of his mouth, the other in his lap and quite simply sighs at me.

"Little bird," he begins, "what's the matter?" My eyes dart frantically. "Isn't this what you need? Isn't fucking war and fucking what you're good at?" His last sentence bullets my hand under the seat to rip free my gun.

Markov's met with the barrel, which makes him sober up, but not enough to put his fucking features back on. "What do you want, Alex?" he asks. I can feel him staring at my half-naked body like *I'm* the confusing creature in this fucking car, speaking fucked up nonsense without any mother*fucking* eyes!

I flick off the safety. "What do **you** want, Mark?!" I roar and *feel* him look at me like I'm some lost, stupid, confused little girl. It's the same *feeling* Tyr gave me so long ago and I don't know what the *fuck* I did to deserve it! A bird flies by the window. I shrink back in horror, gun shaking in my grasp.

He raises his hands. "Where are you right now?" he asks, mimicking Olive's *entire voice* with his actual throat and nothing-lips.

Cornered and terrified, I jack my back against the car door. Squaring my shoulders, my gun is pointed directly at his blurry face. He doesn't even fucking flinch.

"Time is a tricky little minx. One assumes it charts on a straight path, plodding ever forward and leaving our bodies in its wake with each shivering decade. I'm—" says nothing. A swarm of blue locusts shatters the window, scatters glass, I scream and wake up in my bed.

I'm clothed in something soft, sitting in oceans of sheets. Markov— with his face back on—is at my side, drinking a beer and playing with Diana. She mewls at him, boxes with his hands and I can do nothing but gawk.

"W-what happened?" I dribble out, slack-jawed. Markov knits his brows together, takes a swig of his beer and ruffles Diana's ears.

He gives me pity. *No appetizing, no objectifying, no flirting. Pity.* "Alex, I need you to do something for me," he says sternly. He's never stern with me, my leash is long, he's stern and he's never stern and— I stumble off the bed, doe-legged, flap against the wall and feel my insides rot.

Something's breaking, I'm— "Alex," he catches my attention with a whistle that comes out like a Wood Thrush's cry. I rear my ghost-white face to meet that disgusting sound, but *now* I'm staring down the barrel of a gun placed between my fucking eyes. **Boris' fated gun.**

Time is a tricky minx— "Alex, focus," Markov says in Tyr's voice. A long line of tears chart a river down my cheek. Past-me doesn't know what's happening at this moment and as we look at this together, I can only offer you three explanations.

One: the constant trauma has finally burst through my bones, melted my muscles, geared up a gene and I've lost my *fucking* mind. Two: future-me is exerting so much pressure he's ripping up the very fabric of reality.

Or, three: it's both, actually. All of this is just a mass of piddling data failures that ravage a man who kept it together for so many years, and now that his success is within reach, he can't handle winning even just one thing for once in his pathetic, fucked up, tortured little life.

Disheveled and haggard, past-me stares at his hands and sees the blood he's spilled crawling up his wrists, alive, slithering, famished.

"There is punishment for every crime, though it can sometimes take a bit of time," says nothing. *Who the fuck is speaking?!*

Horrified, past-me stares at the fluid air as it fills with something-words from an unseen mouth. A flock of scream-cry human-bird-bleats drips murderously to chase the letters away.

Pale as a sheet, memories tear through him in sticky ephemerality: mint-nurse, enemies, brothers in arms, specters, ghouls, ghosts, phantoms, stream-screaming human-limbed avians. *Sickness.*

He bolts to the bathroom, scrubs the nothing from his flesh with a torrent of water, Markov rounds behind him to drink his beer and watches him with—*No. No, it can't be. He never fucking felt it.*

I see through time the thing that glimmers darkly in Markov's pale green eyes. I see the thing that I erased to make him easier to hate, because anger lets me *live*. It was there, and despite all my inner screeching, *I can see it now.*

I can see it when Markov places his hand to the back of my head and runs his fingers through my short bleached locks. I can see it as I watch myself brace against the toilet to puke bile—a stomach full of absolutely *fucking* nothing. I can see it as he places the beer on the counter and kneels behind me to place his shaking hand to my bony, tattooed back.

He presses his face to my neck as I relive the cataclysms I only ever summon to kickstart the war of survival. *It's killing me.*

The real Markov—not the villain I constructed—can do nothing but hold me as his beautiful mouth quivers against my broken, shaking bird-body, because my terror terrifies even him.

Markov spends the night and we don't fuck but the heat between my legs is scalding. He holds me not like glass, not like a weapon, not like a piece of meat, not like I'm leashed by the throat. He holds me like

Nikolai would, kisses my brow and nestles me to his chest.

Feeling finally safe, I drift off to sleep, but it's a fitful one with no finality. The night's spent pleading with my fucking brain to turn the screaming birds off and stop the searing sensation of my crotch. *It doesn't obey me because nothing ever fucking does.*

When I can no longer force sleep, I wrestle out of bed in the middle of the night and see the plans on my wall are in a neat little pile in a box on the floor. *Markov left me. The haunted home of my body was too much to bear.*

I rub the sleep from my eyes, then walk bloodlessly toward that plain, terrifying box. On top of it is a note, scribbled out in piss-poor Cyrillic.

I pick it up and hold it between my fingers, mouthing the words out loud.

"Alex, I need you to do something for me." Markov's voice rings in my ears as I read, then begin to pace. "When this is all over, promise me something."

I kneel at once, leafing through the chaos in cardboard, one-handed. "You have to promise, little bird. Please." I pick through what's coming to pass, what I've worked so hard to achieve: vengeance, retributive justice, bastardized freedom, 'Something Awesome.'

I pull out Boris' cherry Polaroid. Hunched on the balls of my feet, I stare as it blows wet dollops of smoke into the air. My very normal reaction is to scrutinize it again, see-sawing between a note and a picture. *My brilliant mind can't fathom how truly sick it is, as no truly sick mind ever can. Not even a brilliant one.*

"When this is all over." I mull my lower lip between my teeth. "Leave." My eye twitches. "Leave the business. Leave it all behind. I can't come with you. But I'll help you leave. When it's over, walk away. You can't be a king, little bird. It will kill you."

A knock on my door startles me. I drop the note to the floor. It drifts, nestles itself on top of a million little broken symbols, I crush Boris' smoking Polaroid, jam it into the box, pick the box up, hear another knock and shove the heap of trauma beneath my bed.

Making my way to the door, Diana trails after me, weaving between my ankles. I open the door, peek through and in that moment the prior events erase in a flurry of shadow.

As we witness this together, notice my expression: a blank void where my mind resets. I will never remember that note, not until much later. *It's survival.*

I will never remember how kind Markov had been in this moment, just like how I'll never remember how kind he was despite what he'll eventually do to me. *I will never remember what we felt for each other.* I will only ever remember vengeance, as it's the only thing I can hold onto in this space between the toxic caverns of my skull. *That's the script.*

This is why the future of futures is made of rot: I'm rotten. Everything terrible that humanity faces with the clouds between its thighs will always be my fault, because of what I am. *It's all my fault, really.*

I'm met with Moira's beautiful face. Her eyes crinkle as she smiles. "Hello, darling, can I come in?" Her tone is foreign to my ears. I crack a dry smile, opening the door regardless. Her hair is long and lovely, she's wearing a beautiful indigo velvet slip dress and her heels are taller than anything I've ever owned.

I whistle. "You look *very* fucking clever." I chuckle. Moira steps through my door, heels clicking on hardwood.

I shut it behind her as she stoops to dote on the feline. "Oh, she's absolutely precious." She giggles. "What's her name, darling?" she asks, pulling my cat into her arms.

"I could ask you the same thing, *darling*," I say with a snort. "Diana," I add, then circle my playing piece like a shark, which curiously makes her beam with pride.

Moira chuckles behind her hand like a proper villainess. "I'm working on a clever angle, angel. I've been brushing up on my acting." She pauses. "Say, what's the matter, dear?" she asks, holding up the cat who lovingly licks her nose.

"What do you mean?" I ask.

"You look positively dreadful," she offers, passing Diana into my arms, who digs her claws into my shirt as though that alone can bring me back.

"As though you haven't slept in months." Moira makes pigeon sounds.

My lips part but I don't know what to say. I feel it, but I'm lost.

I just don't— "I don't know, Moi. Ah, anyways," I blurt out, swiping my face with the back of my hand. "Tell me what angle you're working at and let's see if we can't speed it up." I chuckle, making my way to my bedroom.

I want to show her what I've been working on.

"Huh." I look over my naked pock-marked wall and swivel around as the cat makes bread out of my shirt. "Fucking weird. Anyways."

Moira clicks after me, raising a feline brow. "Dear, you seem scattered."

"I am. I am. We're…" The windows shake. "We're almost there, Moira Angela Darling. Let's talk. I want to make sure you know how this has to play out. Because—"

"You need him crippled in any way you can," Moira offers with a beautiful smirk, "because you're desperate."

I nod slowly, Moira smiles weakly, Diana purrs warmly and I feel like I've lost something *acutely* important.

This is why the fated bullet hits its mark. This is why Boris always wins. I blame everything else, but this was *always* here. A thing born, a thing unmade, a thing that makes and remakes itself to survive, a thing that never speaks itself, a thing that begs to be rescued, a thing of avian screams, a victim, a tragedy, a contradiction, a hero, a villain playing hero.

Help, police, stop, murder.

I brush my nose against my cat's head, who holds on for dear life as my new partner in crime spots madness in my eyes and internally vows to protect me, but if Olivia couldn't pull it off, she certainly can't either. Percy never knew where to start, did she? Eric, for all his warmth, is feeble in this, too. What about Lauren? Well, she's far too clever to bother. *Markov fails to save me the way I always need him to. He will never not fail.*

Olivia, I'm sorry. I'm so fucking sorry, princess. I'm dead. I'm lying in the streets with Boris' smoking gun and every single atom in every timeline explodes to push back the clock.

I try again, blood flows back into my dead body and we know why I'm never the hero. *I'm too fucking broken* and— "I'm sorry," I say from past-me's quivering mouth. *What?*

Moira tilts her head to the side and looks at me with something I never earned from her: true empathy.

She shakes her head. "For what, darling?"

"For using you." I rescue myself, squeezed between the panes of madness *and* impossible superpowers I have no concept of.

Moira chuckles behind her hand. "Oh, dear... Well, I'll just have to use you back then, hmm?"

I cock a half-smile, unsure of everything, looking at a woman who is somehow unsure of nothing. "Promise?" I ask as Diana vibrates in my arms.

Moira giggles behind her hand, clicks forward, then raises her arm to present a pinky. "Promise, pet."

We link fingers and a pact is made that spans lifetimes and dimensions. A pact I imagine is nothing but manipulation, because I can never imagine anyone willingly helping me do anything at all. *I'm worthless.*

"Now, why don't you sit with me and explain more? Tell me of your life, tell me of all these," she says, gesturing gracefully at the wall, "quite complicated plans."

"I don't know where the papers went, but it's all up here," I reply, tapping my temple. "Like...a computer." These words are foreign, from another time, one this version of me doesn't understand.

Moira's smile smears. She takes me by the arm to turn me to face the wall with her. She rests her head on my shoulder.

"Don't lose yourself, Alex. Focus."

"What?" I flick my gaze to Moira but she merely stifles a yawn.

"Oh, I didn't say anything," she mumbles while stretching. "So, are you going to fill me in, or will I have to pin you like a Polaroid?"

Moira's mouth moves, Diana purrs, my lips part in reply, but the phone rings off its hook in mere moments.

I look down. Diana isn't in my arms. Confused, I stumble toward the mint-colored beacon and pick it up with a shaking hand.

"Darling, darling, I think this can really work!" Moira says. With the receiver perched at my ear, I glance outside and see the sun setting. *Time is a tricky little minx and I've lost her again.*

I suffer to laugh, pull my mask on and pretend I'm not as sick as a dog. "Tell me everything."

Moira makes a play at quirky villainy, filling me in on her progress. Thankfully, I remember some of it, but not nearly enough.

You may be wondering how I recover from this, what happens when you lose time, see birds where none exist, hear things that aren't real and phase in and out of reality on two fronts.

Let's just say regaining control is gradual and sometimes it takes an inciting action to piece it all together. One's mind can be sick beyond reason and you can still walk through life, unaware for a time. But it never lasts. Worst of all, sometimes it kills you in the end.

Against all odds, I'm trying to choose life this time around. I want to return to you, Olive. I want to wrap my arms around you, kiss your lips and turn your cheeks pinker than your hair. I want to listen to you talk and drift off to sleep with your meandering lullabies.

Olive, please. I need you. Please, help me stop this. Please.

42 / PINK STAR

Someone with fluorescent pink hair rides through the streets of New York on a mustard-colored scooter. Their smile shines bright against a sea of chaotic scents, sensations, colors and conversations. Life is beautiful for Olivia, because she chooses to see it that way. The spies of hard-won living creep the corners of her eyes, her malaise always tucked behind her ear to hold, to keep, to remember. But *never* choose.

She bustles down my street, past Yuen's shop and parks near the trash bins. Pulling the helmet from her head, her unruly pink curls spring free, she locks her scooter to the railing, tucks her headgear under her arm and clops up my steps to knock on the door.

I'm a heap of snapped nothing-twigs bundled in a robe, legs splayed to the hardwood, crouched in my room, staring at nothing, pulling fake things from the air and pinning them with nothing into the nothing-wall of my nothing-life. *I lost the script.*

I crack a taut smile, ignoring Olive's nothing-knocking until she hops to the window and screeches through the wall of glass I'm stuck behind.

"Hey, buddy! Open the heck up!"

A bird bangs at my window as I break apart on the floor like wax and float to the ceiling. Olive screeches again. Noticing her pink hair, I take to standing. Compartmentalizing my rot, I stumble to the window and crack it open.

My smile is a mad, distant brushstroke as the floodlights blind, the blue door opens, my insides bleed out on old linen and my soul finally drifts into the afterlife. *Men like to imagine they've murdered me. Maybe they did. Maybe I'm already fucking dead.*

Olive's gap-toothed smile breaks the spell. She opens her eyes wide, gives me several blinks, then cocks her head to the side.

"Ya look like shit." She snorts like a piglet.

My thinness, faded scars, missing piece and rot-inked-skin makes me self-conscious. The robe is pulled taut over my bag of bones as I float a hand to scrape through my dirty hair.

She wrinkles her nose. "Percy's been tryina call you, she got worried," Olive mutters, then does something impossible. She jacks the window open fully and wriggles inside, but only manages to get partway through before getting stuck on her giant fucking tits.

"Aw, balls," she grunts, tongue sticking out as she teeters, shoes stupidly scraping the bricks outside.

With my one last atom of energy, I stretch out a shaky hand and help her through, pulling her body to my chest as she chortles.

"Heck yeah, we did it!" She's as bright as a pink star. *And just as lovely.*

"Percy..." I test her name in my mouth. "Was worried about me?" Bloodless, I stare at magnetic pink as she stares *through* me.

Olive grimaces at my matted hair. "Oh," she says plainly, as if seeing what I can't, which is *exactly* what she's doing.

Pushing past my comfort zone, she gets as close to my face as she can, grills my mind-fucked head, then takes my hand. *Gravity kicks on all at once.*

She weighs me down from the stars above, tethered and tied to this one point in space, then drifts me in a circle. I'm a mobile, a set of broken novas that hang limply around the orbit of her bright pink star.

"H-how can you live like this?" she asks, gawking at the space around me. *Sparse-nothing, bare-tree furniture and—* "Gross," she mutters and kicks the air. A stack of invisible pizza boxes flicks into view and clatters to the floor.

"Oh, *what*?" She twists around to glare at my bedroom wall. *A wall of nothing, with holes, push-pins and—* "What's this crap?" she asks, pulling the daisy Polaroid free from the plaster.

As quiet as the dead, I scour the room and spot a cardboard box laying sideways on the floor, busted open like a carcass with the fallen bodies of me and mine seeping into the wood. *Gray ink, smeared deaths, oblivion.*

Betamax tapes rest between all the piddling pictures, which makes me step back. *I don't remember taking these back with me.* My gaze drags over their spines. Spotting the name of the corpse I was, I press my hand to my mouth and let loose terrible tears.

"Al, hey. Al. *Alex!*" Olive shouts, snatches my arm, then drags me across the room. "What the heck's goin' on with you?"

I glance at her, say nothing and cry about nothing she can see.

Olive tilts her head, hazel eyes drilling holes in my brutalized walls, as if she blames the very paint itself. I pull away from her, wrapping the robe around my frail, bloodless, muted body. *I don't know what's happening. I don't know what I need. We're so close and yet I can't fucking make it happen. I can't make it to the finish line.*

She must know I'm useless, because she leaves. *She hates me.*

I'm left standing alone in my room as Diana paws at the air on my bed. Bursting apart at the seams, I think Olive's left me forever. *She hears my thoughts and hates me—I'd hate me. I hate me.*

When Olive returns, I'm standing in the same spot, chewing at my fingernails. She tears at my arm, contorts my wrist and plants an orange translucent bottle in my palm. "Here, ya big stupid idiot!"

I gawk at the bottle, turn it in the air, shake it and grimace at her.

Olive grimaces right back. "Fer sleep!" she shouts.

Bottle in hand, my body is spun around in shifting space-time. I watch a ghost of myself staring right back at—*Fuck.*

The gun goes off, I die, wind back, I live and witness my old self staring at me. He *sees* me. This never happened. The timeline is diverging already. *Did—did she hear me?!*

"Hey, buddy!" Olive turns past-me around, pries me from a vision of my death, drags me into the kitchen, yanks open my fridge door, snatches a half-filled bottle of Sprite and shoves it into my hand. "Take one, take a nap, then maybe we'll do somethin', I dunno."

I blink furiously. "What?"

"Gosh yer fuckin' thick," Olive grumbles. "Take. One. And. Go. Tha. Fuck. Ta. Sleep. And. Then. We're. Gonna. Maybe. Do. Somethin'. You—"

"Alright, alright, fuck." I twist the cap, drop a small oval pill in my hand, tip the soda bottle to my lips, knock back the pill and make a show of compliance. "Ahh." I stick out my tongue.

Olive grins at me. "Okey dokey, let's take a nap." She grabs my wrist and drags me to the bed. I stop at the edge of it, prying my bony arm away.

"Why are you doing this?" I ask, the voice distant in my ears. "I'm— Hey!" Ignoring my words, Olive crawls into bed. Diana scuttles under the covers after her and pokes furry her head out to look at us.

"We can't do this, Liv. Percy will—"

"We hadda fight," Olive admits, thin brows twisting. "I don't wanna be alone right now. And you *can't* be, ya big dummy."

Olive pulls the covers over her mouth to glare at me from beyond them. I glance at her, then the cat at her side, grip the back of my head and thread my fingers through my hair to pull and twist. "Liv, this—"

Olive huffs at me and flops over, jerking the covers over her head.

It's not meant to separate here. What the fuck did you do?!

Oh, me? I didn't do a fucking thing.

Diana charts through the waves of sheets, pops free, then finds a comfortable position to curl into a furry circle at the end of the bed. I slide underneath the sheets, Olive lets out a gentle sigh, her eyes flutter closed, my heart jackhammers my ribs and my crotch microwaves itself. *Lust is not my fucking friend.*

A moment passes. Olive fidgets, then whispers, "How's it goin' with tha', uh...whats-his-face?"

"Horrible," I say into Olive's hair, which makes her wiggle her toes under the sheets. "But I've made a new friend, you know...she's helping me. Helping us. Maybe it'll be alright," I whisper bloodlessly as my junk slowly stops exploding.

Olive wriggles around to face me. "Can I meet her? Is she wicked cool?" *Her smile is bright enough to nuke a planet.*

"Yeah, yes. Why—" My eyelids feel heavy, Olive's so warm, the day's been made so simple, my burning thighs cool, the screaming birds are gone and I'm more comfortable than I've been in fucking *years.*

"Why don't we have little—a little party, maybe at Eric's place? I haven't been there much, but could—it could be fun. Invite Percy and everyone too. Maybe you two can make up," I mumble.

"I'm big mad at her," Olive quibbles.

"What did she even fucking do?" I ask, yawning. Our noses are almost close enough to touch, but thankfully the engine between my legs has decided to shut itself off, for both our sakes.

Olive gnaws her dog-bitten lower lip, measuring her words for me.

"You don't have to censor yourself with me, princess," I whisper.

"She won't even hold my hand!" she grumbles. "But *she's* mad about stuff that ain't happenin'." Olive scans my face for a moment too long. "Or maybe stuff that'll happen but not yet. I dunno."

"But not yet," I repeat her words, she turns away from me and I wrap my arms around her body. This is emotional cheating but I think we're *both* too exhausted to care.

As we're carried into drowsy comfort with the warming sun, in too-soft sheets while I breathe into her hair, I do what I have never done in a million lifetimes. I slip my hand under the crux of her arm and place my palm on her stomach. I feel her breathe, my eyes flutter closed and I truly, truly sleep.

I sleep deeply, I dream of nothing horrific, I wake up with no starts and Diana purrs by our feet. As I dream of pink-skies, I accept that I will steal Olive away from my first real, true friend.

Olive rouses, which wakes me, but my eyes stay shut. For a moment, she studies me, then plants a kiss by my mouth. *Too close, just right, so sweet.*

I can't *not* steal her away, not just because I'm a prick with an overclocked libido and blistering sense of entitlement. I can't not, because I promised to give her whatever she wants, and what I'm too stupid to realize right now is she wants *me*. Worthless, useless, evil, broken, crazy me.

Alone? Never.

I wrap my arms around her and know I'm going to hell not just for murder, but for adultery and theft.

43 / WHAT NEVER WAS

Like we vaguely planned, Olive and I host a small get-together to bring Moira into the fold and maybe mend Olive's broken heart.

Like we vaguely planned, I call Eric and with the phone perched at my cheek, I hear him excitedly blurt out his Brit-marble-speech and talk a mile a minute about how much fucking weed we're going to smoke.

Unlike what we planned, the night doesn't yield what I know is meant to happen: I'm meant to party my ass off to pretend I'm fine, get drunk, sneak about Eric's flat, snag his alcohol and watch Olive kiss Percival's cheek.

They're meant to make up and I'm meant to witness it, covet this and steal it at the first available opportunity because I need to solder my mental wound with something made of pink glitter.

I planned this. I instigated this. I pushed Percival to Eric. I made this happen because I'm the villain. That's the script.

But that's not exactly how this will play out. Instead, we're now sitting, smoking from Eric's bong. Moira is swapping clothes with Percival; giddy in their new friendship.

They never grew this close in my memories and now they have. We're witnessing a divergent timeline and yet Boris' bullet is still trying to blow my fucking brains out all over a wet brick wall.

There's the crack of light, there's me dying and yet *everything* has changed.

Drunk, high, fragile, raw, worn and confused I take a bong hit and pass it to Eric. Eric chuckles, inhales far too much, coughs and sputters all over me.

As we've gone off script and death-defying-narrator-meddler-me has far more control than I *ever* thought possible, I try something insane.

"Eric, let's make out," I offer through a thick cloud of musty smoke, passing the bong back. Eric's eyes are the size of saucers.

"Mate, w—" I shove a variable through his mouth with my tongue, time resets and past-me is left thinking he's hallucinated the whole thing because he's insane and *insanely* horny.

"Darling," Moira squeals at Percy, who's now wearing her blue slip dress. "Oh, you look positively *fabulous*."

Percy giggles behind her hand, twirling in place. "Like, oh my god! I *do*!" She cackles, the two women laugh together and I smile a good, true, earnest smile. It dies swiftly.

Standing on shaky limbs, I walk toward Percy, grab her by the arm and pull away despite her protests. "W-what, oh my god, what are you, like, doing?" Percy snaps.

"I'm sorry," I say plainly. "I'm in love with Liv, you know it, you're going to fucking ruin this early and then we're going to hit it off. It's my fault, Percy. All of this is my fucking fault. I'm sorry. I really, really fucking am."

Time resets itself, the reel moves back, and I'm yet again sitting next to Eric, smoking his weed, grimacing and imagining I made the prior conversation up, because I'm just a *little* bit too high and still think I can bargain with undiagnosed brain-rot.

With a sigh, I pass the bong to Eric, who hands it to Olive, who sticks her tongue out at him. "Naw." She rebukes his drugs.

Eric frowns in a thin line, his brows following suit. "Oi, pepto, why not? Ya had too much? Tossed ya lil' candy head is what..."

"Yeah," is all she says, which is another thing that never happened.

Olive locks eyes with me as Eric passes me the bong. I place the glass piece to my lips. Liv narrows her eyes. I push the bong away from my mouth. She nods. Finally, I place the bong down on the table, which makes her smile. Unlike I planned, I smoke no more of Eric's weed and never will for the rest of my short little life.

The night proceeds like it normally would, with Moira now sitting next to me on Eric's small inlet of a porch. We recline in the plastic lawn chairs as we always do.

"Darling, what's going on with you?" Moira asks, slipping her hand into my own.

We lock fingers, I kiss her knuckles and she chuckles. Fast-friends, fast-allies, fast partners in crime. Friends, as if we ever could be, considering how rotten I am. *Must've fucking tricked her.*

A bluebird flies past; fake and horrifying. "I'm losing my fucking mind," I admit with an acidic chuckle.

"Clearly," she says with a short nod, then rests her head on my shoulder. "You know," she begins, as she always does, "he *did* say you were about as stable as a livewire in a swimming pool."

"Who?" I ask, as I always do.

Moira gestures as is her way; a slight tilt of the shoulders, a mildly overwhelmed mouth, then an unacted snarl. "That *terrible* European."

I chuckle, reach for my pack of cigarettes on the railing, clock the butt end on my palm and offer her one, as I always do. She takes one, I pull my own free, light both of them, we smoke and talk of plans that I'm too drunk to remember.

I don't remember Moira holding her cheek pensively as I blather pressure-cooked, rambling nonsense. I don't remember her leaving to call someone, because she's not *supposed* to. We witness this as past-me blurs in time and alcohol-tainted insanity.

Late in the night, I make my way around Eric's flat for more booze. I can't sleep and I *need* to, so I'm intent on getting fucking black-out drunk. Trouble is, I can drink most people under the table and so it takes much more to knock me flat on my ass.

With my hand in the cupboard, I do what I always do and rip free some terrible tasting cinnamon bullshit. Winding back, dripping through time, traipsing through memory, I witness what always happens in the living room we took to like a slumber party. Olive sits up within her mass of pillows, moves a bit of hair from Percy's face and kisses her sweetly.

Blurry eyed, I'm meant to see their tender moment. I'm meant to see it, covet it and want—desperately—what they have. Instead, I feel guilty. Instead of a smile on Olive's face, I spot a frown.

Olive turns, locks eyes with me and begins to cry. Silent tears trail down her cheeks. Stunned, I stand in the doorway of Eric's kitchen with a bottle of alcohol grasped knuckle-white in my fist.

Like it never happens, Percy wakes up to the impossibly soft sound of Olive's tears. She sits, frames Olive's face in her hands, I creep back into the doorframe to hide from sight, but it's too late.

Olive sniffles. "I'm sorry."

Percy reels her head to glare at me. *Ah.* No, this isn't what never was. This is always what it was, wasn't it? I forgot my own backstory in the time of laser-guns and dictators with stolen faces.

They kiss, Percy drags her eyes to rest on my face and what I always labeled jealousy becomes true hatred. A *deserved* hatred, because I'm worth hating. *Loving me costs too fucking much.*

What Never Was is what always happens, yet it's altogether different. We've diverged. Past-me assumes this is just a simple sickness he can fix with sleep. He assumes it's passed like a cloud somebody owns and drags around in the sky. *It hasn't.*

Boris' now-bullet blows my brains out. Time rewinds again, leaving it mere inches from my trembling eye. *Please let me go back. Please let me live and make it right.*

44 / PERCEPTIVE PERCIVAL

The morning after our party, Percy wakes me like she always does. With her hand far too close to my throat, she glares down at me, magenta mouth contorting like a wet slug. "Wake up. We're going for coffee. Or whatever."

"We?" I ask from a dreamy, sleep-addled mouth. I flip about, notice that the others are sleeping and try to quietly slip from the mass of blankets.

"Yeah, we're getting coffee. We need to, like, talk. Or whatever." Percy pulls a chunk of blonde hair behind her ear as she glares holes into my skull. *She must be mining my thoughts like her tiny fucking nightmare girlfriend.*

"You're angry," I mumble, sit and rub my eyes with my fists.

"That's, like, an understatement." She pauses for a moment, then gathers my hand to pull me up like a stubborn, delirious mule. "Let's go. *Now.*"

––––––

Sitting in Olive's favorite cafe (she craves proximity to the woman who won't give it to her) drinking too-strong coffee with a highly-strung Percy, I've defaulted to my devils, because I must. *It's survivalism.*

I feign indifference as she asks me what I've been up to, which isn't the *real* question she wants answered. Her words are waved away as irritants, she gawks at me and I inhale brown sludge.

Why is Percy pretending she gives a flying fuck? Her problems, her life, her issues matter *far* more than anything I could *ever* hope to tell her, not like she ever lets me say a damn thing, my way. *She doesn't care.*

The lightswitch flips, my walls spring up, the birds no longer warble and this feels like stability. It feels like a necessity. *It isn't either.* It's just the tail-end of what happens when a brilliant bird flies too close to the sun and gets set on fire by its own blood.

Guilty no more, I become the evil she thinks I am. "Every little word," I continue as the people around us blur. "You never shut up about work." I move to snatch a sugar packet, tear it open, spill a bit on the table and dump what remains in my coffee.

Stirring the coffee with my finger, I note her reddening face and continue being the evil she assumes. "You can't fault me for taking advantage of the fact that you can't keep your beautiful big mouth shut." *I'm sorry, my beautiful, misunderstood friend.* I simply don't have the energy to be kind right now and I wish you could fucking see that. *You never will.*

"Whatever! I didn't know you, like, did what you did and how you did it, but now I know, and I know I can't know when to stop knowing because I'll just keep talking when I talk!" she screeches at me, jabs her finger into my chest and fails to ask me the *real* questions she wants to ask.

Which are: why are you stuck to Olive's side like glue? What did you do with her the other night? Why did she tell me she's sorry? And— saddest of all—*why are you taking her away from me?*

Percy froths as my smile grows viperine. "You have the right to be angry. But what am I supposed to do when you tell me that the office is busy? Not use it to my advantage?" I shrug, my bright green shirt a contrast to our dark conversation. "That's like telling an addict where to find free drugs."

"That's disgusting," Percy roars, cutting me off. "You're disgusting. You're like, a fucking petty criminal!" Her voice rings in my ears. *The people around us are staring.*

"I wouldn't call what I do 'fucking petty.'" I shrug.

"The hell would you like, call it, or whatever!? You have no rules! You do, like, whatever the hell you want! And you used me to do just that!" Percy continues her tirade.

I take a too-long sip, close my eyes and realize fully what I've been molded into. I accept it, hate myself and offer her nothing real. *Because I'm not real.*

"I'm a businessman," I say beyond the rim of my paper coffee cup. The wheels turn in her head as I offer her fake pity.

"I know what you're thinking. I'm not pretending to be your friend, Percival. You just have certain perks. We're also trying to do something pretty important right now," I say, in full honesty, arrogantly proud that I've deflected her from her important, pink-colored questions.

"What could be, like, *that* important that you'd lie to me about it?" she asks me, lower lip trembling, voice hollow and eyes searching.

"It's a secret." I raise my finger. "But it's 'something awesome.'" The muffled crunching of sweet specks as my digit dots the table froths her further.

I've moved her piece but not for vengeance, not for justice, not for thwarting the one who keeps abducting avians to press them into my mold and break them in half for profit.

It's been years.

"But I will tell you at some point. I promise. Maybe." I lick my finger and she sees me in all my wretched indigo glory. I tilt my Boris-brow in amusement, preen in Tyr's arrogance and smile in Markov-malevolence. I've become the very thing I hoped to destroy when all I wanted was to be myself. *The world's a stage, I play many parts, and never my own.*

Our fight ends with her storming out. Our fight continues when I deliberately invite Olive for coffee later on in the day—treating her, oh so very generously—to her favorite cafe.

Percival watches us from the parking lot, which I know she's doing because I know what time she takes her breaks. *She's a playing piece I watch like a hawk.*

In fact, I force Percival to watch how Olive's face lights up when I compliment her bright pink curls. I imagine she's balling up her fists. Glancing at her, I don't have to imagine any longer. She's pissed.

My hand waves through the glass at her. Olive joins me and waves along. I metaphorically wrap my claws around Olive's guts and eat her neon insides. Percival knows and will do what she does when hurt enough to act. *She's only human. Unlike me.*

Olive, who I assume *doesn't* know, turns to look at me. I meet her hazel gaze as she speaks a line she never says. "I know what yer doin'." Time rewinds, I casually assume I'm simply insane and she resumes huffing down her powdered-sugar donuts.

Smiling at what I've convinced myself I'm entitled to, I feel powerful, and absolutely, positively, dreadfully, irrevocably, entirely *fucking* miserable.

45 / CINDERELLA MACHINE GUN

With a fistful of brightly colored shopping bags, I make my way down loud streets in even louder clothing to congratulate the woman who pulled this whole loud thing off.

Moira peels from an alleyway smoking my brand of cigarettes. I pass her some bags, she peeks inside of them, smiles, then we walk in tandem as a pair of beautifully-dressed devils.

"Oh, dear, you've bought me such lovely clothes," she muses. "Buying my loyalty, hmm?"

I push the circle-glasses up on my nose. "Like I said, clever."

She giggles and stops at a bench to pull free gowns, gold, glory and the stuff of dreams from colorful bags. With bright eyes, she scrutinizes nothing, accepts everything and my potent weapon beams with pride as she spreads a blue dress against her body.

"Tell me, clever girl. Tell me everything." I whirl behind her, she holds up the dress and we make a dance of our victory. She takes my fingers, I twirl her about, she skirts the clothes back where they belong, we snatch them and make our way back to my flat full of glee.

Yuen tries to flag me down as we pass by. I pause for one painstaking moment and look at the man who is possibly the only person who could stop my descent. I ignore him. *My resolve didn't last.*

We scuttle into my biohazard of a flat. Moira knocks over a stack of pizza boxes from Rosalin's and wrinkles her nose. "Oh, dear," she drones, "I guess you really *did* canvas me for years, hmm?"

I place our haul on the coffee table, knocking various things about and turn to look over Moira's smiling face.

"You really don't have a problem with any of this, do you?" I ask.

She shrugs her shoulders, vaguely dances her way toward me, wraps her painted claws around my body and preens a smile into my neck. This is something she mimicked, picked up and will never put down ever again for as long as she lives.

"Not a bit," she admits, pulling back to grin up at me.

"Why not?" I ask, scanning her face. She presses her luck by kissing me with a kiss that's not a kiss. *Moira was a quick study. Quicker than I ever was.*

"I've never had nice things, Alex," she admits. "And I'm not about to malign a fairy godmother." She fusses momentarily with my floral blouse. "Especially not one who wants to do good things in the end. Right, dear?"

I step away from her, unearth a beautiful pair of shoes, inspect them for a moment, raise my brows and place them on the floor. Kicking off my high-tops, I slip into her new indigo weapons and walk in a wide circle.

"Is that what you think?" I ask.

Moira pauses for a moment, hand to her hip, then scans my inked shoulders. "No," she says plainly, glancing at the floor. "No, not really, darling."

I laugh. It's a hollow, bloodless, cruel thing. "Like I said, clever." I click toward her, take her hand, then bring her to sit with me on the sofa. "Now, tell me how you did it. Tell me everything. Every *single* detail."

Moira beams, sits forward as pretty as a posey and places her hands in her lap. "Well, he was *certainly* a lightweight," she says, smirking devilishly.

"And though I *did* have to make a bit too much of a show of the entire ordeal, it was so..."

"Easy." I fill in the rest of her sentence. Her feline brow quirks, she's momentarily pensive and I'm left staring at an imperfect mimic. *Human — is that what you are?* I slide my fingers into a pink bag on the table and remove an expensive lure.

"He's evil, Moira." I pull a flashy watch over my wrist. It catches her eye. "And evil men do *not* deserve your pity." My words melt to native colors.

Her beautiful brown eyes travel from the watch, up my tattooed arms, to my floral shirt, linger on the trick of my lips and finally affix to my baby blues. "Then you don't either. Do you, darling?" Her voice is hollow and brown at the edges. *This is an auditory hallucination.*

Thick silence hangs heavy as my beautiful twin examines me more closely than she ever has before. I'm a motherfucking blood-drinking butterfly skewered into a plastic blue plate and she just *had* to fucking pull my wings off with her demented brown eyes, didn't she? *This is paranoia.*

"I want to show you something," I blurt out, grab her hand, and drag her into my room. With the Polaroids back in place on my wall, she scans them, then watches me curiously as I dig around underneath my bed. Hefting free a box, I drag it to the center of the room, squat and start ripping objects out in chunks with shaking hands. A Polaroid of a carcass framed in a television screen is plucked free. "Cynthia Sinclair—an alias—age sixteen, no known address." I read off the writing under the Polaroid. "That was all I could investigate based on Percy's *politsiya* prattling," I mutter. *A very fantastical set of circumstances. Notice that.*

I'd hoped to terrorize Boris with his crimes; his masterfully molded killer dabbling in backbiting, wheeling him about a room, torturing him, reading off his sins and staining the floor red with his guts. I haven't yet and won't because I'm far too broken. *Imperfect victims are more common than you think.*

The photo flaps to the floor like a molted wax feather, I die her death and pretend I feel nothing in order to survive everything.

Moira, speechless, stoops to peel the memory off the hardwood. She turns it over, the blood flees her face, a card with erratic scribbles slips her fingers, drifts and finally, she places a hand to her mouth. *There isn't a single continuity error in this scene.*

I cut through my pile of thin excuses to pry apart two dead birds. "Unknown boy, unknown age." His death flitters to the floor with an audibly wet flop. "I couldn't figure out who he was. For obvious reasons."

Moira's other hand joins her mouth-framing as her eyes grow dark. Maybe dark like black little buttons. Maybe. *Pay attention.*

Another Polaroid is drawn. I wave it for a moment. "Recognize the bar?" I ask with dead eyes. "It's not just a meeting spot." I smile a smile that's not a smile. "All of Boris' rivers run through it, you know." *My voice is jagged like a fractal migraine.*

"And the *terrible* European. He knows—knew?" she blurts out, but I interrupt her by digging in the box and prying free a Betamax.

"Aleskandra Vosova." He kept them. All of them. Every single one. *Why did Boris know which of his grunts to distract me with, so many years ago?*

"Timeframe unknown, age unknown, no label." I drop it to the floor with a dead thud. Moira winces.

I pull out another. "Aleksandra Vosova, timeframe unknown, age unknown, Betamax A-120P." It joins its fallen comrade with a clatter.

"Aleksandra Vosova, timeframe unknown, age unknown, label too worn to make out," I mumble.

"Aleksandra Vosova, timeframe unknown, age unknown. Label: Bloodsport." My smile twists. "The day I ripped a man's throat out with my fucking teeth." Aleksandra clatters to the floor. She twists, mouth covered in blood as she steels herself to fight men twice her size and miraculously survive against all odds because she's unkillable without her consent.

Moira parts her lips to speak, but says nothing. Shaking her head like a skittish mare, she's naturally dumbfounded. Naturally, I chase her into the corner of the room and hiss into her ear. "So, no, I don't imagine that you need to fucking pity me. I'm the only one who made it out alive by cutting through it all with my mother*fucking* **teeth**."

Moira prepares a dangerous question. "D-darling." She hesitates against the wall I've backed her into. "Knowing where and who," she continues as I begin to sneer. "Couldn't—could you not have gone to the police?"

"Do you want the honest answer or the half-excuse?" I ask in past-something words.

Moira's mouth quivers as she turns her face away from me. "B-both. Both, darling." She winces when I laugh. It's a devastating crack.

"The honest answer is that *I* want to be the one who cuts his wings off. *I deserve it.* I'm fucking *entitled* to it. I *need* it. I've murdered, lied and used the people I *love* for it. I let *them* rot for it." I gesture at the gore all over my hardwood floors. *Metaphor? Hallucination? Literal? Who can say.*

"Collateral *fucking* damage."

Moira stares at me, hesitates, but parts her lips as if I'd dare let her now. I snatch her by the dress and pull her to my face.

"The half-excuse?" I glare, a mad thing torn, twisted, botched and broken and so very damned. "What do you think the *politsiya* would do with an illegal immigrant with no family, no proper education, no life skills beside fucking war and fucking, a boy in the body he *never* asked for?" I pause to laugh a laugh that's not a laugh. She cowers.

"A queer demented fucking bird-snake—with no ID, no one to save him," I simper. "A slave who killed to survive. I asked for *none* of this. *I'm* the blueprint Boris can never, ever replicate. Yet he tries, pathetically! I make so much money by *not* dying, not even from torture! And how? No mother*fucking* clue! Such a lovely *actress.* Such a lovely immortal *fucking* corpse! And where do people like me always end up, *Moira*?!" I'm shaking.

Heart pummeling my ribs, I suck in air to calm down. *She doesn't fucking deserve this.* My fingers relax from her dress, which sets her free to scuttle the wall like a flightless bug. *I've gone too far. I've shown her* my vengeance—an ugly color—and she can do nothing but flee.

After far too long, I snatch up clumps of human remains and drop it into the cardboard box with a collective thud.

"You were all *alone*?" Moira half-shrieks.

My dead blue eyes lock on her earthy browns. I've shown her my most toxic color so she can escape. I've given her an out. Despite me plying her with baubles and bullshit, I've given her a way to *hate* me. *Take it, you stupid fucking child.* Turn this evidence in, make it right, do what I'm too broken to finish. Take the gun, fondle the trigger and blow me—*more* collateral damage—out of the sky along with the man I like least. Take Markov out too. *End this for all of us.*

"You survived *all* this." She pauses, black button eyes darting deplorably. "By *yourself*?!" Her shrill words muffle as she swaddles my corpse.

"You poor, poor dear." I don't fold into this warmth. I don't accept her kindness, her sweet kiss on my temple, her gentle beating heart.

"Why are you hugging me?" I ask, a statue in her pleading arms.

"Why are you crying?" she asks through her own tears.

"I'm not," I grumble.

She leans forward, kneads away the water flooding down my cheeks, finds me beyond a mess of blond and kisses my eyelids. *Moira won't give me any other option besides love. But I'm afraid.*

"You're not alone anymore, darling boy." Her whisper shoots a hole in my guts. All at once, I'm sobbing while feeling absolutely nothing at all.

The scene is ghastly: La Pietà with Mary trying to cradle the sacrificial lamb who thinks himself the Devil. Who wants to *be* the Devil and not the beast of burden who always, always, always fucking suffers when all he wanted was to live his *own* life.

Frozen, I die in her embrace, bleed out within her hands from the bullets her unearned love left me with, the birds scream from the walls, a searing flood of a thousand sparrows erupts across my vision and I'm reduced to catatonic glass.

I emote nothing as I vividly hallucinate, yet the tears keep coming.

"Let's make this right." She sniffles and smooths out my hair. "We'll make it right, pet. *I* will make it right."

I never earned this, Moira. Let me self-destruct. Let me finally die.

46 / YOURS

It's been months since I dropped from the orange sun that blew my mind all over the inside of Markov's car. I sleep fitfully as wax rolls off my back, flick my metaphorical light-switch and wait for the lamp between my thighs to reheat my corpse. *It never turns on no matter what I do.*

Moira claimed the owned-bar, scrubbed it of its disgusting origins and made it into a club. Busy with business, she's kept me at a distance, which gives me more time for romance. I've made meager steps with Markov; my nicer things live in his fancy apartment now. I've even bought a pretty pink Chevy. *For all intents and purposes, it seems I've won.*

I have expensive clothes, a pet, money, human currency, my plans have all worked out, Boris is cut down to his bare bones and Markov runs this city with my mouth on his ear—*I won.*

The warehouse from hell was lit on fire. Boris' associates were gutted and that was blamed on another criminal element. No more bird cards and yet I honor no real victims I let rot for my climb to power. *I fucking won.*

Smiling like I've been paid to, melting on Yuen's hardwood floors, Boris calls me, thin-voiced and frantic. Backed into a corner, he grasps at his one last broken straw—the one *he* fucking broke *himself.*

I laugh-shout into the receiver as Boris quibbles, my mind splits open, nothing-birds deluge me, future-me exerts too much pressure, present-me gets my brains blown out and past-me slams the phone into the wall.

He slams it again and again and again until the plaster cracks.

Curling his fingers around plastic, he rips the phone from its seat, tears the wires, and flings it all against the floor with a deafening thwack.

"I have everything I want," I blurt out, eyes wide as I slink to the floor. I'm an unstable livewire, frayed at the edges, dip-dyed pitch-navy and drowning in a sea of fish shit. *What the fuck is happening to me?*

"I have everything. What *don't* I have?" Blurry-eyed, I fumble across the floor, knock mounds of shopping bags aside, break moldy cups and flatten putrid pizza boxes.

Wraith-like, I skitter toward the pock-marked wall in my room and snatch the daisy-stickered Polaroid. A single tear rolls down my cheek as a plan for happiness forms in the rot of my mind.

Here, I will take, give nothing back and pretend I didn't know a damn thing. That's the plan: hate me so that I can die knowing I deserved all my suffering. *There has to be a reason.*

The club is alight with youths flowing like cells, multiplying and separating in time with organic movement. A band guides their symphony—song is action, movement, life itself. I am a lifeless husk, consuming alcohol and pretending I don't have thoughts in my skull. *I do, they're just tainted with a color so fucking dead I barely recognize them.*

Waves of orange and gold paint the singer's dark skin. The light bounces off of a piercing that hooks from her ear to her nose in a silver wire. Lauren's thin jewels commanded attention. I know her and pretend I don't. *I pretend I keep her away to keep her safe from me.*

Really, I'm keeping *myself* safe, because she *sees* me and hears every fucking thought in my demented head. The magical thinking has turned from oily blood-orange to thick black tar that floods my throat and blocks all airways. I loose all of it with fucking liquor, which is a dire *mistake.*

I take a bright green drink and drip some of the contents onto a woman's navel, who's lying on a long table. She laughs as my corpse licks the salt from her thigh, then sucks the alcohol from her stomach.

She moves to grab my face, but I pull back. "Sorry. I'm just window-shopping. I only buy." I chuckle mindlessly. "One thing at a time."

Possibly rotting in real-time, I spin around, lift my arms into the air and croon. Stupid, kind, simple, useful, wonderful, terrible Eric rounds behind me and slaps my too-thin shoulders. *God, please help me.*

"Mate, this is tha best fuckin' party ever!" He chortles joyfully, dumbly, happily, horribly.

"Fuck yes it is. Hey, Erica," I tease, my pet name for Eric drawn out dramatically. I'm not sober, but I'm sober *enough.*

I spot Percival from the corner of my eye and see a way to gain possible happiness: her daisy. *Maybe that can make me happy.* Hurting terrible people, killing those who've wronged me—that was always the plan—but Percy *isn't* a terrible person and *never* was.

"That girl's pretty cute, huh?" I act, gesturing vaguely at a yellow and magenta shape in the corner of the room.

"Totally. Ey, wait. Why're ya askin' me that?" Eric squints.

As I float above my body, I see his recognition and ignore it because something dead in me feels like *this* will make me *fucking* happy. I am nothing but the chasing of that impulse. Right now, I couldn't stop myself even if I wanted to, or knew how to, for that matter.

"She keeps." I make a play at being blurry-eyed. *Such an actress!* "Makin' eyes at you." I motion with a slowed hand. "And doing that thing with a cherry. You know, the thing. It's red, so it's probably. With. Yeah."

"Mate, she's taken," Eric possibly says as I sway against him. My comfort in Eric's arms grows from rosy to obscene in seconds. *I want his dick in my throat, but that won't make me fucking happy.*

"Where's…Ollie?" Eric asks. I laugh into Eric's chest, he stabilizes himself on my shoulder and I pretend I'm drunker than I am.

"Who?" I narrow my eyes then snort into hysterics. "Aubrey?" I swerve into Eric and feel nothing but navy-pitch despair. "One of Liv's coffee buddies!" I scream into the crowd.

Eric tries to keep me level and that one cut of human kindness knocks my heart's motor back on for a mere fraction of a second.

With my hand against my mouth, I stumble away to scour the club for Markov. Sometimes, he joins us when he can pretend I'm just a friend. Sometimes, he even pretends he loves me. *I want him to fuck me within an inch of my life, but that won't make me **fucking** happy.*

Caught between ten million diverging timelines, stuck in the mire of pitch blackness and hot hellfire, I stagger, float outside my emaciated body and everything *hurts*. I'm lost, as I'm always lost and fumbling for why I'm so mother*fucking* miserable.

"Goddd, I know I'm not fucking supposed to, but, mm." My insides curdle. "We should dance. Even once. Just one dance. Nobody has to know. We could be fucking anybody," I blurt out, bargaining.

Maybe I can pretend he loves me and *then* I'll be happy. Sex is love. Dancing is sex. If I have *someone* to paint my fucking guts, then maybe I can survive the scream-cries of dead-meat-birds eating my fucking brain. *Maybe then, I can finally be fucking happy.*

I wrench my pager from my pocket and page my not-boyfriend, king of the world, ruler of New York, who let my leash go out until it choked me to death on a fence. *God, please help me. Please, don't kill me. Please.*

"Hmm. That fucker could sleep through a damned...er...English. Alex, English. Торнадо. Fuck—ahh whatever," I dribble out, drunker than I think, devolving into umber syllables. He isn't responding to the flashing, beeping, blurry numbers.

Chaotically, I stumble out into the street to smoke a cigarette and try to find the next glimmering object I can lock in my fist and crush. I'm an addict, a nothing-thing. I want to die, but the lights are so bright and lovely. I'm sobbing and smiling while I smoke and everything hurts yet it's so beautiful that I want to throw myself into traffic.

A pink shape greets me. Of course she'd be out here, waiting until we drink ourselves stupid enough to regret it. She's the clever one, the babysitter, the daisy sticker. *Maybe she can make me happy.*

"Hey, Liv, Livvie, Olivia," I dribble out my words, plant my ass beside her with an ungraceful thud, light up a cigarette and lean far too close to her face. Boundaries; I don't know the word. *God, please help me.*

"Hey!" Olive chirps happily, taking the headphones out of her ears.

"Have you seen the guy with the great ass?" I ask her with a short cackle. *I can make it work.* Markov can love me. I can force it. *Please, help me.*

"Oh. Mark? Yeah. He got in the car with...you?" Olivia scrunches up her nose. In this moment, the God of War taps me on the shoulder, possesses my frail body and jolts me from my psychotic depression.

"Fucking *pardon*?" I gawk at Olive like she's grown a second head. Anger gets shit done. Anger makes things clear. Anger gives me control.

Anger lets me live.

47 / US

I'm dead, lying in a heap on wet asphalt as my firing nerves animate my fingers and the hole in my skull gets appetized by pigeons. The machine has finally given out, hobbled by the madness of the past, the death of the present and the chaos of the future. *I've failed to save my own life.*

The cyan letters float, I pulse into the future, slap my synthetic fingers against nonsense code, drop into memories, flood into my dead body, peel back the still-frames like ripping wet concrete and nothing *fucking* works.

I can't make this right. I can't choose life. I'm so fucking sorry, Olive.

"If I don't drive ya, yer gonna try ta walk, huh?" Olivia asks.

"Yeah," I reply with a head full of war, hands braced on the trash can after puking my guts out. *Bile, water, alcohol and nothing else.*

Drinking may make Markov stupid, but it makes me more insane than I already am. I should just fucking drown myself in liquor so I can step out of time completely — *No, Alex, no.*

"And if you walk, yer prolly gonna pass out in a dumpster, huh?" Olive asks softly.

"Yeah," I blurt out, fumbling with the water bottle she's since given me to rinse my mouth out. I spit.

Olivia sighs, I finish off the water and she takes the moment the bottle drops into the can to grab my hand. *Help me.*

"Fine. But if ya do somethin' stupid, I'm gonna have to stop ya," Olive says.

I say nothing in response, because I have nothing, because I *am* nothing. All that remains is raw indigo brittly burning out at the root. I am nothing but a rotten moon tethered to one single pink star. I will destroy her. *What's wrong with me?*

Now inside of Eric's car, which Olive confiscated by running in and stealing his keys, I nearly slam my hand in the door wriggling inside. Pretending I'm normal for her sake, I apologize for my clumsiness and let my head lull back on the seat.

Olive starts the car up, it retches forward and I hold my stomach. *Please, help me.* For a moment, I cast a destroyed glance her way. Her pink curls glisten as I make a decision — one I'd hoped I'd been making until now — but I hadn't. I *choose* to trust she can figure me out, like we agreed to, years ago. *It's up to you, Liv.*

"OK. Where we goin'?" she asks me and it takes everything to respond.

"The address? Oh, fuck damn. Uh..." I drawl, wincing as the sound of dying birds boxes against my ears. *Help me.*

Olive holds up her hand. "Landmarks. C'mon!"

"Penny's Jewelers up the street, hang a left? Then we sweep up, uh..." I rub my eye with my flat, shaky palm. *Olive, I can't —*

"Go through the SoHo district past the drug store, then left up toward...the place with all the...rich shit in it." *Olive, please —*

"Oh, he lives in tha swanky neighborhood with the giant trees 'n crap?" she asks me with a piglet-sneer.

"Yeah. Swanky. Drivin' around with my pink Chevy that fucking-douchepiece of shi—" I can form no English phrases and so I devolve into multiple languages as the sound of bird-screams crack the air.

While we drive, she smiles, but I don't. I bite my nails, smoke and watch my subconscious bleed out in wax, wings, beaks, talons and melt *all* of that together with very-real time powers and skin-splitting flashbacks that churn my empty stomach in knots.

Fuck. We did it a-fucking-gain. How does this happen every time?! We break him every fucking time — restart. I said restart, you fucking shit-for-brains!

"Hey. How ya doin?" Olive asks past-me in a warm voice.

"How do you think I'm doing?" I spit venom on impulse.

"It coulda been nothin'. I coulda jus' been seein' stuff," Olive reassures me as my brain bleeds on asphalt and Boris murders me over and over and over again with his fucking blinding bullet.

"Olive. If you saw something, you saw it. You're the smart one." I look up from my nail-biting at the only person capable of pulling me back together.

"Huh?" she asks, raising a thin brow.

"Everyone freaks out all the time. You keep a cool head. I just... try to punch people. You're the only one who's got their shit together."

I press a cigarette to my lips and stare out at my future-death as it looms and I break. She will never know why I let it happen.

We're meddling too much—look at what we're fucking doing! Restart! Pull back, you fucking psychotic, power-tripping car-battery-ass motherfuck-er!

"I play SNES in my jams on my days off," Olive protests, turning a corner as gently as she can, which isn't gentle enough for me. My vision is buffered by a feathered sea. I'm hallucinating, drunk, enraged, broken, but all I can do is place a hand on the dashboard.

*We went too fucking hard. The compartmentalization isn't failing—when it should. I need to tell her, we need to tell—*I won't pull back.

What?!

It's working. It will work. We can take far more than you think. I won't pull back. Trust me.

Are you seeing this shit?! Yes, I'm talking to you, you fucking shit-head voyeuer-ass motherfucker perched inside my fucking skull! Get him—me—out of there!

I will not pull back. We're diverging. It'll fucking work and he can take it. If you won't trust me, trust her. Trust her, always trust her. Always.

What?!

"Yeah, you also work a real-person job and hustle like a mother-fucker," I add, trying to ignore the sci-fi conversation happening above my head.

"I have pink hair, and my diet is sugar plus more sugar." Olive snorts incredulously.

"And you're the only one not sloshed tonight. That fucking means something." I feel sick again, hold my stomach and stare as my murder blinks in and out of the windshield like broken film.

Olivia quirks a smile and puffs up her feathers with pride. I give her a foggy grin, for that's all I have. That is, until I notice my pink Chevy beyond the bleeding, broken frames.

"Hey! Stop! Right here!" I roar, Olive throttles the breaks and—despite being in no position to save anyone at all—I brace my arm across her chest as the car lurches. I would die for her.

*I will die for her, we would die for—*No, hold on. Hold on, it's fucking working. Just hold on. We're almost there.

"Pull 'round back, I'm coming up...the stairwell," I garble out, a corpse capable of action even though it's been busted open by my oil-slick mind-sun like a radioactive fruit.

"Do ya think that's a good idea? What if you fall?" Olivia warns me, scanning my face for too long.

She can't fix this. Do you hear it? Not the screaming of the birds. Shut the fuck up and listen for once.

"I won't fuckin' fall," I protest, barely sitting in my seat as it is. I tilt my head to the side; a sound besides bird-screams thrums, but I can't tell from where.

"Are ya sure?" Olive questions, gnawing the scar on her lower lip.

Hearing a thud, I assume it's the bleating of my prey-organs. *I'm dying. That's* why I'm seeing and hearing shit. *I'm dying.* My drink must've been spiked. *Help, police, stop, murder.*

The code runs, my mind explodes, yet I still speak to Olive in real-words because she deserves me giving her something real even as my fucking mind skins itself *alive.*

I regale Olive with a story about me lifting a vending machine while drunk, but a beat is blotting my thoughts *and* the avian-butchered wailing. *It's so hard to fucking focus.*

"The moral of the story is that I can do anything drunk that I can do sober. Except, with more vomit, I guess." I finish my compartmentalized trip down memory lane, Olive turns off the engine and I hear it: the beating of her terrified, beautiful heart.

Yes. Hold on. We have to hold on.

After light banter (punctuated by my brain smearing its colorful ink everywhere) we infiltrate via ladder, clop up metal-grate steps, traipse about the place I've all but moved into, and find Markov with his cock buried inside some red-haired woman's body.

This betrayal isn't what's important, though it should be.

It should be, considering it's been relived, written-down, agonized over, rewritten in the future, and yet this is not the climax, not the take-away, not a footnote. *It's barely on the fucking map.*

The take-away is Olive's arms wrapped around my waist as I wave a gun at Markov, who I'm *convinced* never loved me, his cheating being just one piece of evidence. I don't yet understand that *this* was his way of letting me go with *rage* to hold onto. Rage, once my only friend, yet Olive *holds* me. *The only one who ever truly listens to me, holds me.*

Hold on to that thought.

"If you do this, you'll be a monster! A-and I'll hate ya. Forever!" Olive's scream is loud enough to decimate whole continents like a nova shot through a wormhole aimed directly at planet Earth.

I'm frozen, yet *every* fiber of my being is telling me to destroy *everything* in my path because *my* pain deserves that raw, bloody vengeance. *I am the villain.* There's no doubt in my mind of that fact, but as Olive begs *me* to stop, something flicks inside the scooped-out hole where my soul once lived. Something like violets under a pink sky.

Something truly awesome.

   I have to— Yes. Remember what you've survived. Remember what you're capable of. Remember what you can choose. Alex, we need to fucking remember, we need to hold on and ride this out.

   "Stay down. Until we go." My voice is a whisper as my gun points directly at Markov's forehead. With his hands raised, beaten bloody and naked as the day he was born, I choose to let him live. *For her, I choose mercy.*

   "I can't have you hating me, Liv," I say, suffering to smile for her. *For her, I'll smile, because she makes me want to smile.* For her, I won't be just a murderer. For her, despite ruining everything, I will always *try*.

   I flick the safety on my gun, jam it into the back of my pants, turn and rush to scoop Olivia into my arms. We leave in bird-flight, I snag my car keys off a table and we're gone.

   We leave and I know I've set in motion my own breakdown, far worse than even this almost-murder and my hallucinations. Worse, because I dragged *Olive* into it. I know this, because that's the script— *am I wrong?*

   What do you fucking think, dipshit?

   After this heartbreak, the story says I'll pretend to recover. It says we'll dance around love. Olive has her heart broken by Percy, spends the night grieving at my place, we go on a spontaneous date and then she's meant to ask me to a costume party. *That's where our brief love story starts.* It's also the origin of a batshit sci-fi future that's fated to get triply ruined by human stupidity and human madness. *My madness, ruining the future, as I do nothing but destroy everything I touch.*

   That's what fate ordains, but as I run with Olive in my arms to my pink Chevy, place her feet on the asphalt, jam the key into the lock, rip the door open and scoot her inside, she *holds* me.

   Olive holds my corpse and kisses my lips with tears in her eyes. She kisses me, the me she knows, not my ghost, or my trauma, or my specter, or the red-painted girl-meat. She kisses me—Alex.

   The machine hitches, the system fails and space itself cracks in half. The bullet piercing my skull slides back in time and back into Boris' gun. His arm falls. He's jerked—one foot behind the other—as he marches out of the scene in a smear of color. I stand from kneeling, writes a futuristic machine.

   "Liv," I say, breaking away while my brain cooks itself. "What the fuck are you doing?" My voice is as soft as my limbs are brittle. She's stronger than I am, especially now. *Maybe she always was.*

   I pull back in time, away from my murder, take to a reversed-jog, back up the street, farther and farther around a corner, until I'm in front of a building with a blue door. The pen is mighty.

"Shush fer once," Olive mutters, then drags me on top of her as time freezes around us. Her heart beats out of her chest from fear; I can feel it. Terrified, time-stuck, watery-eyed, she's just like me, yet so very different.

Below the enclave of my arms, Olive looks at me like I'm the sun. The terrifying, volatile sun that she's afraid will detonate and leave her with her brutal, lonely thoughts. All she can do is hold me. Hold me, keep me and pray I don't explode and melt down her wrists.

I dare to pull my arm underneath her back, lift her face to mine and kiss her like I've wanted to since the moment I met her. It's gentle and patient; a sign of love by someone given so *very* little.

Olive pushes back to frame my face with her hands. Her comforting gray-hazel meets my caustic blue. "Doncha ever do stupid shit like that, ever again, ya here me, buddy?" She sniffles.

The door behind me opens. I magnetize through the entrance. The system restarts. I bolt from a traumatic response caused by a dickhead named Markov. She's mightier.

My empathy flicks on and I remember my first, real, true friend. "Liv, Liv, Liv—stop. Stop, we can't fucking do this."

As I try to pull away, Olive latches to my arm. A memory surfaces, but this time it's warm and pink and *good*. A memory of a party. A memory where we spoke in the way we can that others can't ever seem to hear.

"Why. Not?!" Olive roars and locks me in place with her arms. I can't escape and don't bother trying. *I have no blood left in my body, anyways.*

The door vanishes. The building vanishes. The street vanishes. The known horrible-future of horrible bullshit quite simply, beautifully, vanishes.

"Percy—" I hesitate.

Olive snarls, shoves me and baps her fist against my chest. "We broke up!" she screeches. "Doncha 'member? Or are ya that fuckin'— oh Jesus." Olivia fusses in place, then full-on punches me right in the chest as hard as she can. *It hurts.*

Kneeling on the squeaky seats, we stare at each other. I'm confused, heartbroken, terrified of everything and she's *absolutely* fucking livid at me. She cares enough to be *this* angry. *Why didn't I know?*

"Didja take tha pills to sleep?" Her face is almost as pink as her hair. "Didja friggin' eat?!"

My mouth opens but no words come out. I'm stunned.

Error 404: Asset not found. Rerouting, please stand by. Error: Connection to database lost. Rerouting, please stand by. Error. yd bnɒts ɘsɒɘlq ,ǫniʇuoɿɘ

< K. LEIGH / 261 >

on tar-date 0/0/at :am. Error, user A-0p doesn't have access privi leges. Error, error, user olive claimed Sudo permissions. error, user olive moved the files on Star-date 06/06/5352 at 5:55am. error, user A-120p doesn't have ac cess privileges.

"Al, you're very strong," she begins, pulling words from thin air that haven't yet come to pass. "Al, you're very strong, but you're also kinda weak. But I need ya to know that I am going to protect you. Okay? We got choices."

As if I didn't have enough to fucking deal with, yellow text crawls my vision, fractal and parasitic. *What the absolute fuck is happening to me?!*

Past-me shakes like a leaf as he assumes *all* his marbles have swirled down the drain at once. A thousand lines of code snap, crackle and pop beyond the panes of time through one single pore in the glass: *Olivia.*

I collect my hands in my lap, draw them to my face, rake my fingers over my skin, rip through my hair, lean forward and sob.

Olive watches me cry, then does something impossible: she stares above my head. *Yes, she sees it.* Remember: I'm a superhero. *What does that make her?*

Scowling, she pulls me to her lap. With my head on her knees, Olive gingerly pries the gun from my pants, then leans to place it on the back seat. She draws me close, lets me cry into her daisy-print shirt and listens to me wail as my wax wings finally melt for good.

"You can't..." I sob hot, wet tears. "You can't be my fucking plot device, Liv." *I'm just using her.* She's fixing me and I'm using her to fix me. That's all. She can't actually fucking care about me; I bargain. *Love is a color that terrifies millions of people, especially me.*

"I'm not," she huffs. "This is *my* goddang choice." Choice. Choices. *Her* choice. This is Olive's choice. I can't take her choice away, but why am I her fucking choice to begin with? *I'm a nothing who has nobody. I don't even fucking exist on paper. I don't fucking exist.*

"Percy, I love her. I really do, ya know." Olive hunts for my eyes as she explains. "But she doesn't even *listen* ta me." She sniffles. "She won't even hold my hand. Cause...ya know?"

I swallow hard. "Because of what she thinks others think, r-right?" I manage. Even now as I break apart across the very spectrum of time and space itself, I manage for *her.*

Olive nods, but something bitter cuts it short. Tears reserved for a future moment threaten to flee from her eyes. When she can hold them back no longer, they fall, each more dreadful than the last. *Heartbreak, isolation, loneliness.* Her beautiful face contorts in agony. It's a wound that will last lifetimes. *I can't let it. I fucking refuse.*

Jerking away, I clasp her to my chest—thrumming with reckless hope, impossible ideas, brilliant blue skies. *Please. Please, God. Let me try.*

"Even if I was still—" My eyes shoot open. "I will always, *forever*, hold your fucking hand." I sob out my promise, screw my eyes shut and clutch her to hold, to keep and to nourish with whatever love I have left.

"I will always, *always* listen to you." I tremble. "But I can't fucking take you from her like this. Do you understand?"

Olive nods softly in my arms, drawing up her hands to hold my tattooed shoulders like Markov *never* could. *My heart breaks and rebuilds all at once.*

"You have no *fucking* idea what I've done. Who I am. I can't lie to you, Liv. Not *you*." Olive listens to me, sniffling into my shirt. She feels what I can't tell her, empathetically not psychically. *That's a superpower neither of us have.*

"I'm not that nice neither, ya know," she mutters, sitting back to scan my face. "I didn't tell her what happened. Member? When we had a nap."

Brave Olivia, who opens up her plucky pink self to a wounded, feral bluebird, kisses my chin like she had on that unfated day. The day that was *never* meant to happen, but did. *I'd forgotten.* She peers up at cowardly blue me, blinks pitifully, feels terrible and I can't make her feel better.

She's wilting and I can't be the one to save her. *Can I?*

48 / USUAL PEOPLE

Smearing tears across my face, I force a smile, then reach out to run my shaking fingers through her curls. *I entertain a possibility,* but a flash of light across cuts the thought in two. Someone must've called the police after I riddled Markov's flat with bullets to kill the metaphorical wound. A metaphorical wound that's still searing my guts. *Fuck.*

"Come," I mutter in Nikolai something-words. "Come." I pull Olive to sit, put the keys in the ignition, slam my door shut and drive.

I drive with no destination because her broken heart needs it. I drive for forever because my damage begs me to. I drive with my most valuable passenger and wait for her to listen to what I can't say. I drive with perpetual pink and wait for her to tell busted blue what she needs.

Silence hovers, but it's comfortable, vulnerable and full of a word we both need more than we're ever willing to admit: *trust.*

No more insane strategies on walls. No more games played to force outcomes that I can't ask for help with. No more time-stopping, no more murder, no more making myself evil because I've convinced myself that's all that I am and that will finally let me die. *No more.*

"Olive. Tell me what you want," I whisper as my heart hammers my ribs. "What you want most of all." I'm sure she finds my extreme emotions confusing. As the lights around us blur in a million bleeding LEDs, I hope I'm wrong about that.

She swipes at her eyes, then looks up at me from beyond her curls. "I wanna go to computer college," she says, kicking at the dash with her foot. *I can arrange that, princess,* I think but don't say. She catches my gentle smile and grins.

My brows raise.

Olive fidgets in her seat and huffs, "I wanna be with somebody who's proud of me. Who wants ta show me off." *I can do that. I'm already fucking proud of you. You're brilliant,* I say with a half-smile. Her eyes shine bright.

"I wanna be with somebody who listens ta me." Olive's cheeks turn pink as I glance at her freckled face.

"I wanna apologize to her, too, ya know," she mumbles through a yawn. "But we don't work. Just like you an' what's-his-face."

Turning a corner, I chuckle drily. "No, no we fucking don't, do we?"

"Naw," she agrees, rolling her lower lip between her teeth. "I think ya prolly got real bad taste in men, huh?" she half-asks.

I burst out a short laugh. "Yeah, yeah I fucking do. Except—" Nikolai's ghost carves out my insides. I'm not supposed to tell her this. I'm not supposed to tell anyone. *The script says I won't.*

Olive cocks an eyebrow at me. "Tell me! I'm tellin' *you* stuff!" she barks. "Sorry, uh. I mean, ya gotta' tell people stuff, ya know? We both gotta talk 'bout it. Yeah?"

Glancing at her, I entertain the possibility of not being a fucking coward and spill my guts. "Nikolai Voronin." I whistle. "Kissed me like dying and loved me even when I bled all over his fuckin' floors, that one. Special." I drift into my native accent, a texture from another time, another life, another tragedy I'd hoped to forget. *I ran from love like a fool.*

Olive pricks up her ears and squints. "Cause ya got, uh...shot?"

"No." I hesitate, but decide to be brave. For her, I'll be brave enough to say plainly what she can't know. "I wasn't born a guy."

Olive narrows her eyes, raises both brows and gives me the most ridiculous shrug. "Did he give ya chocolate 'n stuff?"

I nearly twist my head off to stare at this dork who sees nothing strange at all with who and what I am. "Well, he did feed me good things, but if I'm honest, he mostly got me off. Helps with cramps."

"Oh yah," she says matter-of-factly, like this is a usual conversation between usual people, when it isn't. "Did what's-his-face feed ya good things?"

She's hungry. Spotting a sign in the distance, I drive in that direction, trailing an unseen star fogged by near-morning haze.

"No," I say, shaking my head, "cheap nachos."

"Ya buy people a bunch of crap too, doncha?" she asks, pulling her shirt up. "Cause you dunno how to make friends or nothin'—"

I snort. "Liv, what are you—"

Olive rips her shirt over her head and tosses it in the back seat. "I'm hot!" She grimaces at me, then flops back with a grumble. "And

Percy bought it fer me." *Heartbroken? Me too.*

My strong brows quirk as the haloed sign grows bright and large like the moon. "Liv, we're getting something to eat," I say, flexing my fingers off the wheel in the direction of the sign. "You have to wear a fucking shirt. A superhero bra does *not* count."

She rolls her eyes. *The audacity.* "Do tha drive-thru. Who cares?"

A smirk splits my face, I angle my knee on the wheel, pull my shirt over my head and toss it in the back seat. My body is a story in scars and ink. I hope she doesn't mind. *I hope she understands.*

"Did he buy it fer ya?" she asks, leaning to scan my stars.

I snicker, hands back on the wheel. "No, but now we match. And you're right, 'who cares?'"

Olive beams at me. "You get it." She grins. "It don't matter. Everyone's always so goddang upset about dumb crap. You too, ya know," she huffs and crosses her arms. *How she manages it with those things is beyond me.*

"Oh really?" I ask, brow raising. I wet my lower lip and grow braver than I've ever been in my entire fucking life. "Tell me. Tell me what you see, Liv." *Please say what I can't.*

She twists up her nose at me. "Ya really wanna know?"

I nod, the sign—McDonalds—grows clear. I turn the wheel to merge onto the ramp. As we chart over a sea of asphalt, she holds her breath, rolls her eyes and measures her words. For my comfort, she's trying to be gentle. I'm not used to anyone trying in a way that ever works.

"Yer out of yer dangin mind. Ya don't sleep." She raises a finger. "Ya don't eat real food." She raises another finger. "Yer prolly on drugs." She snorts as she raises the next finger. "Ya don't talk to nobody about nothin'." Another finger is raised. "And you dunno that tellin' people what's up is whatcha gotta do! Yer a big, stupid, idiot." The last finger raises.

"Sorry. Crap." She covers her mouth with her whole hand.

I shake my head, pull through the drive-thru, the speaker crackles and an exhausted-sounding woman asks us what we want to order. "This is good," I say, Russian lilt coloring my words. "What do you want?"

"Whaddaya mean 'this is good?'" Olive snorts, crosses her arms and continues. "Big mac, big fries, two cookies, diet coke, chicken nuggies."

I burst out laughing. "God, you *are* fucking hungry, huh?"

"Yeah! Feed me already, jeez," she fusses, playfully blowing her bangs out of her eyes. *She's trying to make me smile. It's working.*

"I'll have a sal—" Olive yanks my ear violently then flops back in her seat. "I-I'll have two big macs, two large fries, four cookies, two diet cokes and two orders of 'chicken nuggies.'"

Olive grimaces at me. "Ya can't keep doing that, ya know."

"Doing what, Liv?"

"All ya eat is booze and dumplings, mebbe not even *that*. Don't think I didn't notice, *buddy*," she grumbles. "Yer body ain't got nothin' in it to stop it from goin' crazy! Ya know ya need fuel to fall asleep, right?"

Blinking a few times, I dig around in my pocket, take out far too much cash, steer through the drive-thru, shove my hand through the window and pause to wince at Olive's feral scowl.

"You're very smart," I admit. "And I'm very fucking stupid."

"I know!" she says proudly.

I smirk, we get our food, I pass her a brown paper bag and she devours mass quantities of fried things at Olympic speeds.

"Now you," she says, gesturing with her last fry that she then jams into my mouth without so much as a warning.

I gnash it indelicately, which makes her grin. "Do you do this shit with Percy?" I ask, pulling into the parking lot so we can eat together.

"Waddaya mean?" she asks, then digs her hand in my bag to shove another fry in my mouth, which I chew dramatically. She grins.

"I mean." I hesitate. "Bark orders at her." Raising my brows, I rummage around in my bag and pull free a fistful of fries. I stare at them for a moment. Olive glares at me. I jam the mound into my mouth. She nods, crossing her arms again. *She's fucking bossy.*

"No. I just didn't say nothin'," she admits, slurping her soda loudly. "Cause she don't wanna hear it."

Her lips part. Olive breaks character with brutal clarity. "She doesn't want to hear anything that isn't flattering. She never wants to be wrong. She thinks she's always right even when she hurts herself and me," Olive says, childish phrases dashed to the rocks.

I devour my hunk of fries, wipe my mouth and mumble, "Do you speak like a fucking brat *all* the time?" Unwrapping my burger from its silver foil, I take a large bite, and scan her face for a sign I've crossed a line.

"Yes," she admits, sipping her soda on ice cubes.

"Why?" I mumble around the processed meat lodged in my cheek.

Olive shrugs, looks off into the distance and finally decides to let me in. "It's prolly some kinda age regression crap."

Raising my brows, I gorge on a handful of nuggets, then squint. "Why?" I ask, licking my fingers free of salt.

Olive darts her eyes to my face briefly. "I remember bein' happy for a little bit, when I was real young. Sorta carried. But now, that's all people expect from me." She sighs, then scrambles her bright bangs from her eyes.

"No matter what I do. No matter what I say. No matter how smart I am. No matter how hard I work," she admits, scowling. "I'm short. I like comic books and video games. I make stupid jokes and talk funny. I got no tact at all. So, I'm treated like a kid. A kid who can't ever be angry or sad cause people think I don't know nothin'."

Other people must be fucking blind. "I don't know what that's like, being a kid," I reply, chewing.

She turns to look at me, grows quiet, then places her drink on the floor. Hands in her lap, she sighs. "Me neither, not really. I had ta work when I was really young. My parents are older and not," Olive mumbles, pausing on a wounding-word, *"healthy.* I had to make money or we woulda been homeless again."

Homeless? I know the feeling. I eat a handful of nuggets, pass some her way, she inhales them, then jostles back into her seat with a huff.

Her round face contorts in frustration. "I never got to have the stuff you get to have," Olive admits. "And you live in a pigsty, drive a fancy car and buy all of us random crap," she vaguely judges me.

I let her, dive in for more fries and try bravery again. "Would it surprise you to know I've never not worked?" I admit.

She grows quiet, so I offer her a smile, hoping she knows this isn't a contest. Olive perks up instantly. *She makes everything so beautifully simple.*

I gnash my fries for a moment, then speak. "Or that I was hidden away, because I have a powerful father who never wanted me? A powerful mother, most likely ashamed of what was done to me? Worse so when I made myself a guy and put my name on the map. *Then,* I was a fucking threat." My voice is even-keel. These are just statements. *I'm not trying to poison the fucking air around us both.*

"Bein' yourself's a threat?" she asks, nose wrinkling. "And naw, not surprised. Saw tha eyes when I crawled through yer window."

This makes me pause mid-deposit of one very crunchy, very delicious fried piece of potato that I pretend I'm not starving for. "You knew?" I ask, french-fry hovering near my lips.

Olive shimmies closer to me and steals one of my fries. She eats it more delicately than before. "Yeah, I'm clever, 'member? I read a lotta books and yer a book."

I scan her face as she eats my food. "So, you never really had a fucking chance to just live, huh, Liv?" I ask, snagging my soda to take a sip.

"Nope." *Her smile is gorgeous.* "Not until now and even then." Liv punctuates her sentence with a fry. "I don't have a lot, ya know?"

"I don't either," I say between sips. "Seems like I fucking do, but I never asked for this." Olive waits for me to continue as my straw slurps ice. "I've never talked with anyone like this before..." I blurt out.

Olive nestles to my side, rests her head on my arm and lets out a small sigh. "Me neither," she mutters against my skin.

I wrap my arm around her shoulder, drawing her close. "I've held this shit in for years." Olive nods into me. *She has too.*

"So, what do you say, Liv?" I muse into her bright hair.

"Huh?" she asks, tilting to look into my eyes as her nose wrinkles.

"Do you want to just...live?" I ask, punctuating my sentence with an arm squeeze. "With me. If you want." *My heart is beating out of my McFucking chest.* "We can just drive, you know? Drive forever. But..." I pause. "I need to pick up the fucking cat."

Olive's laugh is music. "Yeah, yeah. Let's pick up tha cat. But..." She pauses. "What about tha rest?" A frown tugs her mouth.

A dog-bitten scar, a sad past, joyful, brilliance, maturity, strength, simplicity. *Where did you come from and why do you feel like home?*

I nod, wipe my hands on my pants, turn the car key and start backing up. "Let's take them too." Peeling out of the parking, I merge onto the highway and we're off.

Olive gawks, searching for a serious answer on my face.

My lip quirks. "Leave the business. Leave it all behind. I can't come with you." I pause, regurgitating the words Markov gave me, that I'd erased, that I remember now because I need them. "But I'll help you leave. When it's over, walk away. You can't be a king, little bird. It will kill you."

Olive pulls a clump of curls behind her ear. "What's-his-face?" she says and I nod. "So we can go? Anywhere? All of us, together?" Her expression sours. "But Percy."

"Liv." I clear my throat. "You know she loves you and you love her, right?" I ask and she nods. "Let's make some shit right. Get us all out."

Olive scrunches her nose. "How're we gonna do it? Are ya—"

"I'm fucking loaded, princess. But, we got one problem." I wipe my hand across my mouth. "I have to kill somebody, or he'll follow us forever."

Olive grimaces, bobs her head side to side, fidgets with her hair, raises both brows, then sputters, "Is he *really* bad?"

"He was ordered to keep me in a cage. Or maybe kill me. Not fucking sure which." I pause to drive around an insane rotary. "When he figured out he could make money by breaking me against the bars, he did. Then, I inconveniently hopped trade-dress and stole his muscle. He couldn't have that, for many reasons," I admit as we careen in a circle with colors flooding past the windows.

"Then, when he realized I'm *very* hard to kill, he made it his mission to get me to do it for him." Olive stares at me, but it's a comfortable stare. *She's really listening.*

"But that didn't work, huh?" Olive asks, nestling to my side again as we break from the rotary.

"No, it didn't." I finagle my hand into my pocket, unearth a cigarette, light it and roll down the window. "It..." *These words feel dangerous, but right.* "I might be unkillable. Unless I want to be."

Olive's nod prompts me to continue. "So he tried to recreate me. Sold the films, but never quite got it right, because they died so fast." I flick ash above an asphalt river.

"Kept me leashed so he could pull money out of me. When that didn't work, well." I inhale smoke. "He tried to make me his murder-bitch."

Olive raises her thin brows and sighs enough for the both of us. "Yer life's *heckin'* complicated."

"Too 'heckin' complicated,'" I agree, streaming smoke from my nose. "So I found a bigger dog to take him out, but he broke my heart."

"What's-his-face," Olive whispers, as if it's some big secret. "Mark, right?"

"Yes." We peel down the highway faster than the speed limit, I clutch a very shirtless, very unusual beauty to my side, smoke and imagine a world where neither of our lives are 'heckin' complicated.'

"So, if Boris *doesn't* die, it's bad news for all of us." I tell the one person who takes me at my word. She makes me honest.

Olive grumbles, "Boris, huh?"

"Yes. If I don't take him out, he's just going to keep following me. Especially since I tanked his fucking empire by hacking off his income stream, base of operations, and anyone who could ever fucking help him."

Olive's eyes widen. "Ya did?"

I glance at her face and give her a warm smile. "Mhm." My chuckle is framed in smoke. "Moira helped, you know. Like superhero. She pulled the whole thing—"

"What?!" Olive shouts, bouncing away from me, then curls her fists. "I-I didn't get to help?! What tha heck! I wanna be a superhero too! You big, selfish jerk!"

She punches my shoulder playfully, but she's quite pissed. It stings like hell.

"Ouch, ouch, alright, hey." I snicker. "Enough of my bullshit for now. We're going to take the long way back and you're going to tell me all about this 'computer college.'"

For one impenetrable moment, the light from a series of passing streetlamps hits her bright hair, cascades over round cheeks and bathes Olive in an orange glow. The dawn-sky above gives way to blue with every moment, a blue full of possibilities. Blue, like heaven and not the violet of my violent world.

Her curls lap like waves as the car thrums over an asphalt ocean spanning the entire country. The wind from the window whips my hair. At my side, Olive smiles. *I'm real, I exist, I'm alive and I love her.*

We've diverged from the timeline where she suffers far more than this, my friendships snap and Boris kills me because my trauma *lets* him. *What would a truly clever villain do to an unaware superhero if he stumbled upon one?* **Do you know?** *Does your world have those, too?*

Olive breaks the purple prose with a small sneer. "I wanna be a hero. This is crap," she mumbles.

"Liv." I catch her attention, she parts her lips to speak and I steal her words by kissing her until she burns hot-pink.

You already are.

49 / SPLIT ENDS

When we make it back to the city, I drive us to my apartment, park by the dumpsters, cart Olive up the stairs and pass out with her on my bed with Diana by our feet. I sleep for what feels like centuries, Olive leaves while I'm asleep and comes back with grocery bags. They rustle, rousing me from catatonia. "Mmm," I grumble.

"Oh, yer up!" she chirps, something sizzles and she curses in a language I don't know.

Cocking one eye open, I slip out of bed, stumble, startle the cat and fumble into the kitchen. It smells like meat—smoky, seared, fatty, sticky, sinewy meat. It smells like roasted vegetables—earthy, crunchy, delicious, colorful vegetables.

My explosive appetite has finally returned, all the way back from its trip to Wonderland nearly ten mother*fucking* years ago.

"Hot pot!" she giggles. "I gotta home-one from that dude." She sections choice cuts of raw meat, veggies and things I have no name for onto a big silver platter. "Oh, balls," she curses and jags sharply to fuss with what looks like a— "Rice cooker. From that dude, what's-his-face." Olive pauses, a chopstick raised in the air as she thinks. "Yuen, right? He's always feedin' ya, huh? Like a cat."

Dumbfounded, I rub my hand all over my face, gawk, drag the sleep from my eyes and sputter out only one word. "What?"

Olive sticks out her tongue at me, presses a button on the rice cooker and returns to cordoning delicious, searing, friable morsels on a bright green plate.

"I cheated." She cackles. *Yes, yes you did.* "Already ate some, he-heh." *That's not what you meant, and you know it, you little pink demon.*

"No, uh," I grumble, step forward, remember the stack of trash and knock absolutely *nothing* over. "What the *fuck*?" I gawk at the pile I *didn't* kick and expect to be there.

"We're havin' a lil get tagether, ya know?" she snickers.

My mouth draws into a flat line, I turn around, plod back into my bedroom and lay face down in my sheets.

"H-hey, no! Hey!" Olive shouts, curses about something, then rushes behind me to directly flop onto my body. I groan.

"We gotta tie up some split ends, huh? Before we do stuff?" She slaps my back with her flat palm. "Okey dokey?" she asks.

"You mean 'loose ends,'" I mouth into the sheets.

She jabs her face next to my ear. "What?!" she **screams**. *The audacity.* "I know," she adds. "I'm bein' cute. Keep up!"

Snarling, I tear away, yet she plasters herself against me again.

"Loose ends, not spl—what? Yes we *do* fucking have to tie them up, but mine means murder," I grumble, wrenching my head to glare at my spotless apartment.

"What *is* all this?" I gesture out at my lovely home as she bounces against me with her *entire* body.

"Well, if yer gonna *maybe* move out, we can't leave it crap," she says, squeezing me. "Yuen's real nice, ya know. I like yer apartment, too."

Writhing like a demon, I pry her off of me, sit, look out at the life I could've lived if I hadn't been a useless fucking piece of shit, then turn my attention back to the excitable beauty who cleaned up my entire life in just one night.

"This is unfair to you, you know. You are doing far, far too fucking much—" To shut me up, Olive snatches a pillow and hits me in the face.

"I make tha' choice. *You* don't make it. Eat my whole ass, *buddy*." For a moment she glares at me, I glare at her, she grimaces sheepishly and I split the air with a sharp cackle.

Tackling Olive to the bed, I pin her in place with a feral grin. "I just might, you little shit." I play-bite her, which makes her erupt into a painfully beautiful fit of laughter.

"Promise?" Liv snorts, twists about, then scampers away before I can mock-terrorize her further.

"Rahhh!" I stomp after her as she scream-laughs into the other room.

Chuckling, I stretch my arms over my head. When I put my hand down I find a piece of paper in it. It has scribbled notes, an address and an important-sounding name scrawled on it. "Uh, what the fuck is—"

"I picked tha college," Olive yells from the kitchen. "So now *you* gotta' pick tha adult stuff. No complainin'."

"*Excuse* me?" Gawking at the paper, I twist my brows, then grumble. *A fucking psychologist. I don't like the idea of a shrink digging their fingers around in my goddamn brains.*

"Fine, I will. I *promise,* but Olive…" I race after her as she jags about my apartment doing shit that I've never done before. Shit that I *should've* done as an adult: cook, clean and actually take care of my fucking problems.

"Liv, you're doing *that* thing — you know? You can't do this, I have to do this myse—" Olive throws a can at my head. It hits, dings off my dome and clatters to the ground.

My expression flatlines as she peels from the kitchen and huffs at me.

"Ya gotta let people help you, ya big, stupid, idiot. *Then,*" she grumbles, hands on her hips. "You pay fer *my* school. My rent too. *Their* rent too. Heh." She cackles. "*And,* you give me chocolate *and* we have fun." She snickers and scoots away before I can terrorize her.

"Eat my whole ass, ya know?" she yells from the kitchen as she stirs something into a sizzling frenzy.

"You're a fucking nightmare creature." I hiss after her, round the kitchen and settle at her side to investigate what she's doing. "How the fuck did Percy miss out?" I add with a conflicted smile.

Olive shrugs. "Dunno," she says with a sigh, "but I can't be with somebody who don't even wanna hold my hand 'round coworkers, ya know?"

She stirs vegetables, then taps her spoon on the pan a few times. "Wouldn't even lemme meet her parents." She snorts, then passes me a spoon. "Stir now."

Taking the wooden spoon from her grasp, I vaguely mull the vegetables around in a circle. *I've never cooked a day in my fucking life.* "No 'please?'" I ask, pressing my luck.

"No, you listen ta me. *I'm* tha boss now, dummy." Olive's fearless as fuck, ferocious and five foot two in motherfucking sneakers. *Unbelievable.*

I oblige with a devilish smirk, flip the vegetables in the pan, tilt my head to the side, check the heat like I assume I must, turn it down a little and she beams at me.

"Good, see? Yer learnin'," she says, which makes me grin sheepishly.

Her pink shape flits about the apartment as I watch her from the corner of my eye. My task is vegetables, even if she *is* wildly distracting. Dutifully, I make sure I don't burn the food to fucking cinders. *She's the boss.*

"I like it," I start up, using a spoon to pry free a mushroom, blow across it, then devour the smoky morsel. *I'm fucking starving.*

Olive pops her head from my bathroom, toothbrush lodged in her mouth. "Thwlike whath?" she mumbles.

"I *like* being told what to do," I admit with a salacious grin. "Some-times."

"Oh, *do* ya now?" Olive grins just as demonically. "Gwood thwah knowth," she mumbles through a minty grin.

I toss the vegetables in the pan—they successfully flip. "I cook! Yes!" I chortle triumphantly. Olive is nothing but toothpaste-smiles; proud of me for my one stupid act of adulthood.

The day continues on with playful banter, learning the life skills I never managed, accompanied by the vague residue of hallucinations cropping up every now and then. She helps with these; chamomile tea, grounding techniques, teaching me things I never knew I needed to know to be healthy. Things she knows, because she's brilliant and had to grow up way too fast, far too young. We're similar, yet she makes trying to be healthy look easy, though I know it must be hard for her, too.

War is not healthy, not eating is not healthy, constant trauma is not healthy. I have to truly heal. For that reason, I take another monstrous nap and dream of rivers, catching small fish and picking flowers. I'm fragile and fucking exhausted, but I'm gaining strength, just like my furry orphan cat did so many years ago.

The night comes eventually, and with it, very many wounds that are neither simple nor easy to sear shut. *I'm more nervous than I've ever been in my entire fucking life.*

I dress slowly, dread filling my gut as I pull on a hooded sweat-shirt and a pair of slacks. Olive finds my hand, knits our fingers and gnaws her scarred lower lip.

"Nervous, huh?" I ask and she nods at my question. I nod back, suck in the entire expanse of air in the room, exhale, shake out both our arms and it's time to face what we *both* don't want to.

Markov is the first to arrive. Logic dictates that he'd be the last, and that he'd hate me for trying to murder him, but he doesn't.

He brings me flowers—poppy-red and lovely. Spotting Olive's hand in mine when he opens the door, he pauses for a moment, then hands them to her with a distracting smile on his face.

"Thanks!" Olive says cheerfully and hops away to place the flow-ers in a vase, as if I fucking own one. She makes due with a bong, her nasally giggles clipping the air.

"Alex," Markov says in baritones as I avoid his mouth. "I'm sorry." He shoves his hands in his pockets.

"Come in," I say, my voice taut and shoulders scrunched. "It's—it's not your fault. I fucking get it. I remembered the note."

Markov frowns, passes by my side and I close the door behind him. "I get it," I repeat gruffly.

Markov pinches the bridge of his nose when I turn to look him over. He looks short. Maybe it's because the weight of the world is on his shoulders. *He doesn't want to have this fucking conversation either.*

"You were lost," he says into his hand. "I'm a prick, little bird, but it worked, didn't it?"

My fingers tingle like nettles; birdflight anxiety, but I don't fight, freeze, or flee. *I have to fucking face him.*

"I don't think it always fucking does, though. Because you're just not that fucking smart," I admit, licking my lower lip. "And you tried to play my games, when you should've just gotten me some fucking help. You were a coward." *Honesty. What a novel concept.*

Olive, sitting in the living room, leans back in her chair to look at us. She lifts her chin at me; a question. I raise my chin; an answer. She sits forward once more, satisfied and out of view.

Markov sighs heavily. "I thought that's how you operate, Alex."

"What?" I hiss. "I stick my dick in random people? I make the guy who loves me feel like he's just a fuck-toy? Just a tool he uses to get shit done? No, no, definitely fucking not," I continue, shaking my head.

Markov sighs, then takes to standing with his back to my pock-marked wall. "Alex, I couldn't break it off directly, or you'd have killed me, right?" he asks, raising his brows.

I grimace, then fold my arms across my chest. "Yes, yeah. But, fuck—Mark, I needed help, not *that*."

Markov grows quiet for a moment. Unable to figure out where to put his hands, he rubs his nose again.

"I don't know *how* to do that, Alex. How to be that. *She* does." He gestures at the other room as Olive clinks glasses together.

"Did you do this?" I ask him, mulling my hand over my mouth as I peer into the living room.

Markov's smile burns a hole in my chest. I turn to avoid it. *I have to learn boundaries. I have to unlearn loving him. I have to.*

"Moira," he says with a slight shrug, "is very convincing."

"What?" I scrunch my nose, taking a step forward. "What the fuck does *that* mean?"

On cue, Moira busts through my door and shakes her shoulders as she bounces in. I glare at her, she stops mid-pop to lock eyes with Markov, who covers his face with his whole hand.

"Oh, dear. He told you, didn't he?" Moira's smile is sinful.

Glasses clink from the living room, I drag my searing blue gaze across the air and pin Moira in place with a look pitch-black enough to freeze anyone's blood in their *fucking* veins.

Moira, instead of being intimidated, chortles behind her hand. "Ah, I meddled, darling. Look at me meddling."

This is not part of the run-time protocol. What—

She raises her velvety palm and speaks. "You see, darling, Percival was *very* angry with you. She knew something had happened, and *I* knew something had happened and, well, that man is terrible for you." Moira pauses to raise her hand, princess-like. "And, you'd lost all your *silly* little marbles! So I called the *Terrible European*, played your game, and I won, didn't I, dear?" she says with the casualness of a career criminal.

"You!" My roar is deafening. Olive leans through the doorway, stopping me in my tracks before I can do something I'll fucking regret.

"You're telling me," I stammer, my mouth impossibly dry. "You got Markov to break my heart and *somehow* put all the pieces together while I was losing my shit, to play fucking *matchmaker*?!"

Moira laughs behind her hand like a proper villainess. "*And*, I'm forcing him to help you leave the business *properly*," she says, pausing to wag her annoying finger. "Faking your death won't work, pet. Aren't *I* the truly clever, truly brilliant one?"

"He broke my fucking heart!" I shout, which causes Moira to dance in my direction. "I do not like when you fucking dance, it's like a warning sign for bullshit!" Reeling away, I hiss. "You're more fucking crazy than I'll *ever* be. What if I'd—"

Moira stops her ridiculous antics to place a hand to her hip. "I thought about it. You *are* rather unstable, dear, but I also made sure your *favorite* star was floating outside." Moira grins as my face boils. "And I did something *special*," she coos devilishly.

"And what the fuck was that?!"

Moira puffs up her feathers. "I took care of your little problem for you," she chortles, wagging her finger in the air, "ear-ly."

My eyes go wide. I'm left dumbstruck in the face of this serpentine beast who took a page from my book and ran with it beyond my wildest motherfucking *dreams*. "Fucking *pardon*?"

"We don't *have* to leave the city, is what I'm *saying*, darling," she says with a feline arch of the brow. "*I* popped the cherry." She cackles fiendishly. "Well," Moira continues, "I poisoned him, dear. It was a simple thing, really."

Gawking, I whirl to interrogate the ever-loving-fuck out of Markov to corroborate Moira's story, but he's busy helping Olive set out the food. "You!" I shout, pointing, "Deserve to be *fucking* shot!"

"Yes." Markov sighs, then turns to Olive. "Did Eric pick it up?" he asks her.

"Where's my fucking gun?!"

"Gone, mate," Eric says, barreling through my door with a covered container in tow. He sweeps past me and places it in the kitchen, then rounds to my side to slap me hard on the back.

Shellshocked, I glue my eyes shut and boil inside my very fucking skin. My eyes shoot open when Diana mewls on my bed, then hops to the floor. She perks up her furry tail, wanders toward Eric, he picks her up to coo dumbly and my temples throb. He dotes on my cat with his big dumb fucking eyebrows wagging and a big dumb fucking stupid smile plastered on his big dumb, fucking, stupid, *annoying* face.

"Mate, ya seem tossed 'n all, bit confusin' innit?" Eric asks, nuzzling *my* cat.

"Yes!" I screech, which ushers Percy through the doorway, who grimaces at me, shuts said door, then places her hands to her chest.

"What did *you* do?!" I twist an accusatory snarl in her direction.

Percival jumps as I point at her, then rears her hands up. "I, like, *totally* didn't know what was going on either, or whatever. They're, like, all so *mean*," she pleads with me.

"So they played *both* of us?" I hiss and cross my arms.

Percy sighs. "I'm like, obviously not happy about it, but Liv and I had like, a long talk earlier on the phone—"

Her syllables split when I cleave the air with my hand. "When?! My phone's fucking—" Snapping my head around, I catch a pink landline nestled on the plaster, right where I'd ripped the mint one clean off the mother*fucking* wall. Dragging my eyes across hardwood to where I bludgeoned the thing, I find nothing but a mere *scuff*.

"Al." Olive is at my side and holding a piece of sizzling meat in my face. *It smells divine.* I glare at it as she speaks. "You passed out, ya know? Been sleepin' fer a whole day. We all talked 'bout stuff and did some crap."

I take Olive's peace offering in my teeth, devour it and turn away, arms still crossed. "How the fuck did you know I wouldn't *kill* you?" I hiss-chew at Markov who freezes in the doorway of my bedroom, holding a bottle of pink wine.

Mark hesitates, considers turning right back around, but doesn't. "I didn't," he offers, pops the cork of the wine and nearly downs half the bottle.

Wiping his mouth, he admits everything. "I was very drunk, little bird. And Moira is *very* convincing."

Moira raises her hands and sashays to the side, ridiculously. "I just did what you taught me, darling." She chuckles.

"Which is what?! Fucking with my *life*?!" I bellow in her direction.

She sashays again and says, "Well, yes, darling. Of course. I paid attention. You never pulled one over on little old me." *What?!*

"I've brought the music, but I will only stay for one song." Lauren, the songbird, the one I kept at arm's length, strolls through my door and drags with her an amp and an electric guitar.

Percy closes the door for her and smiles. Lauren smiles back. *Are they fucking friends?!*

"Lauren," I whisper from a too-tight mouth. "You're—"

She offers me a knowing smile, then takes to plugging her amp into the wall. "Who do you suppose Eric gets his weed from?" she asks incredulously. "I have a whole garden in my home, do I not?"

"Wait, wait, wait," I stammer, raise my hand and twist to look over the faces of my friends. "This is too fucking perfect. And this?!" I wave my hand at all the delicious food Eric is now carting about. "And *that*?!" I fling my index finger at Lauren's guitar.

Olive steps from the kitchen with a pink plate of ice cream cake in her hand. It has one single lit candle in it, already melting. "Doncha know what day it is?" Olive asks me, sheepishly.

Moira wraps her arm around my shoulder. "We're guesstimating a little bit," she says, then turns me to face her head-on.

Is there a holiday to celebrate living?

I flick my eyes from Moira to Olive. She stands like a beacon with a large piece of sweet, melting ice cream cake she prepared just for me. *They did this, all for me?*

The horrible pity of my friends shatters my heart. Moira told them *everything* and Markov filled in what he could. That's why they're looking at me like this. *Fucking shit.* I'm naked in my speechlessness as Olive sets the plate on the edge of my bed.

My eyes fill with tears as my friends grow blurry.

Moira hums, catching my attention. "Darling boy," she says in a silky voice, threading her fingers through my hair. "Don't you deserve one nice day?"

My heart jackhammers up into my throat and I can say nothing as Moira soothes me like a mother would. Memories of the subway, the little girl and everything I've never had stream down my face all at once.

"Don't you deserve a life without a monster on your heels? I'm sorry for how I did it," Moira whispers, running her painted claws through my pale hair, "but I am *not* sorry for doing it."

"I've lost my mind. None of this is fucking happening. All of you are figments of my imagination. This is too perfect. I have *never*..." I gulp back terrible tears as Moira swipes her knuckles over my eyes.

"I never get to have this!" I shout, shoving Moira back.

"It *can't* be fucking real! There doesn't **exist** a world where I live and get a-any." I crumple in on myself and ruin my own party. My first and only birthday party. *I don't even know how fucking old I really am.*

"I never get to have a-any of this. *I don't ever get to have this,* don't you fucking people get that?! I'm the *villain!*" I'm a stuttering, coiling, malfunctioning mess and all my friends can do is look at me with disgusting, loathsome, horrible pity.

Smearing tears across my face, I bullet words from the shaky barrel of my throat. "I could think, maybe." I sniffle into my hand. "Maybe if I fucking ran away to fucking *space,* I could have s-something close. But this?!"

I can see nothing but blurry shapes, shadows, figments, specters, ghosts and nothing-things as Olive slides her hand into mine and squeezes my fingers.

"I get to get out of all this, scot-fucking-free—" Lauren cuts me off by strumming her guitar, as though this is a beautiful moment that deserves her music. *Is it? No, it fucking can't be. All of this fake. It's bullshit!*

"Do ya really think ya got outta it scot-free?" Olive asks softly, pressing her face to my arm in an effort to ground me. Pity—the most loathsome word—fades as my distorted thoughts are swept away by Moira's hands returning to my hair and Olive's fingers threading my own.

My friends look at me with *adoration,* not pity. Olive tethers me with her heart and hand, Moira dotes on me like I'm a cat, Lauren plays her guitar, and despite all of it, my self-hatred wins in the end.

This is a fucking hallucination. I cannot *possibly* conceive of a life where I'm given anything without violence in so many horrifying colors. Nobody, not one single person, could ever willingly want to help me, or want me in their life at all, for that matter. *Nobody.*

I'm immediately catatonic, or at least I fucking think so.

50 / MERCY

This is all—Impossible. A simulation. A fabrication. A lie. Is that what you want me to tell you? Can you really not think that maybe, just fucking maybe, there's a timeline where you get to live? Where you get to be happy?

It's not fucking poss—You saw a cosmic shadow when you disassociated from your body. Who was it?

I'm cra—Alex, you were traumatized. You were raped. You never use the real fucking words: abused, trafficked, disassociated, traumatized, manipulated, raped. Who do you think the shadow was?

Well, it's not fucking G—You're right, God isn't real. But you forget, you always fucking forget that you're a superhero. You survived the impossible and came out stronger for it.

I'm a monst—That doesn't mean you're irredeemable. Look at what you've lived through. Look at how you've warped the very fucking fabric of reality to do just that. Look at what you have now. Look at what you've been given.

No one would ever—Who's the cosmic shadow, whose story is this, who the fuck am I and why can you hear me now?

It's—Turn and face yourself.

Processing. Please stand by.

Standing in a space with softly smiling faces, I'm judged by no one for ruining a day not meant for my tears. A day I didn't know I could have. A day I never even thought existed. The universe expands and contracts around me as I entertain *a possibility*. Rivers trail my cheeks as I suck in jagged, rib-cracking bolts of air.

Open your eyes.

Moira's blurry face comes into view. *She's real.* Her bright red smile hitches awkwardly. She flutters her fingers through my hair, pushing mercy through my skin. **Mercy.** I want to believe.

Do you feel it? Do you hear it? Do you see it?

As I feel Moira's breath on my skin, hear Olive's heart thumping my side and see the bittersweet faces of my friends, I entertain something *impossible*: a dream I escaped to, so many years ago.

In a mind stuck between bars, in symbols made to hide agony, in a life pressed into a mold, in a lack of choices, I allow just one, fleeting, rose-colored possibility.

In strategies as cries for help, in a chess game I played alone, in an ocean of tears, in mimicking the evil around me just to survive, I imagine an outcome where I get to be myself. Just a man, just a boy, just a person. *Just 'Alex' and nothing more than that.*

In terrifying silence, in mindless violet violence and in reacting and reacting and reacting until I was nothing *but* a nuclear reaction, I imagine that I could possibly, *maybe*—my brows twist—*maybe. It's finally...*

Light hovers above you and hardwood cools your feet. The warmest color holds your side, your fists overflow with metaphorical fish and nothing *has* to hurt. *It doesn't have to hurt, if you don't want it to.*

A kiss on the eyelids from a blue-dipped savior washes away pain lived and long dead while an awkward sage sentinel stands guard over your vulnerable heart.

A russet wound that's finally brave enough to close itself protects you from a forever-dead enemy while a friendship you wish to mend smiles in magenta gentleness.

A translucent dove circles the ceiling, possesses nothing no longer and flits out a window, never to return. You couldn't save them, because you're just simply, imperfectly, foreverly *human.*

A furry orphan who loves you patters on the floors of the father-figure you never had, who would love you if you let him. A talented friend in gold plays music to celebrate you being alive—for once—*truly* living.

Look at your friends and their beautiful faces. And just look at that sky beyond your window! Look at the orange circle dripping in the heat of city streets. A cloud rescues you from the sun. Know that *nobody* owns that cloud, for nobody can. See that blue sky for what it is—no violet-violence, no indigo war—just crystal clear and full of real, true *possibilities.*

Breathe, for the first time in your life, as yourself. *Breathe* and know your enemies are gone. Breathe, choose life, choose love, find a way to make things right, spread your wings and know that your cage was broken so very many years ago. *You're you.*

"I'm free?" I whisper to a patient Moira who steps back, glassy-eyed, gracefully overwhelmed and permanently beautiful in my permanent indigo. She adopted it for me, more capable than I ever was, because she can do it without breaking. *I'm so fragile.*

"Well…" Moira sniffles. "We all are, darling." Her smile blossoms like a poppy. "It feels so different now, doesn't it, dear?" she asks, voice cracking. "I'm not sure what I'm saying," she admits, eyes filling with tears. "Ignore me, dear. I'm just a bit…" Moira turns away, overcome.

Olive, quiet in all this, leans up to plant a chaste kiss, but I meet her mouth; butterfly-light, slow-lashed, gentle, open, patient, *good.* My hand scoops behind her to lift her body, her arms drift down over my slim shoulders to shield me and I feel her *breathe.* **She's real.**

This is all real and true. We've changed fate itself. For all of us.

I soak in the warmth of her heart and fall in love again as her lashes kiss my skin. *Let loose that dead life, little bird. You're home.*

Olive dots her lips to my nose, then draws to my side to grin rosy into my sweatshirt.

"So…" I sniffle, wiping my face with the back of my hand. "What happens now?" I ask in Olive's direction.

"Anything ya want," she whispers with a gap-toothed grin, "it's yer party, doncha know?" She squeezes my arm.

"Anything *we* want," I correct her, glancing warmly at the faces of people who love me. I'm loved not just by 'anyone at all' but the *best* of someones: true superheroes.

EPILOGUE

We start where all things end, with time. This time, I managed to live past my predetermined bullet. Even so, I infect dimensions, my corpses fall and the fated fucked up future flickers distantly. But in *this* timeline, *I get to live.* I get to live and learn from all the living I've done. *What a novel concept.*

We didn't move out of the city—fleeing as I always do—yet tell myself I don't. However, I *did* pay rent for my friends and *did* throw cash at anything Olive wanted, namely 'computer college.'

It was the only way I knew to thank them for tolerating my breakdown. The problem here is that Markov *did* actually get me the fuck out of 'the business' the right way, which means I went broke, because usual jobs are unusual for a guy like me.

I'm only good at two employable things, you know. Both of which are illegal and only one for real reasons. As expected, I couldn't hold down anything 'usual' for a very long time.

Because we're all poor planners for our own messy lives, Markov floated a few of us, until Liv and I didn't need it, because I stumbled into something unexpectedly perfect: I became a self-defense instructor at a local gym. *And I love every minute of it.*

How'd I manage to score such a sweet fucking gig? Well, let's just say Yuen had a friend of a friend who saw me stop just-shy of kicking Markov's head off. Impressing someone with my natural skills, I settled into teaching others what I know so they could defend against a world that would see them only *just* survive.

Knowing that I could do some good for once, I took to it like a fly on shit and trained an army, but not for my own brand of justice.

Helping people for the sake of helping them feels *really* fucking good. Getting paid to help people feels *really* fucking good. I never knew I could do that. I never thought I could be anything more.

There's been ups and downs, of course. My mental health diagnosis is some bullshit I don't *quite* understand. I have to take a pill every day—come hell or high water—because if I don't, my mind unravels. Late nights pinning memories, an impossible libido, hallucinations, grandiosity and then a psychotic depression chaser. *I barely survived the first time, thank you very fucking much.*

Olive's been patient with me, as has everyone else, which I'm not used to. All my symptoms are apparently very manageable with a bit of love, a lot of sobriety and restraint. Whodathunkit?

On that note, Percy's my shopaholic watchdog; we made up. I apologized for everything, she's still upset, but we're *trying*. We're also holding each other accountable for not buying bullshit we can't afford. So far? It's working. She lets me stumble on honesty now, versus finding new problems to solve. She still wants to feel all my feelings with me and I'm *still* fucking terrible at it, but we're *trying*.

As for making it right, Markov, Percy and myself figured out how to put real names to the victims I couldn't save and give their loved ones some closure. They deserve that and Percy *does* deserve to be a superhero. She's far more clever than anyone gives her credit for, including me. Did you know she can pick locks? Neither did I!

Percy and Eric are dating now, which isn't surprising, considering her bottle-blonde mind-flayer shit doesn't work on him. Eric's very happy these days. I think he's going to ask her to marry him, based on all the awkward half-questions he keeps only half-asking me. I'm happy for them, though it's still bittersweet for Olive, for obvious reasons.

Moira's club brings in bank. She throws money at us frivolously, but it feels warm, not venomous. I think giving gifts might be her 'love language.' That's what this crunchy-ass book Lauren gave me says, anyways.

Yes, I'm reading crunchy-ass books. Lauren and I are book buddies. I get to learn things *not* under duress for *once* in my fucking life *and* drink lavender lemonade while basking in the beauty of her home.

She puts me to work, of course. Her amps are heavier than her dead fucking tree chunks and she plays a lot of shows. I go to as many as I can, but leave before it gets too late. Sleep is something I took for granted for far too long. It's also *not* fucking negotiable.

Markov and I don't talk much, but when we do, it's not as painful as I imagined. Little by little, I'm learning to forgive him and I think he's coming to terms with his *actual* alcoholism. He also made me a promise; there's just some shit he won't let fly in his city.

I don't know if I trust him to keep that promise to me, but I *do* trust him to keep that promise to Moira or she'll poison him. She's somehow more cold-blooded than I ever was. How did *that* fucking happen?

At the end of all things, we only have time *and* each other. We're all flawed, unique people trying to live our lives in a brutal world. We try our best, we're not perfect, but we try. The clock ticks and I try my best to let it.

It should be obvious that I've been domesticated like a stray cat. Sometimes I don't know if I like it and coil in on myself. Sometimes I don't think I can be anything more than trauma and have to talk my brain chemicals down like chastising a spoiled brat. Sometimes, a memory drops like ink into my eyes and I haunt myself, blinded by all I barely survived.

On a day in the brighter, more usual future, I fumble into my bathroom, step into the tub and twist the knob to let too-cold water batter me. Nikolai's ghost greets me like a stab in the chest, but the pain is replaced by a warm hand that slides across my damp skin.

Olive is naked, pressed to my back and smiling against me. Impossibly gorgeous, she reaches for a bar of lavender soap Lauren made us, just because she wanted to. Lathering her hands, Olive scrubs my scarred, inked skin and hums to herself as sweet scents surround us.

I allow myself to look at her and describe nothing in detail because her face-flushing beauty isn't something you get to fucking see. *Imagine it, because that's all I'm going to give you.*

Twisting, I catch her soapy wrist and stare into her hazel eyes. I place my flat palm over what saved me: her beating heart. "Thank you," I whisper.

"Fer what?" Olive asks in pink stars, LED lights and clear blue mornings where nothing really, truly hurts.

"For loving me."

My name is Alex Voss. I'm a piss-poor role model, necessary lesson and survivor. This is my superhero origin story, with an ending I never expected, but truly deserved. We all deserve a happy ending. **Yes, even you.**

Choosing life will not come easy if you're like me: a broken breed born of horrible memories that cage us in trauma through countless shivering decades. But people like us *do* have a choice, you know.

We don't have to war with the world. We don't have to fly into the sun and melt our fucking brains. We don't have to fall like a stone into tar-pit hell. We don't have to haunt ourselves and react until we're nothing *but* a nuclear reaction.

We have a choice. It's not an easy choice to make, but I promise that you'll find it if you hold on, let people in and ride it out together.

Choose to defy fate at every single turn of the page and you might just find that the superhero you need to truly live is the one you left behind to barely survive.

Have you been listening, princess?

ABOUT THE AUTHOR

K. Leigh is a 35-year-old once-painter, sometimes-freelancer, for-ever-artist living in Providence, RI. They write hopeful/ tragic stories full of funny, horrible characters, in various genres.

Enter the world of CONSTELIS VOSS: constelisvoss.com

Read nonfiction by K. Leigh: blog.constelisvoss.com